The Young

Earl of Beaconsfield Benjamin Disraeli

Alpha Editions

This edition published in 2024

ISBN : 9789362997562

Design and Setting By
Alpha Editions
www.alphaedis.com
Email - info@alphaedis.com

As per information held with us this book is in Public Domain.
This book is a reproduction of an important historical work. Alpha Editions uses
the best technology to reproduce historical work in the same manner it was first
published to preserve its original nature. Any marks or number seen are left
intentionally to preserve its true form.

Contents

BOOK I. ....- 1 -

CHAPTER I. ....- 3 -

CHAPTER II. ....- 6 -

CHAPTER III. ....- 10 -

CHAPTER IV. ....- 12 -

CHAPTER V. ....- 16 -

CHAPTER VI. ....- 18 -

CHAPTER VII. ....- 20 -

CHAPTER VIII. ....- 22 -

CHAPTER IX. ....- 26 -

CHAPTER X. ....- 28 -

CHAPTER XI. ....- 31 -

CHAPTER XII. ....- 36 -

CHAPTER XIII. ....- 37 -

CHAPTER XIV. ....- 38 -

BOOK II. ....- 41 -

CHAPTER I. ....- 43 -

CHAPTER II. ....- 46 -

CHAPTER III. ....- 51 -

CHAPTER IV. ....- 58 -

CHAPTER V. ....- 63 -

CHAPTER VI. ....- 71 -

CHAPTER VII. ....- 76 -

CHAPTER VIII. ....- 80 -

CHAPTER IX. ....- 83 -

CHAPTER X. ....- 87 -

CHAPTER XI. ....- 90 -

CHAPTER XII. ....- 96 -

CHAPTER XIII. ....- 98 -

CHAPTER XIV. ....- 102 -

BOOK III. ....- 109 -

CHAPTER I. ....- 111 -

CHAPTER II. ....- 116 -

CHAPTER III. ....- 118 -

CHAPTER IV. ....- 121 -

CHAPTER V. ....- 127 -

CHAPTER VI. ....- 131 -

CHAPTER VII. ....- 136 -

CHAPTER VIII. ....- 142 -

CHAPTER IX. ....- 150 -

CHAPTER X. ....- 153 -

CHAPTER XI. ....- 161 -

CHAPTER XII. ....- 164 -

CHAPTER XIII. ....- 167 -

CHAPTER XIV. ....- 170 -

CHAPTER XV ....- 173 -

CHAPTER XVI. ....- 178 -

CHAPTER XVII. ....- 180 -

CHAPTER XVIII. ....- 185 -

BOOK IV. ....- 195 -

CHAPTER I. ....- 197 -

CHAPTER II. ....- 199 -

CHAPTER III. ....- 201 -

CHAPTER IV. ....- 203 -

CHAPTER V. ....- 206 -

CHAPTER VI. ....- 208 -

CHAPTER VII. ....- 214 -

CHAPTER VIII. ....- 217 -

CHAPTER IX. ....- 221 -

CHAPTER X. ....- 226 -

CHAPTER XI. ....- 228 -

CHAPTER XII. ....- 231 -

BOOK V. ....- 237 -

CHAPTER I. ....- 239 -

CHAPTER II. ....- 241 -

CHAPTER III. ....- 246 -

CHAPTER IV. ....- 249 -

CHAPTER V. ....- 252 -

CHAPTER VI. ....- 254 -

BOOK V [CONTINUED] ....- 261 -

CHAPTER VII. ....- 263 -

CHAPTER VIII. ....- 274 -

CHAPTER IX. ....- 281 -

CHAPTER X. ....- 285 -

CHAPTER XI. ....- 288 -

CHAPTER XII. ....- 290 -

CHAPTER XIII. ....- 294 -

BOOK I.

CHAPTER I.

Fortune's Favourite

GEORGE AUGUSTUS FREDERICK, DUKE OF ST. JAMES, completed his twenty-first year, an event which created almost as great a sensation among the aristocracy of England as the Norman Conquest. A minority of twenty years had converted a family always amongst the wealthiest of Great Britain into one of the richest in Europe. The Duke of St. James possessed estates in the north and in the west of England, besides a whole province in Ireland. In London there were a very handsome square and several streets, all made of bricks, which brought him in yearly more cash than all the palaces of Vicenza are worth in fee-simple, with those of the Grand Canal of Venice to boot. As if this were not enough, he was an hereditary patron of internal navigation; and although perhaps in his two palaces, three castles, four halls, and lodges *ad libitum*, there were more fires burnt than in any other establishment in the empire, this was of no consequence, because the coals were his own. His rent-roll exhibited a sum total, very neatly written, of two hundred thousand pounds; but this was independent of half a million in the funds, which we had nearly forgotten, and which remained from the accumulations occasioned by the unhappy death of his father.

The late Duke of St. James had one sister, who was married to the Earl of Fitz-pompey. To the great surprise of the world, to the perfect astonishment of the brother-in-law, his Lordship was not appointed guardian to the infant minor. The Earl of Fitz-pompey had always been on the best possible terms with his Grace: the Countess had, only the year before his death, accepted from his fraternal hand a diamond bracelet; the Lord Viscount St. Maurice, future chief of the house of Fitz-pompey, had the honour not only of being his nephew, but his godson. Who could account, then, for an action so perfectly unaccountable? It was quite evident that his Grace had no intention of dying.

The guardian, however, that he did appoint was a Mr. Dacre, a Catholic gentleman of ancient family and large fortune, who had been the companion of his travels, and was his neighbour in his county. Mr. Dacre had not been honoured with the acquaintance of Lord Fitz-pompey previous to the decease of his noble friend; and after that event such an acquaintance would probably not have been productive of agreeable reminiscences; for from the moment of the opening of the fatal will the name of Dacre was wormwood to the house of St. Maurice. Lord Fitz-pompey, who, though the brother-in-law of a Whig magnate, was a Tory, voted against the Catholics with renewed fervour.

- 3 -

Shortly after the death of his friend, Mr. Dacre married a beautiful and noble lady of the house of Howard, who, after having presented him with a daughter, fell ill, and became that common character, a confirmed invalid. In the present day, and especially among women, one would almost suppose that health was a state of unnatural existence. The illness of his wife and the non-possession of parliamentary duties rendered Mr. Dacre's visits to his town mansion rare, and the mansion in time was let.

The young Duke, with the exception of an occasional visit to his uncle, Lord Fitz-pompey, passed the early years of his life at Castle Dacre. At seven years of age he was sent to a preparatory school at Richmond, which was entirely devoted to the early culture of the nobility, and where the principal, the Reverend Doctor Coronet, was so extremely exclusive in his system that it was reported that he had once refused the son of an Irish peer. Miss Coronet fed her imagination with the hope of meeting her father's noble pupils in after-life, and in the meantime read fashionable novels.

The moment that the young Duke was settled at Richmond, all the intrigues of the Fitz-pompey family were directed to that quarter; and as Mr. Dacre was by nature unsuspicious, and was even desirous that his ward should cultivate the friendship of his only relatives, the St. Maurice family had the gratification, as they thought, of completely deceiving him. Lady Fitz-pompey called twice a week at Crest House with a supply of pine-apples or bonbons, and the Rev. Dr. Coronet bowed in adoration. Lady Isabella St. Maurice gave a china cup to Mrs. Coronet, and Lady Augusta a paper-cutter to Miss. The family was secured. All discipline was immediately set at defiance, and the young Duke passed the greater part of the half-year with his affectionate relations. His Grace, charmed with the bonbons of his aunt and the kisses of his cousins, which were even sweeter than the sugar-plums; delighted with the pony of St. Maurice, which immediately became his own; and inebriated by the attentions of his uncle,—who, at eight years of age, treated him, as his Lordship styled it, 'like a man'—contrasted this life of early excitement with what now appeared the gloom and the restraint of Castle Dacre, and he soon entered into the conspiracy, which had long been hatching, with genuine enthusiasm. He wrote to his guardian, and obtained permission to spend his vacation with his uncle. Thus, through the united indulgence of Dr. Coronet and Mr. Dacre, the Duke of St. James became a member of the family of St. Maurice.

No sooner had Lord Fitz-pompey secured the affections of the ward than he entirely changed his system towards the guardian. He wrote to Mr. Dacre, and in a manner equally kind and dignified courted his acquaintance. He dilated upon the extraordinary, though extremely natural, affection which Lady Fitz-pompey entertained for the only offspring of her beloved brother, upon the happiness which the young Duke enjoyed with his cousins, upon the great and evident advantages which his Grace would derive from companions of his own age, of the singular friendship which he had already formed with St. Maurice; and then, after paying Mr. Dacre many compliments upon the admirable manner in which he had already fulfilled the duties of his important office, and urging the lively satisfaction that a visit from their brother's friend would confer both upon Lady Fitz-pompey and himself, he requested permission for his nephew to renew the visit in which he had been 'so happy!' The Duke seconded the Earl's diplomatic scrawl in the most graceful round-text. The masterly intrigues of Lord Fitz-pompey, assisted by Mrs. Dacre's illness, which daily increased, and which rendered perfect quiet indispensable, were successful, and the young Duke arrived at his twelfth year without revisiting Dacre. Every year, however, when Mr. Dacre made a short visit to London, his ward spent a few days in his company, at the house of an old-fashioned Catholic nobleman; a visit which only afforded a dull contrast to the gay society and constant animation of his uncle's establishment.

It would seem that fate had determined to counteract the intentions of the late Duke of St. James, and to achieve those of the Earl of Fitz-pompey. At the moment that the noble minor was about to leave Dr. Coronet for Eton, Mrs. Dacre's state was declared hopeless, except from the assistance of an Italian sky, and Mr. Dacre, whose attachment to his lady was romantic, determined to leave England immediately.

It was with deep regret that he parted from his ward, whom he tenderly loved; but all considerations merged in the paramount one; and he was consoled by the reflection that he was, at least, left to the care of his nearest connections. Mr. Dacre was not unaware of the dangers to which his youthful pledge might be exposed by the indiscriminate indulgence of his uncle, but he trusted to the impartial and inviolable system of a public school to do much; and he anticipated returning to England before his ward was old enough to form those habits which are generally so injurious to young nobles. In this hope Mr. Dacre was disappointed. Mrs. Dacre lingered, and revived, and lingered, for nearly eight years; now filling the mind of her husband and her daughter with unreasonable hope, now delivering them to that renewed anguish, that heart-rending grief, which the attendant upon a declining relative can alone experience, additionally agonizing because it cannot be indulged. Mrs. Dacre died, and the widower and his daughter returned to England. In the meantime, the Duke of St. James had not been idle.

CHAPTER II.

Tender Relatives

THE departure and, at length, the total absence of Mr. Dacre from England yielded to Lord Fitz-pompey all the opportunity he had long desired. Hitherto he had contented himself with quietly sapping the influence of the guardian: now that influence was openly assailed. All occasions were seized of depreciating the character of Mr. Dacre, and open lamentations were poured forth on the strange and unhappy indiscretion of the father who had confided the guardianship of his son, not to his natural and devoted friends, but to a harsh and repulsive stranger. Long before the young Duke had completed his sixteenth year all memory of the early kindness of his guardian, if it had ever been imprinted on his mind, was carefully obliterated from it. It was constantly impressed upon him that nothing but the exertions of his aunt and uncle had saved him from a life of stern privation and irrational restraint: and the man who had been the chosen and cherished confidant of the father was looked upon by the son as a grim tyrant, from whose clutches he had escaped, and in which he determined never again to find himself. 'Old Dacre,' as Lord Fitz-pompey described him, was a phantom enough at any time to frighten his youthful ward. The great object of the uncle was to teaze and mortify the guardian into resigning his trust, and infinite were the contrivances to bring about this desirable result; but Mr. Dacre was obstinate, and, although absent, contrived to carry on and complete the system for the management of the Hauteville property which he had so beneficially established and so long pursued.

In quitting England, although he had appointed a fixed allowance for his noble ward, Mr. Dacre had thought proper to delegate a discretionary authority to Lord Fitz-pompey to furnish him with what might be called extraordinary necessaries. His Lordship availed himself with such dexterity of this power that his nephew appeared to be indebted for every indulgence to his uncle, who invariably accompanied every act of this description with an insinuation that he might thank Mrs. Dacre's illness for the boon.

'Well, George,' he would say to the young Etonian, 'you shall have the boat, though I hardly know how I shall pass the account at head-quarters; and make yourself easy about Flash's bill, though I really cannot approve of such proceedings. Thank your stars you have not got to present that account to old Dacre. Well, I am one of those who are always indulgent to young blood. Mr. Dacre and I differ. He is your guardian, though. Everything is in his power; but you shall never want while your uncle can help you; and so run off to Caroline, for I see you want to be with her.'

The Lady Isabella and the Lady Augusta, who had so charmed Mrs. and Miss Coronet, were no longer in existence. Each had knocked down her earl. Brought up by a mother exquisitely adroit in female education, the Ladies St. Maurice had run but a brief, though a brilliant, career. Beautiful, and possessing every accomplishment which renders beauty valuable, under the unrivalled chaperonage of the Countess they had played their popular parts without a single blunder. Always in the best set, never flirting with the wrong man, and never speaking to the wrong woman, all agreed that the Ladies St. Maurice had fairly won their coronets. Their sister Caroline was much younger; and although she did not promise to develop so unblemished a character as themselves, she was, in default of another sister, to be the Duchess of St. James.

Lady Caroline St. Maurice was nearly of the same age as her cousin, the young Duke. They had been play-fellows since his emancipation from the dungeons of Castle Dacre, and every means had been adopted by her judicious parents to foster and to confirm the kind feelings which had been first engendered by being partners in the same toys and sharing the same sports. At eight years old the little Duke was taught to call Caroline his 'wife;' and as his Grace grew in years, and could better appreciate the qualities of his sweet and gentle cousin, he was not disposed to retract the title. When George rejoined the courtly Coronet, Caroline invariably mingled her tears with those of her sorrowing spouse; and when the time at length arrived for his departure for Eton, Caroline knitted him a purse and presented him with a watch-ribbon. At the last moment she besought her brother, who was two years older, to watch over him, and soothed the moment of final agony by a promise to correspond. Had the innocent and soft-hearted girl been acquainted with, or been able to comprehend, the purposes of her crafty parents, she could not have adopted means more calculated to accomplish them. The young Duke kissed her a thousand times, and loved her better than all the world.

In spite of his private house and his private tutor, his Grace did not make all the progress in his classical studies which means so calculated to promote abstraction and to assist acquirement would seem to promise. The fact is, that as his mind began to unfold itself he found a perpetual and a more pleasing source of study in the contemplation of himself. His early initiation in the school of Fitz-pompey had not been thrown away. He had heard much of nobility, and beauty, and riches, and fashion, and power; he had seen many individuals highly, though differently, considered for the relative quantities which they possessed of these qualities; it appeared to the Duke of St. James that among the human race he possessed the largest quantity of them all: he cut his private tutor. His private tutor, who had been appointed by Mr. Dacre, remonstrated to Lord Fitz-pompey, and with such success that he thought proper shortly after to resign his situation. Dr. Coronet begged to recommend his son, the Rev. Augustus Granville Coronet. The Duke of St. James now got on rapidly, and also found sufficient time for his boat, his tandem, and his toilette.

The Duke of St. James appeared at Christ Church. His conceit kept him alive for a few terms. It is delightful to receive the homage of two thousand young men of the best families in the country, to breakfast with twenty of them, and to cut the rest. In spite, however, of the glories of the golden tuft and a delightful private establishment which he and his followers maintained in the chaste suburbs of Alma Mater, the Duke of St. James felt ennuied. Consequently, one clear night, they set fire to a pyramid of caps and gowns in Peckwater. It was a silly thing for any one: it was a sad indiscretion for a Duke; but it was done. Some were expelled; his Grace had timely notice, and having before cut the Oxonians, now cut Oxford.

Like all young men who get into scrapes, the Duke of St. James determined to travel. The Dacres returned to England before he did. He dexterously avoided coming into contact with them in Italy. Mr. Dacre had written to him several times during the first years of his absence; and although the Duke's answers were short, seldom, and not very satisfactory, Mr. Dacre persisted in occasionally addressing him. When, however, the Duke had arrived at an age when he was at least morally responsible for his own conduct, and entirely neglected answering his guardian's letters, Mr. Dacre became altogether silent.

The travelling career of the young Duke may be conceived by those who have wasted their time, and are compensated for that silliness by being called men of the world. He gamed a little at Paris; he ate a good deal at Vienna; and he studied the fine arts in Italy. In all places his homage to the fair sex was renowned. The Parisian duchess, the Austrian princess, and the Italian countess spoke in the most enthusiastic terms of the English nobility. At the end of three years the Duke of St. James was of opinion that he had obtained a great knowledge of mankind. He was mistaken; travel is not, as is imagined, the best school for that sort of science. Knowledge of mankind is a knowledge of their passions. The traveller is looked upon as a bird of passage, whose visit is short, and which the vanity of the visited wishes to make agreeable. All is show, all false, and all made up. Coterie succeeds coterie, equally smiling—the explosions take place in his absence. Even a grand passion, which teaches a man more, perhaps, than anything else, is not very easily excited by the traveller. The women know that, sooner or later, he must disappear; and though this is the case with all lovers, they do not like to miss the possibility of delusion. Thus the heroines keep in the background, and the visitor, who is always in a hurry, falls into the net of the first flirtation that offers.

The Duke of St. James had, however, acquired a great knowledge; if not of mankind, at any rate of manners. He had visited all Courts, and sparkled in the most brilliant circles of the Continent. He returned to his own country with a taste extremely refined, a manner most polished, and a person highly accomplished.

CHAPTER III.

The Duke Returns

A SORT of scrambling correspondence had been kept up between the young Duke and his cousin, Lord St. Maurice, who had for a few months been his fellow-traveller. By virtue of these epistles, notice of the movements of their interesting relative occasionally reached the circle at Fitz-pompey House, although St. Maurice was scanty in the much-desired communications; because, like most young Englishmen, he derived singular pleasure from depriving his fellow-creatures of all that small information which every one is so desirous to obtain. The announcement, however, of the approaching arrival of the young Duke was duly made. Lord Fitz-pompey wrote and offered apartments at Fitz-pompey House. They were refused. Lord Fitz-pompey wrote again to require instructions for the preparation of Hauteville House. His letter was unanswered. Lord Fitz-pompey was quite puzzled.

'When does your cousin mean to come, Charles?' 'Where does your cousin mean to go, Charles?' 'What does your cousin mean to do, Charles?' These were the hourly queries of the noble uncle.

At length, in the middle of January, when no one expected him, the Duke of St. James arrived at Mivart's.

He was attended by a French cook, an Italian valet, a German jÃ¤ger, and a Greek page. At this dreary season of the year this party was, perhaps, the most distinguished in the metropolis.

Three years' absence and a little knowledge of life had somewhat changed the Duke of St. James's feelings with regard to his noble relatives. He was quite disembarrassed of that Panglossian philosophy which had hitherto induced him to believe that the Earl of Fitz-pompey was the best of all possible uncles. On the contrary, his Grace rather doubted whether the course which his relations had pursued towards him was quite the most proper and the most prudent; and he took great credit to himself for having, with such unbounded indulgence, on the whole deported himself with so remarkable a temperance. His Grace, too, could no longer innocently delude himself with the idea that all the attention which had been lavished upon him was solely occasioned by the impulse of consanguinity. Finally, the young Duke's conscience often misgave him when he thought of Mr. Dacre. He determined, therefore, on returning to England, not to commit himself too decidedly with the Fitz-pompeys, and he had cautiously guarded himself from being entrapped into becoming their guest. At the same time, the recollection of old intimacy, the general regard which he really felt for them all, and the sincere affection which he entertained for his cousin Caroline, would have deterred him from giving any outward signs of his altered feelings, even if other considerations had not intervened.

And other considerations did intervene. A Duke, and a young Duke, is an important personage; but he must still be introduced. Even our hero might make a bad tack on his first cruise. Almost as important personages have committed the same blunder. Talk of Catholic emancipation! O! thou Imperial Parliament, emancipate the forlorn wretches who have got into a bad set! Even thy omnipotence must fail there!

Now, the Countess of Fitz-pompey was a brilliant of the first water. Under no better auspices could the Duke of St. James bound upon the stage. No man in town could arrange his club affairs for him with greater celerity and greater tact than the Earl; and the married daughters were as much like their mother as a pair of diamond ear-rings are like a diamond necklace.

The Duke, therefore, though he did not choose to get caged in Fitz-pompey House, sent his page, Spiridion, to the Countess, on a special embassy of announcement on the evening of his arrival, and on the following morning his Grace himself made his appearance at an early hour.

Lord Fitz-pompey, who was as consummate a judge of men and manners as he was an indifferent speculator on affairs, and who was almost as finished a man of the world as he was an imperfect philosopher, soon perceived that considerable changes had taken place in the ideas as well as in the exterior of his nephew. The Duke, however, was extremely cordial, and greeted the family in terms almost of fondness. He shook his uncle by the hand with a fervour with which few noblemen had communicated for a considerable period, and he saluted his aunt on the cheek with a delicacy which did not disturb the rouge. He turned to his cousin.

Lady Caroline St. Maurice was indeed a right beautiful being. She, whom the young Duke had left merely a graceful and kind-hearted girl, three years had changed into a somewhat dignified but most lovely woman. A little perhaps of her native ease had been lost; a little perhaps of a manner rather too artificial had supplanted that exquisite address which Nature alone had prompted; but at this moment her manner was as unstudied and as genuine as when they had gambolled together in the bowers of Malthorpe. Her white and delicate arm was extended with cordial grace, her full blue eye beamed with fondness, and the soft blush that rose on her fair cheek exquisitely contrasted with the clusters of her dark brown hair.

The Duke was struck, almost staggered. He remembered their infant loves; he recovered with ready address. He bent his head with graceful affection and pressed her lips. He almost repented that he had not accepted his uncle's offer of hospitality.

CHAPTER IV.

A Social Triumph

LORD FITZ-POMPEY was a little consoled for the change which he had observed in the character of the Duke by the remembrance of the embrace with which his Grace had greeted Lady Caroline. Never indeed did a process which has, through the lapse of so many ages, occasioned so much delight, produce more lively satisfaction than the kiss in question. Lord Fitz-pompey had given up his plan of managing the Duke after the family dinner which his nephew had the pleasure to join the first day of his first visit. The Duke and he were alone, and his Lordship availed himself of the rare opportunity with that adroitness for which he was celebrated. Nothing could be more polite, more affable, more kind, than his Grace's manner! but the uncle cared little for politeness, or affability, or kindness. The crafty courtier wanted candour, and that was absent. That ingenuous openness of disposition, that frank and affectionate demeanour, for which the Duke of St. James had been so remarkable in his early youth, and with the aid of which Lord Fitz-pompey had built so many Spanish castles, had quite disappeared.

Nothing could be more artificial, more conventional, more studied, than his whole deportment. In vain Lord Fitz-pompey pumped; the empty bucket invariably reminded him of his lost labour. In vain his Lordship laid his little diplomatic traps to catch a hint of the purposes or an intimation of the inclinations of his nephew; the bait was never seized. In vain the Earl affected unusual conviviality and boundless affection; the Duke sipped his claret and admired his pictures. Nothing would do. An air of habitual calm, a look of kind condescension, and an inclination to a smile, which never burst into a beam, announced that the Duke of St. James was perfectly satisfied with existence, and conscious that he was himself, of that existence, the most distinguished ornament. In fact, he was a sublime coxcomb; one of those rare characters whose finished manner and shrewd sense combined prevent their conceit from being contemptible. After many consultations it was determined between the aunt and uncle that it would be most prudent to affect a total non-interference with their nephew's affairs, and in the meantime to trust to the goodness of Providence and the charms of Caroline.

Lady Fitz-pompey determined that the young Duke should make his debut at once, and at her house. Although it was yet January, she did not despair of collecting a select band of guests, Brahmins of the highest caste. Some choice spirits were in office, like her lord, and therefore in town; others were only passing through; but no one caught a flying-fish with more dexterity than the Countess. The notice was short, the whole was unstudied. It was a felicitous impromptu, and twenty guests were assembled, who were the Corinthian capitals of the temple of fashion.

There was the Premier, who was invited, not because he was a minister, but because he was a hero. There was another Duke not less celebrated, whose palace was a breathing shrine which sent forth the oracles of mode. True, he had ceased to be a young Duke; but he might be consoled for the vanished lustre of youth by the recollection that he had enjoyed it, and by the present inspiration of an accomplished manhood. There were the Prince and the Princess Protocoli: his Highness a first-rate diplomatist, unrivalled for his management of an opera; and his consort, with a countenance like Cleopatra and a tiara like a constellation, famed alike for her shawls and her snuff. There were Lord and Lady Bloomerly, who were the best friends on earth: my Lord a sportsman, but soft withal, his talk the Jockey Club, filtered through White's; my Lady a little blue, and very beautiful. Their daughter, Lady Charlotte, rose by her mother's side like a tall bud by a full-blown flower. There were the Viscountess Blaze, a peeress in her own right, and her daughter, Miss Blaze Dash-away, who, besides the glory of the future coronet, moved in all the confidence of independent thousands. There was the Marquess of Macaroni, who was at the same time a general, an ambassador, and a dandy; and who, if he had liked, could have worn twelve orders; but this day, being modest, only wore six. There, too, was the Marchioness, with a stomacher stiff with brilliants extracted from the snuffboxes presented to her husband at a Congress.

There were Lord Sunium, who was not only a peer but a poet; and his lady, a Greek, who looked just finished by Phidias. There, too, was Pococurante, the epicurean and triple millionaire, who in a political country dared to despise politics, in the most aristocratic of kingdoms had refused nobility, and in a land which showers all its honours upon its cultivators invested his whole fortune in the funds. He lived in a retreat like the villa of Hadrian, and maintained himself in an elevated position chiefly by his wit and a little by his wealth. There, too, were his noble wife, thoroughbred to her fingers' tips, and beaming like the evening star; and his son, who was an M.P., and thought his father a fool. In short, our party was no common party, but a band who formed the very core of civilisation; a high court of last appeal, whose word was a fiat, whose sign was a hint, whose stare was death, and sneer——— damnation!

The Graces befriend us! We have forgotten the most important personage. It is the first time in his life that Charles Annesley has been neglected. It will do him good.

Dandy has been voted vulgar, and beau is now the word. It may be doubted whether the revival will stand; and as for the exploded title, though it had its faults at first, the muse of Byron has made it not only English, but classical. Charles Annesley could hardly be called a dandy or a beau. There was nothing in his dress—though some mysterious arrangement in his costume, some rare simplicity, some curious happiness, always made it distinguished—there was nothing, however, in his dress, which could account for the influence which he exercised over the manners of his contemporaries. Charles Annesley was about thirty. He had inherited from his father, a younger brother, a small estate; and, though heir to a wealthy earldom, he had never abused what the world called 'his prospects.' Yet his establishment, his little house in Mayfair, his horses, his moderate stud at Melton, were all unique, and everything connected with him was unparalleled for its elegance, its invention, and its refinement. But his manner was his magic. His natural and subdued nonchalance, so different from the assumed non-emotion of a mere dandy; his coldness of heart, which was hereditary, not acquired; his cautious courage, and his unadulterated self-love, had permitted him to mingle much with mankind without being too deeply involved in the play of their passions; while his exquisite sense of the ridiculous quickly revealed those weaknesses to him which his delicate satire did not spare, even while it refrained from wounding. All feared, marry admired, and none hated him. He was too powerful not to dread, too dexterous not to admire, too superior to hate. Perhaps the great secret of his manner was his exquisite superciliousness, a quality which, of all, is the most difficult to manage. Even with his intimates he was never confidential, and perpetually assumed his public character with the private coterie which he loved to rule. On the whole, he was unlike any of the leading men of modern days, and rather reminded one of the fine gentlemen of our old brilliant comedy, the Dorimants, the Bellairs, and the Mirabels.

Charles Annesley was a member of the distinguished party who were this day to decide the fate of the young Duke. Let him come forward!

His Grace moved towards them, tall and elegant in figure, and with that air of affable dignity which becomes a noble, and which adorns a court; none of that affected indifference which seems to imply that nothing can compensate for the exertion of moving, and 'which makes the dandy, while it mars the man.' His large and somewhat sleepy grey eye, his clear complexion, his small mouth, his aquiline nose, his transparent forehead, his rich brown hair, and the delicacy of his extremities, presented, when combined, a very excellent specimen of that style of beauty for which the nobility of England are remarkable. Gentle, for he felt the importance of the tribunal, never loud, ready, yet a little reserved, he neither courted nor shunned examination. His finished manner, his experience of society, his pretensions to taste, the gaiety of his temper, and the liveliness of his imagination, gradually developed themselves with the developing hours.

The banquet was over: the Duke of St. James passed his examination with unqualified approval; and having been stamped at the mint of fashion as a sovereign of the brightest die, he was flung forth, like the rest of his golden brethren, to corrupt the society of which he was the brightest ornament.

CHAPTER V.

Sweeping Changes

THE morning after the initiatory dinner the young Duke drove to Hauteville House, his family mansion, situated in his family square. His Grace particularly prided himself on his knowledge of the arts; a taste for which, among other things, he intended to introduce into England. Nothing could exceed the horror with which he witnessed the exterior of his mansion, except the agony with which he paced through the interior.

'Is this a palace?' thought the young Duke; 'this hospital a palace!'

He entered. The marble hall, the broad and lofty double staircase painted in fresco, were not unpromising, in spite of the dingy gilding; but with what a mixed feeling of wonder and disgust did the Duke roam through clusters of those queer chambers which in England are called drawing-rooms!

'Where are the galleries, where the symmetrical saloons, where the lengthened suite, where the collateral cabinets, sacred to the statue of a nymph or the mistress of a painter, in which I have been customed to reside? What page would condescend to lounge in this ante-chamber? And is this gloomy vault, that you call a dining-room, to be my hall of Apollo? Order my carriage.'

The Duke sent immediately for Sir Carte Blanche, the successor, in England, of Sir Christopher Wren. His Grace communicated at the same time his misery and his grand views. Sir Carte was astonished with his Grace's knowledge, and sympathised with his Grace's feelings. He offered consolation and promised estimates. They came in due time. Hauteville House, in the drawing of the worthy Knight, might have been mistaken for the Louvre. Some adjoining mansions were, by some magical process for which Sir Carte was famous, to be cleared of their present occupiers, and the whole side of the square was in future to be the site of Hauteville House. The difficulty was great, but the object was greater. The expense, though the estimate made a bold assault on the half million, was a mere trifle, 'considering.' The Duke was delighted. He condescended to make a slight alteration in Sir Carte's drawing, which Sir Carte affirmed to be a great improvement. Now it was Sir Carte's turn to be delighted. The Duke was excited by his architect's admiration, and gave him a dissertation on Schönbrunn.

Although Mr. Dacre had been disappointed in his hope of exercising a personal influence over the education of his ward, he had been more fortunate in his plans for the management of his ward's property. Perhaps there never was an instance of the opportunities afforded by a long minority

- 16 -

having been used to greater advantage. The estates had been increased and greatly improved, all and very heavy mortgages had been paid off, and the rents been fairly apportioned. Mr. Dacre, by his constant exertions and able dispositions since his return to England, also made up for the neglect with which an important point had been a little treated; and at no period had the parliamentary influence of the house of Hauteville been so extensive, so decided, and so well bottomed as when our hero became its chief.

In spite of his proverbial pride, it seemed that Mr. Dacre was determined not to be offended by the conduct of his ward. The Duke had not yet announced his arrival in England to his guardian; but about a month after that event he received a letter of congratulation from Mr. Dacre, who at the same time expressed a desire to resign a trust into his Grace's hand which, he believed, had not been abused. The Duke, who rather dreaded an interview, wrote in return that he intended very shortly to visit Yorkshire, when he should have the pleasure of availing himself of the kind invitation to Castle Dacre; and having thus, as he thought, dexterously got rid of the old gentleman for the present, he took a ride with Lady Caroline St. Maurice.

CHAPTER VI.

The Duke Visits Hauteville

PARLIAMENT assembled, the town filled, and every moment in the day of the Duke of St. James was occupied. Sir Carte and his tribe filled up the morning. Then there were endless visits to endless visitors; dressing; riding, chiefly with Lady Caroline; luncheons, and the bow window at White's. Then came the evening with all its crash and glare; the banquet, the opera, and the ball.

The Duke of St. James took the oaths and his seat. He was introduced by Lord Fitz-pompey. He heard a debate. We laugh at such a thing, especially in the Upper House; but, on the whole, the affair is imposing, particularly if we take part in it. Lord Ex-Chamberlain thought the nation going on wrong, and he made a speech full of currency and constitution. Baron Deprivyseal seconded him with great effect, brief but bitter, satirical and sore. The Earl of Quarterday answered these, full of confidence in the nation and in himself. When the debate was getting heavy, Lord Snap jumped up to give them something light. The Lords do not encourage wit, and so are obliged to put up with pertness. But Viscount Memoir was very statesmanlike, and spouted a sort of universal history. Then there was Lord Ego, who vindicated his character, when nobody knew he had one, and explained his motives, because his auditors could not understand his acts. Then there was a maiden speech, so inaudible that it was doubted whether, after all, the young orator really did lose his virginity. In the end, up started the Premier, who, having nothing to say, was manly, and candid, and liberal; gave credit to his adversaries and took credit to himself, and then the motion was withdrawn.

While all this was going on, some made a note, some made a bet, some consulted a book, some their ease, some yawned, a few slept; yet, on the whole, there was an air about the assembly which can be witnessed in no other in Europe. Even the most indifferent looked as if he would come forward if the occasion should demand him, and the most imbecile as if he could serve his country if it required him. When a man raises his eyes from his bench and sees his ancestor in the tapestry, he begins to understand the pride of blood.

The young Duke had not experienced many weeks of his career before he began to sicken of living in an hotel. Hitherto he had not reaped any of the fruits of the termination of his minority. He was a *cavalier seul*, highly considered, truly, but yet a mere member of society. He had been this for years. This was not the existence to enjoy which he had hurried to England. He aspired to be society itself. In a word, his tastes were of the most magnificent description, and he sighed to be surrounded by a court. As

Hauteville House, even with Sir Carte's extraordinary exertions, could not be ready for his reception for three years, which to him appeared eternity, he determined to look about for an establishment. He was fortunate. A nobleman who possessed an hereditary mansion of the first class, and much too magnificent for his resources, suddenly became diplomatic, and accepted an embassy. The Duke of St. James took everything off his hands: house, furniture, wines, cooks, servants, horses. Sir Carte was sent in to touch up the gilding and make a few temporary improvements; and Lady Fitz-pompey pledged herself to organise the whole establishment ere the full season commenced and the early Easter had elapsed, which had now arrived.

It had arrived, and the young Duke had departed to his chief family seat, Hauteville Castle, in Yorkshire. He intended at the same time to fulfil his long-pledged engagement at Castle Dacre. He arrived at Hauteville amid the ringing of bells, the roasting of oxen, and the crackling of bonfires. The Castle, unlike most Yorkshire castles, was a Gothic edifice, ancient, vast, and strong; but it had received numerous additions in various styles of architecture, which were at the same time great sources of convenience and great violations of taste. The young Duke was seized with a violent desire to live in a genuine Gothic castle: each day his refined taste was outraged by discovering Roman windows and Grecian doors. He determined to emulate Windsor, and he sent for Sir Carte.

Sir Carte came as quick as thunder after lightning. He was immediately struck with Hauteville, particularly with its capabilities. It was a superb place, certainly, and might be rendered unrivalled. The situation seemed made for the pure Gothic. The left wing should decidedly be pulled down, and its site occupied by a Knight's hall; the old terrace should be restored; the donjon keep should be raised, and a gallery, three hundred feet long, thrown through the body of the castle. Estimates, estimates, estimates! But the time? This was a greater point than the expense. Wonders should be done. There were now five hundred men working for Hauteville House; there should be a thousand for Hauteville Castle. Carte Blanche, Carte Blanche, Carte Blanche!

On his arrival in Yorkshire the Duke had learnt that the Dacres were in Norfolk on a visit. As the Castle was some miles off, he saw no necessity to make a useless exertion, and so he sent his jÃ¤ger with his card. He had now been ten days in his native county. It was dull, and he was restless. He missed the excitement of perpetual admiration, and his eye drooped for constant glitter. He suddenly returned to town, just when the county had flattered itself that he was about to appoint his public days.

CHAPTER VII.

The First Fancy

EASTER was over, the sun shone, the world was mad, and the young Duke made his dÃ©but at Almack's. He determined to prove that he had profited by a winter at Vienna. His dancing was declared consummate. He galloped with grace and waltzed with vigour. It was difficult to decide which was more admirable, the elegance of his prance or the precision of his whirl. A fat Russian Prince, a lean Austrian Count, a little German Baron, who, somehow or other, always contrived to be the most marked characters of the evening, disappeared in despair.

There was a lady in the room who attracted the notice of our hero. She was a remarkable personage. There are some sorts of beauty which defy description, and almost scrutiny. Some faces rise upon us in the tumult of life like stars from out the sea, or as if they had moved out of a picture. Our first impression is anything but fleshly. We are struck dumb, we gasp, our limbs quiver, a faintness glides over our frame, we are awed; instead of gazing upon the apparition, we avert the eyes, which yet will feed upon its beauty. A strange sort of unearthly pain mixes with the intense pleasure. And not till, with a struggle, we call back to our memory the commonplaces of existence, can we recover our commonplace demeanour. These, indeed, are rare visions, early feelings, when our young existence leaps with its mountain torrents; but as the river of our life rolls on, our eyes grow dimmer or our blood more cold.

Some effect of this kind was produced on the Duke of St. James by the unknown dame. He turned away his head to collect his senses. His eyes again rally; and this time, being prepared, he was more successful in his observations.

The lady was standing against the wall; a young man was addressing some remarks to her which apparently were not very interesting. She was tall and young, and, as her tiara betokened, married; dazzling fair, but without colour; with locks like night and features delicate, but precisely defined. Yet all this did not at first challenge the observation of the young Duke. It was the general and peculiar expression of her countenance which had caused in him such emotion. There was an expression of resignation, or repose, or sorrow, or serenity, which in these excited chambers was strange, and singular, and lone. She gazed like some genius invisible to the crowd, and mourning over its degradation.

He stopped St. Maurice, as his cousin passed by, to inquire her name, and learnt that she was Lady Aphrodite Grafton, the wife of Sir Lucius Grafton.

'What, Lucy Grafton!' exclaimed the Duke. 'I remember; I was his fag at Eton. He was a handsome dog; but I doubt whether he deserves such a wife. Introduce me.'

Lady Aphrodite received our hero with a gentle bow, and did not seem quite as impressed with his importance as most of those to whom he had been presented in the course of the evening. The Duke had considerable tact with women, and soon perceived that the common topics of a hack flirtation would not do in the present case. He was therefore mild and modest, rather piquant, somewhat rational, and apparently perfectly unaffected. Her Ladyship's reserve wore away. She refused to dance, but conversed with more animation. The Duke did not leave her side. The women began to stare, the men to bet: Lady Aphrodite against the field. In vain his Grace laid a thousand plans to arrange a tea-room tÃªte-Ã -tÃªte. He was unsuccessful. As he was about to return to the charge her Ladyship desired a passer-by to summon her carriage. No time was to be lost. The Duke began to talk hard about his old friend and schoolfellow, Sir Lucius. A greenhorn would have thought it madness to take an interest in such a person of all others; but women like you to enter their house as their husband's friend. Lady Aphrodite could not refrain from expressing her conviction that Sir Lucius would be most happy to renew his acquaintance with the Duke of St. James, and the Duke of St. James immediately said that he would take the earliest opportunity of giving him that pleasure.

CHAPTER VIII.

A Noble Reprobate

SIR LUCIUS GRAFTON was five or six years older than the Duke of St. James, although he had been his contemporary at Eton. He, too, had been a minor, and had inherited an estate capable of supporting the becoming dignity of an ancient family. In appearance he was an Antinous. There was, however, an expression of firmness, almost of ferocity, about his mouth, which quite prevented his countenance from being effeminate, and broke the dreamy voluptuousness of the rest of his features. In mind he was a rouÃ©. Devoted to pleasure, he had racked the goblet at an early age; and before he was five-and-twenty procured for himself a reputation which made all women dread and some men shun him. In the very wildest moment of his career, when he was almost marked like Cain, he had met Lady Aphrodite Maltravers. She was the daughter of a nobleman who justly prided himself, in a degenerate age, on the virtue of his house. Nature, as if in recompense for his goodness, had showered all her blessings on his only daughter. Never was daughter more devoted to a widowed sire; never was woman influenced by principles of purer morality.

This was the woman who inspired Sir Lucius Grafton with an ungovernable passion. Despairing of success by any other method, conscious that, sooner or later, he must, for family considerations, propagate future baronets of the name of Grafton, he determined to solicit her hand. But for him to obtain it, he was well aware, was difficult. Confident in his person, his consummate knowledge of the female character, and his unrivalled powers of dissimulation, Sir Lucius arranged his dispositions. The daughter feared, the father hated him. There was indeed much to be done; but the remembrance of a thousand triumphs supported the adventurer. Lady Aphrodite was at length persuaded that she alone could confirm the reformation which she alone had originated. She yielded to a passion which her love of virtue had alone kept in subjection. Sir Lucius and Lady Aphrodite knelt at the feet of the old Earl. The tears of his daughter, ay! and of his future son-in-law—for Sir Lucius knew when to weep—were too much for his kind and generous heart. He gave them his blessing, which faltered on his tongue.

A year had not elapsed ere Lady Aphrodite woke to all the wildness of a deluded woman. The idol on whom she had lavished all the incense of her innocent affections became every day less like a true divinity. At length even the ingenuity of a passion could no longer disguise the hideous and bitter truth. She was no longer loved. She thought of her father. Ah, what was the madness of her memory!

The agony of her mind disappointed her husband's hope of an heir, and the promise was never renewed.

In vain she remonstrated with the being to whom she was devoted: in vain she sought by meek endurance again to melt his heart. It was cold; it was callous. Most women would have endeavoured to recover their lost influence by different tactics; some, perhaps, would have forgotten their mortification in their revenge. But Lady Aphrodite had been the victim of passion, and now was its slave. She could not dissemble.

Not so her spouse. Sir Lucius knew too well the value of a good character to part very easily with that which he had so unexpectedly regained. Whatever were his excesses, they were prudent ones. He felt that boyhood could alone excuse the folly of glorying in vice; and he knew that, to respect virtue, it was not absolutely necessary to be virtuous. No one was, apparently, more choice in his companions than Sir Lucius Grafton; no husband was seen oftener with his wife; no one paid more respect to age, or knew better when to wear a grave countenance. The world praised the magical influence of Lady Aphrodite; and Lady Aphrodite, in private, wept over her misery. In public she made an effort to conceal all she felt; and, as it is a great inducement to every woman to conceal that she is neglected by the man whom she adores, her effort was not unsuccessful. Yet her countenance might indicate that she was little interested in the scene in which she mixed. She was too proud to weep, but too sad to smile. Elegant and lone, she stood among her crushed and lovely hopes like a column amid the ruins of a beautiful temple.

The world declared that Lady Aphrodite was desperately virtuous, and the world was right. A thousand fireflies had sparkled round this myrtle, and its fresh and verdant hue was still unsullied and un-scorched. Not a very accurate image, but pretty; and those who have watched a glancing shower of these glittering insects will confess that, poetically, the bush might burn. The truth is, that Lady Aphrodite still trembled when she recalled the early anguish of her broken sleep of love, and had not courage enough to hope that she might dream again. Like the old Hebrews, she had been so chastened for her wild idolatry that she dared not again raise an image to animate the wilderness of her existence. Man she at the same time feared and despised. Compared with her husband, all who surrounded her were, she felt, in appearance inferior, and were, she believed, in mind the same.

We know not how it is, but love at first sight is a subject of constant ridicule; but, somehow, we suspect that it has more to do with the affairs of this world than the world is willing to own. Eyes meet which have never met before, and glances thrill with expression which is strange. We contrast these pleasant sights and new emotions with hackneyed objects and worn sensations.

Another glance and another thrill, and we spring into each other's arms. What can be more natural?

Ah, that we should awake so often to truth so bitter! Ah, that charm by charm should evaporate from the talisman which had enchanted our existence!

And so it was with this sweet woman, whose feelings grow under the pen. She had repaired to a splendid assembly to play her splendid part with the consciousness of misery, without the expectation of hope. She awaited without interest the routine which had been so often uninteresting; she viewed without emotion the characters which had never moved. A stranger suddenly appeared upon the stage, fresh as the morning dew, and glittering like the morning star. All eyes await, all tongues applaud him. His step is grace, his countenance hope, his voice music! And was such a being born only to deceive and be deceived? Was he to run the same false, palling, ruinous career which had filled so many hearts with bitterness and dimmed the radiancy of so many eyes? Never! The nobility of his soul spoke from his glancing eye, and treated the foul suspicion with scorn. Ah, would that she had such a brother to warn, to guide, to love!

So felt the Lady Aphrodite! So felt; we will not say so reasoned. When once a woman allows an idea to touch her heart, it is miraculous with what rapidity the idea is fathered by her brain. All her experience, all her anguish, all her despair, vanished like a long frost, in an instant, and in a night. She felt a delicious conviction that a knight had at length come to her rescue, a hero worthy of an adventure so admirable. The image of the young Duke filled her whole mind; she had no ear for others' voices; she mused on his idea with the rapture of a votary on the mysteries of a new faith.

Yet strange, when he at length approached her, when he addressed her, when she replied to that mouth which had fascinated even before it had spoken, she was cold, reserved, constrained. Some talk of the burning cheek and the flashing eye of passion; but a wise man would not, perhaps, despair of the heroine who, when he approaches her, treats him almost with scorn, and trembles while she affects to disregard him.

Lady Aphrodite has returned home: she hurries to her apartment, she falls in a sweet reverie, her head leans upon her hand. Her soubrette, a pretty and chattering Swiss, whose republican virtue had been corrupted by Paris, as Rome by Corinth, endeavours to divert Mer lady's ennui: she excruciates her beautiful mistress with tattle about the admiration of Lord B———and the sighs of Sir Harry. Her Ladyship reprimands her for her levity, and the soubrette, grown sullen, revenges herself for her mistress's reproof by converting the sleepy process of brushing into lively torture.

The Duke of St. James called upon Lady Aphrodite Grafton the next day, and at an hour when he trusted to find her alone. He was not disappointed. More than once the silver-tongued pendule sounded during that somewhat protracted but most agreeable visit. He was, indeed, greatly interested by her, but he was an habitual gallant, and always began by feigning more than he felt. She, on the contrary, who was really in love, feigned much less. Yet she was no longer constrained, though calm. Fluent, and even gay, she talked as well as listened, and her repartees more than once called forth the resources of her guest. She displayed a delicate and even luxurious taste, not only in her conversation, but (the Duke observed it with delight) in her costume. She had a passion for music and for flowers; she sang a romance, and she gave him a rose. He retired perfectly fascinated.

CHAPTER IX.

Old Friends Meet

SIR LUCIUS GRAFTON called on the Duke of St. James. They did not immediately swear an eternal friendship, but they greeted each other with considerable warmth, talked of old times and old companions, and compared their former sensations with their present. No one could be a more agreeable companion than Sir Lucius, and this day he left a very favourable impression with his young friend. From this day, too, the Duke's visits at the Baronet's were frequent; and as the Graftons were intimate with the Fitz-pompeys, scarcely a day elapsed without his having the pleasure of passing a portion of it in the company of Lady Aphrodite: his attentions to her were marked, and sometimes mentioned. Lord Fitz-pompey was rather in a flutter. George did not ride so often with Caroline, and never alone with her. This was disagreeable; but the Earl was a man of the world, and a sanguine man withal. These things will happen. It is of no use to quarrel with the wind; and, for his part, he was not sorry that he had the honour of the Grafton acquaintance; it secured Caroline her cousin's company; and as for the *liaison*, if there were one, why it must end, and probably the difficulty of terminating it might even hasten the catastrophe which he had so much at heart. 'So, Laura, dearest! let the Graftons be asked to dinner.'

In one of those rides to which Caroline was not admitted, for Lady Aphrodite was present, the Duke of St. James took his way to the Regent's Park, a wild sequestered spot, whither he invariably repaired when he did not wish to be noticed; for the inhabitants of this pretty suburb are a distinct race, and although their eyes are not unobserving, from their inability to speak the language of London they are unable to communicate their observations.

The spring sun was setting, and flung a crimson flush over the blue waters and the white houses. The scene was rather imposing, and reminded our hero of days of travel. A sudden thought struck him. Would it not be delightful to build a beautiful retreat in this sweet and retired land, and be able in an instant to fly from the formal magnificence of a London mansion? Lady Aphrodite was charmed with the idea; for the enamoured are always delighted with what is fanciful. The Duke determined immediately to convert the idea into an object. To lose no time was his grand motto. As he thought that Sir Carte had enough upon his hands, he determined to apply to an artist whose achievements had been greatly vaunted to him by a distinguished and noble judge.

M. Bijou de Millecolonnes, Chevalier of the Legion of Honour and member of the Academy of St. Luke's, except in his title, was the antipodes of Sir Carte Blanche. Sir Carte was all solidity, solemnity, and correctness; Bijou de

Millecolonnes all lightness, gaiety, and originality. Sir Carte was ever armed with the Parthenon, Palladio, and St. Peter's; Bijou de Millecolonnes laughed at the ancients, called Palladio and Michel barbarians of the middle ages, and had himself invented an order. Bijou was not so plausible as Sir Carte; but he was infinitely more entertaining. Far from being servile, he allowed no one to talk but himself, and made his fortune by his elegant insolence. How singular it is that those who love servility are always the victims of impertinence!

Gaily did Bijou de Millecolonnes drive his pea-green cabriolet to the spot in question. He formed his plan in an instant. 'The occasional retreat of a noble should be something picturesque and poetical. The mind should be led to voluptuousness by exquisite associations, as well as by the creations of art. It is thus their luxury is rendered more intense by the reminiscences that add past experience to present enjoyment! For instance, if you sail down a river, imitate the progress of Cleopatra. And here, here, where the opportunity is so ample, what think you of reviving the Alhambra?'

Splendid conception! The Duke already fancied himself a Caliph. 'Lose no time, Chevalier! Dig, plant, build!'

Nine acres were obtained from the Woods and Forests; mounds were thrown up, shrubs thrown in; the paths emulated the serpent; the nine acres seemed interminable. All was surrounded by a paling eight feet high, that no one might pierce the mystery of the preparations.

A rumour was soon current that the Zoological Society intended to keep a Bengal tiger *au naturel*, and that they were contriving a residence which would amply compensate him for his native jungle. The Regent's Park was in despair, the landlords lowered their rents, and the tenants petitioned the King. In a short time some hooded domes and some Saracenic spires rose to sight, and the truth was then made known that the young Duke of St. James was building a villa. The Regent's Park was in rapture, the landlords raised their rents, and the tenants withdrew their petition.

CHAPTER X.

His Grace Entertains

MR. DACRE again wrote to the Duke of St. James. He regretted that he had been absent from home when his Grace had done him the honour of calling at Castle Dacre. Had he been aware of that intended gratification, he could with ease, and would with pleasure, have postponed his visit to Norfolk. He also regretted that it would not be in his power to visit London this season; and as he thought that no further time should be lost in resigning the trust with which he had been so honoured, he begged leave to forward his accounts to the Duke, and with them some notes which he believed would convey some not unimportant information to his Grace for the future management of his property. The young Duke took a rapid glance at the sum total of his rental, crammed all the papers into a cabinet with a determination to examine them the first opportunity, and then rolled off to a morning concert of which he was the patron.

The intended opportunity for the examination of the important papers was never caught, nor was it surprising that it escaped capture. It is difficult to conceive a career of more various, more constant, or more distracting excitement than that in which the Duke of St. James was now engaged. His life was an ocean of enjoyment, and each hour, like each wave, threw up its pearl. How dull was the ball in which he did not bound! How dim the banquet in which he did not glitter! His presence in the Gardens compensated for the want of flowers; his vision in the Park for the want of sun. In public breakfasts he was more indispensable than pine-apples; in private concerts more noticed than an absent prima donna. How fair was the dame on whom he smiled! How dark was the tradesman on whom he frowned! Think only of prime ministers and princes, to say nothing of princesses; nay! think only of managers of operas and French actors, to say nothing of French actresses; think only of jewellers, milliners, artists, horse-dealers, all the shoals who hurried for his sanction; think only of the two or three thousand civilised beings for whom all this population breathed, and who each of them had claims upon our hero's notice! Think of the statesmen, who had so much to ask and so much to give; the dandies to feed with and to be fed; the dangerous dowagers and the desperate mothers; the widows, wild as early partridges; the budding virgins, mild as a summer cloud and soft as an opera hat! Think of the drony bores, with their dull hum; think of the chivalric guardsmen, with their horses to sell and their bills to discount; think of Willis, think of Crockford, think of White's, think of Brooks', and you may form a faint idea how the young Duke had to talk, and eat, and flirt, and cut, and pet, and patronise!

You think it impossible for one man to do all this. There is yet much behind. You may add to the catalogue Melton and Newmarket; and if to hunt without an appetite and to bet without an object will not sicken you, why, build a yacht!

The Duke of St. James gave his first grand entertainment for the season. It was like the assembly of the immortals at the first levee of Jove. All hurried to pay their devoirs to the young king of fashion; and each who succeeded in becoming a member of the Court felt as proud as a peer with a new title, or a baronet with an old one. An air of regal splendour, an almost imperial assumption, was observed in the arrangements of the fÃªte. A troop of servants in rich liveries filled the hall; grooms lined the staircase; Spiridion, the Greek page, lounged on an ottoman in an ante-chamber, and, with the assistance of six young gentlemen in crimson-and-silver uniforms, announced the coming of the cherished guests. Cartloads of pine-apples were sent up from the Yorkshire Castle, and waggons of orange-trees from the Twickenham Villa.

A brilliant coterie, of which his Grace was a member, had amused themselves a few nights before by representing in costume the Court of Charles the First. They agreed this night to reappear in their splendid dresses; and the Duke, who was Villiers, supported his character, even to the gay shedding of a shower of diamonds. In his cap was observed an hereditary sapphire, which blazed like a volcano, and which was rumoured to be worth his rent-roll.

There was a short concert, at which the most celebrated Signora made her dÃ©but; there was a single vaudeville, which a white satin play-bill, presented to each guest as they entered the temporary theatre, indicated to have been written for the occasion; there was a ball, in which was introduced a new dance. Nothing for a moment was allowed to lag. *Longueurs* were skilfully avoided, and the excitement was so rapid that every one had an appetite for supper.

A long gallery lined with bronzes and *bijouterie*, with cabinets and sculpture, with china and with paintings, all purchased for the future ornament of Hauteville House, and here stowed away in unpretending, but most artificial, confusion, offered accommodation to all the guests. To a table covered with gold, and placed in a magnificent tent upon the stage, his Grace loyally led two princes of the blood and a child of France. Madame de Protocoli, Lady Aphrodite Grafton, the Duchess of Shropshire, and Lady Fitz-pompey, shared the honours of the pavilion, and some might be excused for envying a party so brilliant and a situation so distinguished. Yet Lady Aphrodite was an unwilling member of it; and nothing but the personal solicitation of Sir Lucius would have induced her to consent to the wish of their host.

A pink *carte* succeeded to the satin play-bill. Vi-tellius might have been pleased with the banquet. Ah, how shall we describe those soups, which surely must have been the magical elixir! How paint those ortolans dressed by the inimitable artist, Ã la St. James, for the occasion, and which look so beautiful in death that they must surely have preferred such an euthanasia even to flying in the perfumed air of an Auso-nian heaven!

Sweet bird! though thou hast lost thy plumage, thou shalt fly to my mistress! Is it not better to be nibbled by her than mumbled by a cardinal? I, too, will feed on thy delicate beauty. Sweet bird! thy companion has fled to my mistress; and now thou shalt thrill the nerves of her master! Oh! doff, then, thy waistcoat of wine-leaves, pretty rover! and show me that bosom more delicious even than woman's. What gushes of rapture! What a flavour! How peculiar! Even how sacred I Heaven at once sends both manna and quails. Another little wanderer! Pray follow my example! Allow me. All Paradise opens! Let me die eating ortolans to the sound of soft music!

Even the supper was brief, though brilliant; and again the cotillon and the quadrille, the waltz and the galoppe! At no moment of his life had the young Duke felt existence so intense. Wherever he turned his eye he found a responding glance of beauty and admiration; wherever he turned his ear the whispered tones were soft and sweet as summer winds. Each look was an offering, each word adoration! His soul dilated; the glory of the scene touched all his passions. He almost determined not again to mingle in society; but, like a monarch, merely to receive the world which worshipped him. The idea was sublime: was it even to him impracticable? In the midst of his splendour he fell into a reverie, and mused on his magnificence. He could no longer resist the conviction that he was a superior essence, even to all around him. The world seemed created solely for his enjoyment. Nor man nor woman could withstand him. From this hour he delivered himself up to a sublime selfishness. With all his passions and all his profusion, a callousness crept over his heart. His sympathy for those he believed his inferiors and his vassals was slight. Where we do not respect we soon cease to love; when we cease to love, virtue weeps and flies. His soul wandered in dreams of omnipotence.

This picture perhaps excites your dislike; perchance your contempt. Pause! Pity him! Pity his fatal youth!

CHAPTER XI.

Love at a Bazaar

THE Lady Aphrodite at first refused to sit in the Duke's pavilion. Was she, then, in the *habit* of refusing? Let us not forget our Venus of the Waters. Shall we whisper where the young Duke first dared to hope? No, you shall guess. *Je vous le donne en trois.* The Gardens? The opera? The tea-room? No! no! no! You are conceiving a locality much more romantic. Already you have created the bower of a Parisina, where the waterfall is even more musical than the birds, more lulling than the evening winds; where all is pale, except the stars; all hushed, except their beating pulses! Will this do? No! What think you, then, of a *Bazaar?*

O thou wonderful nineteenth century! thou that believest in no miracles and doest so many, hast thou brought this, too, about, that ladies' hearts should be won, and gentlemen's also, not in courts of tourney or halls of revel, but over a counter and behind a stall? We are, indeed, a nation of shopkeepers!

The king of Otaheite, though a despot, was a reformer. He discovered that the eating of bread-fruit was a barbarous custom, which would infallibly prevent his people from being a great nation. He determined to introduce French rolls. A party rebelled; the despot was energetic; some were executed; the rest ejected. The vagabonds arrived in England. As they had been banished in opposition to French rolls, they were declared to be a British interest. They professed their admiration of civil and religious liberty, and also of a subscription. When they had drunk a great deal of punch, and spent all their money, they discovered that they had nothing to eat, and would infallibly have been starved, had not an Hibernian Marchioness, who had never been in Ireland, been exceedingly shocked that men should die of hunger; and so, being one of the bustlers, she got up a fancy sale and a *Sandwich Isle Bazaar.*

All the world was there and of course our hero. Never was the arrival of a comet watched by astronomers who had calculated its advent with more anxiety than was the appearance of the young Duke. Never did man pass through such dangers. It was the fiery ordeal. St. Anthony himself was not assailed by more temptations. Now he was saved from the lustre of a blonde face by the superior richness of a blonde lace. He would infallibly have been ravished by that ringlet had he not been nearly reduced by that ring which sparkled on a hand like the white cat's. He was only preserved from his unprecedented dangers by their number. No, no! He had a better talisman: his conceit.

'Ah, Lady Balmont!' said his Grace to a smiling artist, who offered him one of her own drawings of a Swiss cottage, 'for me to be a tenant, it must be love and a cottage!'

'What! am I to buy this ring, Mrs. Abercroft? *Point de jour.* Oh! dreadful phrase! Allow me to present it to you, for you are the only one whom such words cannot make tremble.'

'This chain, Lady Jemima, for my glass! It will teach me where to direct it.'

'Ah! Mrs. Fitzroy!' and he covered his face with affected fear. 'Can you forgive me? Your beautiful note has been half an hour unanswered. The box is yours for Tuesday.'

He tried to pass the next stall with a smiling bow, but he could not escape. It was Lady de Courcy, a dowager, but not old. Once beautiful, her charms had not yet disappeared. She had a pair of glittering eyes, a skilfully-carmined cheek, and locks yet raven. Her eloquence made her now as conspicuous as once did her beauty. The young Duke was her constant object and her occasional victim. He hated above all things a talking woman; he dreaded above all others Lady de Courcy.

He could not shirk. She summoned him by name so loud that crowds of barbarians stared, and a man called to a woman, and said, 'My dear! make haste; here's a Duke!'

Lady de Courcy was prime confidant of the Irish Marchioness. She affected enthusiasm about the poor sufferers. She had learnt Otaheitan, she lectured about the bread-fruit, and she played upon a barbarous thrum-thrum, the only musical instrument in those savage wastes, ironically called the Society Islands, because there is no society. She was dreadful. The Duke in despair took out his purse, poured forth from the pink and silver delicacy, worked by the slender fingers of Lady Aphrodite, a shower of sovereigns, and fairly scampered off. At length he reached the lady of his heart.

'I fear,' said the young Duke with a smile, and in a soft sweet voice, 'that you will never speak to me again, for I am a ruined man.'

A beam of gentle affection reprimanded him even for badinage on such a subject.

'I really came here to buy up all your stock, but that gorgon, Lady de Courcy, captured me, and my ransom has sent me here free, but a beggar. I do not know a more ill-fated fellow than myself. Now, if you had only condescended to take me prisoner, I might have saved my money; for I should have kissed my chain.'

'My chains, I fear, are neither very alluring nor very strong.' She spoke with a thoughtful air, and he answered her only with his eye.

'I must bear off something from your stall,' he resumed in a more rapid and gayer tone, 'and, as I cannot purchase you must present. Now for a gift!'

'Choose!'

'Yourself.'

'Your Grace is really spoiling my sale. See! poor Lord Bagshot. What a valuable purchaser.'

'Ah! Bag, my boy!' said the Duke to a slang young nobleman whom he abhorred, but of whom he sometimes made a butt, 'am I in your way? Here! take this, and this, and this, and give me your purse. I'll pay Lady Aphrodite.' And so the Duke again showered some sovereigns, and returned the shrunken silk to its defrauded owner, who stared, and would have remonstrated, but the Duke turned his back upon him.

'There now,' he continued to Lady Aphrodite; 'there is two hundred per cent, profit for you. You are not half a *marchande*. I will stand here and be your shopman. Well, Annesley,' said he, as that dignitary passed, 'what will you buy? I advise you to get a place. 'Pon my soul, 'tis pleasant! Try Lady de Courcy. You know you are a favourite.'

'I assure your Grace,' said Mr. Annesley, speaking slowly, 'that that story about Lady de Courcy is quite untrue and very rude. I never turn my back on any woman; only my heel. We are on the best possible terms. She is never to speak to me, and I am always to bow to her. But I really must purchase. Where did you get that glass-chain, St. James? Lady Afy, can you accommodate me?'

'Here is one prettier! But are you near-sighted, too, Mr. Annesley?'

'Very. I look upon a long-sighted man as a brute who, not being able to see with his mind, is obliged to see with his body. The price of this?'

'A sovereign,' said the Duke; 'cheap; but we consider you as a friend.'

'A sovereign! You consider me a young Duke rather. Two shillings, and that a severe price; a charitable price. Here is half-a-crown; give me sixpence. I was not a minor. Farewell! I go to the little Pomfret. She is a sweet flower, and I intend to wear her in my button-hole. Good-bye, Lady Afy!'

The gay morning had worn away, and St. James never left his fascinating position. Many a sweet and many a soft thing he uttered. Sometimes he was baffled, but never beaten, and always returned to the charge with spirit. He was confident, because he was reckless: the lady had less trust in herself,

- 33 -

because she was anxious. Yet she combated well, and repressed the feelings which she could hardly conceal.

Many of her colleagues had already departed. She requested the Duke to look after her carriage. A bold plan suddenly occurred to him, and he executed it with rare courage and rarer felicity.

'Lady Aphrodite Grafton's carriage!'

'Here, your Grace!'

'Oh! go home. Your lady will return with Madame de Protocoli.'

He rejoined her.

'I am sorry, that, by some blunder, your carriage has gone. What could you have told them?'

'Impossible! How provoking! How stupid!'

'Perhaps you told them that you would return with the Fitz-pompeys, but they are gone; or Mrs. Aberleigh, and she is not here; or perhaps—but they have gone too. Everyone has gone.'

'What shall I do? How distressing! I had better send. Pray send; or I will ask Lady de Courcy.'

'Oh! no, no! I really did not like to see you with her. As a favour—as a favour to me, I pray you not.'

'What can I do? I must send. Let me beg your Grace to send.'

'Certainly, certainly; but, ten to one, there will be some mistake. There always is some mistake when you send these strangers. And, besides, I forgot all this time my carriage is here. Let it take you home.'

'No, no!'

'Dearest Lady Aphrodite, do not distress yourself. I can wait here till the carriage returns, or I can walk; to be sure, I can walk. Pray, pray take the carriage! As a favour—as a favour to me!'

'But I cannot bear you to walk. I know you dislike walking.'

'Well, then, I will wait.'

'Well, if it must be so; but I am ashamed to inconvenience you. How provoking of these men! Pray, then, tell the coachman to drive fast, that you may not have to wait. I declare there is scarcely a human being in the room; and those odd people are staring so!'

He pressed her arm as he led her to his carriage. She is in; and yet, before the door shuts, he lingers.

'I shall certainly walk,' said he. 'I do not think the easterly wind will make me very ill. Good-bye! Oh, what a *coup-de-vent*!'

'Let me get out, then; and pray, pray take the carriage. I would much sooner do anything than go in it. I would much rather walk. I am sure you will be ill!'

'Not if I be with you.'

CHAPTER XII.

Royal Favour

THERE was a brilliant levee, all stars and garters; and a splendid drawing-room, all plumes and *sÃ©duisantes*. Many a bright eye, as its owner fought his way down St. James's Street, shot a wistful glance at the enchanted bow-window where the Duke and his usual companions, Sir Lucius, Charles Annesley, and Lord Squib, lounged and laughed, stretched themselves and sneered: many a bright eye, that for a moment pierced the futurity that painted her going in state as Duchess of St. James.

His Majesty summoned a dinner party, a rare but magnificent event, and the chief of the house of Hauteville appeared among the chosen vassals. This visit did the young Duke good; and a few more might have permanently cured the conceit which the present one momentarily calmed. His Grace saw the plate, and was filled with envy; his Grace listened to his Majesty, and was filled with admiration. O, father of thy people! if thou wouldst but look a little oftener on thy younger sons, their morals and their manners might be alike improved.

His Majesty, in the course of the evening, with his usual good-nature, signalled out for his notice the youngest, and not the least distinguished, of his guests. He complimented the young Duke on the accession to the ornaments of his court, and said, with a smile, that he had heard of conquests in foreign ones. The Duke accounted for his slight successes by reminding his Majesty that he had the honour of being his godson, and this he said in a slight and easy way, not smart or quick, or as a repartee to the royal observation; for 'it is not decorous to bandy compliments with your Sovereign.' His Majesty asked some questions about an Emperor or an Archduchess, and his Grace answered to the purpose, but short, and not too pointed. He listened rather than spoke, and smiled more assents than he uttered. The King was pleased with his young subject, and marked his approbation by conversing with that unrivalled affability which is gall to a Roundhead and inspiration to a Cavalier. There was a *bon mot*, which blazed with all the soft brilliancy of sheet lightning. What a contrast to the forky flashes of a regular wit! Then there was an anecdote of Sheridan—the royal Sheridaniana are not thrice-told tales—recounted with that curious felicity which has long stamped the illustrious narrator as a consummate *raconteur*. Then——but the Duke knew when to withdraw; and he withdrew with renewed loyalty.

CHAPTER XIII.

A Lover's Trick

ONE day, looking in at his jeweller's, to see some models of a shield and vases which were executing for him in gold, the young Duke met Lady Aphrodite and the Fitz-pompeys. Lady Aphrodite was speaking to the jeweller about her diamonds, which were to be reset for her approaching fÃªte. The Duke took the ladies upstairs to look at the models, and while they were intent upon them and other curiosities, his absence for a moment was unperceived. He ran downstairs and caught Mr. Garnet.

'Mr. Garnet! I think I saw Lady Aphrodite give you her diamonds?' 'Yes, your Grace.'

'Are they valuable?' in a careless tone. 'Hum! pretty stones; very pretty stones, indeed. Few Baronets' ladies have a prettier set; worth perhaps a 1000L.; say 1200L. Lady Aphrodite Grafton is not the Duchess of St. James, you know,' said Mr. Garnet, as if he anticipated furnishing that future lady with a very different set of brilliants.

'Mr. Garnet, you can do me the greatest favour.' 'Your Grace has only to command me at all times.'

'Well, then, in a word, for time presses, can you contrive, without particularly altering—that is, without altering the general appearance of these diamonds—can you contrive to change the stones, and substitute the most valuable that you have; consistent, as I must impress upon you, with maintaining their general appearance as at present?'

'The most valuable stones,' musingly repeated Mr. Garnet; 'general appearance as at present? Your Grace is aware that we may run up some thousands even in this set?'

'I give you no limit.'

'But the time,' rejoined Mr. Garnet. 'They must be ready for her Ladyship's party. We shall be hard pressed. I am afraid of the time.'

'Cannot the men work all night? Pay them anything.'

'It shall be done, your Grace. Your Grace may command me in anything.'

'This is a secret between us, Garnet. Your partners————'

'Shall know nothing. And as for myself, I am as close as an emerald in a seal-ring.'

CHAPTER XIV.

Close of the Season

HUSSEIN PACHA, 'the favourite,' not only of the Marquess of Mash, but of Tattersall's, unaccountably sickened and died. His noble master, full of chagrin took to his bed, and followed his steed's example. The death of the Marquess caused a vacancy in the stewardship of the approaching Doncaster. Sir Lucius Grafton was the other steward, and he proposed to the Duke of St. James, as he was a Yorkshireman, to become his colleague. His Grace, who wished to pay a compliment to his county, closed with the proposition. Sir Lucius was a first-rate jockey; his colleague was quite ignorant of the noble science in all its details; but that was of slight importance. The Baronet was to be the working partner, and do the business; the Duke the show member of the concern, and do the magnificence; as one banker, you may observe, lives always in Portland Place, reads the Court Journal all the morning, and has an opera-box, while his partner lodges in Lombard Street, thumbs a price-current, and only has a box at Clapham.

The young Duke, however, was ambitious of making a good book; and, with all the calm impetuosity which characterises a youthful Hauteville, determined to have a crack stud at once. So at Ascot, where he spent a few pleasant hours, dined at the Cottage, was caught in a shower, in return caught a cold, a slight influenza for a week, and all the world full of inquiries and anxiety; at Ascot, I say, he bought up all the winning horses at an average of three thousand guineas for each pair of ears. Sir Lucius stared, remonstrated, and, as his remonstrances were in vain, assisted him.

As people at the point of death often make a desperate rally, so this, the most brilliant of seasons, was even more lively as it nearer approached its end. The *dÃ©jeÃ»ner* and the *villa fÃªte* the water party and the rambling ride, followed each other with the bright rapidity of the final scenes in a pantomime. Each *dama* seemed only inspired with the ambition of giving the last ball; and so numerous were the parties that the town really sometimes seemed illuminated. To breakfast at Twickenham, and to dine in Belgrave Square; to hear,' or rather to honour, half an act of an opera; to campaign through half a dozen private balls, and to finish with a romp at the rooms, as after our wine we take a glass of liqueur; all this surely required the courage of an Alexander and the strength of a Hercules, and, indeed, cannot be achieved without the miraculous powers of a Joshua. So thought the young Duke, as with an excited mind and a whirling head he threw himself at half-past six o'clock on a couch which brought him no sleep.

Yet he recovered, and with the aid of the bath, the soda, and the coffee, and all the thousand remedies which a skilful valet has ever at hand, at three o'clock on the same day he rose and dressed, and in an hour was again at the illustrious bow-window, sneering with Charles Annesley, or laughing downright with Lord Squib.

The Duke of St. James gave a water party, and the astounded Thames swelled with pride as his broad breast bore on the ducal barges. St. Maurice, who was in the Guards, secured his band; and Lord Squib, who, though it was July, brought a furred great coat, secured himself. Lady Afy looked like Amphitrite, and Lady Caroline looked in love. They wandered in gardens like Calypso's; they rambled over a villa which reminded them of Baise; they partook of a banquet which should have been described by Ariosto. All were delighted; they delivered themselves to the charms of an unrestrained gaiety. Even Charles Annesley laughed and romped.

This is the only mode in which public eating is essentially agreeable. A banqueting-hall is often the scene of exquisite pleasure; but that is not so much excited by the gratification of a delicate palate as by the magnificent effect of light and shade; by the beautiful women, the radiant jewels, the graceful costume, the rainbow glass, the glowing wines, the glorious plate. For the rest, all is too hot, too crowded, and too noisy, to catch a flavour; to analyse a combination, to dwell upon a gust. To eat, *really* to eat, one must eat alone, with a soft light, with simple furniture, an easy dress, and a single dish, at a time. Hours of bliss! Hours of virtue! for what is more virtuous than to be conscious of the blessings of a bountiful Nature? A good eater must be a good man; for a good eater must have a good digestion, and a good digestion depends upon a good conscience.

But to our tale. If we be dull, skip: time will fly, and beauty will fade, and wit grow dull, and even the season, although it seems, for the nonce, like the existence of Olympus, will nevertheless steal away. It is the hour when trade grows dull and tradesmen grow duller; it is the hour that Howell loveth not and Stultz cannot abide; though the first may be consoled by the ghosts of his departed millions of *mouchoirs*, and the second by the vision of coming millions of shooting-jackets. Oh, why that sigh, my gloomy Mr. Gunter? Oh, why that frown, my gentle Mrs. Grange?

One by one the great houses shut; shoal by shoal the little people sail away. Yet beauty lingers still. Still the magnet of a straggling ball attracts the remaining brilliants; still a lagging dinner, like a sumpter-mule on a march, is a mark for plunder. The Park, too, is not yet empty, and perhaps is even more fascinating; like a beauty in a consumption, who each day gets thinner and more fair. The young Duke remained to the last; for we linger about our first season, as we do about our first mistress, rather wearied, yet full of delightful reminiscences.

BOOK II.

CHAPTER I.

His Grace Meets an Early Love

LADY APHRODITE and the Duke of St. James were for the first time parted; and with an absolute belief on the lady's side, and an avowed conviction on the gentleman's, that it was impossible to live asunder, they separated, her Ladyship shedding some temporary tears, and his Grace vowing eternal fidelity.

It was the crafty Lord Fitz-pompey who brought about this catastrophe. Having secured his nephew as a visitor to Malthorpe, by allowing him to believe that the Graftons would form part of the summer coterie, his Lordship took especial care that poor Lady Aphrodite should not be invited. 'Once part them, once get him to Malthorpe alone,' mused the experienced Peer, 'and he will be emancipated. I am doing him, too, the greatest kindness. What would I have given, when a young man, to have had such an uncle!'

The Morning Post announced with a sigh the departure of the Duke of St. James to the splendid festivities of Malthorpe; and also apprised the world that Sir Lucius and Lady Aphrodite were entertaining a numerous and distinguished party at their seat, Cleve Park, Cambridgeshire.

There was a constant bustle kept up at Malthorpe, and the young Duke was hourly permitted to observe that, independent of all private feeling, it was impossible for the most distinguished nobleman to ally himself with a more considered family. There was a continual swell of guests dashing down and dashing away, like the ocean; brilliant as its foam, numerous as its waves. But there was one permanent inhabitant of this princely mansion far more interesting to our hero than the evanescent crowds who rose like bubbles, glittered, broke, and disappeared.

Once more wandering in that park of Malthorpe where had passed the innocent days of his boyhood, his thoughts naturally recurred to the sweet companion who had made even those hours of happiness more felicitous. Here they had rambled, here they had first tried their ponies, there they had nearly fallen, there he had quite saved her; here were the two very elms where St. Maurice made for them a swing, here was the very keeper's cottage of which she had made for him a drawing, and which he still retained. Dear girl! And had she disappointed the romance of his boyhood; had the experience the want of which had allowed him then to be pleased so easily, had it taught him to be ashamed of those days of affection? Was she not now the most gentle, the most graceful, the most beautiful, the most kind? Was she not the most wife-like woman whose eyes had ever beamed with tenderness? Why, why not at once close a career which, though short, yet already could yield

- 43 -

reminiscences which might satisfy the most craving admirer of excitement? But there was Lady Aphrodite; yet that must end. Alas! on his part, it had commenced in levity; he feared, on hers, it must terminate in anguish. Yet, though he loved his cousin; though he could not recall to his memory the woman who was more worthy of being his wife, he could not also conceal from himself that the feelings which impelled him were hardly so romantic as he thought should have inspired a youth of one-and-twenty when he mused on the woman he loved best. But he knew life, and he felt convinced that a mistress and a wife must always be different characters. A combination of passion with present respect and permanent affection he supposed to be the delusion of romance writers. He thought he must marry Caroline, partly because he must marry sooner or later; partly because he had never met a woman whom he had loved so much, and partly because he felt he should be miserable if her destiny in life were not, in some way or other, connected with his own. 'Ah! if she had but been my sister!'

After a little more cogitation, the young Duke felt much inclined to make his cousin a Duchess; but time did not press. After Doncaster he must spend a few weeks at Cleve, and then he determined to come to an explanation with Lady Aphrodite. In the meantime, Lord Fitz-pompey secretly congratulated himself on his skilful policy, as he perceived his nephew daily more engrossed with his daughter. Lady Caroline, like all unaffected and accomplished women, was seen to great effect in the country.

There, while they feed their birds, tend their flowers, and tune their harp, and perform those more sacred, but not less pleasing, duties which become the daughter of a great proprietor, they favourably contrast with those more modish damsels who, the moment they are freed from the Park and from Willis's, begin fighting for silver arrows and patronising county balls.

September came, and brought some relief to those who were suffering in the inferno of provincial ennui; but this is only the purgatory to the Paradise of *battues*. Yet September has its days of slaughter; and the young Duke gained some laurels, with the aid of friend Egg, friend Purdy, and Manton. And the Premier galloped down sixty miles in one morning. He sacked his cover, made a light bet with St. James on the favourite, lunched standing, and was off before night; for he had only three days' holiday, and had to visit Lord Protest, Lord Content, and Lord Proxy. So, having knocked off four of his crack peers, he galloped back to London to flog up his secretaries.

And the young Duke was off too. He had promised to spend a week with Charles Annesley and Lord Squib, who had taken some Norfolk Baronet's seat for the autumn, and while he was at Spa were thinning his preserves. It

- 44 -

was a week! What fantastic dissipation! One day, the brains of three hundred hares made a *pâté* for Charles Annesley. Oh, Heliogabalus! you gained eternal fame for what is now 'done in a corner!'

CHAPTER II.

A New Charmer

THE Carnival of the North at length arrived. All civilised eyes were on the most distinguished party of the most distinguished steward, who with his horse Sanspareil seemed to share universal favour. The French Princes and the Duke of Burlington; the Protocolis, and the Fitz-pompeys, and the Bloomerlys; the Duke and Duchess of Shropshire, and the three Ladies Wrekin, who might have passed for the Graces; Lord and Lady Vatican on a visit from Rome, his Lordship taking hints for a heat in the Corso, and her Ladyship, a classical beauty with a face like a cameo; St. Maurice, and Annesley, and Squib, composed the party. The Premier was expected, and there was murmur of an Archduke. Seven houses had been prepared, a party-wall knocked down to make a dining-room, the plate sent down from London, and venison and wine from Hauteville.

The assemblage exceeded in quantity and quality all preceding years, and the Hauteville arms, the Hauteville liveries, and the Hauteville outriders, beat all hollow in blazonry, and brilliancy, and number. The North countrymen were proud of their young Duke and his carriages and six, and longed for the Castle to be finished. Nothing could exceed the propriety of the arrangements, for Sir Lucius was an unrivalled hand, and, though a Newmarket man, gained universal approbation even in Yorkshire. Lady Aphrodite was all smiles and new liveries, and the Duke of St. James reined in his charger right often at her splendid equipage.

The day's sport was over, and the evening's sport begun, to a quiet man, who has no bet more heavy than a dozen pair of gloves, perhaps not the least amusing. Now came the numerous dinner-parties, none to be compared to that of the Duke of St. James. Lady Aphrodite was alone wanting, but she had to head the *mÂ©nage* of Sir Lucius. Every one has an appetite after a race: the Duke of Shropshire attacked the venison as Samson the Philistines; and the French princes, for once in their life, drank real champagne.

Yet all faces were not so serene as those of the party of Hauteville. Many a one felt that strange mixture of fear and exultation which precedes a battle. To-morrow was the dreaded St. Leger.

'Tis night, and the banquet is over, and all are hastening to the ball.

In spite of the brilliant crowd, the entrance of the Hauteville party made a sensation. It was the crowning ornament to the scene, the stamp of the sovereign, the lamp of the Pharos, the flag of the tower. The party dispersed, and the Duke, after joining a quadrille with Lady Caroline, wandered away to make himself generally popular.

As he was moving along, he turned his head; he started.

'Ah!' exclaimed his Grace.

The cause of this sudden and ungovernable exclamation can be no other than a woman. You are right. The lady who had excited it was advancing in a quadrille, some ten yards from her admirer. She was very young; that is to say, she had, perhaps, added a year or two to sweet seventeen, an addition which, while it does not deprive the sex of the early grace of girlhood, adorns them with that indefinable dignity which is necessary to constitute a perfect woman. She was not tall, but as she moved forward displayed a figure so exquisitely symmetrical that for a moment the Duke forgot to look at her face, and then her head was turned away; yet he was consoled a moment for his disappointment by watching the movements of a neck so white, and round, and long, and delicate, that it would have become Psyche, and might have inspired Praxiteles. Her face is again turning towards him. It stops too soon; yet his eye feeds upon the outline of a cheek not too full, yet promising of beauty, like hope of Paradise.

She turns her head, she throws around a glance, and two streams of liquid light pour from her hazel eyes on his. It was a rapid, graceful movement, unstudied as the motion of a fawn, and was in a moment withdrawn, yet was it long enough to stamp upon his memory a memorable countenance. Her face was quite oval, her nose delicately aquiline, and her high pure forehead like a Parian dome. The clear blood coursed under her transparent cheek, and increased the brilliancy of her dazzling eyes. His never left her. There was an expression of decision about her small mouth, an air of almost mockery in her curling lip, which, though in themselves wildly fascinating, strangely contrasted with all the beaming light and beneficent lustre of the upper part of her countenance. There was something, too, in the graceful but rather decided air with which she moved, that seemed to betoken her self-consciousness of her beauty or her rank; perhaps it might be her wit; for the Duke observed that while she scarcely smiled, and conversed with lips hardly parted, her companion, with whom she was evidently intimate, was almost constantly convulsed with laughter, although, as he never spoke, it was clearly not at his own jokes.

Was she married? Could it be? Impossible! Yet there was a richness in her costume which was not usual for unmarried women. A diamond arrow had pierced her clustering and auburn locks; she wore, indeed, no necklace; with such a neck it would have been sacrilege; no ear-rings, for her ears were too small for such a burthen; yet her girdle was of brilliants; and a diamond cross worthy of Belinda and her immortal bard hung upon her breast.

The Duke seized hold of the first person he knew: it was Lord Bagshot.

'Tell me,' he said, in the stern, low voice of a despot; 'tell me who that creature is.'

'Which creature?' asked Lord Bagshot.

'Booby! brute! Bag, that creature of light and love!'

'Where?'

'There!

'What, my mother?'

'Your mother! cub! cart-horse! answer me, or I will run you through.'

'Who do you mean?'

'There, there, dancing with that raw-boned youth with red hair.'

'What, Lord St. Jerome! Lor! he is a Catholic. I never speak to them. My governor would be so savage.'

'But the girl?'

'Oh! the girl! Lor! she is a Catholic, too.'

'But who is she?'

'Lor! don't you know?'

'Speak, hound; speak!'

'Lor! that is the beauty of the county; but then she is a Catholic. How shocking! Blow us all up as soon as look at us.'

'If you do not tell me who she is directly, you shall never get into White's. I will black-ball you regularly.'

'Lor! man, don't be in a passion. I will tell. But then I know you know all the time. You are joking. Everybody knows the beauty of the county; everybody knows May Dacre.'

'May Dacre!' said the Duke of St. James, as if he were shot.

'Why, what is the matter now?' asked Lord Bag-shot.

'What, the daughter of Dacre of Castle Dacre?' pursued his Grace.

'The very same; the beauty of the county. Everybody knows May Dacre. I knew you knew her all the time. You did not take me in. Why, what is the matter?'

'Nothing; get away!'

'Civil! But you will remember your promise about White's?'

'Ay! ay! I shall remember you when you are proposed.'

'Here, here is a business!' soliloquized the young Duke. 'May Dacre! What a fool I have been! Shall I shoot myself through the head, or embrace her on the spot? Lord St. Jerome, too! He seems mightily pleased. And my family have been voting for two centuries to emancipate this fellow! Curse his grinning face! I am decidedly anti-Catholic. But then she is a Catholic! I will turn Papist. Ah! there is Lucy. I want a counsellor.'

He turned to his fellow-steward. 'Oh, Lucy! such a woman! such an incident!'

'What! the inimitable Miss Dacre, I suppose. Everybody speaking of her; wherever I go, one subject of conversation. Burlington wanting to waltz with her, Charles Annesley being introduced, and Lady Bloomerly decidedly of opinion that she is the finest creature in the county. Well, have you danced with her?'

'Danced, my dear fellow! Do not speak to me.'

'What is the matter?'

'The most diabolical matter that you ever heard of.'

'Well, well?'

'I have not even been introduced.'

'Well! come on at once.'

'I cannot.'

'Are you mad?'

'Worse than mad. Where is her father?'

'Who cares?'

'I do. In a word, my dear Lucy, her father is that guardian whom I have perhaps mentioned to you, and to whom I have behaved so delicately.'

'Why! I thought your guardian was an old curmudgeon.'

'What does that signify, with such a daughter!'

'Oh! here is some mistake. This is the only child of Dacre of Castle Dacre, a most delightful fellow; one of the first fellows in the county; I was introduced to him to-day on the course. I thought you knew them. You were admiring his outriders to-day, the green and silver.'

'Why, Bag told me they were old Lord Sunderland's.'

'Bag! How can you believe a word that booby says? He always has an answer. To-day, when Afy drove in, I asked Bag who she was, and he said it was his

- 49 -

aunt, Lady de Courcy. I begged to be introduced, and took over the blushing Bag and presented him.'

'But the father; the father, Lucy! How shall I get out of this scrape?'

'Oh! put on a bold face. Here! give him this ring, and swear you procured it for him at Genoa, and then say that, now you are here, you will try his pheasants.'

'My dear fellow, you always joke. I am in agony. Seriously, what shall I do?'

'Why, seriously, be introduced to him, and do what you can.'

'Which is he?'

'At the extreme end, next to the very pretty woman, who, by-the-bye, I recommend to your notice: Mrs. Dallington Vere. She is amusing. I know her well. She is some sort of relation to your Dacres. I will present you to both at once.'

'Why! I will think of it.'

'Well, then! I must away. The two stewards knocking their heads together is rather out of character. Do you know it is raining hard? I am cursedly nervous about to-morrow.'

'Pooh! pooh! If I could get through to-night, I should not care for to-morrow.'

CHAPTER III.

The Duke Apologises

AS SIR LUCIUS hurried off his colleague advanced towards the upper end of the room, and, taking up a position, made his observations, through the shooting figures of the dancers, on the dreaded Mr. Dacre. The late guardian of the Duke of St. James was in the perfection of manhood; perhaps five-and-forty by age; but his youth had lingered long. He was tall, thin, and elegant, with a mild and benevolent expression of countenance, not unmixed, however, with a little reserve, the ghost of youthly pride. Listening with polished and courtly bearing to the pretty Mrs. Dallington Vere, assenting occasionally to her piquant observations by a slight bow, or expressing his dissent by a still slighter smile, seldom himself speaking, yet always with that unembarrassed manner which makes a saying listened to, Mr. Dacre was altogether, in appearance, one of the most distinguished personages in this distinguished assembly. The young Duke fell into an attitude worthy of Hamlet: 'This, then, is *old* Dacre! O deceitful Fitz-pompey! O silly St. James! Could I ever forget that tall, mild man, who now is perfectly fresh in my memory? Ah! that memory of mine; it has been greatly developed to-night. Would that I had cultivated that faculty with a little more zeal! But what am I to do? The case is urgent. What must the Dacres think of me? What must May Dacre think? On the course the whole day, and I the steward, and not conscious of the presence of the first family in the Riding! Fool, fool! Why, why did I accept an office for which I was totally unfitted? Why, why must I flirt away a whole morning with that silly Sophy Wrekin? An agreeable predicament, truly, this! What would I give now once more to be in St. James's Street! Confound my Yorkshire estates! How they must dislike, how they must despise me! And now, truly, I am to be *introduced* to him! The Duke of St. James, Mr. Dacre! Mr. Dacre, the Duke of St. James! What an insult to all parties! How supremely ludicrous! What a mode of offering my gratitude to the man to whom I am under solemn and inconceivable obligations! A choice way, truly, to salute the bosom-friend of my sire, the guardian of my interests, the creator of my property, the fosterer of my orphan infancy! It is useless to conceal it; I am placed in the most disagreeable, the most inextricable situation. 'Inextricable! Am I, then, the Duke of St. James? Am I that being who, two hours ago, thought that the world was formed alone for my enjoyment, and I quiver and shrink here like a common hind? Out, out on such craven cowardice! I am no Hauteville! I am bastard! Never! I will not be crushed. I will struggle with this emergency; I will conquer it. Now aid me, ye heroes of my house! On the sands of Palestine, on the plains of France, ye were not in a more difficult situation than is your descendant in a ball-room in his own county. My mind elevates itself to the occasion, my courage

- 51 -

expands with the enterprise; I will right myself with these Dacres with honour, and without humiliation.'

The dancing ceased, the dancers disappeared. There was a blank between the Duke of St. James on one side of the broad room, and Mr. Dacre and those with whom he was conversing on the other. Many eyes were on his Grace, and he seized the opportunity to execute his purpose. He advanced across the chamber with the air of a young monarch greeting a victorious general. It seemed that, for a moment, his Majesty wished to destroy all difference of rank between himself and the man that he honoured. So studied and so inexpressibly graceful were his movements that the gaze of all around involuntarily fixed upon him. Mrs. Dallington Vere unconsciously refrained from speaking as he approached; and one or two, without actually knowing his purpose, made way. They seemed awed by his dignity, and shuffled behind Mr. Dacre, as if he were the only person who was the Duke's match.

'Mr. Dacre,' said his Grace, in the softest but still audible tones, and he extended, at the same time, his hand; 'Mr. Dacre, our first meeting should have been neither here nor thus; but you, who have excused so much, will pardon also this!'

Mr. Dacre, though a calm personage, was surprised by this sudden address. He could not doubt who was the speaker. He had left his ward a mere child. He saw before him the exact and breathing image of the heart-friend of his ancient days. He forgot all but the memory of a cherished friendship.

He was greatly affected; he pressed the offered hand; he advanced; he moved aside. The young Duke followed up his advantage, and, with an air of the greatest affection, placed Mr. Dacre's arm in his own, and then bore off his prize in triumph.

Right skilfully did our hero avail himself of his advantage. He spoke, and he spoke with emotion. There is something inexpressibly captivating in the contrition of a youthful and a generous mind. Mr. Dacre and his late ward soon understood each other; for it was one of those meetings which sentiment makes sweet.

'And now,' said his Grace, 'I have one more favour to ask, and that is the greatest: I wish to be recalled to the recollection of my oldest friend.'

Mr. Dacre led the Duke to his daughter; and the Earl of St. Jerome, who was still laughing at her side, rose.

'The Duke of St. James, May, wishes to renew his acquaintance with you.'

She bowed in silence. Lord St. Jerome, who was the great oracle of the Yorkshire School, and who had betted desperately against the favourite, took Mr. Dacre aside to consult him about the rain, and the Duke of St. James dropped into his chair. That tongue, however, which had never failed him, for once was wanting. There was a momentary silence, which the lady would not break; and at last her companion broke it, and not felicitously.

'I think there is nothing more delightful than meeting with old friends.'

'Yes! that is the usual sentiment; but I half suspect that it is a commonplace, invented to cover our embarrassment under such circumstances; for, after all, "an old friend" so situated is a person whom we have not seen for many years, and most probably not cared to see.'

'You are indeed severe.'

'Oh! no. I think there is nothing more painful than parting with old friends; but when we have parted with them, I am half afraid they are lost.'

'Absence, then, with you is fatal?'

'Really, I never did part with any one I greatly loved; but I suppose it is with me as with most persons.'

'Yet you have resided abroad, and for many years?'

'Yes; but I was too young then to have many friends; and, in fact, I accompanied perhaps all that I possessed.'

'How I regret that it was not in my power to accept your kind invitation to Dacre in the Spring!'

'Oh! My father would have been very glad to see you; but we really are dull kind of people, not at all in your way, and I really do not think that you lost much amusement.'

'What better amusement, what more interesting occupation, could I have had than to visit the place where I passed my earliest and my happiest hours? 'Tis nearly fifteen years since I was at Dacre.'

'Except when you visited us at Easter. We regretted our loss.'

'Ah! yes! except that,' exclaimed the Duke, remembering his jÃ¤ger's call; 'but that goes for nothing. I of course saw very little.'

'Yet, I assure you, you made a great impression. So eminent a personage, of course, observes less than he himself is observed. We had a graphical description of you on our return, and a very accurate one, too; for I recognised your Grace to-night merely from the report of your visit.'

The Duke shot a shrewd glance at his companion's face, but it betrayed no indication of badinage, and so, rather puzzled, he thought it best to put up with the parallel between himself and his servant. But Miss Dacre did not quit this agreeable subject with all that promptitude which he fondly anticipated.

'Poor Lord St. Jerome,' said she, 'who is really the most unaffected person I know, has been complaining most bitterly of his deficiency in the *air noble*. He is mistaken for a groom perpetually; and once, he says, had a *douceur* presented to him in his character of an ostler. Your Grace must be proud of your advantage over him. You would have been gratified by the universal panegyric of our household. They, of course, you know, are proud of their young Duke, a real Yorkshire Duke, and they love to dwell upon your truly imposing appearance. As for myself, who am true Yorkshire also, I take the most honest pride in hearing them describe your elegant attitude, leaning back in your britzska, with your feet on the opposite cushions, your hat arranged aside with that air of undefinable grace characteristic of the Grand Seigneur, and, which is the last remnant of the feudal system, your reiterated orders to drive over an old woman. You did not even condescend to speak English, which made them quite enthusiastic—'

'Oh, Miss Dacre, spare me!'

'Spare you! I have heard of your Grace's modesty; but this excessive sensibility, under well-earned praise, surprises me!'

'But, Miss Dacre, you cannot indeed really believe that this vulgar ruffian, this grim scarecrow, this Guy Faux, was—was—myself.'

'Not yourself! Really, I am a simple personage. I believe in my eyes and trust to my ears. I am at a loss for your meaning.'

'I mean, then,' said the Duke, who had gained time to rally, 'that this monster was some impostor, who must have stolen my carriage, picked my pocket, and robbed me of my card, which, next to his reputation, is a man's most delicate possession.'

'Then you never called upon us?'

'I blush to confess it, never; but I will call, in future, every day.'

'Your ingenuousness really rivals your modesty.'

'Now, after these confessions and compliments, may I suggest a waltz?'

'No one is waltzing now.'

'When the quadrille, then, is finished?'

'Then I am engaged.'

'After your engagement?'

'That is indeed making a business of pleasure. I have just refused a similar request of your fellow-steward. We damsels shall soon be obliged to carry a book to enrol our engagements as well as our bets, if this system of reversionary dancing be any longer encouraged.'

'But you must dance with me!' said the Duke, imploringly.

'Oh! you will stumble upon me in the course of the evening, and I shall probably be more fortunate.

I suppose you feel nervous about to-morrow?'

'Not at all.'

'Ah! I forgot. Your Grace's horse is the favourite. Favourites always win.'

'Have I a horse?'

'Why, Lord St. Jerome says he doubts whether it be one.'

'Lord St. Jerome seems a vastly amusing personage; and, as he is so often taken for an ostler, I have no doubt is an exceedingly good judge of horse-flesh.'

Miss Dacre smiled. It was that wild, but rather wicked, gleam which sometimes accompanies the indulgence of innocent malice. It seemed to insinuate, 'I know you are piqued, and I enjoy it' But here her hand was claimed for the waltz.

The young Duke remained musing.

'There she swims away! By heavens! unrivalled! And there is Lady Afy and Burlington; grand, too. Yet there is something in this little Dacre which touches my fancy more. What is it? I think it is her impudence. That confounded scrape of Carlstein! I will cashier him to-morrow. Confound his airs! I think I got out of it pretty well. To-night, on the whole, has been a night of triumph; but if I do not waltz with the little Dacre I will only vote myself an ovation. But see, here comes Sir Lucius. Well! how fares my brother consul?'

'I do not like this rain. I have been hedging with Hounslow, having previously set Bag at his worthy sire with a little information. We shall have a perfect swamp, and then it will be strength against speed; the old story. Damn the St. Leger. I am sick of it.'

'Pooh! pooh! think of the little Dacre!'

'Think of her, my dear fellow! I think of her too much. I should absolutely have diddled Hounslow, if it had not been for her confounded pretty face flitting about my stupid brain. I saw you speaking to Guardy. You managed that business well.'

'Why, as I do all things, I flatter myself, Lucy. Do you know Lord St. Jerome?'

'Verbally. We have exchanged monosyllables; but he is of the other set.'

'He is cursedly familiar with the little Dacre. As the friend of her father, I think I shall interfere. Is there anything in it, think you?'

'Oh! no; she is engaged to another.'

'Engaged!' said the Duke, absolutely turning pale.

'Do you remember a Dacre at Eton?'

'A Dacre at Eton!' mused the Duke. At another time it would not have been in his power to have recalled the stranger to his memory; but this evening the train of association had been laid, and after struggling a moment with his mind he had the man. 'To be sure I do: Arundel Dacre, an odd sort of a fellow; but he was my senior.'

'Well, that is the man; a nephew of Guardy, and cousin, of course, to La Bellissima. He inherits, you know, all the property. She will not have a sou; but old Dacre, as you call him, has managed pretty well, and Monsieur Arundel is to compensate for the entail by presenting him with a grandson.'

'The deuce!'

'The deuce, indeed! Often have I broken his head. Would that I had to a little more purpose!'

'Let us do it now!'

'He is not here, otherwise——One dislikes a spooney to be successful.'

'Where are our friends?'

'Annesley with the Duchess, and Squib with the Duke at écarté.'

'Success attend them both!'

'Amen!'

CHAPTER IV.

Innocence and Experience

TO FEEL that the possessions of an illustrious ancestry are about to slide from out your line for ever; that the numerous tenantry, who look up to you with the confiding eye that the most liberal parvenu cannot attract, will not count you among their lords; that the proud park, filled with the ancient and toppling trees that your fathers planted, will yield neither its glory nor its treasures to your seed, and that the old gallery, whose walls are hung with pictures more cherished than the collections of kings, will not breathe with your long posterity; all these are feelings sad and trying, and are among those daily pangs which moralists have forgotten in their catalogue of miseries, but which do not the less wear out those heart-strings at which they are so constantly tugging.

This was the situation of Mr. Dacre. The whole of his large property was entailed, and descended to his nephew, who was a Protestant; and yet, when he looked upon the blooming face of his enchanting daughter, he blessed the Providence which, after all his visitations, had doomed him to be the sire of a thing so lovely. An exile from her country at an early age, the education of May Dacre had been completed in a foreign land; yet the mingling bloods of Dacre and of Howard would not in a moment have permitted her to forget The inviolate island of the sage and free! even if the unceasing and ever-watchful exertions of her father had been wanting to make her worthy of so illustrious an ancestry.

But this, happily, was not the case; and to aid the development of the infant mind of his young child, to pour forth to her, as she grew in years and in reason, all the fruits of his own richly-cultivated intellect, was the solitary consolation of one over whose conscious head was impending the most awful of visitations. May Dacre was gifted with a mind which, even if her tutor had not been her father, would have rendered tuition a delight. Her lively imagination, which early unfolded itself; her dangerous yet interesting vivacity; the keen delight, the swift enthusiasm, with which she drank in knowledge, and then panted for more; her shrewd acuteness, and her innate passion for the excellent and the beautiful, filled her father with rapture which he repressed, and made him feel conscious how much there was to check, to guide, and to form, as well as to cherish, to admire, and to applaud.

As she grew up the bright parts of her character shone with increased lustre; but, in spite of the exertions of her instructor, some less admirable qualities had not yet disappeared. She was still too often the dupe of her imagination, and though perfectly inexperienced, her confidence in her theoretical knowledge of human nature was unbounded. She had an idea that she could penetrate the characters of individuals at a first meeting; and the consequence of this fatal axiom was, that she was always the slave of first impressions, and constantly the victim of prejudice. She was ever thinking individuals better or worse than they really were, and she believed it to be out of the power of anyone to deceive her. Constant attendance during many years on a dying and beloved mother, and her deeply religious feelings, had first broken, and then controlled, a spirit which nature had intended to be arrogant and haughty. Her father she adored; and she seemed to devote to him all that consideration which, with more common characters, is generally distributed among their acquaintance. We hint at her faults. How shall we describe her virtues? Her unbounded generosity, her dignified simplicity, her graceful frankness, her true nobility of thought and feeling, her firmness, her courage and her truth, her kindness to her inferiors, her constant charity, her devotion to her parents, her sympathy with sorrow, her detestation of oppression, her pure unsullied thoughts, her delicate taste, her deep religion. All these combined would have formed a delightful character, even if unaccompanied with such brilliant talents and such brilliant beauty. Accustomed from an early age to the converse of courts and the forms of the most polished circles, her manner became her blood, her beauty, and her mind. Yet she rather acted in unison with the spirit of society than obeyed its minutest decree. She violated etiquette with a wilful grace which made the outrage a precedent, and she mingled with princes without feeling her inferiority. Nature, and art, and fortune were the graces which had combined to form this girl. She was a jewel set in gold, and worn by a king.

Her creed had made her, in ancient Christendom, feel less an alien; but when she returned to that native country which she had never forgotten, she found that creed her degradation. Her indignant spirit clung with renewed ardour to the crushed altars of her faith; and not before those proud shrines where cardinals officiate, and a thousand acolytes fling their censers, had she bowed with half the abandonment of spirit with which she invoked the Virgin in her oratory at Dacre.

The recent death of her mother rendered Mr. Dacre and herself little inclined to enter society; and as they were both desirous of residing on that estate from which they had been so long and so unwillingly absent, they had not yet visited London. The greater part of their time had been passed chiefly in communication with those great Catholic families with whom the Dacres were allied, and to which they belonged. The modern race of the Howards and the Cliffords, the Talbots, the Arundels, and the Jerninghams, were not unworthy of their proud progenitors. Miss Dacre observed with respect, and assuredly with sympathy, the mild dignity, the noble patience, the proud humility, the calm hope, the uncompromising courage, with which her father and his friends sustained their oppression and lived as proscribed in the realm which they had created. Yet her lively fancy and gay spirit found less to admire in the feelings which influenced these families in their intercourse with the world, which induced them to foster but slight intimacies out of the pale of the proscribed, and which tinged their domestic life with that formal and gloomy colouring which ever accompanies a monotonous existence. Her disposition told her that all this affected non-interference with the business of society might be politic, but assuredly was not pleasant; her quick sense whispered to her it was unwise, and that it retarded, not advanced, the great result in which her sanguine temper dared often to indulge. Under any circumstances, it did not appear to her to be wisdom to second the efforts of their oppressors for their degradation or their misery, and to seek no consolation in the amiable feelings of their fellow-creatures for the stern rigour of their unsocial government. But, independently of all general principles, Miss Dacre could not but believe that it was the duty of the Catholic gentry to mix more with that world which so misconceived their spirit. Proud in her conscious knowledge of their exalted virtues, she felt that they had only to be known to be recognised as the worthy leaders of that nation which they had so often saved and never betrayed.

She did not conceal her opinions from the circle in which they had grown up. All the young members were her disciples, and were decidedly of opinion that if the House of Lords would but listen to May Dacre, emancipation would be a settled thing. Her logic would have destroyed Lord Liverpool's arguments; her wit extinguished Lord Eldon's jokes. But the elder members only shed a solemn smile, and blessed May Dacre's shining eyes and sanguine spirit.

Her greatest supporter was Mrs. Dallington Vere. This lady was a distant relation of Mr. Dacre. At seventeen she, herself a Catholic, had married Mr. Dallington Vere, of Dallington House, a Catholic gentleman of considerable fortune, whose age resembled his wealth. No sooner had this incident taken place than did Mrs. Dallington Vere hurry to London, and soon evinced a most laudable determination to console herself for her husband's political disabilities. Mrs. Dallington Vere went to Court; and Mrs. Dallington Vere gave suppers after the opera, and concerts which, in number and brilliancy, were only equalled by her balls. The dandies patronised her, and selected her for their Muse. The Duke of Shropshire betted on her always at écarté; and, to crown the whole affair, she made Mr. Dallington Vere lay claim to a dormant peerage. The women were all pique, the men all patronage. A Protestant minister was alarmed; and Lord Squib supposed that Mrs. Dallington must be the Scarlet Lady of whom they had heard so often.

Season after season she kept up the ball; and although, of course, she no longer made an equal sensation, she was not less brilliant, nor her position less eminent. She had got into the best set, and was more quiet, like a patriot in place. Never was there a gayer lady than Mrs. Dallington Vere, but never a more prudent one. Her virtue was only equalled by her discretion; but, as the odds were equal, Lord Squib betted on the last. People sometimes indeed did say—they always will—but what is talk? Mere breath. And reputation is marble, and iron, and sometimes brass; and so, you see, talk has no chance. They did say that Sir Lucius Grafton was about to enter into the Romish communion; but then it turned out that it was only to get a divorce from his wife, on the plea that she was a heretic.

The fact was, Mrs. Dallington Vere was a most successful woman, lucky in everything, lucky even in her husband; for he died. He did not only die; he left his whole fortune to his wife. Some said that his relations were going to set aside the will, on the plea that it was written with a crow-quill on pink paper; but this was false; it was only a codicil.

All eyes were on a very pretty woman, with fifteen thousand a year, and only twenty-three. The Duke of Shropshire wished he were disembarrassed. Such a player of écarté might double her income. Lord Raff advanced, trusting to his beard, and young Amadée de Rouerie mortgaged his dressing-case, and came post from Paris; but in spite of his sky-blue nether garments and his Hessians, he followed my Lord's example, and re-crossed the water. It is even said that Lord Squib was sentimental; but this must have been the malice of Charles Annesley.

All, however, failed. The truth is, Mrs. Dallington Vere had nothing to gain by re-entering Paradise, which matrimony, of course, is; and so she determined to remain mistress of herself. She had gained fashion, and fortune, and rank; she was young, and she was pretty. She thought it might be possible for a discreet, experienced little lady to lead a very pleasant life without being assisted in her expenses or disturbed in her diversion by a gentleman who called himself her husband, occasionally asked her how she slept in a bed which he did not share, or munificently presented her with a necklace purchased with her own money. Discreet Mrs. Dallington Vere!

She had been absent from London during the past season, having taken it also into her head to travel.

She was equally admired and equally plotted for at Rome, at Paris, and at Vienna, as at London; but the bird had not been caught, and, flying away, left many a despairing prince and amorous count to muse over their lean visages and meagre incomes.

Dallington House made its fair mistress a neighbour of her relations, the Dacres. No one could be a more fascinating companion than Mrs. Dallington Vere. May Dacre read her character at once, and these ladies became great allies. She was to assist Miss Dacre in her plans for rousing their Catholic friends, as no one was better qualified to be her adjutant. Already they had commenced their operations, and balls at Dallington and Dacre, frequent, splendid, and various, had already made the Catholic houses the most eminent in the Riding, and their brilliant mistresses the heroines of all the youth.

CHAPTER V.

Ruined Hopes

IT RAINED all night without ceasing yet the morrow was serene. Nevertheless the odds had shifted. On the evening, thy had not been more than two to one against the first favourite, the Duke of St. James's ch. c. Sanspareil, by Ne Plus Ultra; while they were five to one against the second favourite, Mr. Dash's gr. c. The Dandy, by Banker, and nine and ten to one against the next in favour. This morning, however, affairs were altered. Mr. Dash and his Dandy were at the head of the poll; and as the owner rode his own horse, being a jockey and a fit rival for the Duke of St. James, his backers were sanguine. Sanspareil, was, however, the second favourite.

The Duke, however, was confident as an universal conqueror, and came on in his usual state, rode round the course, inspirited Lady Aphrodite, who was all anxiety, betted with Miss Dacre, and bowed to Mrs. Dallington.

There were more than ninety horses, and yet the start was fair. But the result? Pardon me! The fatal remembrance overpowers my pen. An effort and some *Eau de Portingale*, and I shall recover. The first favourite was never heard of, the second favourite was never seen after the distance post, all the ten-to-oners were in the rear, and a *dark* horse, which had never been thought of, and which the careless St. James had never even observed in the list, rushed past the grand stand in sweeping triumph. The spectators were almost too surprised to cheer; but when the name of the winner was detected there was a deafening shout, particularly from the Yorkshiremen. The victor was the Earl of St. Jerome's b. f. May Dacre, by Howard.

Conceive the confusion! Sanspareil was at last discovered, and immediately shipped off for Newmarket, as young gentlemen who get into scrapes are sent to travel. The Dukes of Burlington and Shropshire exchanged a few hundreds; the Duchess and Charles Annesley a few gloves. The consummate Lord Bloomerly, though a backer of the favourite, in compliment to his host, contrived to receive from all parties, and particularly from St. Maurice. The sweet little Wrekins were absolutely ruined. Sir Lucius looked blue, but he had hedged; and Lord Squib looked yellow, but some doubted. Lord Hounslow was done, and Lord Bagshot was diddled.

The Duke of St. James was perhaps the heaviest sufferer on the field, and certainly bore his losses the best. Had he seen the five-and-twenty thousand he was minus counted before him, he probably would have been staggered; but as it was, another crumb of his half-million was gone. The loss existed only in idea. It was really too trifling to think of, and he galloped up to Miss Dacre, and was among the warmest of her congratulators.

- 63 -

'I would offer your Grace my sympathy for your congratulations,' said Miss Dacre, in a rather amiable tone; 'but' (and here she resumed her air of mockery) 'you are too great a man to be affected by so light a casualty. And, now that I recollect myself, did you run a horse?'

'Why, no; the fault was, I believe, that he would not run; but Sanspareil is as great a hero as ever. He has only been conquered by the elements.'

The dinner at the Duke of St. James's was this day more splendid even than the preceding. He was determined to show that the disappointment had produced no effect upon the temper of so imperial a personage as himself, and he invited several of the leading gentry to join his coterie. The Dacres were among the solicited; but they were, during the races, the guests of Mrs. Dallington Vere, whose seat was only a mile off, and therefore were unobtainable.

Blazed the plate, sparkled the wine, and the aromatic venison sent forth its odourous incense to the skies. The favourite cook had done wonders, though a Sanspareil pâté, on which he had been meditating for a week, was obliged to be suppressed, and was sent up as a tourte à la Bourbon, in compliment to his Royal Highness. It was a delightful party: all the stiffness of metropolitan society disappeared. All talked, and laughed, and ate, and drank; and the Protocolis and the French princes, who were most active members of a banquet, ceased sometimes, from want of breath, to moralize on the English character. The little Wrekins, with their well-acted lamentations over their losses, were capital; and Sophy nearly smiled and chattered her head this day into the reversion of the coronet of Fitz-pompey. May she succeed! For a wilder little partridge never yet flew. Caroline St. Maurice alone was sad, and would not be comforted; although St. James, observing her gloom, and guessing at its cause, had in private assured her that, far from losing, on the whole he was perhaps even a winner.

None, however, talked more agreeable nonsense and made a more elegant uproar than the Duke of St. James.

'These young men,' whispered Lord Squib to Annesley, 'do not know the value of money. We must teach it them. I know too well; I find it very dear.'

If the old physicians are correct in considering from twenty-five to thirty-five as the period of lusty youth, Lord Squib was still a lusty youth, though a very corpulent one indeed. The carnival of his life, however, was nearly over, and probably the termination of the race-week might hail him a man. He was the best fellow in the world; short and sleek, half bald, and looked fifty; with a waist, however, which had not yet vanished, and where Art successfully controlled rebellious Nature, like the Austrians the Lombards. If he were not exactly a wit, he was still, however, full of unaffected fun, and threw out the

- 64 -

results of a *rouÃ©* life with considerable ease and point. He had inherited a fair and peer-like property, which he had contrived to embarrass in so complicated and extraordinary a manner that he had been a ruined man for years, and yet lived well on an income allowed him by his creditors to manage his estate for their benefit. The joke was, he really managed it well. It was his hobby, and he prided himself especially upon his character as a man of business.

The banquet is certainly the best preparative for the ball, if its blessings be not abused, for then you get heavy. Your true votary of Terpsichore, and of him we only speak, requires, particularly in a land of easterly winds, which cut into his cab-head at every turn of every street, some previous process to make his blood set him an example in dancing. It is strong Burgundy and his sparkling sister champagne that make a race-ball always so amusing a *divertissement*. One enters the room with a gay elation which defies rule without violating etiquette, and in these county meetings there is a variety of character, and classes, and manners, which is interesting, and affords an agreeable contrast to those more brilliant and refined assemblies the members of which, being educated by exactly the same system and with exactly the same ideas, think, look, move, talk, dress, and even eat, alike; the only remarkable personage being a woman somewhat more beautiful than the beauties who surround her, and a man rather more original in his affectations than the puppies that surround him. The proof of the general dulness of polite circles is the great sensation that is always produced by a new face. The season always commences briskly, because there are so many. Ball, and dinner, and concert collect then plentiful votaries; but as we move on the dulness will develop itself, and then come the morning breakfast, and the water party, and the *fÃªte champÃªtre*, all desperate attempts to produce variety with old materials, and to occasion a second effect by a cause which is already exhausted.

These philosophical remarks precede another introduction to the public ball-room at Doncaster. Mrs. Dallington Vere and Miss Dacre are walking arm in arm at the upper end of the room.

'You are disappointed, love, about Arundel?' said Mrs. Dallington.

'Bitterly; I never counted on any event more certainly than on his return this summer.'

'And why tarrieth the wanderer? unwillingly of course?'

'Lord Darrell, who was to have gone over as *ChargÃ© d'affaires*, has announced to his father the impossibility of his becoming a diplomatist, so our poor *attachÃ©* suffers, and is obliged to bear the *portefeuille ad interim.*'

'Does your cousin like Vienna?'

'Not at all. He is a regular John Bull; and, if I am to judge from his correspondence, he will make an excellent ambassador in one sense, for I think his fidelity and his patriotism may be depended on. We seldom serve those whom we do not love; and, if I am to believe Arundel, there is neither a person nor a place on the whole Continent that affords him the least satisfaction.'

'How singular, then, that he should have fixed on such a *mÃ©tier*; but, I suppose, like other young men, his friends fixed for him?'

'Not at all. No step could be less pleasing to my father than his leaving England; but Arundel is quite unmanageable, even by papa. He is the oddest but the dearest person in the world!'

'He is very clever, is he not?'

'I think so. I have no doubt he will distinguish himself, whatever career he runs; but he is so extremely singular in his manner that I do not think his general reputation harmonises with my private opinion.'

'And will his visit to England be a long one?'

'I hope that it will be a permanent one. I, you know, am his confidant, and entrusted with all his plans. If I succeed in arranging something according to his wishes, I hope that he will not again quit us.'

'I pray you may, sweet! and wish, love, for your sake, that he would enter the room this moment.'

'This is the most successful meeting, I should think, that ever was known at Doncaster,' said Miss Dacre. 'We are, at least, indebted to the Duke of St. James for a very agreeable party, to say nothing of all the gloves we have won.'

'How do you like the Duke of Burlington?'

'Much. There is a calm courtliness about him which I think very imposing. He is the only man I ever saw who, without being very young, was not an unfit companion for youth. And there is no affectation of juvenility about him. He involuntarily reminds you of youth, as an empty orchestra does of music.'

'I shall tell him this. He is already your devoted; and I have no doubt that, inspired at the same time by your universal charms and our universal hints, I shall soon hail you Duchess of Burlington. Don Arundel will repent his diplomacy.'

'I thought I was to be another Duchess this morning.'

'You deserve to be a triple one. But dream not of the unhappy patron of Sanspareil. There is something in his eyes which tells me he is not a marrying man.'

There was a momentary pause, and Miss Dacre spoke.

'I like his brother steward, Bertha. Sir Lucius is witty and candid. It is an agreeable thing to see a man who had been so gay, and who has had so many temptations to be gay, turn into a regular domestic character, without losing any of those qualities which made him an ornament to society. When men of the world terminate their career as prudently as Sir Lucius, I observe that they are always amusing companions, because they are perfectly unaffected.'

'No one is more unaffected than Lucius Grafton. I am quite happy to find you like him; for he is an old friend of mine, and I know that he has a good heart.'

'I like him especially because he likes you.'

'Dearest!'

'He introduced me to Lady Afy. I perceive that she is very attached to her husband.'

'Lady Afy is a charming woman. I know no woman so truly elegant as Lady Afy. The young Duke, you know they say, greatly admires Lady Afy.'

'Oh! does he? Well now, I should have thought her rather a sentimental and serious donna; one very unlikely————'

'Hush! here come two cavaliers.'

The Dukes of Burlington and St. James advanced.

'We are attracted by observing two nymphs wandering in this desert,' said his Grace of Burlington. This was the Burgundy.

'And we wish to know whether there be any dragon to destroy, any ogre to devour, any magician to massacre, or how, when, and where we can testify our devotion to the ladies of our love,' added his Grace of St. James. This was the champagne.

'The age of chivalry is past,' said Miss Dacre. 'Bores have succeeded to dragons, and I have shivered too many lances in vain ever to hope for their extirpation; and as for enchantments————'

'They depend only upon yourself,' gallantly interrupted the Duke of Burgundy. Psha!—Burlington.

'Our spells are dissolved, our wands are sunk five fathom deep; we had retired to this solitude, and we were moralising,' said Mrs. Dallington Vere.

'Then you were doing an extremely useless and not very magnanimous thing,' said the Duke of St. James; 'for to moralise in a desert is no great exertion of philosophy. You should moralise in a drawing-room; and so let me propose our return to that world which must long have missed us. Let us do something to astound these elegant barbarians. Look at that young gentleman: how stiff he is! A Yorkshire Apollo! Look at that old lady; how elaborately she simpers! The Venus of the Riding! They absolutely attempt to flirt. Let us give them a gallop!'

He was advancing to salute this provincial couple; but his more mature companion repressed him.

'Ah! I forgot,' said the young Duke. 'I am Yorkshire. If I were a western, like yourself, I might compromise my character. Your Grace monopolises the fun.'

'I think you may safely attack them,' said Miss Dacre. 'I do not think you will be recognised. People entertain in this barbarous country, such vulgar, old-fashioned notions of a Duke of St. James, that I have not the least doubt your Grace might have a good deal of fun without being found out.'

'There is no necessity,' said the Duke, 'to fly from Miss Dacre for amusement. By-the-bye, you make a good repartee. You must permit me to introduce you to my friend, Lord Squib. I am sure you would agree so.'

'I have been introduced to Lord Squib.'

'And you found him most amusing? Did he say anything which vindicates my appointment of him as my court jester?'

'I found him modest. He endeavoured to excuse his errors by being your companion; and to prove his virtues by being mine.'

'Treacherous Squib! I positively must call him out. Duke, bear him a cartel.'

'The quarrel is ours, and must be decided here,' said Mrs. Dallington Vere. 'I second Miss Dacre.'

'We are in the way of some good people here, I think,' said the Duke of Burlington, who, though the most dignified, was the most considerate of men; 'at least, here are a stray couple or two staring as if they wished us to understand we prevented a set.'

'Let them stare,' said the Duke of St. James; 'we were made to be looked at. 'Tis our vocation, Hal, and they are gifted with vision purposely to behold us.'

'Your Grace,' said Miss Dacre, 'reminds me of my old friend, Prince Rubarini, who told me one day that when he got up late he always gave orders to have the sun put back a couple of hours.'

'And you, Miss Dacre, remind me of my old friend, the Duchess of Nevers, who told me one day that in the course of her experience she had only met one man who was her rival in repartee.'

'And that man,' asked Mrs. Vere.

'Was your slave, Mrs. Dallington,' said the young Duke, bowing profoundly, with his hand on his heart.

'I remember she said the same thing to me,' said the Duke of Burlington, 'about ten years before.'

'That was her grandmother, Burley,' said the Duke of St. James.

'Her grandmother!' said Mrs. Dallington, exciting the contest.

'Decidedly,' said the young Duke. 'I remember my friend always spoke of the Duke of Burlington as grandpapa.'

'You will profit, I have no doubt, then, by the company of so venerable a friend,' said Miss Dacre.

'Why,' said the young Duke, 'I am not a believer in the perfectibility of the species; and you know, that when we come to a certain point——'

'We must despair of improvement,' said the Duke of Burlington.

'Your Grace came forward, like a true knight, to my rescue,' said Miss Dacre, bowing to the Duke of Burlington.

'Beauty can inspire miracles,' said the Duke of St. James.

'This young gentleman has been spoiled by travel, Miss Dacre,' said the Duke of Burlington. 'You have much to answer for, for he tells every one that you were his guardian.'

The eyes of Miss Dacre and the Duke of St. James met. He bowed with that graceful impudence which is, after all, the best explanation for every possible misunderstanding.

'I always heard that the Duke of St. James was born of age,' said Miss Dacre.

'The report was rife on the Continent when I travelled,' said Mrs. Dallington Vere.

'That was only a poetical allegory, which veiled the precocious results of my fair tutor's exertions.'

'How discreet he is!' said the Duke of Burlington. 'You may tell immediately that he is two-and-forty.'

'We are neither of us, though, off the *pavÃ©* yet, Burlington; so what say you to inducing these inspiring muses to join the waltz which is just now commencing?'

The young Duke offered his hand to Miss Dacre, and, followed by their companions, they were in a few minutes lost in the waves of the waltzers.

CHAPTER VI.

A Complaisant Spouse

THE gaieties of the race-week closed with a ball at Dallington House. As the pretty mistress of this proud mansion was acquainted with all the members of the ducal party, our hero and his noble band were among those who honoured it with their presence.

We really have had so many balls both in this and other as immortal works that, in a literary point of view, we think we must give up dancing; nor would we have introduced you to Dallington House if there had been no more serious business on hand than a flirtation with a lady or a lobster salad. Ah! why is not a little brief communion with the last as innocent as with the first?

Small feet are flitting in the mazy dance and music winds with inspiring harmony through halls whose lofty mirrors multiply beauty and add fresh lustre to the blazing lights. May Dacre there is wandering like a peri in Paradise, and Lady Aphrodite is glancing with her dazzling brow, yet an Asmodeus might detect an occasional gloom over her radiant face. It is but for an instant, yet it thrills. She looks like some favoured sultana, who muses for a moment amid her splendour on her early love.

And she, the sparkling mistress of this scene; say, where is she? Not among the dancers, though a more graceful form you could scarcely look upon; not even among her guests, though a more accomplished hostess it would be hard to find. Gaiety pours forth its flood, and all are thinking of themselves, or of some one sweeter even than self-consciousness, or else perhaps one absent might be missed.

Leaning on the arm of Sir Lucius Grafton, and shrouded in her cashmere, Mrs. Dallington Vere paces the terrace in earnest conversation.

'If I fail in this,' said Sir Lucius, 'I shall be desperate. Fortune seems to have sent him for the very purpose. Think only of the state of affairs for a moment. After a thousand plots on my part; after having for the last two years never ceased my exertions to make her commit herself; when neither a love of pleasure, nor a love of revenge, nor the thoughtlessness to which women in her situation generally have recourse, produced the slightest effect; this stripling starts upon the stage, and in a moment the iceberg melts. Oh! I never shall forget the rapture of the moment when the faithful Lachen announced the miracle!'

'But why not let the adventure take the usual course? You have your evidence, or you can get it. Finish the business. The *exposA©s*, to be sure, are disagreeable enough; but to be the talk of the town for a week is no great suffering. Go to Baden, drink the waters, and it will be forgotten. Surely this is an inconvenience not to be weighed for a moment against the great result.'

'Believe me, my dearest friend, Lucy Grafton cares very little about the babble of the million, provided it do not obstruct him in his objects. Would to Heaven I could proceed in the summary and effectual mode you point out; but that I much doubt. There is about Afy, in spite of all her softness and humility, a strange spirit, a cursed courage or obstinacy, which sometimes has blazed out, when I have over-galled her, in a way half-awful. I confess I dread her standing at bay. I am in her power, and a divorce she could successfully oppose if I appeared to be the person who hastened the catastrophe and she were piqued to show that she would not fall an easy victim. No, no! I have a surer, though a more difficult, game. She is intoxicated with this boy. I will drive her into his arms.'

'A probable result, forsooth! I do not think your genius has particularly brightened since we last met. I thought your letters were getting dull. You seem to forget that there is a third person to be consulted in this adventure. And why in the name of Doctors' Commons, the Duke is to close his career by marrying a woman of whom, with your leave, he is already, if experience be not a dream, half-wearied, is really past my comprehension, although as Yorkshire, Lucy, I should not, you know, be the least apprehensive of mortals.'

'I depend upon my unbounded influence over St. James.'

'What! do you mean to recommend the step, then?'

'Hear me! At present I am his confidential counsellor on all subjects——'

'But one.'

'Patience, fair dame; and I have hitherto imperceptibly, but efficiently, exerted my influence to prevent his getting entangled with any other nets.'

'Faithful friend!'

'*Point de moquerie!* Listen. I depend further upon his perfect inexperience of women; for, in spite of his numerous gallantries, he has never yet had a grand passion, and is quite ignorant, even at this moment, how involved his feelings are with his mistress. He has not yet learnt the bitter lesson that, unless we despise a woman when we cease to love her, we are still a slave, without the consolement of intoxication. I depend further upon his strong feelings; for strong I perceive they are, with all his affectation; and on his weakness of character, which will allow him to be the dupe of his first great emotion. It is to prevent that explosion from taking place under any other roof than my own that I now require your advice and assistance; that advice and assistance which already have done so much for me. I like not this sudden and uncontemplated visit to Castle Dacre. I fear these Dacres; I fear the revulsion of his feelings. Above all, I fear that girl.'

'But her cousin; is he not a talisman? She loves him.'

'Pooh! a cousin! Is not the name an answer? She loves him as she loves her pony; because he was her companion when she was a child, and kissed her when they gathered strawberries together. The pallid, moonlight passion of a cousin, and an absent one, too, has but a sorry chance against the blazing beams that shoot from the eyes of a new lover. Would to Heaven that I had not to go down to my boobies at Cleve! I should like nothing better than to amuse myself an autumn at Dallington with the little Dacre, and put an end to such an unnatural and irreligious connection. She is a splendid creature! Bring her to town next season.'

'But to the point. You wish me, I imagine, to act the same part with the lady as you have done with the gentleman. I am to step in, I suppose, as the confidential counsellor on all subjects of sweet May. I am to preserve her from a youth whose passions are so impetuous and whose principles are so unformed.'

'Admirable Bertha! You read my thoughts.'

'But suppose I endanger, instead of advance, your plans. Suppose, for instance, I captivate his Grace. As extraordinary things have happened, as you know. High place must be respected, and the coronet of a Duchess must not be despised.'

'All considerations must yield to you, as do all men,' said Sir Lucius, with ready gallantry, but not free from anxiety.

'No, no; there is no danger of that. I am not going to play traitress to my system, even for the Duke of St. James; therefore, anything that occurs between us shall be merely an incident *pour passer le temps seulement*, and to preserve our young friend from the little Dacre. I have no doubt he will behave very well, and that I shall send him safe to Cleve Park in a fortnight with a good character. I would recommend you, however, not to encourage any unreasonable delay.'

'Certainly not; but I must, of course, be guided by circumstances.' Sir Lucius observed truly. There were other considerations besides getting rid of his spouse which cemented his friendship with the young Duke. It will be curious if lending a few thousands to the husband save our hero from the wife. There is no such thing as unmixed evil. A man who loses his money gains, at least, experience, and sometimes something better. But what the Duke of St. James gained is not yet to be told.

'And you like Lachen?' asked Mrs. Dallington.

'Very much.'

'I formed her with great care, but you must keep her in good humour.'

'That is not difficult. *Elle est trÂ's jolie*; and pretty women, like yourself, are always good-natured.'

'But has she really worked herself into the confidence of the virtuous Aphrodite?'

'Entirely. And the humour is, that Lachen has persuaded her that Lachen herself is on the best possible terms with my confidential valet, and can make herself at all times mistress of her master's secrets. So it is always in my power, apparently without taking the slightest interest in Afy's conduct, to regulate it as I will. At present she believes that my affairs are in a distracted state, and that I intend to reside solely on the Continent, and to bear her off from her Cupidon. This thought haunts her rest, and hangs heavy on her waking mind. I think it will do the business.'

'We have been too long absent. Let us return.'

'I accompany you, my charming friend. What should I do without such an ally? I only wish that I could assist you in a manner equally friendly. Is there no obdurate hero who wants a confidential adviser to dilate upon your charms, or to counsel him to throw himself at your feet; or are that beautiful in face and lovely form, as they must always be, invincible?'

'I assure you quite disembarrassed of any attentions whatever. But, I suppose, when I return to Athens, I must get Platonic again.'

'Let me be the philosopher!'

'No, no; we know each other too well. I have been free ever since that fatal affair of young Darrell, and travel has restored my spirits a little. They say his brother is just as handsome. He was expected at Vienna, but I could not meet him, although I suppose, as I made him a Viscount, I am rather popular than not with him.'

'Pooh! pooh! think not of this. No one blames you. You are still a universal favourite. But I would recommend you, nevertheless, to take me as your cavalier.'

'You are too generous, or too bold. No, man! I am tired of flirtation, and really think, for variety's sake, I must fall in love. After all, there is nothing like the delicious dream, though it be but a dream. Spite of my discretion, I sometimes tremble lest I should end by making myself a fool, with some grand passion. You look serious. Fear not for the young Duke. He is a dazzling gentleman, but not a hero exactly to my taste.'

CHAPTER VII.

At Castle Dacre

THE moment that was to dissolve the spell which had combined and enchanted so many thousands of human beings arrived. Nobles and nobodies, beauties and blacklegs, dispersed in all directions. The Duke of Burlington carried off the French princes and the Protocolis, the Bloomerlys and the Vaticans, to his Paradise of Marringworth. The Fitz-pompeys cantered off with the Shropshires; omen of felicity to the enamoured St. Maurice and the enamouring Sophy. Annesley and Squib returned to their pÃ¢tÃ©s. Sir Lucius and Lady Aphrodite, neither of them with tempers like summer skies, betook their way to Cambridgeshire, like Adam and Eve from the glorious garden. The Duke of St. James, after a hurried visit to London, found himself, at the beginning of October, on his way to Dacre.

As his carriage rolled on he revelled in delicious fancies. The young Duke built castles not only at Hauteville, but in less substantial regions. Reverie, in the flush of our warm youth, generally indulges in the future. We are always anticipating the next adventure and clothe the coming heroine with a rosy tint. When we advance a little on our limited journey, and an act or two of the comedy, the gayest in all probability, are over, the wizard Memory dethrones the witch Imagination, and 'tis the past on which the mind feeds in its musings. 'Tis then we ponder on each great result which has stolen on us without the labour of reflection; 'tis then we analyse emotions which, at the time, we could not comprehend, and probe the action which passion inspired, and which prejudice has hitherto defended. Alas! who can strike these occasional balances in life's great ledger without a sigh! Alas! how little do they promise in favour of the great account! What whisperings of final bankruptcy! what a damnable consciousness of present insolvency! My friends! what a blunder is youth! Ah! why does Truth light her torch but to illume the ruined temple of our existence! Ah! why do we know we are men only to be conscious of our exhausted energies!

And yet there is a pleasure in a deal of judgment which your judicious man alone can understand. It is agreeable to see some younkers falling into the same traps which have broken our own shins; and, shipwrecked on the island of our hopes, one likes to mark a vessel go down full in sight. 'Tis demonstration that we are not branded as Cains among the favoured race of man. Then giving advice: that *is* delicious, and perhaps repays one all. It is a privilege your grey-haired signors solely can enjoy; but young men now-a-days may make some claims to it. And, after all, experience is a thing that all men praise. Bards sing its glories, and proud Philosophy has long elected it her favourite child. 'Tis the '*rÃ² KaxÃ v*', in spite of all its ugliness, and the *elixir vitÃ*¦, though we generally gain it with a shattered pulse.

No more! no more! it is a bitter cheat, the consolation of blunderers, the last refuge of expiring hopes, the forlorn battalion that is to capture the citadel of happiness; yet, yet impregnable! Oh! what is wisdom, and what is virtue, without youth! Talk not to me of knowledge of mankind; give, give me back the sunshine of the breast which they o'erclouded! Talk not to me of proud morality; oh! give me innocence!

Amid the ruins of eternal Rome I scribble pages lighter than the wind, and feed with fancies volumes which will be forgotten ere I can hear that they are even published. Yet am I not one insensible to the magic of my memorable abode, and I could pour my passion o'er the land; but I repress my thoughts, and beat their tide back to their hollow caves!

The ocean of my mind is calm, but dim, and ominous of storms that may arise. A cloud hangs heavy o'er the horizon's verge, and veils the future. Even now a star appears, steals into light, and now again 'tis gone! I hear the proud swell of the growing waters; I hear the whispering of the wakening winds; but reason lays her trident on the cresting waves, and all again is hushed.

For I am one, though young, yet old enough to know ambition is a demon; and I fly from what I fear. And fame has eagle wings, and yet she mounts not so high as man's desires. When all is gained, how little then is won! And yet to gain that little how much is lost! Let us once aspire and madness follows. Could we but drag the purple from the hero's heart; could we but tear the laurel from the poet's throbbing brain, and read their doubts, their dangers, their despair, we might learn a greater lesson than we shall ever acquire by musing over their exploits or their inspiration. Think of unrecognised Caesar, with his wasting youth, weeping over the Macedonian's young career! Could Pharsalia compensate for those withering pangs? View the obscure Napoleon starving in the streets of Paris! What was St. Helena to the bitterness of such existence? The visions of past glory might illumine even that dark-imprisonment; but to be conscious that his supernatural energies might die away without creating their miracles: can the wheel or the rack rival the torture of such a suspicion? Lo! Byron bending o'er his shattered lyre, with inspiration in his very rage. And the pert taunt could sting even this child of light! To doubt of the truth of the creed in which you have been nurtured is not so terrific as to doubt respecting the intellectual vigour on whose strength you have staked your happiness. Yet these were mighty ones; perhaps the records of the world will not yield us threescore to be their mates! Then tremble, ye whose cheek glows too warmly at their names! Who would be more than man should fear lest he be less.

Yet there is hope, there should be happiness, for them, for all. Kind Nature, ever mild, extends her fond arms to her truant children, and breathes her words of solace. As we weep on her indulgent and maternal breast, the exhausted passions, one by one, expire like gladiators in yon huge pile that has made barbarity sublime. Yes! there is hope and joy; and it is here!

Where the breeze wanders through a perfumed sky, and where the beautiful sun illumines beauty.

On the poet's farm and on the conqueror's arch thy beam is lingering! It lingers on the shattered porticoes that once shrouded from thy o'erpowering glory the lords of earth; it lingers upon the ruined temples that even in their desolation are yet sacred! 'Tis gone, as if in sorrow! Yet the woody lake still blushes with thy warm kiss; and still thy rosy light tinges the pine that breaks the farthest heaven!

A heaven all light, all beauty, and all love! What marvel men should worship in these climes? And lo! a small and single cloud is sailing in the immaculate ether, burnished with twilight, like an Olympian chariot from above, with the fair vision of some graceful god!

It is the hour that poets love; but I crush thoughts that rise from out my mind, like nymphs from out their caves, when sets the sun. Yes, 'tis a blessing here to breathe and muse. And cold his clay, indeed, who does not yield to thy Ausonian beauty! Clime where the heart softens and the mind expands! Region of mellowed bliss! O most enchanting land!

But we are at the park gates.

They whirled along through a park which would have contained half a hundred of those Patagonian paddocks of modern times which have usurped the name. At length the young Duke was roused from his reverie by Carlstein, proud of his previous knowledge, leaning over and announcing—

'ChÃ¢teau de Dacre, your Grace!'

The Duke looked up. The sun, which had already set, had tinged with a dying crimson the eastern sky, against which rose a princely edifice. Castle Dacre was the erection of Vanbrugh, an imaginative artist, whose critics we wish no bitterer fate than not to live in his splendid creations. A spacious centre, richly ornamented, though broken, perhaps, into rather too much detail, was joined to wings of a corresponding magnificence by fanciful colonnades. A terrace, extending the whole front, was covered with orange trees, and many a statue, and many an obelisk, and many a temple, and many a fountain, were tinted with the warm twilight. The Duke did not view the forgotten scene of youth without emotion. It was a palace worthy of the heroine on whom he had been musing. The carriage gained the lofty portal. Luigi and Spiridion, who had preceded their master, were ready to receive the Duke, who was immediately ushered to the rooms prepared for his reception. He was later than he had intended, and no time was to be unnecessarily lost in his preparation for his appearance.

His Grace's toilet was already prepared: the magical dressing-box had been unpacked, and the shrine for his devotions was covered with richly-cut bottles of all sizes, arranged in all the elegant combinations which the picturesque fancy of his valet could devise, adroitly intermixed with the golden instruments, the china vases, and the ivory and rosewood brushes, which were worthy even of Delcroix's exquisite inventions.

The Duke of St. James was master of the art of dress, and consequently consummated that paramount operation with the decisive rapidity of one whose principles are settled. He was cognisant of all effects, could calculate in a second all consequences, and obtained his result with that promptitude and precision which stamp the great artist. For a moment he was plunged in profound abstraction, and at the same time stretched his legs after his drive. He then gave his orders with the decision of Wellington on the arrival of the Prussians, and the battle began.

His Grace had a taste for magnificence in costume; but he was handsome, young, and a duke. Pardon him. Yet to-day he was, on the whole, simple. Confident in a complexion whose pellucid lustre had not yielded to a season of dissipation, his Grace did not dread the want of relief which a white face, a white cravat, and a white waistcoat would seem to imply.

A hair chain set in diamonds, worn in memory of the absent Aphrodite, and to pique the present Dacre, is annexed to a glass, which reposes in the waistcoat pocket. This was the only weight that the Duke of St. James ever carried. It was a bore, but it was indispensable.

It is done. He stops one moment before the long pier-glass, and shoots a glance which would have read the mind of Talleyrand. It will do. He assumes the look, the air that befit the occasion: cordial, but dignified; sublime, but sweet. He descends like a deity from Olympus to a banquet of illustrious mortals.

CHAPTER VIII.

'Fair Women and Brave Men.'

MR. DACRE received him with affection: his daughter with a cordiality which he had never yet experienced from her. Though more simply dressed than when she first met his ardent gaze, her costume again charmed his practised eye. 'It must be her shape,' thought the young Duke; 'it is magical!'

The rooms were full of various guests, and some of these were presented to his Grace, who was, of course, an object of universal notice, but particularly by those persons who pretended not to be aware of his entrance. The party assembled at Castle Dacre consisted of some thirty or forty persons, all of great consideration, but of a different character from any with whom the Duke of St. James had been acquainted during his short experience of English society. They were not what are called fashionable people. We have no princes and no ambassadors, no duke who is a gourmand, no earl who is a jockey, no manoeuvring mothers, no flirting daughters, no gambling sons, for your entertainment. There is no superfine gentleman brought down specially from town to gauge the refinement of the manners of the party, and to prevent them, by his constant supervision and occasional sneer, from losing any of the beneficial results of their last campaign. We shall sadly want, too, a Lady Patroness to issue a decree or quote her code of consolidated etiquette. We are not sure that Almack's will ever be mentioned: quite sure that Maradan has never yet been heard of. The Jockey Club may be quoted, but Crockford will be a dead letter. As for the rest, Boodle's is all we can promise; miserable consolation for the bow-window. As for buffoons and artists, to amuse a vacant hour or sketch a vacant face, we must frankly tell you at once that there is not one. Are you frightened? Will you go on? Will you trust yourself with these savages? Try. They are rude, but they are hospitable.

The party, we have said, were all persons of great consideration; some were noble, most were rich, all had ancestors. There were the Earl and Countess of Faulconcourt. He looked as if he were fit to reconquer Palestine, and she as if she were worthy to reward him for his valour. Misplaced in this superior age, he was *sans peur* and she *sans reproche*. There was Lord Mildmay, an English peer and a French colonel. Methinks such an incident might have been a better reason for a late measure than an Irishman being returned a member of our Imperial Parliament. There was our friend Lord St. Jerome; of course his stepmother, yet young, and some sisters, pretty as nuns. There were some cousins from the farthest north, Northumbria's bleakest bound, who came down upon Yorkshire like the Goths upon Italy, and were revelling in what they considered a southern clime.

There was an M.P. in whom the Catholics had hopes. He had made a great speech; not only a great speech, but a great impression. His matter certainly was not new, but well arranged, and his images not singularly original, but appositely introduced; in short, a bore, who, speaking on a subject in which a new hand is indulged, and connected with the families whose cause he was pleading, was for once courteously listened to by the very men who determined to avenge themselves for their complaisance by a cough on the first opportunity. But the orator was prudent; he reserved himself, and the session closed with his fame yet full-blown.

Then there were country neighbours in great store, with wives that were treasures, and daughters fresh as flowers. Among them we would particularise two gentlemen. They were great proprietors, and Catholics and Baronets, and consoled themselves by their active maintenance of the game-laws for their inability to regulate their neighbours by any other. One was Sir Chetwode Chetwode of Chetwode; the other was Sir Tichborne Tichborne of Tichborne. It was not easy to see two men less calculated to be the slaves of a foreign and despotic power, which we all know Catholics are. Tall, and robust, and rosy, with hearts even stouter than their massy frames, they were just the characters to assemble in Runnymede, and probably, even at the present day, might have imitated their ancestors, even in their signatures. In disposition they were much the same, though they were friends. In person there were some differences, but they were slight. Sir Chetwode's hair was straight and white; Sir Tichborne's brown and curly. Sir Chetwode's eyes were blue; Sir Tichborne's grey.

Sir Chetwode's nose was perhaps a snub; Sir Tichborne's was certainly a bottle. Sir Chetwode was somewhat garrulous, and was often like a man at a play, in the wrong box! Sir Tichborne was somewhat taciturn; but when he spoke, it was always to the purpose, and made an impression, even if it were not new. Both were kind hearts; but Sir Chetwode was jovial, Sir Tichborne rather stern. Sir Chetwode often broke into a joke; Sir Tichborne sometimes backed into a sneer. .

A few of these characters were made known by Mr. Dacre to his young friend, but not many, and in an easy way; those that stood nearest. Introduction is a formality and a bore, and is never resorted to by your well-bred host, save in a casual way. When proper people meet at proper houses, they give each other credit for propriety, and slide into an acquaintance by degrees. The first day they catch a name; the next, they ask you whether you are the son of General———. 'No; he was my uncle.' 'Ah! I knew him well. A worthy soul!' And then the thing is settled. You ride together, shoot, or fence, or hunt. A game of billiards will do no great harm; and when you part, you part with a hope that you may meet again.

Lord Mildmay was glad to meet with the son of an old friend. He knew the late Duke well, and loved him better. It is pleasant to hear our fathers praised. We, too, may inherit their virtues with their lands, or cash, or bonds; and, scapegraces as we are, it is agreeable to find a precedent for the blood turning out well. And, after all, there is no feeling more thoroughly delightful than to be conscious that the kind being from whose loins we spring, and to whom we cling with an innate and overpowering love, is viewed by others with regard, with reverence, or with admiration. There is no pride like the pride of ancestry, for it is a blending of all emotions. How immeasurably superior to the herd is the man whose father only is famous! Imagine, then, the feelings of one who can trace his line through a thousand years of heroes and of princes!

'Tis dinner! hour that I have loved as loves the bard the twilight; but no more those visions rise that once were wont to spring in my quick fancy. The dream is past, the spell is broken, and even the lore on which I pondered in my first youth is strange as figures in Egyptian tombs.

No more, no more, oh! never more to me, that hour shall bring its rapture and its bliss! No more, no more, oh! never more for me, shall Flavour sit upon her thousand thrones, and, like a syren with a sunny smile, win to renewed excesses, each more sweet! My feasting days are over: me no more the charms of fish, or flesh, still less of fowl, can make the fool of that they made before. The fricandeau is like a dream of early love; the fricassee, with which I have so often flirted, is like the tattle of the last quadrille; and no longer are my dreams haunted with the dark passion of the rich ragoÃ»t. Ye soups! o'er whose creation I have watched, like mothers o'er their sleeping child! Ye sauces! to which I have even lent a name, where are ye now? Tickling, perchance, the palate of some easy friend, who quite forgets the boon companion whose presence once lent lustre even to his ruby wine and added perfume to his perfumed hock!

Our Duke, however, had not reached the age of retrospection. He pecked as prettily as any bird. Seated on the right hand of his delightful hostess, nobody could be better pleased; supervised by his jÃ¤ger, who stood behind his chair, no one could be better attended. He smiled, with the calm, amiable complacency of a man who feels the world is quite right.

CHAPTER IX.

The Châtelaine of Castle Dacre

HOW is your Grace's horse, Sans-pareil?' asked Sir Chetwode Chetwode of Chetwode of the Duke of St. James, shooting at the same time a sly glance at his opposite neighbour, Sir Tichborne Tichborne of Tichborne.

'Quite well, sir,' said the Duke in his quietest tone, but with an air which, he flattered himself, might repress further inquiry.

'Has he got over his fatigue?' pursued the dogged Baronet, with a short, gritty laugh, that sounded like a loose drag-chain dangling against the stones. 'We all thought the Yorkshire air would not agree with him.'

'Yet, Sir Chetwode, that could hardly be your opinion of Sanspareil,' said Miss Dacre, 'for I think, if I remember right, I had the pleasure of making you encourage our glove manufactory.'

Sir Chetwode looked a little confused. The Duke of St. James, inspirited by his fair ally, rallied, and hoped Sir Chetwode did not back his steed to a fatal extent. 'If,' continued he, 'I had had the slightest idea that any friend of Miss Dacre was indulging in such an indiscretion, I certainly would have interfered, and have let him known that the horse was not to win.'

'Is that a fact?' asked Sir Tichborne Tichborne of Tichborne, with a sturdy voice.

'Can a Yorkshireman doubt it?' rejoined the Duke. 'Was it possible for anyone but a mere Newmarket dandy to have entertained for a moment the supposition that anyone but May Dacre should be the Queen of the St. Leger?'

'I have heard something of this before,' said Sir Tichborne, 'but I did not believe it. A young friend of mine consulted me upon the subject. "Would you advise me," said he, "to settle?" "Why," said I, "if you can prove any bubble, my opinion is, don't; but if you cannot prove anything, my opinion is, do."'

'Very just! very true!' were murmured by many in the neighbourhood of the oracle; by no one with more personal sincerity than Lady Tichborne herself.

'I will write to my young friend,' continued the Baronet.

'Oh, no!' said Miss Dacre. 'His Grace's candour must not be abused. I have no idea of being robbed of my well-earned honours. Sir Tichborne, private conversation must be respected, and the sanctity of domestic life must not be profaned. If the tactics of Doncaster are no longer to be fair war, why, half the families in the Riding will be ruined!'

- 83 -

'Still,'—said Sir Tichborne.

But Mr. Dacre, like a deity in a Trojan battle, interposed, and asked his opinion of a keeper.

'I hope you are a sportsman,' said Miss Dacre to the Duke, 'for this is the palace of Nimrod!'

'I have hunted; it was not very disagreeable. I sometimes shoot; it is not very stupid.'

'Then, in fact, I perceive that you are a heretic. Lord Faulconcourt, his Grace is moralising on the barbarity of the chase.'

'Then he has never had the pleasure of hunting in company with Miss Dacre.'

'Do you indeed follow the hounds?' asked the Duke.

'Sometimes do worse, ride over them; but Lord Faulconcourt is fast emancipating me from the trammels of my frippery foreign education, and I have no doubt that, in another season, I shall fling off quite in style.'

'You remember Mr. Annesley?' asked the Duke.

'It is difficult to forget him. He always seemed to me to think that the world was made on purpose for him to have the pleasure of "cutting" it.'

'Yet he was your admirer!'

'Yes, and once paid me a compliment. He told me it was the only one that he had ever uttered.'

'Oh, Charley, Charley! this is excellent. We shall have a tale when we meet. What was the compliment?'

'It would be affectation in me to pretend that I have forgotten it. Nevertheless, you must excuse me.'

'Pray, pray let me have it!'

'Perhaps you will not like it?'

'Now, I must hear it.'

'Well then, he said that talking to me was the only thing that consoled him for having to dine with you and to dance with Lady Shropshire.'

'Charles is jealous,' drawled the Duke.

'Of her Grace?' asked Miss Dacre, with much anxiety.

'No; but Charles is aged, and once, when he dined with me, was taken for my uncle.'

The ladies retired, and the gentlemen sat barbarously long. Sir Chetwode Chetwode of Chetwode and Sir Tichborne Tichborne of Tichborne were two men who drank wine independent of fashion, and exacted, to the last glass, the identical quantity which their fathers had drunk half a century before, and to which they had been used almost from their cradle. The only subject of conversation was sporting. Terrible shots, more terrible runs, neat barrels, and pretty fencers. The Duke of St. James was not sufficiently acquainted with the geography of the mansion to make a premature retreat, an operation which is looked upon with an evil eye, and which, to be successful, must be prompt and decisive, and executed with supercilious nonchalance. So he consoled himself by a little chat with Lord Mildmay, who sat smiling, handsome, and mustachioed, with an empty glass, and who was as much out of water as he was out of wine. The Duke was not very learned in Parisian society; but still, with the aid of the Duchess de Berri and the Duchess de Duras, LÃ©ontine Fay, and Lady Stuart de Rothesay, they got on, and made out the time until Purgatory ceased and Paradise opened.

For Paradise it was, although there were there assembled some thirty or forty persons not less dull than the majority of our dull race, and in those little tactics that make society less burdensome perhaps even less accomplished. But a sunbeam will make even the cloudiest day break into smiles; a bounding fawn will banish monotony even from a wilderness; and a glass of claret, or perchance some stronger grape, will convert even the platitude of a goblet of water into a pleasing beverage, and so May Dacre moved among her guests, shedding light, life, and pleasure.

She was not one who, shrouded in herself, leaves it to chance or fate to amuse the beings whom she has herself assembled within her halls. Nonchalance is the *mÃ©tier* of your modern hostess; and so long as the house be not on fire, or the furniture not kicked, you may be even ignorant who is the priestess of the hospitable fane in which you worship.

They are right; men shrink from a fussy woman. And few can aspire to regulate the destinies of their species, even in so slight a point as an hour's amusement, without rare powers. There is no greater sin than to be *trop prononcÃ©e*. A want of tact is worse than a want of virtue. Some women, it is said, work on pretty well against the tide without the last: I never knew one who did not sink who ever dared to sail without the first.

Loud when they should be low, quoting the wrong person, talking on the wrong subject, teasing with notice, excruciating with attentions, disturbing a tÃªte-Ã -tÃªte in order to make up a dance; wasting eloquence in persuading a man to participate in amusement whose reputation depends on his social sullenness; exacting homage with a restless eye, and not permitting the least worthy knot to be untwined without their divinityships' interference;

patronising the meek, anticipating the slow, intoxicated with compliment, plastering with praise, that you in return may gild with flattery; in short, energetic without elegance, active without grace, and loquacious without wit; mistaking bustle for style, raillery for badinage, and noise for gaiety, these are the characters who mar the very career they think they are creating, and who exercise a fatal influence on the destinies of all those who have the misfortune to be connected with them.

Not one of these was she, the lady of our tale. There was a quiet dignity lurking even under her easiest words and actions which made you feel her notice a compliment: there was a fascination in her calm smile and in her sunlit eye which made her invitation to amusement itself a pleasure. If you refused, you were not pressed, but left to that isolation which you appeared to admire; if you assented, you were rewarded with a word which made you feel how sweet was such society! Her invention never flagged, her gaiety never ceased; yet both were spontaneous, and often were unobserved. All felt amused, and all were unconsciously her agents. Her word and her example seemed, each instant, to call forth from her companions new accomplishments, new graces, new sources of joy and of delight. All were surprised that they were so agreeable.

CHAPTER X.

Love's Young Dream

MORNING came, and the great majority of the gentlemen rose early as Aurora. The chase is the favourite pastime of man and boy; yet some preferred plundering their host's preserves, by which means their slumbers were not so brief and their breakfast less disturbed. The *battue*, however, in time, called forth its band, and then one by one, or two by two, or sometimes even three, leaning on each other's arms and smiling in each other's faces, the ladies dropped into the breakfast-room at Castle Dacre. There, until two o'clock, a lounging meal might always be obtained, but generally by twelve the coast was clear; for our party were a natural race of beings, and would have blushed if flaming noon had caught them napping in their easy couches. Our bright bird, May Dacre, too, rose from her bower, full of the memory of the sweetest dreams, and fresh as lilies ere they kiss the sun.

She bends before her ivory crucifix, and gazes on her blessed mother's face, where the sweet Florentine had tinged with light a countenance

Too fair for worship, too divine for love!

And innocence has prayed for fresh support, and young devotion told her holy beads. She rises with an eye of mellowed light, and her soft cheek is tinted with the flush that comes from prayer. Guard over her, ye angels! wheresoe'er and whatsoe'er ye are! For she shall be your meet companion in an after-day. Then love your gentle friend, this sinless child of clay!

The morning passed as mornings ever pass where twenty women, for the most part pretty, are met together. Some read, some drew, some worked, all talked. Some wandered in the library, and wondered why such great books were written. One sketched a favourite hero in the picture gallery, a Dacre, who had saved the State or Church, had fought at Cressy, or flourished at Windsor: another picked a flower out of the conservatory, and painted its powdered petals. Here, a purse, half-made, promised, when finished quite, to make some hero happy. Then there was chat about the latest fashions, caps and bonnets, sÃ©duisantes, and sleeves. As the day grew' old, some rode, some walked, some drove. A pony-chair was Lady Faulconcourt's delight, whose arm was roundly turned and graced the whip; while, on the other hand, Lady St. Jerome rather loved to try the paces of an ambling nag, because her figure was of the sublime; and she looked not unlike an Amazonian queen, particularly when Lord Mildmay was her Theseus.

He was the most consummate, polished gentleman that ever issued from the court of France. He did his friend Dacre the justice to suppose that he was a victim to his barbarous guests; but for the rest of the galloping crew, who rode and shot all day, and in the evening fell asleep just when they were wanted, he shrugged his shoulders, and he thanked his stars! In short, Lord Mildmay was the ladies' man; and in their morning dearth of beaux, to adopt their unanimous expression, 'quite a host!'

Then there was archery for those who could draw a bow or point an arrow; and we are yet to learn the sight that is more dangerous for your bachelor to witness, or the ceremony which more perfectly develops all that the sex would wish us to remark, than this 'old English' custom.

With all these resources, all was, of course, free and easy as the air. Your appearance was your own act. If you liked, you might have remained, like a monk or nun, in your cell till dinner-time, but no later. Privacy and freedom are granted you in the morning, that you may not exhaust your powers of pleasing before night, and that you may reserve for those favoured hours all the new ideas that you have collected in the course of your morning adventures.

But where was he, the hero of our tale? Fencing? Craning? Hitting? Missing? Is he over, or is he under? Has he killed, or is he killed? for the last is but the chance of war, and pheasants have the pleasure of sometimes seeing as gay birds as themselves with plumage quite as shattered. But there is no danger of the noble countenance of the Duke of St. James bearing to-day any evidence of the exploits of himself or his companions. His Grace was in one of his sublime fits, and did not rise. Luigi consoled himself for the bore of this protracted attendance by diddling the page-in-waiting at dominos.

The Duke of St. James was in one of his sublime fits. He had commenced by thinking of May Dacre, and he ended by thinking of himself. He was under that delicious and dreamy excitement which we experience when the image of a lovely and beloved object begins to mix itself up with our own intense self-love. She was the heroine rather of an indefinite reverie than of definite romance. Instead of his own image alone playing about his fancy, her beautiful face and springing figure intruded their exquisite presence. He no longer mused merely on his own voice and wit: he called up her tones of thrilling power; he imagined her in all the triumph of her gay repartee. In his mind's eye, he clearly watched all the graces of her existence. She moved, she gazed, she smiled. Now he was alone, and walking with her in some rich wood, sequestered, warm, solemn, dim, feeding on the music of her voice, and gazing with intenseness on the wakening passion of her devoted eye. Now they rode together, scudded over champaign, galloped down hills, scampered through valleys, all life, and gaiety, and vivacity, and spirit. Now they were in courts and crowds; and he led her with pride to the proudest kings. He covered her with jewels; but the world thought her brighter than his gems. Now they met in the most unexpected and improbable manner:

now they parted with a tenderness which subdued their souls even more than rapture. Now he saved her life: now she blessed his existence. Now his reverie was too vague and misty to define its subject. It was a stream of passion, joy, sweet voices, tender tones, exulting hopes, beaming faces, chaste embraces, immortal transports!

It was three o'clock, and for the twentieth time our hero made an effort to recall himself to the realities of life. How cold, how tame, how lifeless, how imperfect, how inconsecutive, did everything appear! This is the curse of reverie. But they who revel in its pleasures must bear its pains, and are content. Yet it wears out the brain, and unfits us for social life. They who indulge in it most are the slaves of solitude. They wander in a wilderness, and people it with their voices. They sit by the side of running waters, with an eye more glassy than the stream. The sight of a human being scares them more than a wild beast does a traveller; the conduct of life, when thrust upon their notice, seems only a tissue of adventures without point; and, compared with the creatures of their imagination, human nature seems to send forth only abortions.

'I must up,' said the young Duke; 'and this creature on whom I have lived for the last eight hours, who has, in herself, been to me the universe, this constant companion, this cherished friend, whose voice was passion and whose look was love, will meet me with all the formality of a young lady, all the coldness of a person who has never even thought of me since she saw me last. Damnable delusion! To-morrow I will get up and hunt.'

He called Luigi, and a shower-bath assisted him in taking a more healthy view of affairs. Yet his faithful fancy recurred to her again. He must indulge it a little. He left off dressing and flung himself in a chair.

'And yet,' he continued, 'when I think of it again, there surely can be no reason that this should not turn into a romance of real life. I perceived that she was a little piqued when we first met at Don-caster. Very natural! Very flattering! I should have been piqued. Certainly, I behaved decidedly ill. But how, in the name of Heaven, was I to know that she was the brightest little being that ever breathed! Well, I am here now! She has got her wish. And I think an evident alteration has already taken place. But she must not melt too quickly. She will not; she will do nothing but what is exquisitely proper. How I do love this child! I dote upon her very image. It is the very thing that I have always been wanting. The women call me inconstant. I have never been constant. But they will not listen to us without we feign feelings, and then they upbraid us for not being influenced by them. I have sighed, I have sought, I have wept, for what I now have found. What would she give to know what is passing in my mind! By Heavens! there is no blood in England that has a better chance of being a Duchess!'

CHAPTER XI.

Le Roi S'Amuse

A CANTER is the cure for every evil, and brings the mind back to itself sooner than all the lessons of Chrysippus and Crantor. It is the only process that at the same time calms the feelings and elevates the spirits, banishes blue devils and raises one to the society of 'angels ever bright and fair.' It clears the mind; it cheers the heart. It is the best preparation for all enterprises, for it puts a man in good humour both with the world and himself; and, whether you are going to make a speech or scribble a scene, whether you are about to conquer the world or yourself, order your horse. As you bound along, your wit will brighten and your eloquence blaze, your courage grow more adamantine, and your generous feelings burn with a livelier flame. And when the exercise is over the excitement does not cease, as when it grows from music, for your blood is up, and the brilliancy of your eye is fed by your bubbling pulses. Then, my young friend, take my advice: rush into the world, and triumph will grow out of your quick life, like Victory bounding from the palm of Jove!

Our Duke ordered his horses, and as he rattled along recovered from the enervating effects of his soft reverie. On his way home he fell in with Mr. Dacre and the two Baronets, returning on their hackneys from a hard fought field.

'Gay sport?' asked his Grace.

'A capital run. I think the last forty minutes the most splitting thing we have had for a long time!' answered Sir Chetwode. 'I only hope Jack Wilson will take care of poor Fanny. I did not half like leaving her. Your Grace does not join us?'

'I mean to do so; but I am, unfortunately, a late riser.'

'Hem!' said Sir Tichborne. The monosyllable meant much.

'I have a horse which I think will suit your Grace,' said Mr. Dacre, 'and to which, in fact, you are entitled, for it bears the name of your house. You have ridden Hauteville, Sir Tichborne?'

'Yes; fine animal!'

'I shall certainly try his powers,' said the Duke. 'When is your next field-day?'

'Thursday,' said Sir Tichborne; 'but we shall be too early for you, I am afraid,' with a gruff smile.

'Oh, no!' said the young Duke, who saw his man; 'I assure you I have been up to-day nearly two hours. Let us get on.'

The first person that his Grace's eye met, when he entered the room in which they assembled before dinner, was Mrs. Dallington Vere.

Dinner was a favourite moment with the Duke of St. James during this visit at Castle Dacre, since it was the only time in the day that, thanks to his rank, which he now doubly valued, he could enjoy a tÃªte-Ã -tÃªte with its blooming mistress.

'I am going to hunt,' said the Duke, 'and I am to ride Hauteville. I hope you will set me an example on Thursday, and that I shall establish my character with Sir Tichborne.'

'I am to lead on that day a bold band of archers. I have already too much neglected my practising, and I fear that my chance of the silver arrow is slight.'

'I have betted upon you with everybody,' said the Duke of St. James.

'Remember Doncaster! I am afraid that May Dacre will again be the occasion of your losing your money.'

'But now I am on the right side. Together we must conquer.'

'I have a presentiment that our union will not be a fortunate one.'

'Then I am ruined,' said his Grace with rather a serious tone.

'I hope you have not really staked anything upon such nonsense?' said Miss Dacre.

'I have staked everything,' said his Grace.

'Talking of stakes,' said Lord St. Jerome, who pricked up his ears at a congenial subject, 'do you know what they are going to do about that affair of Anderson's?'

'What does he say for himself?' asked Sir Chetwode.

'He says that he had no intention of embezzling the money, but that, as he took it for granted the point could never be decided, he thought it was against the usury laws to allow money to lie idle.'

'That fellow has always got an answer,' said Sir Tichborne. 'I hate men who have always got an answer. There is no talking common sense with them.'

The Duke made his escape to-day, and, emboldened by his illustrious example, Charles Faulcon, Lord St. Jerome, and some other heroes followed, to the great disgust of Sir Chetwode and Sir Tichborne.

As the evening glided on conversation naturally fell upon the amusements of society.

'I am sure we are tired of dancing every night,' said Miss Dacre. 'I wonder if we could introduce any novelty. What think you, Bertha? You can always suggest.'

'You remember the *tableaux vivants?*' said Mrs. Dallington Vere.

'Beautiful! but too elaborate a business, I fear, for us. We want something more impromptu. The *tableaux* are nothing without brilliant and accurate costume, and to obtain that we must work at least for a week, and then, after all, in all probability, a failure. *Ils sont trop recherchÂ©s,*' she said, lowering her voice to Mrs. Dallington, '*pour nous ici.* They must spring out of a society used to such exhibitions.'

'I have a costume dress here,' said the Duke of

St. James.

'And I have a uniform,' said Lord Mildmay.

'And then,' said Mrs. Dallington, 'there are cashmeres, and scarfs, and jewels to be collected. I see, however, you think it impossible.'

'I fear so. However, we will think of it. In the meantime, what shall we do now? Suppose we act a fairy tale?'

'None of the girls can act,' said Mrs. Dallington, with a look of kind pity.

'Let us teach them. That itself will be an amusement. Suppose we act Cinderella? There is the music of Cendrillon, and you can compose, when necessary, as you go on. Clara Howard!' said May Dacre, 'come here, love! We want you to be Cinderella in a little play.'

'I act! oh! dear May! How can you laugh at me so! I cannot act.'

'You will not have to speak. Only just move about as I direct you while Bertha plays music.'

'Oh! dear May, I cannot, indeed! I never did act. Ask Eugenia!'

'Eugenia! If you are afraid, I am sure she will faint. I asked you because I thought you were just the person for it.'

'But only think,' said poor Clara, with an imploring voice, 'to act, May! Why, acting is the most difficult thing in the world. Acting is quite a dreadful thing. I know many ladies who will not act.'

'But it is not acting, Clara. Well! I will be Cinderella, and you shall be one of the sisters.'

'No, dear May!'

'Well, then, the Fairy?' 'No, dear, dear, dear May!'

'Well, Duke of St. James, what am I to do with this rebellious troop?'

'Let me be Cinderella!'

'It is astonishing,' said Miss Dacre, 'the difficulty which you encounter in England, if you try to make people the least amusing or vary the regular dull routine, which announces dancing as the beautiful of diversions and cards as the sublime.'

'We are barbarians,' said the Duke. 'We were not,' said May Dacre. 'What are *tableaux*, or acted charades, or romances, to masques, which were the splendid and various amusement of our ancestors. Last Christmas we performed "Comus" here with great effect; but then we had Arundel, and he is an admirable actor.'

'Curse Arundel!' thought the Duke. 'I had forgotten him.'

'I do not wonder,' said Mrs. Dallington Vere, 'at people objecting to act regular plays, for, independently of the objections, not that I think anything of them myself, which are urged against "private theatricals," the fact is, to get up a play is a tremendous business, and one or two is your bound. But masques, where there is so little to learn by rote, a great consideration, where music and song are so exquisitely introduced, where there is such an admirable opportunity for brilliant costume, and where the scene may be beautiful without change—such an important point—I cannot help wondering that this national diversion is not revived.'

'Suppose we were to act a romance without the costume?' said the Duke. 'Let us consider it a rehearsal. And perhaps the Misses Howard will have no objection to sing?'

'It is difficult to find a suitable romance,' said Miss Dacre. 'All our modern English ones are too full of fine poetry. We tried once an old ballad, but it was too long. Last Christmas we got up a good many, and Arundel, Isabella, and myself used to scribble some nonsense for the occasion. But I am afraid they are all either burnt or taken away. I will look in the music-case.'

She went to the music-case with the Duke and Mrs. Dallington.

'No,' she continued; 'not one, not a single one. But what are these?' She looked at some lines written in pencil in a music-book. 'Oh! here is something; too slight, but it will do. You see,' she continued, reading it to the Duke, 'by the introduction of the same line in every verse, describing the same action, a back-scene is, as it were, created, and the story, if you can call it such, proceeds in front. Really, I think, we might make something of this.'

Mr. Dacre and some others were at whist. The two Baronets were together, talking over the morning's sport. EcartÃ© covered a flirtation between Lord

- 93 -

Mildmay and Lady St. Jerome. Miss Dacre assembled her whole troop; and, like a manager with a new play, read in the midst of them the ballad, and gave them directions for their conduct. A japan screen was unfolded at the end of the room. Two couches indicated the limits of the stage. Then taking her guitar, she sang with a sweet voice and arch simplicity these simpler lines:—

I.

Childe Dacre stands in his father's hall,

While all the rest are dancing;

Childe Dacre gazes on the wall,

While brightest eyes are glancing.

Then prythee tell me, gentles gay!

What makes our Childe so dull to-day?

Each verse was repeated.

In the background they danced a cotillon.

In the front, the Duke of St. James, as Childe Dacre, leant against the wall, with arms folded and eyes fixed; in short, in an attitude which commanded great applause.

II.

I cannot tell, unless it be,

While all the rest are dancing,

The Lady Alice, on the sea,

With brightest eyes is glancing,

Or muses on the twilight hour

Will bring Childe Dacre to her bower.

Mrs. Dallington Vere advances as the Lady Alice. Her walk is abrupt, her look anxious and distracted; she seems to be listening for some signal. She falls into a musing attitude, motionless and graceful as a statue. Clara Howard alike marvels at her genius and her courage.

III.

Childe Dacre hears the curfew chime,

While all the rest are dancing;

Unless I find a fitting rhyme,

Oh! here ends my romancing!

But see! her lover's at her feet!

Oh! words of joy! oh! meeting sweet!

The Duke advances, chivalric passion in his every gesture. The Lady Alice rushes to his arms with that look of trembling transport which tells the tale of stolen love. They fall into a group which would have made the fortune of an Annual.

IV.

Then let us hope, when next I sing,

And all the rest are dancing,

Our Childe a gentle bride may bring,

All other joys enhancing.

Then we will bless the twilight hour

That call'd him to a lady's bower.

The Duke led Mrs. Dallington to the dancers with courtly grace. There was great applause, but the spirit of fun and one-and-twenty inspired him, and he led off a gallop. In fact, it was an elegant romp. The two Baronets started from their slumbers, and Lord Mildmay called for Mademoiselle Dacre. The call was echoed. Miss Dacre yielded to the public voice, and acted to the life the gratified and condescending air of a first-rate performer. Lord Mildmay called for Madame Dallington. Miss Dacre led on her companion as Sontag would Malibran. There was no wreath at hand, but the Duke of St. James robbed his coat of its rose, and offered it on his knee to Mademoiselle, who presented it with Parisian feeling to her rival. The scene was as superb as anything at the *AcadÃ©mie*.

CHAPTER XII.

An Impromptu Excursion

'WE CERTAINLY must have a masque,' said the young Duke, as he threw himself into his chair, satisfied with his performance.

'You must open Hauteville with one,' said Mrs. Dallington.

'A capital idea; but we will practise at Dacre first.'

'When is Hauteville to be finished?' asked Mrs. Dallington. 'I shall really complain if we are to be kept out of it much longer. I believe I am the only person in the Riding who has not been there.'

'I have been there,' said the Duke, 'and am afraid I must go again; for Sir Carte has just come down for a few days, and I promised to meet him. It is a sad bore. I wish it were finished.'

'Take me with you,' said Mrs. Dallington; 'take us all, and let us make a party.'

'An admirable idea,' exclaimed the young Duke, with a brightening countenance. 'What admirable ideas you have, Mrs. Dallington! This is, indeed, turning business into pleasure! What says our hostess?'

'I will join you.'

'To-morrow, then?' said the Duke.

'To-morrow! You are rapid!'

'Never postpone, never prepare: that is your own rule. To-morrow, to-morrow, all must go.'

'Papa, will you go to-morrow to Hauteville?'

'Are you serious?'

'Yes,' said Miss Dacre: 'we never postpone; we never prepare.'

'But do not you think a day, at least, had better intervene?' urged Mr. Dacre; 'we shall be unexpected.'

'I vote for to-morrow,' said the Duke.

'To-morrow!' was the universal exclamation. Tomorrow was carried.

'I will write to Blanche at once,' said the Duke.

Mrs. Dallington Vere ran for the writing materials, and his Grace indicted the following pithy note:—

'Half-past Ten, Castle Dacre.

'Dear Sir Carte,

'Our party here intend to honour Hauteville with a visit to-morrow, and anticipate the pleasure of viewing the improvements, with yourself for their cicerone. Let Rawdon know immediately of this. They tell me here that the sun rises about six. As we shall not be with you till noon, I have no doubt your united energies will be able to make all requisite preparations. We may be thirty or forty. Believe me, dear Sir Carte,

'Your faithful servant,

'St. James.

'Carlstein bears this, which you will receive in an hour. Let me have a line by return.'

CHAPTER XIII.

The Charms of Hauteville

IT WAS a morning all dew and sunshine, soft yet bright, just fit for a hawking party, for dames of high degree, feathered cavaliers, ambling palfreys, and tinkling bells. Our friends rose early, and assembled punctually. All went, and all went on horseback; but they sent before some carriages for the return, in case the ladies should be wearied with excessive pleasure. The cavalcade, for it was no less, broke into parties which were often out of sight of each other. The Duke and Lord St. Jerome, Clara Howard and Charles Faulcon, Miss Dacre and Mrs. Dallington, formed one, and, as they flattered themselves, not the least brilliant. They were all in high spirits, and his Grace lectured on riding-habits with erudite enthusiasm.

Their road lay through a country wild and woody, where crag and copse beautifully intermixed with patches of rich cultivation. Halfway, they passed Rosemount, a fanciful pavilion where the Dukes of St. James sometimes sought that elegant simplicity which was not afforded by all the various charms of their magnificent Hauteville. At length they arrived at the park-gate of the castle, which might itself have passed for a tolerable mansion. It was ancient and embattled, flanked by a couple of sturdy towers, and gave a noble promise of the baronial pile which it announced. The park was a petty principality; and its apparently illimitable extent, its rich variety of surface, its ancient woods and numerous deer, attracted the attention and the admiration even of those who had been born in such magical enclosures.

Away they cantered over the turf, each moment with their blood more sparkling. A turn in the road, and Hauteville, with its donjon keep and lordly flag, and many-windowed line of long perspective, its towers, and turrets, and terraces, bathed with the soft autumnal sun, met their glad sight.

'Your Majesty is welcome to my poor castle!' said the young Duke, bowing with head uncovered to Miss Dacre.

'Nay, we are at the best but captive princesses about to be immured in that fearful keep; and this is the way you mock us!'

'I am content that you shall be my prisoner.'

'A struggle for freedom!' said Miss Dacre, looking back to Mrs. Dallington, and she galloped towards the castle.

Lord Mildmay and Lady St. Jerome cantered up, and the rest soon assembled. Sir Carte came forward, all smiles, with a clerk of the works bearing a portfolio of plans. A crowd of servants, for the Duke maintained an establishment at Hauteville, advanced, and the fair equestrians were dismounted. They shook their habits and their curls, vowed that riding was your only exercise, and that dust in the earthly economy was a blunder. And then they entered the castle.

Room after room, gallery after gallery; you know the rest. Shall we describe the silk hangings and the reverend tapestry, the agate tables and the tall screens, the china and the armour, the state beds and the curious cabinets, and the family pictures mixed up so quaintly with Italian and Flemish art? But we pass from meek Madonnas and seraphic saints, from gleaming Claudes and Guidos soft as Eve, from Rubens's satyrs and Albano's boys, and even from those gay and natural medleys, paintings that cheer the heart, where fruit and flower, with their brilliant bloom, call to a feast the butterfly and bee; we pass from these to square-headed ancestors by Holbein, all black velvet and gold chains; cavaliers, by Vandyke, all lace and spurs, with pointed beards, that did more execution even than their pointed swords; patriots and generals, by Kneller, in Blenheim wigs and Steen-kirk cravats, all robes and armour; scarlet judges that supported ship-money, and purple bishops, who had not been sent to the Tower. Here was a wit who had sipped his coffee at Button's, and there some mad Alcibiades duke who had exhausted life ere he had finished youth, and yet might be consoled for all his flashing follies could he witness the bright eyes that lingered on his countenance, while they glanced over all the patriotism and all the piety, all the illustrious courage and all the historic craft, which, when living, it was daily told him that he had shamed. Ye dames with dewy eyes that Lely drew! have we forgotten you? No! by that sleepy loveliness that reminds us that night belongs to beauty, ye were made for memory! And oh! our grandmothers, that we now look upon as girls, breathing in Reynolds's playful canvas, let us also pay our homage to your grace!

The chapel, where you might trace art from the richly Gothic tomb, designed by some neighbouring abbot, to the last effort of Flaxman; the riding-house, where, brightly framed, looked down upon you with a courtly smile the first and gartered duke, who had been Master of the Horse, were alike visited, and alike admired. They mounted the summit of the round tower, and looked around upon the broad county, which they were proud to call their own. Amid innumerable seats, where blazed the hearths of the best blood of England, they recognised, with delight, the dome of Dacre and the woods of Dallington. They walked along a terrace not unworthy of the promenade of a court; they visited the flower gardens, where the peculiar style of every nation was in turn imitated; they loitered in the vast conservatories, which were themselves a palace; they wandered in the wilderness, where the invention of consummate art presented them with the ideal of nature. In this poetic solitude, where all was green, and still, and sweet, or where the only sound was falling water or fluttering birds, the young Duke recurred to the feelings which, during the last momentous week, had so mastered his nature, and he longed to wind his arm round the beautiful being without whom this enchanting domain was a dreary waste.

They assembled in a green retreat, where the energetic Sir Carte had erected a marquÃ©e, and where a collation greeted the eyes of those who were well prepared for it. Rawdon had also done his duty, and the guests, who were aware of the sudden manner in which the whole affair had arisen, wondered at the magic which had produced a result worthy of a week's preparation. But it is a great thing to be a young Duke. The pasties, and the venison, and the game, the pines, and the peaches, and the grapes, the cakes, and the confectionery, and the ices, which proved that the still-room at Hauteville was not an empty name, were all most popular. But the wines, they were marvellous! And as the finest cellars in the country had been ransacked for excellence and variety, it is not wonderful that their produce obtained a panegyric. There was hock of a century old, which made all stare, though we, for our part, cannot see, or rather taste, the beauty of this antiquity. Wine, like woman, in our opinion, should not be too old, so we raise our altar to the infant Bacchus; but this is not the creed of the million, nor was it the persuasion of Sir Chetwode Chetwode or of Sir Tichborne Tichborne, good judges both. The Johannisberger quite converted them. They no longer disliked the young Duke. They thought him a fool, to be sure, but at the same time a good-natured one. In the meantime, all were interested, and Carlstein with his key bugle, from out a neighbouring brake, afforded the only luxury that was wanting.

It is six o'clock, carriages are ordered, and horses are harnessed. Back, back to Dacre! But not at the lively rate at which they had left that lordly hall this morning. They are all alike inclined to move slowly; they are silent, yet serene and satisfied; they ponder upon the reminiscences of a delightful morning, and also of a delightful meal. Perhaps they are a little weary; perhaps they wish to gaze upon the sunset.

It is eight o'clock, and they enter the park gates. Dinner is universally voted a bore, even by the Baronets. Coffee covers the retreat of many a wearied bird to her evening bower. The rest lounge on a couch or sofa, or chew the cud of memory on an ottoman. It was a day of pleasure which had been pleasant. That was certain: but that was past. Who is to be Duchess of St. James? Answer this. May Dacre, or Bertha Vere, or Clara Howard? Lady St. Jerome, is it to be a daughter of thy house? Lady Faulconcourt, art thou to be hailed as the unrivalled mother?' Tis mystery all, as must always be the future of this world. We muse, we plan, we hope, but naught is certain but that which is naught; for, a question answered, a doubt satisfied, an end attained; what are they but fit companions for clothes out of fashion, cracked china, and broken fans?

Our hero was neither wearied nor sleepy, for his mind was too full of exciting fancies to think of the interests of his body. As all were withdrawing, he threw his cloak about him and walked on the terrace. It was a night soft as the rhyme that sighs from Rogers' shell, and brilliant as a phrase just turned by Moore. The thousand stars smiled from their blue pavilions, and the moon shed the mild light that makes a lover muse. Fragrance came in airy waves from trees rich with the golden orange, and from out the woods there ever and anon arose a sound, deep and yet hushed, and mystical, and soft. It could not be the wind!

His heart was full, his hopes were sweet, his fate pledged on a die. And in this shrine, where all was like his love, immaculate and beautiful, he vowed a faith which had not been returned. Such is the madness of love! Such is the magic of beauty!

Music rose upon the air. Some huntsmen were practising their horns. The triumphant strain elevated his high hopes, the tender tone accorded with his emotions. He paced up and down the terrace in excited reverie, fed by the music. In imagination she was with him: she spoke, she smiled, she loved. He gazed upon her beaming countenance: his soul thrilled with tones which, only she could utter. He pressed her to his throbbing and tumultuous breast!

The music stopped. He fell from his seventh heaven. He felt all the exhaustion of his prolonged reverie. All was flat, dull, unpromising. The moon seemed dim, the stars were surely fading, the perfume of the trees was faint, the wind of the woods was a howling demon. Exhausted, dispirited, ay! almost desperate, with a darkened soul and staggering pace, he regained his chamber.

CHAPTER XIV.

Pride Has a Fall

THERE is nothing more strange, but nothing more certain, than the different influence which the seasons of night and day exercise upon the moods of our minds. Him whom the moon sends to bed with a head full of misty meaning the sun-will summon in the morning with a brain clear and lucid as his beam. Twilight makes us pensive; Aurora is the goddess of activity. Despair curses at midnight; Hope blesses at noon.

And the bright beams of Phoebus—why should this good old name be forgotten?—called up our Duke rather later than a monk at matins, in a less sublime disposition than that in which he had paced among the orange-trees of Dacre. His passion remained, but his poetry was gone. He was all confidence, and gaiety, and love, and panted for the moment when he could place his mother's coronet on the only head that was worthy to share the proud fortunes of the house of Hauteville.

'Luigi, I will rise. What is going on to-day?' 'The gentlemen are all out, your Grace.'

'And the ladies?'

'Are going to the Archery Ground, your Grace.'

'Ah! she will be there, Luigi?'

'Yes, your Grace.'

'My robe, Luigi.'

'Yes, your Grace.'

'I forgot what I was going to say. Luigi!'

'Yes, your Grace.'

'Luigi, Luigi, Luigi,' hummed the Duke, perfectly unconscious, and beating time with his brush. His valet stared, but more when his lord, with eyes fixed on the ground, fell into a soliloquy, not a word of which, most provokingly, was audible, except to my reader.

'How beautiful she looked yesterday upon the keep when she tried to find Dacre! I never saw such eyes in my life! I must speak to Lawrence immediately. I think I must have her face painted in four positions, like that picture of Lady Alice Gordon by Sir Joshua. Her full face is sublime; and yet there is a piquancy in the profile, which I am not sure—and yet again, when her countenance is a little bent towards you, and her neck gently turned, I think that is, after all—but then when her eyes meet yours, full! oh! yes! yes!

yes! That first look at Doncaster! It is impressed upon my brain like self-consciousness. I never can forget it. But then her smile! When she sang on Tuesday night! By Heavens!' he exclaimed aloud, 'life with such a creature is immortality!'

About one o'clock the Duke descended into empty chambers. Not a soul was to be seen. The birds had flown. He determined to go to the Archery Ground. He opened the door of the music-room.

He found Miss Dacre alone at a table, writing. She looked up, and his heart yielded as her eye met his.

'You do not join the nymphs?' asked the Duke.

'I have lent my bow,' she said, 'to an able substitute.'

She resumed her task, which he perceived was copying music. He advanced, he seated himself at the table, and began playing with a pen. He gazed upon her, his soul thrilled with unwonted sensations, his frame shook with emotions which, for a moment, deprived him even of speech. At length he spoke in a low and tremulous tone:—

'I fear I am disturbing you, Miss Dacre?'

'By no means,' she said, with a courteous air; and then, remembering she was a hostess, 'Is there anything that you require?'

'Much; more than I can hope. O Miss Dacre! suffer me to tell you how much I admire, how much I love you!'

She started, she stared at him with distended eyes, and her small mouth was open like a ring.

'My Lord!'

'Yes!' he continued in a rapid and impassioned tone. 'I at length find an opportunity of giving way to feelings which it has been long difficult for me to control. O beautiful being! tell me, tell me that I am blessed!'

'My Lord! I—I am most honoured; pardon me if I say, most surprised.'

'Yes! from the first moment that your ineffable loveliness rose on my vision my mind has fed upon your image. Our acquaintance has only realised, of your character, all that my imagination had preconceived, Such unrivalled beauty, such unspeakable grace, could only have been the companions of that exquisite taste and that charming delicacy which, even to witness, has added great felicity to my existence. Oh! tell me—tell me that they shall be for me something better than a transient spectacle. Condescend to share the fortune and the fate of one who only esteems his lot in life because it enables him to offer you a station not utterly unworthy of your transcendent excellence!'

'I have permitted your Grace to proceed too far. For your—for my own sake, I should sooner have interfered, but, in truth, I was so astounded at your unexpected address that I have but just succeeded in recalling my scattered senses. Let me again express to you my acknowledgments for an honour which I feel is great; but permit me to regret that for your offer of your hand and fortune these acknowledgments are all I can return.'

'Miss Dacre! am I then to wake to the misery of being rejected?'

'A little week ago, Duke of St. James, we were strangers. It would be hard if it were in the power of either of us now to deliver the other to misery.'

'You are offended, then, at the presumption which, on so slight an acquaintance, has aspired to your hand. It is indeed a high possession. I thought only of you, not of myself. Your perfections require no time for recognition. Perhaps my imperfections require time for indulgence. Let me then hope!'

'You have misconceived my meaning, and I regret that a foolish phrase should occasion you the trouble of fresh solicitude, and me the pain of renewed refusal. In a word, it is not in my power to accept your hand.'

He rose from the table, and stifled the groan which struggled in his throat. He paced up and down the room with an agitated step and a convulsed brow, which marked the contest of his passions. But he was not desperate. His heart was full of high resolves and mighty meanings, indefinite but great, He felt like some conqueror, who, marking the battle going against him, proud in his infinite resources and invincible power, cannot credit the madness of a defeat. And the lady, she leant her head upon her delicate arm, and screened her countenance from his scrutiny.

He advanced.

'Miss Dacre! pardon this prolonged intrusion; forgive this renewed discourse. But let me only hope that a more favoured rival is the cause of my despair, and I will thank you——'

'My Lord Duke,' she said, looking up with a faint blush, but with a flashing eye, and in an audible and even energetic tone, 'the question you ask is neither fair nor manly; but, as you choose to press me, I will say that it requires no recollection of a third person to make me decline the honour which you intended me.'

'Miss Dacre! you speak in anger, almost in bitterness. Believe me,' he added, rather with an air of pique, 'had I imagined from your conduct towards me that I was an object of dislike, I would have spared you this inconvenience and myself this humiliation.'

'At Castle Dacre, my conduct to all its inmates is the same. The Duke of St. James, indeed, hath both hereditary and personal claims to be considered here as something better than a mere inmate; but your Grace has elected to dissolve all connection with our house, and I am not desirous of assisting you in again forming any.'

'Harsh words, Miss Dacre!'

'Harsher truth, my Lord Duke,' said Miss Dacre, rising from her seat, and twisting a pen with agitated energy. 'You have prolonged this interview, not I. Let it end, for I am not skilful in veiling my mind; and I should regret, here at least, to express what I have hitherto succeeded in concealing.'

'It cannot end thus,' said his Grace: 'let me, at any rate, know the worst. You have, if not too much kindness, at least too much candour, to part so!' 'I am at a loss to understand,' said Miss Dacre, 'what other object our conversation can have for your Grace than to ascertain my feelings, which I have already declared more than once, upon a point which you have already more than once urged. If I have not been sufficiently explicit or sufficiently clear, let me tell you, sir, that nothing but the request of a parent whom I adore would have induced me even to speak to the person who had dared to treat him with contempt.' 'Miss Dacre!'

'You are moved, or you affect to be moved. 'Tis well: if a word from a stranger can thus affect you, you may be better able to comprehend the feelings of that person whose affections you have so long outraged; your equal in blood, Duke of St. James, your superior in all other respects.'

'Beautiful being!' said his Grace, advancing, falling on his knee, and seizing her hand. 'Pardon, pardon, pardon! Like your admirable sire, forgive; cast into oblivion all remembrance of my fatal youth. Is not your anger, is not this moment, a bitter, an utter expiation for all my folly, all my thoughtless, all my inexperienced folly; for it was no worse? On my knees, and in the face of Heaven, let me pray you to be mine. I have staked my happiness upon this venture. In your power is my fate. On you it depends whether I shall discharge my duty to society, to the country to which I owe so much, or whether I shall move in it without an aim, an object, or a hope. Think, think only of the sympathy of our dispositions; the similarity of our tastes. Think, think only of the felicity that might be ours. Think of the universal good we might achieve! Is there anything that human reason could require that we could not command? any object which human mind could imagine that we could not obtain? And, as for myself, I swear that I will be the creature of your will. Nay, nay! oaths are mockery, vows are idle! Is it possible to share existence with you, beloved girl! without watching for your every wish, without—'

'My Lord Duke, this must end. You do not recommend yourself to me by this rhapsody. What do you know of me, that you should feel all this? I may be different from what you expected; that is all. Another week, and another woman may command a similar effusion. I do not believe you to be insincere. There would be more hope for you if you were. You act from impulse, and not from principle. This is your best excuse for your conduct to my father. It is one that I accept, but which will certainly ever prevent me from becoming your wife. Farewell!' 'Nay, nay! let us not part in enmity!' 'Enmity and friendship are strong words; words that are much abused. There is another, which must describe our feelings towards the majority of mankind, and mine towards you. Substitute for enmity indifference.'

She quitted the room: he remained there for some minutes, leaning on the mantelpiece, and then rushed into the park. He hurried for some distance with the rapid and uncertain step which betokens a tumultuous and disordered mind. At length he found himself among the ruins of Dacre Abbey. The silence and solemnity of the scene made him conscious, by the contrast, of his own agitated existence; the desolation of the beautiful ruin accorded with his own crushed and beautiful hopes. He sat himself at the feet of the clustered columns, and, covering his face with his hands, he wept.

They were the first tears that he had shed since childhood, and they were agony. Men weep but once, but then their tears are blood. We think almost their hearts must crack a little, so heartless are they ever after. Enough of this.

It is bitter to leave our fathers hearth for the first time; bitter is the eve of our return, when a thousand fears rise in our haunted souls. Bitter are hope deferred, and self-reproach, and power unrecognised. Bitter is poverty; bitterer still is debt. It is bitter to be neglected; it is more bitter to be misunderstood. It is bitter to lose an only child. It is bitter to look upon the land which once was ours. Bitter is a sister's woe, a brother's scrape; bitter a mother's tear, and bitterer still a father's curse. Bitter are a briefless bag, a curate's bread, a diploma that brings no fee. Bitter is half-pay!

It is bitter to muse on vanished youth; it is bitter to lose an election or a suit. Bitter are rage suppressed, vengeance unwreaked, and prize-money kept back. Bitter are a failing crop, a glutted market, and a shattering spec. Bitter are rents in arrear and tithes in kind. Bitter are salaries reduced and perquisites destroyed. Bitter is a tax, particularly if misapplied; a rate, particularly if embezzled. Bitter is a trade too full, and bitterer still a trade that has worn out. Bitter is a bore!

It is bitter to lose one's hair or teeth. It is bitter to find our annual charge exceed our income. It is bitter to hear of others' fame when we are boys. It is bitter to resign the seals we fain would keep. It is bitter to hear the winds blow when we have ships at sea, or friends. Bitter are a broken friendship and a dying love. Bitter a woman scorned, a man betrayed!

Bitter is the secret woe which none can share. Bitter are a brutal husband and a faithless wife, a silly daughter and a sulky son. Bitter are a losing card, a losing horse. Bitter the public hiss, the private sneer. Bitter are old age without respect, manhood without wealth, youth without fame. Bitter is the east wind's blast; bitter a stepdame's kiss. It is bitter to mark the woe which we cannot relieve. It is bitter to die in a foreign land.

But bitterer far than this, than these, than all, is waking from our first delusion! For then we first feel the nothingness of self; that hell of sanguine spirits. All is dreary, blank, and cold. The sun of hope sets without a ray, and the dim night of dark despair shadows only phantoms. The spirits that guard round us in our pride have gone. Fancy, weeping, flies. Imagination droops her glittering pinions and sinks into the earth. Courage has no heart, and love seems a traitor. A busy demon whispers in our ear that all is vain and worthless, and we among the vainest of a worthless crew!

And so our young friend here now depreciated as much as he had before exaggerated his powers. There seemed not on the earth's face a more forlorn, a more feeble, a less estimable wretch than himself, but just now a hero. O! what a fool, what a miserable, contemptible fool was he! With what a light tongue and lighter heart had he spoken of this woman who despised, who spurned him! His face blushed, ay! burnt, at the remembrance of his reveries and his fond monologues! the very recollection made him shudder with disgust. He looked up to see if any demon were jeering him among the ruins.

His heart was so crushed that hope could not find even one desolate chamber to smile in. His courage was so cowed that, far from indulging in the distant romance to which, under these circumstances, we sometimes fly, he only wondered at the absolute insanity which, for a moment, had permitted him to aspire to her possession. 'Sympathy of dispositions! Similarity of tastes, forsooth! Why, we are different existences! Nature could never have made us for the same world or with the same clay! O consummate being! why, why did we meet? Why, why are my eyes at length unsealed? Why, why do I at length feel conscious of my utter worthlessness? O God! I am miserable!' He arose and hastened to the house. He gave orders to Luigi and his people to follow him to Rosemount with all practicable speed, and having left a note for his host with the usual excuse, he mounted his horse, and in half an hour's time, with a countenance like a stormy sea, was galloping through the park gates of Dacre.

BOOK III.

CHAPTER I.

'If She Be Not Fair For Me.'

THE day after the arrival of the Duke of St. James at Cleve Park, his host, Sir Lucius Grafton, received the following note from Mrs. Dallington Vere:

'Castle Dacre,————, 182—.

'My dear Baronet,

'Your pigeon has flown, otherwise I should have tied this under his wing, for I take it for granted he is trained too dexterously to alight anywhere but at Cleve.

'I confess that in this affair your penetration has exceeded mine. I hope throughout it will serve you as well. I kept my promise, and arrived here only a few hours after him. The prejudice which I had long observed in the little Dacre against your protÃ©gÃ© was too marked to render any interference on my part at once necessary, nor did I anticipate even beginning to give her good advice for a month to come. Heaven knows what a month of his conduct might have done! A month achieves such wonders! And, to do him justice, he was most agreeable; but our young gentleman grew impetuous, and so the day before yesterday he vanished, and in the most extraordinary manner! Sudden departure, unexpected business, letter and servants both left behind; Monsieur grave, and a little astonished; and the demoiselle thoughtful at the least, but not curious. Very suspicious this last circumstance! A flash crossed my mind, but I could gain nothing, even with my most dexterous wiles, from the little Dacre, who is a most unmanageable heroine. However, with the good assistance of a person who in a French tragedy would figure as my confidante, and who is the sister of your Lachen, something was learnt from Monsieur le valet, to say nothing of the page. All agree; a countenance pale as death, orders given in a low voice of suppressed passion and sundry oaths. I hear he sulked the night at Rosemount.

'Now, my good Lucy, listen to me. Lose no time about the great object. If possible, let this autumn be distinguished. You have an idea that our friend is a very manageable sort of personage; in phrase less courteous, is sufficiently weak for all reasonable purposes. I am not quite so clear about this. He is at present very young, and his character is not formed; but there is a something about him which makes me half fear that, if you permit his knowledge of life to increase too much, you may quite fear having neglected my admonitions. At present his passions are high. Use his blood while it is hot, and remember that if you count on his rashness you may, as nearly in the present instance, yourself rue it. In a word, despatch. The deed that is done, you know—

'My kindest remembrances to dear Lady Afy, and tell her how much I regret I cannot avail myself of her most friendly invitation. Considering, as I know, she hates me, I really do feel flattered.

'You cannot conceive what Vandals I am at present among! Nothing but my sincere regard for you, my much-valued friend, would induce me to stay here a moment. I have received from the countenance of the Dacres all the benefit which a marked connection with so respectable and so moral a family confers, and I am tired to death. But it is a well-devised plan to have a reserve in the battles of society. You understand me; and I am led to believe that it has had the best effect, and silenced even the loudest. "Confound their politics!" as dear little Squib says, from whom I had the other day the funniest letter, which I have half a mind to send you, only you figure in it so much!

'Burlington is at Brighton, and all my friends, except yourself. I have a few barbarians to receive at Dallington, and then I shall be off there. Join us as quickly as you can. Do you know, I think that it would be an excellent *locale* for the *scena*. We might drive them over to Dieppe: only do not put off your visit too long, or else there will be no steamers.

'The Duke of Shropshire has had a fit, but rallied. He vows he was only picking up a letter, or tying his shoestring, or something of that kind; but Ruthven says he dined off *boudins Ã la Sefton*, and that, after a certain age, you know—

'Lord Darrell is with Annesley and Co. I understand, most friendly towards me, which is pleasant; and Charles, who is my firm ally, takes care to confirm the kind feeling. I am glad about this.

'Felix Crawlegh, or Crawl*ey*, as some say, has had an affair with Tommy Seymour, at Grant's. Felix was grand about porter, or something, which he never drank, and all that. Tommy, Who knew nothing about the brewing father, asked him, very innocently, why malt liquors had so degenerated. Conceive the agony, particularly as Lady Selina is said to have no violent aversion to quartering her arms with a mash-tub, argent.

'The Macaronis are most hospitable this year; and the Marquess says that the only reason that they kept in before was because he was determined to see whether economy was practicable. He finds it is not; so now expense is no object.

'Augustus Henley is about to become a senator! What do you think of this? He says he has tried everything for an honest livelihood, and even once began a novel, but could not get on; which, Squib says, is odd, because there is a receipt going about for that operation which saves all trouble:

- 112 -

'"Take a pair of pistols and a pack of cards, a cookery-book and a set of new quadrilles; mix them up with half an intrigue and a whole marriage, and divide them into three equal portions." Now, as Augustus has both fought and gamed, dined and danced, I suppose it was the morality which posed him, or perhaps the marriage.

'They say there is something about Lady Flutter, but, I should think, all talk. Most probably a report set about by her Ladyship. Lord Flame has been blackballed, that is certain. But there is no more news, except that the Wiltshires are going to the Continent: we know why; and that the Spankers are making more dash than ever: God knows how! Adieu!

'B. D. V.'

The letter ended; all things end at last. A she-correspondent for our money; provided always that she does not *cross*.

Our Duke—in spite of his disgrace, he still is ours, and yours too, I hope, gentlest reader—our Duke found himself at Cleve Park again, in a different circle from the one to which he had been chiefly accustomed. The sporting world received him with open arms. With some of these worthies, as owner of Sanspareil, he had become slightly acquainted. But what is half a morning at Tattersall's, or half a week at Doncaster, compared with a meeting at Newmarket? There your congenial spirits congregate. Freemasons every man of them! No uninitiated wretch there dares to disturb, with his profane presence, the hallowed mysteries. There the race is not a peg to hang a few days of dissipation on, but a sacred ceremony, to the celebration of which all men and all circumstances tend and bend. No balls, no concerts, no public breakfasts, no bands from Litolf, no singers from Welsh, no pineapples from Gunter, are there called for by thoughtless thousands, who have met, not from any affection for the turfs delights or their neighbour's cash, but to sport their splendid liveries and to disport their showy selves.

The house was full of men, whose talk was full of bets. The women were not as bad, but they were not plentiful. Some lords and signors were there without their dames. Lord Bloomerly, for instance, alone, or rather with his eldest son, Lord Bloom, just of age, and already a knowing hand. His father introduced him to all his friends with that smiling air of self-content which men assume when they introduce a youth who may show the world what they were at his years; so the Earl presented the young Viscount as a lover presents his miniature to his mistress. Lady Afy shone in unapproached perfection. A dull Marchioness, a *gauche* Viscountess, and some other dames, who did not look like the chorus of this Diana, acted as capital foils, and permitted her to meet her cavalier under what are called the most favourable auspices.

They dined, and discussed the agricultural interest in all its exhausted ramifications. Wheat was sold over again, even at a higher price; poachers were recalled to life, or from beyond seas, to be re-killed or re-transported. The poor-laws were a very rich topic, and the poor lands a very ruinous one. But all this was merely the light conversation, just to vary, in an agreeable mode, which all could understand, the regular material of discourse, and that was of stakes and stallions, pedigrees and plates.

Our party rose early, for their pleasure was their business. Here were no lounging dandies and no exclusive belles, who kept their bowers until hunger, which also drives down wolves from the Pyrenees, brought them from their mystical chambers to luncheon and to life. In short, an air of interest, a serious and a thoughtful look, pervaded every countenance. Fashion was kicked to the devil, and they were all too much in earnest to have any time for affectation. Breakfast was over, and it was a regular meal at which all attended, and they hurried to the course. It seems, when the party arrive, that they are the only spectators. A party or two come on to keep them company. A club discharges a crowd of gentlemen, a stable a crowd of grooms. At length a sprinkling of human beings is collected, but all is wondrous still and wondrous cold. The only thing that gives sign of life is Lord Breedall's movable stand; and the only intimation that fire is still an element is the sailing breath of a stray cigar.

'This, then, is Newmarket!' exclaimed the young Duke. 'If it required five-and-twenty thousand pounds to make Doncaster amusing, a plum, at least, will go in rendering Newmarket endurable.'

But the young Duke was wrong. There was a fine race, and the connoisseurs got enthusiastic. Sir Lucius Grafton was the winner. The Duke sympathised with his friend's success.

He began galloping about the course, and his blood warmed. He paid a visit to Sanspareil. He heard his steed was still a favourite for a coming race. He backed his steed, and Sanspareil won. He began to find Newmarket not so disagreeable. In a word, our friend was in an entirely new scene, which was exactly the thing he required. He was interested, and forgot, or rather forcibly expelled from his mind, his late overwhelming adventure. He grew popular with the set. His courteous manners, his affable address, his gay humour, and the facility with which he adopted their tone and temper, joined with his rank and wealth, subdued the most rugged and the coldest hearts. Even the jockeys were civil to him, and welcomed him with a sweet smile and gracious nod, instead of the sour grin and malicious wink with which those characters generally greet a stranger; those mysterious characters who, in their influence over their superiors, and their total want of sympathy with their species, are our only match for the oriental eunuch.

- 114 -

He grew, we say, popular with the set. They were glad to see among them a young nobleman of spirit. He became a member of the Jockey Club, and talked of taking a place in the neighbourhood. All recommended the step, and assured him of their readiness to dine with him as often as he pleased. He was a universal favourite; and even Chuck Farthing, the gentleman jockey, with a cock-eye and a knowing shake of his head, squeaked out, in a sporting treble, one of his monstrous fudges about the Prince in days of yore, and swore that, like his Royal Highness, the young Duke made the Market all alive.

The heart of our hero was never insensible to flattery. He could not refrain from comparing his present with his recent situation. The constant consideration of all around him, the affectionate cordiality of Sir Lucius, and the unobtrusive devotion of Lady Afy, melted his soul. These agreeable circumstances graciously whispered to him each hour that he could scarcely be the desolate and despicable personage which lately, in a moment of madness, he had fancied himself. He began to indulge the satisfactory idea, that a certain person, however unparalleled in form and mind, had perhaps acted with a little precipitation. Then his eyes met those of Lady Aphrodite; and, full of these feelings, he exchanged a look which reminded him of their first meeting; though now, mellowed by gratitude, and regard, and esteem, it was perhaps even more delightful. He was loved, and he was loved by an exquisite being, who was the object of universal admiration. What could he desire more? Nothing but the wilfulness of youth could have induced him for a moment to contemplate breaking chains which had only been formed to secure his felicity. He determined to bid farewell for ever to the impetuosity of youth. He had not been three days under the roof of Cleve before he felt that his happiness depended upon its fairest inmate. You see, then, that absence is not always fatal to love!

CHAPTER II.

Fresh Entanglements

HIS Grace completed his stud, and became one of the most distinguished votaries of the turf. Sir Lucius was the inspiring divinity upon this occasion. Our hero, like all young men, and particularly young nobles, did everything in extremes; and extensive arrangements were made by himself and his friend for the ensuing campaign. Sir Lucius was to reap half the profit, and to undertake the whole management. The Duke was to produce the capital and to pocket the whole glory. Thus rolled on some weeks, at the end of which our hero began to get a little tired. He had long ago recovered all his self-complacency, and if the form of May Dacre ever flitted before his vision for an instant, he clouded it over directly by the apparition of a bet, or thrust it away with that desperate recklessness with which we expel an ungracious thought. The Duke sighed for a little novelty. Christmas was at hand. He began to think that a regular country Christmas must be a sad bore. Lady Afy, too, was rather *exigeante*. It destroys one's nerves to be amiable every day to the same human being. She was the best creature in the world; but Cambridgeshire was not a pleasant county. He was most attached; but there was not another agreeable woman in the house. He would not hurt her feelings for the world; but his own were suffering desperately. He had no idea that he ever should get so entangled. Brighton, they say, is a pleasant place.

To Brighton he went; and although the Graftons were to follow him in a fortnight, still even these fourteen days were a holiday. It is extraordinary how hourly, and how violently, change the feelings of an inexperienced young man.

Sir Lucius, however, was disappointed in his Brighton trip. Ten days after the departure of the young Duke the county member died. Sir Lucius had been long maturing his pretensions to the vacant representation. He was strongly supported; for he was a personal favourite, and his family had claims; but he was violently opposed; for a *novus homo* was ambitious, and the Baronet was poor. Sir Lucius was a man of violent passions, and all feelings and considerations immediately merged in his paramount ambition. His wife, too, at this moment, was an important personage. She was generally popular; she was beautiful, highly connected, and highly considered. Her canvassing was a great object. She canvassed with earnestness and with success; for since her consolatory friendship with the Duke of St. James her character had greatly changed, and she was now as desirous of conciliating her husband and the opinion of society as she was before disdainful of the one and fearless of the other. Sir Lucius and Lady Aphrodite Grafton were indeed on the best possible terms, and the whole county admired his conjugal attentions and her wifelike affections.

The Duke, who had no influence in this part of the world, and who was not at all desirous of quitting Brighton, compensated for his absence at this critical moment by a friendly letter and the offer of his purse. By this good aid, his wife's attractions, and his own talents, Sir Lucy succeeded, and by the time Parliament had assembled he was returned member for his native county.

In the meantime, his friend had been spending his time at Brighton in a far less agitated manner, but, in its way, not less successful; for he was amused, and therefore gained his object as much as the Baronet. The Duke liked Brighton much. Without the bore of an establishment, he found himself among many agreeable friends, living in an unostentatious and impromptu, though refined and luxurious, style. One day a new face, another day a new dish, another day a new dance, successively interested his feelings, particularly if the face rode, which they all do; the dish was at Sir George Sauceville's, and the dance at the Duke of Burlington's. So time flew on, between a canter to Rottindean, the flavours of a Perigord, and the blunders of the mazurka.

But February arrived, and this agreeable life must end. The philosophy of society is so practical that it is not allowed, even to a young Duke, absolutely to trifle away existence. Duties will arise, in spite of our best endeavours; and his Grace had to roll up to town, to dine with the Premier, and to move the Address.

CHAPTER III.

A New Star Rises

ANOTHER season had arrived, another of those magical periods of which one had already witnessed his unparalleled triumphs, and from which he had derived such exquisite delight. To his surprise, he viewed its arrival without emotion; if with any feeling, with disgust.

He had quaffed the cup too eagerly. The draught had been delicious; but time also proved that it had been satiating. Was it possible for his vanity to be more completely gratified than it had been? Was it possible for victories to be more numerous and more unquestioned during the coming campaign than during the last? Had not his life, then, been one long triumph? Who had not offered their admiration? Who had not paid homage to his all-acknowledged empire? Yet, even this career, however dazzling, had not been pursued, even this success, however brilliant, had not been attained, without some effort and some weariness, also some exhaustion. Often, as he now remembered, had his head ached; more than once, as now occurred to him, had his heart faltered. Even his first season had not passed over without his feeling lone in the crowded saloon, or starting at the supernatural finger in the banqueting-hall. Yet then he was the creature of excitement, who pursued an end which was as indefinite as it seemed to be splendid. All had now happened that could happen. He drooped. He required the impulse which we derive from an object unattained.

Yet, had he exhausted life at two-and-twenty? This must not be. His feelings must be more philosophically accounted for. He began to suspect that he had lived too much for the world and too little for himself; that he had sacrificed his ease to the applause of thousands, and mistaken excitement for enjoyment. His memory dwelt with satisfaction on the hours which had so agreeably glided away at Brighton, in the choice society of a few intimates. He determined entirely to remodel the system of his life; and with the sanguine impetuosity which characterised him, he, at the same moment, felt that he had at length discovered the road to happiness, and determined to pursue it without the loss of a precious moment.

The Duke of St. James was seen less in the world, and he appeared but seldom at the various entertainments which he had once so adorned. Yet he did not resign his exalted position in the world of fashion; but, on the contrary, adopted a course of conduct which even increased his consideration. He received the world not less frequently or less splendidly than heretofore; and his magnificent mansion, early in the season, was opened to the favoured crowd. Yet in that mansion, which had been acquired with such energy and at such cost, its lord was almost as strange, and certainly

- 118 -

not as pleased, an inmate as the guests, who felt their presence in his chambers a confirmation, or a creation, of their claims to the world's homage. The Alhambra was finished, and there the Duke of St. James entirely resided; but its regal splendour was concealed from the prying eye of public curiosity with a proud reserve, a studied secrecy, and stately haughtiness becoming a caliph. A small band of initiated friends alone had the occasional entrÃ©e, and the mysterious air which they provokingly assumed whenever they were cross-examined on the internal arrangements of this mystical structure, only increased the number and the wildness of the incidents which daily were afloat respecting the fantastic profusion and scientific dissipation of the youthful sultan and his envied viziers.

The town, ever since the season commenced, had been in feverish expectation of the arrival of a new singer, whose fame had heralded her presence in all the courts of Christendom. Whether she were an Italian or a German, a Gaul or a Greek, was equally unknown. An air of mystery environed the most celebrated creature in Europe. There were odd whispers of her parentage. Every potentate was in turn entitled to the gratitude of mankind for the creation of this marvel. Now it was an emperor, now a king. A grand duke then put in his claim, and then an archduke. To-day she was married, tomorrow she was single. To-day her husband was a prince incog., to-morrow a drum-major well known. Even her name was a mystery; and she was known and worshipped throughout the whole civilised world by the mere title of '*The Bird of Paradise!*'

About a month before Easter telegraphs announced her arrival. The Admiralty yacht was too late. She determined to make her first appearance at the opera: and not only the young Duke, but even a far more exalted personage, was disappointed in the sublime idea of anticipating the public opinion by a private concert. She was to appear for the first time on Tuesday; the House of Commons adjourned.

The curtain is drawn up, and the house is crowded. Everybody is there who is anybody. Protocoli, looking as full of fate as if the French were again on the Danube; Macaroni, as full of himself as if no other being were engrossing universal attention. The Premier appears far more anxious than he does at Council, and the Duke of Burlington arranges his fanlike screen with an agitation which, for a moment, makes him forget his unrivalled nonchalance. Even Lady Bloomerly is in suspense, and even Charles Annesley's heart beats. But ah! (or rather, bah!) the enthusiasm of Lady de Courcy! Even the young Guardsman, who paid her Ladyship for her ivory franks by his idle presence, even he must have felt, callous as those young Guardsmen are.

Will that bore of a tenor ever finish that provoking aria, that we have heard so often? How drawlingly he drags on his dull, deafening—

- 119 -

Àŝccola!

Have you seen the primal dew ere the sun has lipped the pearl? Have you seen a summer fly, with tinted wings of shifting light, glance in the liquid noontide air? Have you marked a shooting star, or watched a young gazelle at play? Then you have seen nothing fresher, nothing brighter, nothing wilder, nothing lighter, than the girl who stands before you! She was infinitely small, fair, and bright. Her black hair was braided in Madonnas over a brow like ivory; a deep pure pink spot gave lustre to each cheek. Her features were delicate beyond a dream! her nose quite straight, with a nostril which would have made you crazy, if you had not already been struck with idiocy by gazing on her mouth. She a singer! Impossible! She cannot speak. And, now we look again, she must sing with her eyes, they are so large and lustrous!

The Bird of Paradise curtsied as if she shrunk under the overwhelming greeting, and crossed her breast with arms that gleamed like moonbeams and hands that glittered like stars. This gave time to the *cognoscenti* to remark her costume, which was ravishing, and to try to see her feet; but they were too small. At last Lord Squib announced that he had discovered them by a new glass, and described them as a couple of diamond-claws most exquisitely finished.

She moved her head with a faint smile, as if she distrusted her powers and feared the assembly would be disappointed, and then she shot forth a note which thrilled through every heart and nearly cracked the chandelier. Even Lady Fitz-pompey said 'Brava!' As she proceeded the audience grew quite frantic. It was agreed on all hands that miracles had recommenced. Each air was sung only to call forth fresh exclamations of 'Miracolo!' and encores were as unmerciful as an usurper.

Amid all this rapture the young Duke was not silent. His box was on the stage; and ever and anon the syren shot a glance which seemed to tell him that he was marked out amid this brilliant multitude. Each round of applause, each roar of ravished senses, only added a more fearful action to the wild purposes which began to flit about his Grace's mind. His imagination was touched. His old passion to be distinguished returned in full force. This creature was strange, mysterious, celebrated. Her beauty, her accomplishments, were as singular and as rare as her destiny and her fame. His reverie absolutely raged; it was only disturbed by her repeated notice and his returned acknowledgments. He arose in a state of mad excitation, once more the slave or the victim of his intoxicated vanity. He hurried behind the scenes. He congratulated her on her success, her genius, and her beauty; and, to be brief, within a week of her arrival in our metropolis, the Bird of Paradise was fairly caged in the Alhambra.

CHAPTER IV.

The Bird is Caged

HITHERTO the Duke of St. James had been a celebrated personage, but his fame had been confined to the two thousand Brahmins who constitute the world. His patronage of the Signora extended his celebrity in a manner which he had not anticipated; and he became also the hero of the ten, or twelve, or fifteen millions of pariahs for whose existence philosophers have hitherto failed to adduce a satisfactory cause.

The Duke of St. James was now, in the comprehensive sense of the phrase, a public character. Some choice spirits took the hint from the public feeling, and determined to dine on the public curiosity. A Sunday journal was immediately established. Of this epic our Duke was the hero. His manners, his sayings, his adventures, regularly regaled, on each holy day, the Protestant population of this Protestant empire, who in France or Italy, or even Germany, faint at the sight of a peasantry testifying their gratitude for a day of rest by a dance or a tune. 'Sketches of the Alhambra,' '*Soupers* in the Regent's Park,' 'The Court of the Caliph,' 'The Bird Cage,' &c, &c, &c, were duly announced and duly devoured. This journal, being solely devoted to the illustration of the life of a single and a private individual, was appropriately entitled 'The Universe.' Its contributors were eminently successful. Their pure inventions and impure details were accepted as delicate truth; and their ferocious familiarity with persons with whom they were totally unacquainted demonstrated at the same time their knowledge both of the forms and the personages of polite society.

At the first announcement of this hebdomadal his Grace was a little annoyed, and 'Noctes Hautevillienses' made him fear treason; but when he had read a number, he entirely acquitted any person of a breach of confidence. On the whole he was amused. A variety of ladies in time were introduced, with many of whom the Duke had scarcely interchanged a bow; but the respectable editor was not up to Lady Afy.

If his Grace, however, were soon reconciled to this not very agreeable notoriety, and consoled himself under the activity of his libellers by the conviction that their prolusions did not even amount to a caricature, he was less easily satisfied with another performance which speedily advanced its claims to public notice.

There is an unavoidable reaction in all human affairs. The Duke of St. James had been so successfully attacked that it became worth while successfully to defend him, and another Sunday paper appeared, the object of which was to maintain the silver side of the shield. Here everything was *couleur de rose*. One

- 121 -

week the Duke saved a poor man from the Serpentine; another a poor woman from starvation; now an orphan was grateful; and now Miss Zouch, impelled by her necessity and his reputation, addressed him a column and a half, quite heart-rending. Parents with nine children; nine children without parents; clergymen most improperly unbeneficed; officers most wickedly reduced; widows of younger sons of quality sacrificed to the Colonies; sisters of literary men sacrificed to national works, which required his patronage to appear; daughters who had known better days, but somehow or other had not been so well acquainted with their parents; all advanced with multiplied petitions, and that hackneyed, heartless air of misery which denotes the mumper. His Grace was infinitely annoyed, and scarcely compensated for the inconvenience by the prettiest little creature in the world, who one day forced herself into his presence to solicit the honour of dedicating to him her poems.

He had enough on his hands, so he wrote her a cheque and, with a courtesy which must have made Sappho quite desperate, put her out of the room.

We forgot to say that the name of the new journal was 'The New World.' The new world is not quite so big as the universe, but then it is as large as all the other quarters of the globe together. The worst of this business was, 'The Universe' protested that the Duke of St. James, like a second Canning, had called this 'New World' into existence, which was too bad, because, in truth, he deprecated its discovery scarcely less than the Venetians.

Having thus managed, in the course of a few weeks, to achieve the reputation of an unrivalled rouÃ©, our hero one night betook himself to Almack's, a place where his visits, this season, were both shorter and less frequent.

Many an anxious mother gazed upon him, as he passed, with an eye which longed to pierce futurity; many an agitated maiden looked exquisitely unembarrassed, while her fluttering memory feasted on the sweet thought that, at any rate, another had not captured this unrivalled prize. Perhaps she might be the Anson to fall upon this galleon. It was worth a long cruise, and even a chance of shipwreck.

He danced with Lady Aphrodite, because, since the affair of the Signora, he was most punctilious in his attentions to her, particularly in public. That affair, of course, she passed over in silence, though it was bitter. She, however, had had sufficient experience of man to feel that remonstrance is a last resource, and usually an ineffectual one. It was something that her rival— not that her ladyship dignified the Bird by that title—it was something that she was not her equal, that she was not one with whom she could be put in painful and constant collision. She tried to consider it a freak, to believe only half she heard, and to indulge the fancy that it was a toy which would soon tire. As for Sir Lucius, he saw nothing in this adventure, or indeed in the Alhambra system at all, which militated against his ulterior views. No one more constantly officiated at the ducal orgies than himself, both because he was devoted to self-gratification, and because he liked ever to have his protégé in sight. He studiously prevented any other individual from becoming the Petronius of the circle. His deep experience also taught him that, with a person of the young Duke's temper, the mode of life which he was now leading was exactly the one which not only would insure, but even hurry, the catastrophe his faithful friend so eagerly desired. His pleasures, as Sir Lucius knew, would soon pall; for he easily perceived that the Duke was not heartless enough for a roué. When thorough satiety is felt, young men are in the cue for desperate deeds. Looking upon happiness as a dream, or a prize which, in life's lottery, they have missed; worn, hipped, dissatisfied, and desperate, they often hurry on a result which they disapprove, merely to close a miserable career, or to brave the society with which they cannot sympathise.

The Duke, however, was not yet sated. As after a feast, when we have despatched a quantity of wine, there sometimes, as it were, arises a second appetite, unnatural to be sure, but very keen; so, in a career of dissipation, when our passion for pleasure appears to be exhausted, the fatal fancy of man, like a wearied hare, will take a new turn, throw off the hell-hounds of ennui, and course again with renewed vigour.

And to-night the Duke of St. James was, as he had been for some weeks, all life, and fire, and excitement; and his eye was even now wandering round the room in quest of some consummate spirit whom he might summon to his Saracenic Paradise.

A consummate spirit his eye lighted on. There stood May Dacre. He gasped for breath. He turned pale. It was only for a moment, and his emotion was unperceived. There she stood, beautiful as when she first glanced before him; there she stood, with all her imperial graces; and all surrounding splendour seemed to fade away before her dazzling presence, like mournful spirits of a lower world before a radiant creature of the sky.

She was speaking with her sunlight smile to a young man whose appearance attracted his notice. He was dressed entirely in black, rather short, but slenderly made; sallow, but clear, with long black curls and a Murillo face, and looked altogether like a young Jesuit or a Venetian official by Giorgone or Titian. His countenance was reserved and his manner not easy: yet, on the whole, his face indicated intellect and his figure blood. The features haunted the Duke's memory. He had met this person before. There are some countenances which when once seen can never be forgotten, and the young man owned one of these. The Duke recalled him to his memory with a pang.

Our hero—let him still be ours, for he is rather desolate, and he requires the backing of his friends—our hero behaved pretty well. He seized the first favourable opportunity to catch Miss Dacre's eye, and was grateful for her bow. Emboldened, he accosted her, and asked after Mr. Dacre. She was courteous, but unembarrassed. Her calmness, however, piqued him sufficiently to allow him to rally. He was tolerably easy, and talked of calling. Their conversation lasted only for a few minutes, and was fortunately terminated without his withdrawal, which would have been awkward. The young man whom we have noticed came up to claim her hand.

'Arundel Dacre, or my eyes deceive me?' said the young Duke. 'I always consider an old Etonian a friend, and therefore I address you without ceremony.'

The young man accepted, but not with readiness, the offered hand. He blushed and spoke, but in a hesitating and husky voice. Then he cleared his throat, and spoke again, but not much more to the purpose. Then he looked to his partner, whose eyes were on the ground, and rose as he endeavoured to catch them. For a moment he was silent again; then he bowed slightly to Miss Dacre and solemnly to the Duke, and then he carried off his cousin.

'Poor Dacre!' said the Duke; 'he always had the worst manner in the world. Not in the least changed.'

His Grace wandered into the tea-room. A knot of dandies were in deep converse. He heard his own name and that of the Duke of Burlington; then came 'Doncaster beauty.' 'Don't you know?' 'Oh! yes.' 'All quite mad,' &c, &c, &c. As he passed he was invited in different ways to join the coterie of his admirers, but he declined the honour, and passed them with that icy hauteur which he could assume, and which, judiciously used, contributed not a little to his popularity.

He could not conquer his depression; and, although it was scarcely past midnight, he determined to disappear. Fortunately his carriage was waiting. He was at a loss what to do with himself. He dreaded even to be alone. The Signora was at a private concert, and she was the last person whom, at this moment, he cared to see. His low spirits rapidly increased. He got terribly nervous, and felt miserable. At last he drove to White's.

The House had just broken up, and the political members had just entered, and in clusters, some standing and some yawning, some stretching their arms and some stretching their legs, presented symptoms of an escape from boredom. Among others, round the fire, was a young man dressed in a rough great coat all cords and sables, with his hat bent aside, a shawl tied round his neck with boldness, and a huge oaken staff clenched in his left hand. With the other he held the 'Courier,' and reviewed with a critical eye the report of the speech which he had made that afternoon. This was Lord Darrell.

We have always considered the talents of younger brothers as an unanswerable argument in favour of a Providence. Lord Darrell was the younger son of the Earl of Darleyford, and had been educated for a diplomatist. A report some two years ago had been very current that his elder brother, then Lord Darrell, was, against the consent of his family, about to be favoured with the hand of Mrs. Dallington Vere. Certain it is he was a devoted admirer of that lady. Of that lady, however, a less favoured rival chose one day to say that which staggered the romance of the impassioned youth. In a moment of rashness, impelled by sacred feelings, it is reported, at least, for the whole is a mystery, he communicated what he had heard with horror to the mistress of his destinies. Whatever took place, certain it is Lord Darrell challenged the indecorous speaker, and was shot through the heart. The affair made a great sensation, and the Darleyfords and their connections said bitter things of Mrs. Dallington, and talked much of rash youth and subtle women of discreeter years, and passions shamefully inflamed and purposes wickedly egged on. We say nothing of all this; nor will we dwell upon it. Mrs. Dallington Vere assuredly was no slight sufferer. But she conquered the cabal that was formed against her, for the dandies were her friends, and gallantly supported her through a trial under which some women would have sunk. As it was, at the end of the season she did travel, but all is now forgotten; and Hill Street, Berkeley Square, again contains, at the moment of our story, its brightest ornament.

The present Lord Darrell gave up all idea of being an ambassador, but he was clever; and though he hurried to gratify a taste for pleasure which before had been too much mortified, he could not relinquish the ambitious prospects with which he had, during the greater part of his life, consoled himself for his cadetship. He piqued himself upon being at the same time a dandy and a statesman. He spoke in the House, and not without effect. He was one of those who make themselves masters of great questions; that is to say, who read a great many reviews and newspapers, and are full of others' thoughts without ever having thought themselves. He particularly prided himself upon having made his way into the Alhambra set. He was the only man of business among them. The Duke liked him, for it is agreeable to be courted by those who are themselves considered.

Lord Darrell was a favourite with women. They like a little intellect. He talked fluently on all subjects. He was what is called 'a talented young man.' Then he had mind, and soul, and all that. The miracles of creation have long agreed that body without soul will not do; and even a coxcomb in these days must be original, or he is a bore. No longer is such a character the mere creation of his tailor and his perfumer. Lord Darrell was an avowed admirer of Lady Caroline St. Maurice, and a great favourite with her parents, who both considered him an oracle on the subjects which respectively interested them. You might dine at Fitz-pompey House and hear his name quoted at both ends of the table; by the host upon the state of Europe, and by the hostess upon the state of the season. Had it not been for the young Duke, nothing would have given Lady Fitz-pompey greater pleasure than to have received him as a son-in-law; but, as it was, he was only kept in store for the second string to Cupid's bow.

Lord Darrell had just quitted the House in a costume which, though rough, was not less studied than the finished and elaborate toilet which, in the course of an hour, he will exhibit in the enchanted halls of Almack's. There he will figure to the last, the most active and the most remarked; and though after these continued exertions he will not gain his couch perhaps till seven, our Lord of the Treasury, for he is one, will resume his official duties at an earlier hour than any functionary in the kingdom.

Yet our friend is a little annoyed now. What is the matter? He dilates to his uncle, Lord Seymour Temple, a greyheaded placeman, on the profligacy of the press. What is this? The Virgilian line our orator introduced so felicitously is omitted. He panegyrizes the 'Mirror of Parliament,' where, he has no doubt, the missing verse will appear. The quotation was new, 'Timeo Danaos.'

Lord Seymour Temple begins a long story about Fox and General Fitzpatrick. This is a signal for a general retreat; and the bore, as Sir Boyle Roche would say, like the last rose of summer, remains talking to himself.

CHAPTER V.

His Grace's Rival

ARUNDEL DACRE was the only child of Mr. Dacre's only and deceased brother, and the heir to the whole of the Dacre property. His father, a man of violent passions, had married early in life, against the approbation of his family, and had revolted from the Catholic communion. The elder brother, however mortified by this great deed, which passion had prompted, and not conscience, had exerted his best offices to mollify their exasperated father, and to reconcile the sire to the son. But he had exerted them ineffectually; and, as is not unusual, found, after much harrowing anxiety and deep suffering, that he was not even recompensed for his exertions and his sympathy by the gratitude of his brother. The younger Dacre was not one of those minds whose rashness and impetuosity are counterbalanced, or rather compensated, by a generous candour and an amiable remorse. He was headstrong, but he was obstinate: he was ardent, but he was sullen: he was unwary, but he was suspicious. Everyone who opposed him was his enemy: all who combined for his preservation were conspirators. His father, whose feelings he had outraged and never attempted to soothe, was a tyrant; his brother, who was devoted to his interests, was a traitor.

These were his living and his dying thoughts. While he existed, he was one of those men who, because they have been imprudent, think themselves unfortunate, and mistake their diseased mind for an implacable destiny. When he died, his deathbed was consoled by the reflection that his persecutors might at last feel some compunction; and he quitted the world without a pang, because he flattered himself that his departure would cost them one.

His father, who died before him, had left him no fortune, and even had not provided for his wife or child. His brother made another ineffectual attempt to accomplish a reconciliation; but his proffers of love and fortune were alike scorned and himself insulted, and Arundel Dacre seemed to gloat on the idea that he was an outcast and a beggar.

Yet even this strange being had his warm feelings. He adored his wife, particularly because his father had disowned her. He had a friend whom he idolised, and who, treating his occasional conduct as a species of insanity, had never deserted him. This friend had been his college companion, and, in the odd chapter of circumstances, had become a powerful political character. Dacre was a man of talent, and his friend took care that he should have an opportunity of displaying it. He was brought into Parliament, and animated by the desire, as he thought, of triumphing over his family, he exerted himself with success. But his infernal temper spoiled all. His active quarrels and his

- 127 -

noisy brawls were even more endurable than his sullen suspicions, his dark hints, and his silent hate. He was always offended and always offending. Such a man could never succeed as a politician, a character who, of all others, must learn to endure, to forget, and to forgive. He was soon universally shunned; but his first friend was faithful, though bitterly tried, and Dacre retired from public life on a pension.

His wife had died, and during the latter years of his life almost his only companion was his son. He concentrated on this being all that ardent affection which, had he diffused among his fellow-creatures, might have ensured his happiness and his prosperity. Yet even sometimes he would look in his child's face with an anxious air, as if he read incubating treason, and then press him to his bosom with unusual fervour, as if he would stifle the idea, which alone was madness.

This child was educated in an hereditary hate of the Dacre family. His uncle was daily painted as a tyrant, whom he classed in his young mind with Phalaris or Dionysius. There was nothing that he felt keener than his father's wrongs, and nothing which he believed more certain than his uncle's wickedness. He arrived at his thirteenth year when his father died, and he was to be consigned to the care of that uncle.

Arundel Dacre had left his son as a legacy to his friend; but that friend was a man of the world; and when the elder brother not only expressed his willingness to maintain the orphan, but even his desire to educate and adopt him as his son, he cheerfully resigned all his claims to the forlorn boy, and felt that, by consigning him to his uncle, he had most religiously discharged the trust of his confiding friend.

The nephew arrived at Castle Dacre with a heart equally divided between misery and hatred. It seemed to him that a fate more forlorn than his had seldom been awarded to mortal. Although he found his uncle diametrically opposite to all that his misled imagination had painted him, although he was treated with a kindness and indulgence which tried to compensate for their too long estranged affections, Arundel Dacre could never conquer the impressions of his boyhood; and had it not been for his cousin, May, a creature of whom he had not heard, and of whom no distorted image had therefore haunted his disturbed imagination; had it not been for this beautiful girl, who greeted him with affection which warmed and won his heart, so morbid were his feelings, that he would in all probability have pined away under the roof which he should have looked upon as his own.

His departure for Eton was a relief. As he grew up, although his knowledge of life and man had long taught him the fallacy of his early feelings, and although he now yielded a tear of pity, rather than of indignation, to the adored manes of his father, his peculiar temper and his first education never allowed him entirely to emancipate himself from his hereditary feelings. His character was combined of many and even of contrary qualities.

His talents were great, but his want of confidence made them more doubtful to himself than to the world; yet, at times, in his solitary musings, he perhaps even exaggerated his powers. He was proud, and yet worldly. He never forgot that he was a Dacre; but he desired to be the architect of his own fortune; and his very love of independence made him, at an early period, meditate on the means of managing mankind. He was reserved and cold, for his imagination required much; yet he panted for a confidant and was one of those youths with whom friendship is a passion. To conclude, he was a Protestant among Catholics; and although this circumstance, inasmuch as it assisted him in the views which he had early indulged, was not an ungracious one, he felt that, till he was distinguished, it had lessened his consideration, since he could not count upon the sympathy of hereditary connections and ancient party. Altogether, he was one who, with the consciousness of ancient blood, the certainty of future fortune, fine talents, great accomplishments, and not slight personal advantages, was unhappy. Yet, although not of a sanguine temper, and occasionally delivered to the darkest spleen, his intense ambition sustained him, and he lived on the hope, and sometimes on the conviction, that a bright era would, some day, console him for the bitterness of his past and present life.

At school and at college he equally distinguished himself, and was everywhere respected and often regarded; yet he had never found that friend on whom his fancy had often busied itself, and which one whose alternations of feeling were so violent peremptorily required. His uncle and himself viewed each other with mutual respect and regard, but confidence did not exist between them. Mr. Dacre, in spite of his long and constant efforts, despaired of raising in the breast of his nephew the flame of filial love; and had it not been for his daughter, who was the only person in the world to whom Arundel ever opened his mind, and who could, consequently, throw some light upon his wants and wishes, it would not have been in his power to evince to his nephew that this disappointment had not affected his uncle's feelings in his favour.

When his education was completed, Mr. Dacre had wished him to take up his residence in Yorkshire, and, in every sense, to act as his son, as he was his successor. But Arundel declined this proposition. He obtained from his father's old political connection the appointment of *attachÃ©* to a foreign embassy, and he remained on the Continent, with the exception of a yearly visit to Yorkshire, three or four years. But his views were not in the diplomatic line, and this appointment only served as a political school until he could enter Parliament. May Dacre had wormed from him his secret, and worked with energy in his cause. An opportunity appeared to offer itself, and, under the patronage of a Catholic nobleman, he was to appear as a candidate for an open borough. It was on this business that he had returned to England.

CHAPTER VI.

Birds of a Feather

WE WILL go and make a morning call. The garish light of day, that never suits a chamber, was broken by a muslin veil, which sent its softened twilight through a room of moderate dimensions but of princely decoration, and which opened into a conservatory. The choice saloon was hung with rose-coloured silk, which diffused a delicate tint over the inlaid and costly cabinets. It was crowded with tables covered with *bijouterie*. Apparently, however, a road had been cut through the furniture, by which you might wind your way up to the divinity of the temple. A ravishing perfume, which was ever changing, wandered through the apartment. Now a violet breeze made you poetical; now a rosy gale called you to love. And ever and anon the strange but thrilling breath of some rare exotic summoned you, like an angel, to opening Eden. All was still and sweet, save that a fountain made you, as it were, more conscious of silence; save that the song of birds made you, as it were, more sensible of sweetness.

Upon a couch, her small head resting upon an arm covered with bracelets, which blazed like a Sol-dan's treasure, reclined Mrs. Dallington Vere.

She is in thought. Is her abstracted eye fixed in admiration upon that twinkling foot which, clothed in its Russian slipper, looks like a serpent's tongue, small, red, and pointed; or does a more serious feeling than self-admiration inspire this musing? Ah! a cloud courses over that pellucid brow. Tis gone, but it frowned like the harbinger of a storm. Again! A small but blood-red blush rises into that clear cheek. It was momentary, but its deep colour indicated that it came from the heart. Her eye lights up with a wild and glittering fire, but the flash vanishes into darkness, and gloom follows the unnatural light. She clasps her hands; she rises from an uneasy seat, though supported by a thousand pillows, and she paces the conservatory.

A guest is announced. It is Sir Lucius Grafton.

He salutes her with that studied courtesy which shows they are only friends, but which, when maintained between intimate acquaintance, sometimes makes wicked people suspect that they once perhaps were more. She resumes her seat, and he throws himself into an easy chair which is opposite.

'Your note I this moment received, Bertha, and I am here. You perceive that my fidelity is as remarkable as ever.'

'We had a gay meeting last night.'

'Very much so. So Lady Araminta has at last shown mercy.'

'I cannot believe it.'

'I have just had a note from Challoner, preliminary, I suppose, to my trusteeship. You are not the only person who holds my talents for business in high esteem.'

'But Ballingford; what will he say?'

'That is his affair; and as he never, to my knowledge, spoke to the purpose, his remarks now, I suppose, are not fated to be much more apropos.'

'Yet he can say things. We all know——'

'Yes, yes, we all know; but nobody believes. That is the motto of the present day; and the only way to neutralise scandal, and to counteract publicity.'

Mrs. Dallington was silent, and looked uneasy; and her friend perceiving that, although she had sent to him so urgent a billet, she did not communicate, expressed a little surprise.

'But you wish to see me, Bertha?'

'I do very much, and to speak to you. For these many days I have intended it; but I do not know how it is, I have postponed and postponed our interview. I begin to believe,' she added, looking up with a faint smile, 'I am half afraid to speak.'

'Good God!' said the Baronet, really alarmed, 'you are in no trouble?'

'Oh, no! make yourself easy. Trouble, trouble! No, no! I am not exactly in trouble. I am not in debt; I am not in a scrape; but—but—but I am in something—something worse, perhaps: I am in love.'

The Baronet looked puzzled. He did not for a moment suspect himself to be the hero; yet, although their mutual confidence was illimitable, he did not exactly see why, in the present instance, there had been such urgency to impart an event not altogether either unnatural or miraculous.

'In love!' said Sir Lucius; 'a very proper situation for the prettiest woman in London. Everybody is in love with you; and I heartily rejoice that some one of our favoured sex is about to avenge our sufferings.'

'*Point de moquerie*, Lucy! I am miserable.'

'Dear little pigeon, what is the matter?'

'Ah, me!'

'Speak,-speak,' said he, in a gay tone; 'you were not made for sighs, but smiles. Begin——'

'Well, then, the young Duke——'

'The deuce!' said Sir Lucius, alarmed.

- 132 -

'Oh! no! make yourself easy,' said Mrs. Dallington, smiling; 'no counterplot, I assure you, although really you do not deserve to succeed.'

'Then who is it?' eagerly asked Sir Lucius.

'You will not let me speak. The young Duke——'

'Damn the Duke!'

'How impatient you are, Lucy! I must begin with the beginning. Well, the young Duke has something to do with it.'

'Pray be explicit.'

'In a word, then,' said Mrs. Dallington, in a low voice, but with an expression of earnestness which Sir Lucius had never before remarked, 'I am in love, desperately in love, with one whom hitherto, in accordance with your wishes, I have been driving into the arms of another. Our views, our interests are opposite; but I wish to act fairly, if possible; I wish to reconcile them; and it is for this purpose that I have summoned you this morning.'

'Arundel Dacre!' said Sir Lucius, quietly, and he rapped his cane on his boot. The blood-red spot again rose in his companion's cheek.

There was silence for a moment. Sir Lucius would not disturb it, and Mrs. Dallington again spoke.

'St. James and the little Dacre have again met. You have my secret. I do not ask your good services with Arundel, which I might at another time; but you cannot expect me to work against myself. Depend, then, no longer on my influence with May Dacre; for to be explicit, as we have always been, most heartily should I rejoice to see her a duchess.'

'The point, Bertha,' said Sir Lucius, very quietly, 'is not that I can no longer count upon you as an ally; but I must, I perceive, reckon you an opponent.'

'Cannot we prevent this?' asked Mrs. Dallington with energy.

'I see no alternative,' said Sir Lucius, shaking his head with great unconcern. 'Time will prove who will have to congratulate the other.'

'My friend,' said Mrs. Dallington, with briskness and decision, 'no affectation between us. Drop this assumed unconcern. You know, you know well, that no incident could occur to you at this moment more mortifying than the one I have communicated, which deranges your plans, and probably may destroy your views. You cannot misconceive my motives in making this not very agreeable communication. I might have pursued my object without your knowledge and permission. In a word, I might have betrayed you. But with me every consideration has yielded to friendship. I cannot forget how often, and how successfully, we have combined. I should grieve to see our ancient

- 133 -

and glorious alliance annulled. I am yet in hopes that we may both obtain our objects through its medium.'

'I am not aware,' said Sir Lucius, with more feeling, 'that I have given you any cause to complain of my want of candour. We are in a difficult position. I have nothing to suggest, but I am ready to listen. You know how ready I am to adopt all your suggestions; and I know how seldom you have wanted an expedient.'

'The little Dacre, then, must not marry her cousin; but we cannot flatter ourselves that such a girl will not want to marry some one; I have a conviction that this is her decisive season. She must be occupied. In a word, Lucy, some one must be found.'

The Baronet started from his chair, and nearly knocked down a table.

'Confound your tables, Bertha,' said he, in a pettish tone; 'I can never consult in a room full of tables.' He walked into the conservatory, and she followed him. He seemed plunged in thought. They were again silent. Suddenly he seized her hand and led her back to the sofa, on which they both sat down.

'My dear friend,' he said, in a tone of agitated solemnity. 'I will conceal no longer from you what I have sometimes endeavoured to conceal from myself: I love that girl to distraction.' 'You!'

'Yes; to distraction. Ever since we first met her image has haunted me. I endeavoured to crush a feeling which promised only to plunge me into anxiety, and to distract my attention from my important objects; but in vain, in vain. Her unexpected appearance yesterday has revived my passion with triple fervour. I have passed a sleepless night, and rise with the determination to obtain her.'

'You know your own power, Lucius, better perhaps than I do, or the world. We rank it high; none higher; yet, nevertheless, I look upon this declaration as insanity.'

He raised her hand to his lips, and pressed it with delicate warmth, and summoned his most insinuating tone. 'With your aid, Bertha, I should not despair!'

'Lucy, I am your friend; perhaps your best friend: but these Dacres! Would it were anyone but a Dacre! No, no, this cannot be.'

'Bertha, you know me better than the world: I am a rouÃ©, and you are my friend; but, believe me, I am not quite so vain as to indulge for a moment in the idea that May Dacre should be aught to me but what all might approve and all might honour. Yes, I intend her for my wife.'

'Your wife! You are, indeed, premature.'

'Not quite so premature as you perhaps imagine. Know, then, that the great point is on the eve of achievement. Urged by the information which Afy thinks she unconsciously obtains from Lachen, and harrowed by the idea that I am about to tear her from England, she has appealed to the Duke in a manner to which they were both unused. Hitherto her docile temper has not permitted her to abuse her empire. Now she exerts her power with an energy to which he believed her a stranger. He is staggered by his situation. He at the same time repents having so rashly engaged the feelings of a woman, and is flattered that he is so loved. They have more than once consulted upon the expediency of an elopement.'

'This is good news.'

'O! Bertha, you must feel like me before you can estimate it. Yes!' he clenched his fist with horrible energy, 'there is no hell like a detested wife!'

They were again silent; but when she thought that his emotion had subsided, she again recalled their consideration to the object of their interview.

'You play a bold game, indeed; but it shall not fail from any deficiency on my part. But how are we to proceed at present? Who is to interest the feelings of the little Dacre at once?'

'Who but her future husband? What I want you to do is this: we shall call; but prepare the house to receive us not only as acquaintances, but as desirable intimates. You know what to say. I have an idea that the divine creature entertains no very unfavourable opinion of your obedient slave; and with her temper I care not for what she will not probably hear, the passing opinion of a third person. I stand at present, thanks to Afy, very high with the public; and you know, although my life has not the least altered, that my indiscretions have now a dash of discretion in them; and a reformed rake, as all agree, is the personification of morality. Prepare my way with the Dacres, and all will go right. And as for this Arundel, I know him not; but you have told me enough to make me consider him the most fortunate of men. As for love between cousins, I laugh at it. A glance from you will extinguish the feeble flame, as a sunbeam does a fire: and for the rest, the world does me the honour to believe that, if Lucius Grafton be remarkable for one thing more than another, it is for the influence he attains over young minds. I will get acquainted with this boy; and, for once, let love be unattended by doubt.'

Long was their counsel. The plans we have hinted at were analysed, canvassed, weighed, and finally matured. They parted, after a long morning, well aware of the difficulties which awaited their fulfilment, but also full of hope.

CHAPTER VII.

A Dangerous Guide

SUCH able and congenial spirits as Mrs. Dallington Vere and Sir Lucius Grafton prosecuted their plans with the success which they had a right to anticipate. Lady Aphrodite, who was proud of her previous acquaintance, however slight, with the most distinguished girl in London, and eager to improve it, unconsciously assisted their operations. Society is so constituted that it requires no little talent and no slight energy to repel the intimacy even of those whose acquaintance is evidently not desirable; and there are many people in this world mixing, apparently, with great spirit and self-esteem in its concerns, who really owe their constant appearance and occasional influence in circles of consideration to no other qualities than their own callous impudence, and the indolence and the irresolution of their victims. They, who at the same time have no delicacy and no shame, count fearful odds; and, much as is murmured about the false estimation of riches, there is little doubt that the parvenus as often owe their advancement in society to their perseverance as to their pelf.

When, therefore, your intimacy is courted by those whose intimacy is an honour, and that, too, with an art, which conceals its purpose, you often find that you have, and are a devoted friend, really before you have felt sufficient gratitude for the opera-box which has been so often lent, the carriage which has been ever at hand, the brother who has received such civilities, or the father who has been requested to accept some of the unattainable tokay which he has charmed you by admiring at your own table.

The manoeuvres and tactics of society are infinitely more numerous and infinitely finer than those of strategy. Woe betide the rash knight who dashes into the thick of the polished melÂ©e without some slight experience of his barb and his lance! Let him look to his arms! He will do well not to appear before his helm be plumed with some reputation, however slight. He may be very rich, or even very poor. We have seen that answer with a Belisarius-like air; and more than one hero without an obolus has stumbled upon a fortune merely from his contempt of riches. If to fight, or write, or dress be above you, why, then, you can ride, or dance, or even skate; but do not think, as many young gentlemen are apt to believe, that *talking* will serve your purpose. That is the quicksand of your young beginners. All can talk in a public assembly; that is to say, all can give us exhortations which do not move, and arguments which do not convince; but to converse in a private assembly is a different affair, and rare are the characters who can be endured if they exceed a whisper to their neighbours. But though mild and silent, be ever ready with the rapier of repartee, and be ever armed with the breastplate of good temper.

You will infallibly gather laurels if you add to these the spear of sarcasm and the shield of nonchalance.

The high style of conversation where eloquence and philosophy emulate each other, where principles are profoundly expounded and felicitously illustrated, all this has ceased. It ceased in this country with Johnson and Burke, and it requires a Johnson and a Burke for its maintenance. There is no mediocrity in such discourse, no intermediate character between the sage and the bore. The second style, where men, not things, are the staple, but where wit, and refinement, and sensibility invest even personal details with intellectual interest, does flourish at present, as it always must in a highly civilised society. S. is, or rather was, a fine specimen of this school, and M. and L. are his worthy rivals. This style is indeed, for the moment, very interesting. Then comes your conversation man, who, we confess, is our aversion. His talk is a thing apart, got up before he enters the company from whose conduct it should grow out. He sits in the middle of a large table, and, with a brazen voice, bawls out his anecdotes about Sir Thomas or Sir Humphry, Lord Blank, or my Lady Blue. He is incessant, yet not interesting; ever varying, yet always monotonous. Even if we were amused, we are no more grateful for the entertainment than we are to the lamp over the table for the light which it universally sheds, and to yield which it was obtained on purpose. We are more gratified by the slight conversation of one who is often silent, but who speaks from his momentary feelings, than by all this hullaballoo. Yet this machine is generally a favourite piece of furniture with the hostess. You may catch her eye as he recounts some adventure of the morning, which proves that he not only belongs to every club, but goes to them, light up with approbation; and then, when the ladies withdraw, and the female senate deliver their criticism upon the late actors, she will observe, with a gratified smile, to her confidante, that the dinner went off well, and that Mr. Bellow was very strong to-day.

All this is horrid, and the whole affair is a delusion. A variety of people are brought together, who all come as late as possible, and retire as soon, merely to show they have other engagements. A dinner is prepared for them, which is hurried over, in order that a certain number of dishes should be, not tasted, but seen: and provided that there is no moment that an absolute silence reigns; provided that, besides the bustling of the servants, the clattering of the plates and knives, a stray anecdote is told, which, if good, has been heard before, and which, if new, is generally flat; provided a certain number of certain names of people of consideration are introduced, by which some stranger, for whom the party is often secretly given, may learn the scale of civilisation of which he this moment forms a part; provided the senators do not steal out too soon to the House, and their wives to another party, the hostess is congratulated on the success of her entertainment.

And this glare, and heat, and noise, these *congeries* of individuals without sympathy and dishes without flavour; this is society! What an effect without a cause! A man must be green indeed to stand this for two seasons. One cannot help thinking that one consequence of the increased intelligence of the present day will be a great change in the habits of our intercourse.

To our tale; we linger. Few who did not know too much of Sir Lucius Grafton could refrain from yielding him their regard when he chose to challenge it, and with the Dacres he was soon an acknowledged favourite. As a new M.P., and hitherto doubtful supporter of the Catholic cause, it was grateful to Mr. Dacre's feelings to find in him an ally, and flattering to Mr. Dacre's judgment when that ally ventured to consult him on his friendly operations. With Miss Dacre he was a mild, amiable man, who knew the world; thoroughly good, but void of cant, and owner of a virtue not less to be depended on because his passions had once been strong, and he had once indulged them. His experience of life made him value domestic felicity; because he knew that there was no other source of happiness which was at once so pure and so permanent. But he was not one of those men who consider marriage as an extinguisher of all those feelings and accomplishments which throw a lustre on existence; and he did not consider himself bound, because he had plighted his faith to a beautiful woman, immediately to terminate the very conduct which had induced her to join him in the sacred and eternal pledge. His gaiety still sparkled, his wit still flashed; still he hastened to be foremost among the courteous; and still his high and ready gallantry indicated that he was not prepared to yield the fitting ornament of his still blooming youth. A thousand unobtrusive and delicate attentions which the innocent now received from him without a thought, save of Lady Aphrodite's good fortune; a thousand gay and sentimental axioms, which proved not only how agreeable he was, but how enchanting he must have been; a thousand little deeds which struggled to shun the light, and which palpably demonstrated that the gaiety of his wit, the splendour of his accomplishments, and the tenderness of his soul were only equalled by his unbounded generosity and unparalleled good temper; all these combined had made Sir Lucius Grafton, to many, always a delightful, often a dangerous, and sometimes a fatal, companion. He was one of those whose candour is deadly. It was when he least endeavoured to conceal his character that its hideousness least appeared. He confessed sometimes so much, that you yielded that pity which, ere the shrived culprit could receive, by some fatal alchemy was changed into passion. His smile was a lure, his speech was a spell; but it was when he was silent, and almost gloomy, when you caught his serious eye, charged, as it were, with emotion, gazing on yours, that if you had a guardian sylph you should have invoked its aid; and we pray, if ever you meet the man of whom we write, your invocation may not be forgotten, or be, what is more likely, too late.

The Dacres, this season, were the subject of general conversation. She was the distinguished beauty, and the dandies all agreed that his dinner was worthy of his daughter. Lady Fitz-pompey was not behind the welcoming crowd. She was too politic a leader not to feel anxious to enlist under her colours a recruit who was so calculated to maintain the reputation of her forces. Fitz-pompey House must not lose its character for assembling the most distinguished, the most agreeable, and the most refined, and May Dacre was a divinity who would summon many a crowd to her niche in this Pantheon of fashion.

If any difficulty were for a moment anticipated in bringing about this arrangement, a fortunate circumstance seemed sufficient to remove it. Lord St. Maurice and Arundel Dacre had been acquainted at Vienna, and, though the intimacy was slight, it was sweet. St. Maurice had received many favours from the *attachÃ©*, and, as he was a man of family and reputation, had been happy to greet him on his arrival in London. Before the Dacres made their appearance in town for the season Arundel had been initiated in the mysteries of Fitz-pompey House, and therefore a desire from that mansion to cultivate the good graces of his Yorkshire relation seemed not only not forced, but natural. So, the families met, and, to the surprise of each other, became even intimate, for May Dacre and Lady Caroline soon evinced a mutual regard for each other. Female friendships are of rapid growth, and in the present instance, when there was nothing on either side which was not lovable, it was quite miraculous, and the friendship, particularly on the part of Lady Caroline, shot up in one night, like a blooming aloe.

Perhaps there is nothing more lovely than the love of two beautiful women, who are not envious of each other's charms. How delightfully they impart to each other the pattern of a cap, or flounce, or frill! how charmingly they entrust some slight, slender secret about tinting a flower or netting a purse! Now one leans over the other, and guides her inexperienced hand, as it moves in the mysteries of some novel work, and then the other looks up with an eye beaming with devotion; and then again the first leans down a little lower, and gently presses her aromatic lips upon her friend's polished forehead.

These are sights which we quiet men, who, like 'little Jack Horner,' know where to take up a safe position, occasionally enjoy, but which your noisy fellows, who think that women never want to be alone—a sad mistake—and consequently must be always breaking or stringing a guitar, or cutting a pencil, or splitting a crowquill, or overturning the gold ink, or scribbling over a pattern, or doing any other of the thousand acts of mischief, are debarred from.

Not that these bright flowers often bloomed alone; a blossom not less brilliant generally shared with them the same parterre. Mrs. Dallington completed the bouquet, and Arundel Dacre was the butterfly, who, she was glad to perceive, was seldom absent when her presence added beauty to the beautiful. Indeed, she had good reason to feel confidence in her attractions. Independently of her charms, which assuredly were great, her fortune, which was even greater, possessed, she was well aware, no slight allurement to one who ever trembled when he thought of his dependence, and often glowed when he mused over his ambition. His slight but increasing notice was duly estimated by one who was perfectly acquainted with his peculiar temper, and daily perceived how disregardful he was of all others, except her and his cousin. But a cousin! She felt confidence in the theory of Sir Lucius Grafton.

And the young Duke; have we forgotten him? Sooth to say, he was seldom with our heroine or heroines. He had called on Mr. Dacre, and had greeted him with marked cordiality, and he had sometimes met him and his daughter in society. But although invited, he had hitherto avoided being their visitor; and the comparatively secluded life which he now led prevented him from seeing them often at other houses. Mr. Dacre, who was unaware of what had passed between him and his daughter, thought his conduct inexplicable; but his former guardian remembered that it was not the first time that his behaviour had been unusual, and it was never the disposition of Mr. Dacre to promote explanations.

Our hero felt annoyed at his own weakness. It would have been infinitely more worthy of so celebrated, so unrivalled a personage as the Duke of St. James not to have given the woman who had rejected him this evidence of her power. According to etiquette, he should have called there daily and have dined there weekly, and yet never have given the former object of his adoration the slightest idea that he cared a breath for her presence. According to etiquette, he should never have addressed her but in a vein of persiflage, and with a smile which indicated his perfect heartease and her bad taste. According to etiquette, he should have flirted with every woman in her company, rode with her in the Park, walked with her in the Gardens, chatted with her at the opera, and drunk wine with her at a water party; and finally, to prove how sincere he was in his former estimation of her judgment, have consulted her on the presents which he should make to some intimate friend of hers, whom he announces as his future bride. This is the way to manage a woman; and the result may be conceived. She stares, she starts, she sighs, she weeps; feels highly offended at her friend daring to accept him; writes a letter of rejection herself to the affianced damsel, which she makes him sign, and then presents him with the hand which she always meant to be his.

But this was above our hero. The truth is, whenever he thought of May Dacre his spirit sank. She had cowed him; and her arrival in London had made him as dissatisfied with his present mode of life as he had been with his former career. They had met again, and under circumstances apparently, to him, the most unfavourable. Although he was hopeless, yet he dreaded to think what she might hear of him. Her contempt was bitter; her dislike would even be worse. Yet it seemed impossible to retrieve. He was plunged deeper than he imagined. Embarrassed, entangled, involved, he flew to Lady Afy, half in pique and half in misery. Passion had ceased to throw a glittering veil around this idol; but she was kind, and pure, and gentle, and devoted. It was consoling to be loved to one who was so wretched. It seemed to him that life must ever be a blank without the woman who, a few months ago, he had left an encumbrance. The recollection of past happiness was balm to one who was so forlorn. He shuddered at the thought of losing his only precious possession, and he was never more attached to his mistress than when the soul of friendship rose from the body of expired love.

CHAPTER VIII.

An Epicurean Feast

THE Duke of St. James dines to-day with Mr. Annesley. Men and things should be our study; and it is universally acknowledged that a dinner is the most important of affairs, and a dandy the most important of individuals. If we liked, we could give you a description of the fÃªte which should make all your mouths water; but everyone cooks now, and ekes out his page by robbing Jarrin and by rifling Ude.

Charles Annesley was never seen to more advantage than when a host. Then his superciliousness would, if not vanish, at least subside. He was not less calm, but somewhat less cold, like a summer lake. Therefore we will have an eye upon his party; because, to dine with dandies should be a prominent feature in your career, and must not be omitted in this sketch of the 'Life and Times' of our young hero. The party was of that number which at once secures a variety of conversation and the impossibility of two persons speaking at the same time. The guests were his Grace, Lord Squib, and Lord Darrell. The repast, like everything connected with Mr. Annesley, was refined and exquisite, rather slight than solid, and more novel than various. There was no affectation of *gourmandise,* the vice of male dinners. Your imagination and your sight were not at the same time dazzled and confused by an agglomeration of the peculiar luxuries of every clime and every season. As you mused over a warm and sunny flavour of a brown soup, your host did not dilate upon the milder and moonlight beauties of a white one. A gentle dallying with a whiting, that chicken of the ocean, was not a signal for a panegyric of the darker attraction of a *matelotte Ã la royale.* The disappearance of the first course did not herald a catalogue of discordant dainties. You were not recommended to neglect the *croquettes* because the *boudins* might claim attention; and while you were crowning your important labours with a quail you were not reminded that the *pÃ¢tÃ© de Troyes,* unlike the less reasonable human race, would feel offended if it were not cut. Then the wines were few. Some sherry, with a pedigree like an Arabian, heightened the flavour of the dish, not interfered with it; as a toady keeps up the conversation which he does not distract. A goblet of Graffenburg, with a bouquet like woman's breath, made you, as you remembered some liquid which it had been your fate to fall upon, suppose that German wines, like German barons, required some discrimination, and that hock, like other titles, was not always the sign of the high nobility of its owner. A glass of claret was the third grace. But, if we had been there, we should have devoted ourselves to one of the sparkling sisters; for one wine, like one woman, is sufficient to interest one's feelings for four-and-twenty hours. Fickleness we abhor.

'I observed you riding to-day with the gentle Leonora, St. James,' said Mr. Annesley.

'No! her sister.'

'Indeed! Those girls are uncommonly alike. The fact is, now, that neither face nor figure depends upon nature.'

'No,' said Lord Squib; 'all that the artists of the present day want is a model. Let a family provide one handsome sister, and the hideousness of the others will not prevent them, under good management, from being mistaken, by the best judges, for the beauty, six times in the same hour.'

'You are trying, I suppose, to account for your unfortunate error at Cleverley's, on Monday, Squib?' said Lord Darrell, laughing.

'Pooh! all nonsense.'

'What was it?' said Mr. Annesley.

'Not a word true,' said Lord Squib, stifling curiosity.

'I believe it,' said the Duke, without having heard a syllable. 'Come, Darrell, out with it!'

'It really is nothing very particular, only it is whispered that Squib said something to Lady Clever-ley which made her ring the bell, and that he excused himself to his Lordship by protesting that, from their similarity of dress and manner and strong family likeness, he had mistaken the Countess for her sister.'

Omnes. 'Well done, Squib! And were you introduced to the right person?'

'Why,' said his Lordship, 'fortunately I contrived to fall out about the settlements, and so I escaped.'

'So the chaste Diana is to be the new patroness?' said Lord Darrell.

'So I understand,' rejoined Mr. Annesley. 'This is the age of unexpected appointments.'

'*On dit* that when it was notified to the party most interested, there was a rider to the bill, excluding my Lord's relations.'

'Ha, ha, ha,' faintly laughed Mr. Annesley. 'What have they been doing so remarkable?'

'Nothing,' said Lord Squib. 'That is just their fault. They have every recommendation; but when any member of that family is in a room, everybody feels so exceedingly sleepy that they all sink to the ground. That is the reason that there are so many ottomans at Heavyside House.'

'Is it true,' asked the Duke, 'that his Grace really has a flapper?'

'Unquestionably,' said Lord Squib. 'The other day I was announced, and his attendant was absent. He had left his instrument on a sofa. I immediately took it up, and touched my Lord upon his hump. I never knew him more entertaining. He really was quite lively.'

'But Diana is a favourite goddess of mine,' said Annesley; 'taste that hock.'

'Superb! Where did you get it?'

'A present from poor Raffenburg.'

'Ah! where is he now?'

'At Paris, I believe.'

'Paris! and where is she?'

'I liked Raffenburg,' said Lord Squib; 'he always reminded me of a country innkeeper who supplies you with pipes and tobacco gratis, provided that you will dine with him.'

'He had unrivalled meerschaums,' said Mr. Annesley, 'and he was most liberal. There are two. You know I never use them, but they are handsome furniture.'

'Those Dalmaines are fine girls,' said the Duke of St. James.

'Very pretty creatures! Do you know, Duke,' said Annesley, 'I think the youngest one something like Miss Dacre.'

'Indeed! I cannot say the resemblance struck me.'

'I see old mother Dalmaine dresses her as much like the Doncaster belle as she possibly can.'

'Yes, and spoils her,' said Lord Squib; 'but old mother Dalmaine, with all her fuss, was ever a bad cook, and overdid everything.'

'Young Dalmaine, they say,' observed Lord Darrell, 'is in a sort of a scrape.'

'Ah! what?'

'Oh! some confusion at head-quarters. A great tallow-chandler's son got into the regiment, and committed some heresy at mess.'

'I do not know the brother,' said the Duke.

'You are fortunate, then. He is unendurable. To give you an idea of him, suppose you met him here (which you never will), he would write to you the next day, "My dear St. James."'

'My tailor presented me his best compliments, the other morning,' said the Duke.

'The world is growing familiar,' said Mr. Annesley.

'There must be some remedy,' said Lord Darrell.

'Yes!' said Lord Squib, with indignation. 'Tradesmen now-a-days console themselves for not getting their bills paid by asking their customers to dinner.'

'It is shocking,' said Mr. Annesley, with a forlorn air. 'Do you know, I never enter society now without taking as many preliminary precautions as if the plague raged in all our chambers. In vain have I hitherto prided myself on my existence being unknown to the million. I never now stand still in a street, lest my portrait be caught for a lithograph; I never venture to a strange dinner, lest I should stumble upon a fashionable novelist; and even with all this vigilance, and all this denial, I have an intimate friend whom I cannot cut, and who, they say, writes for the Court Journal.'

'But why cannot you cut him?' asked Lord Darrell.

'He is my brother; and, you know, I pride myself upon my domestic feelings.'

'Yes!' said Lord Squib, 'to judge from what the world says, one would think, Annesley, you were a Brummel!'

'Squib, not even in jest couple my name with one whom I will not call a savage, merely because he is unfortunate.'

'What did you think of little Eugenie, Annesley, last night?' asked the Duke.

'Well, very well, indeed; something like Brocard's worst.'

'I was a little disappointed in her dÃ©but, and much interested in her success. She was rather a favourite of mine in Paris, so I invited her to the Alhambra yesterday, with Claudius Piggott and some more. I had half a mind to pull you in, but I know you do not much admire Piggott.'

'On the contrary, I have been in Piggott's company without being much offended.'

'I think Piggott improves,' said Lord Darrell. 'It was those waistcoats which excited such a prejudice against him when he first came over.'

'What! a prejudice against Peacock Piggott!' said Lord Squib; 'pretty Peacock Piggott! Tell it not in Gath, whisper it not in Ascalon; and, above all, insinuate it not to Lady de Courcy.'

'There is not much danger of my insinuating anything to her,' said Mr. Annesley.

'Your compact, I hope, is religiously observed,' said the Duke.

'Yes, very well. There was a slight infraction once, but I sent Charles Fitzroy as an ambassador, and war was not declared.'

'Do you mean,' asked Lord Squib, 'when your cabriolet broke down before her door, and she sent out to request that you would make yourself quite at home?'

'I mean that fatal day,' replied Mr. Annesley. 'I afterwards discovered she had bribed my tiger.'

'Do you know Eugenie's sister, St. James?' asked Lord Darrell.

'Yes: she is very clever; very popular at Paris. But I like Eugenie, because she is so good-natured. Her laugh is so hearty.'

'So it is,' said Lord Squib. 'Do you remember that girl at Madrid, Annesley, who used to laugh so?'

'What, Isidora? She is coming over.'

'But I thought it was high treason to plunder the grandees' dovecotes?'

'Why, all our regular official negotiations have failed. She is not permitted to treat with a foreign manager; but the new ambassador has a secretary, and that secretary has some diplomatic ability, and so Isidora is to be smuggled over.'

'In a red box, I suppose,' said Lord Squib.

'I rather admire our AdÃ"le,' said the Duke of St. James. 'I really think she dances with more *aplomb* than any of them.'

'Oh! certainly; she is a favourite of mine.'

'But I like that wild little Ducis,' said Lord Squib. 'She puts me in mind of a wild cat.'

'And Marunia of a Bengal tiger,' said his Grace.

'She is a fine woman, though,' said Lord Darrell.

'I think your cousin, St. James,' said Lord Squib, 'will get into a scrape with Marunia. I remember Chetwynd telling me, and he was not apt to complain on that score, that he never should have broken up if it had not been for her.'

'But he was an extravagant fellow,' said Mr. Annesley: 'he called me in at his *bouleversement* for advice, as I have the reputation of a good economist. I do not know how it is, though I see these things perpetually happen; but why men, and men of small fortunes, should commit such follies, really exceeds my comprehension. Ten thousand pounds for trinkets, and nearly as much for old furniture!'

'Chetwynd kept it up a good many years, though, I think,' said Lord Darrell. 'I remember going to see his rooms when I first came over. You recollect his pearl fountain of Cologne water?'

'Millecolonnes fitted up his place, I think?' asked the young Duke; 'but it was before my time.'

'Oh! yes; little Bijou,' said Annesley. 'He has done you justice, Duke. I think the Alhambra much the prettiest thing in town.'

'I was attacked the other day most vigorously by Mrs. Dallington to obtain a sight,' said Lord Squib. 'I referred her to Lucy Grafton. Do you know, St. James, I have half a strange idea that there is a renewal in that quarter?'

'So they say,' said the Duke; 'if so, I confess I am surprised.' But they remembered Lord Darrell, and the conversation turned.

'Those are clever horses of Lincoln Graves,' said Mr. Annesley.

'Neat cattle, as Bagshot says,' observed Lord Squib.

'Is it true that Bag is going to marry one of the Wrekins?' asked the Duke.

'Which?' asked Lord Squib; 'not Sophy, surely I thought she was to be your cousin. I dare say,' he added, 'a false report. I suppose, to use a Bagshotism, his governor wants it; but I should think Lord Cub would not yet be taken in. By-the-bye, he says you have promised to propose him at White's, St. James.'

'Oppose him, I said,' rejoined the Duke. 'Bag really never understands English. However, I think it as probable that he will lounge there as on the Treasury bench. That was his "governor's" last shrewd plan.'

'Darrell,' said Lord Squib, 'is there any chance of my being a commissioner for anything? It struck me last night that I had never been in office.'

'I do not think, Squib, that you ever will be in office, if even you be appointed.'

'On the contrary, my good fellow, my punctuality should surprise you. I should like very much to be a lay lord, because I cannot afford to keep a yacht, and theirs, they say, are not sufficiently used, for the Admirals think it spooney, and the landlubbers are always sick.'

'I think myself of having a yacht this summer,' said the Duke of St. James. 'Be my captain, Squib.'

'If you be serious I will commence my duties tomorrow.'

- 147 -

'I am serious. I think it will be amusing. I give you full authority to do exactly what you like, provided, in two months' time, I have the crack vessel in the club.'

'I begin to press. Annesley, your dinner is so good that you shall be purser; and Darrell, you are a man of business, you shall be his clerk. For the rest, I think St. Maurice may claim a place, and——'

'Peacock Piggott, by all means,' said the Duke. 'A gay sailor is quite the thing.'

'And Charles Fitzroy,' said Annesley, 'because I am under obligations to him, and promised to have him in my eye.'

'And Bagshot for a butt,' said the Duke.

'And Backbite for a buffoon,' said Mr. Annesley.

'And for the rest,' said the young Duke, 'the rest of the crew, I vote, shall be women. The Dalmaines will just do.'

'And the little Trevors,' said Lord Darrell.

'And Long Harrington,' said Lord Squib. 'She is my beauty.'

'And the young Ducie,' said Annesley. 'And Mrs. Dallington of course, and Caroline St. Maurice, and Charlotte Bloomerly; really, she was dressed most prettily last night; and, above all, the queen bee of the hive, May Dacre, eh! St. James? And I have another proposition,' said Annesley, with unusual animation. 'May Dacre won the St. Leger, and ruled the course; and May Dacre shall win the cup, and rule the waves. Our yacht shall be christened by the Lady Bird of Yorkshire.'

'What a delightful thing it would be,' said the Duke of St. James, 'if, throughout life, we might always choose our crew; cull the beauties, and banish the bores.'

'But that is impossible,' said Lord Darrell. 'Every ornament of society is counterbalanced by some accompanying blur. I have invariably observed that the ugliness of a chaperon is exactly in proportion to the charms of her charge; and that if a man be distinguished for his wit, his appearance, his style, or any other good quality, he is sure to be saddled with some family or connection, who require all his popularity to gain them a passport into the crowd.'

'One might collect an unexceptionable coterie from our present crowd,' said Mr. Annesley. 'It would be curious to assemble all the pet lambs of the flock.'

'Is it impossible?' asked the Duke.

'Burlington is the only man who dare try,' said Lord Darrell.

'I doubt whether any individual would have sufficient pluck,' said Lord Squib.

'Yes,' said the Duke, 'it must, I think, be a joint-stock company to share the glory and the odium. Let us do it!'

There was a start, and a silence, broken by Annesley in a low voice:

'By Heavens it would be sublime, if practicable; but the difficulty does indeed seem insurmountable.'

'Why, we would not do it,' said the young Duke, 'if it were not difficult. The first thing is to get a frame for our picture, to hit upon some happy pretence for assembling in an impromptu style the young and gay. Our purpose must not be too obvious. It must be something to which all expect to be asked, and where the presence of all is impossible; so that, in fixing upon a particular member of a family, we may seem influenced by the wish that no circle should be neglected. Then, too, it should be something like a water-party or a fÃªte champÃªtre, where colds abound and fits are always caught, so that a consideration for the old and the infirm may authorise us not to invite them; then, too——'

Omnes. 'Bravo! bravo! St. James. It shall be! it shall be!'

'It must be a fÃªte champÃªtre,' said Annesley, decidedly, 'and as far from town as possible.'

'Twickenham is at your service,' said the Duke.

'Just the place, and just the distance. The only objection is, that, by being yours, it will saddle the enterprise too much upon you. We must all bear our share in the uproar, for, trust me, there will be one; but there are a thousand ways by which our responsibility may be insisted upon. For instance, let us make a list of all our guests, and then let one of us act as secretary, and sign the invitations, which shall be like tickets. No other name need appear, and the hosts will indicate themselves at the place of rendezvous.'

'My Lords,' said Lord Squib, 'I rise to propose the health of Mr. Secretary Annesley, and I think if anyone carry the business through, it will be he.'

'I accept the trust. At present be silent as night; for we have much to mature, and our success depends upon our secrecy.'

CHAPTER IX.

The FÃᵃte of Youth and Beauty

ARUNDEL DACRE, though little apt to cultivate an acquaintance with anyone, called on the young Duke the morning after their meeting. The truth is, his imagination was touched by our hero's appearance. His Grace possessed all that accomplished manner of which Arundel painfully felt the want, and to which he eagerly yielded his admiration. He earnestly desired the Duke's friendship, but, with his usual *mauvaise honte*, their meeting did not advance his wishes. He was as shy and constrained as usual, and being really desirous of appearing to advantage, and leaving an impression in his favour, his manner was even divested of that somewhat imposing coldness which was not altogether ineffective. In short, he was rather disagreeable. The Duke was courteous, as he usually was, and ever to the Da-cres, but he was not cordial. He disliked Arundel Dacre; in a word, he looked upon him as his favoured rival. The two young men occasionally met, but did not grow more intimate. Studiously polite the young Duke ever was both to him and to his lovely cousin, for his pride concealed his pique, and he was always afraid lest his manner should betray his mind.

In the meantime Sir Lucius Grafton apparently was running his usual course of triumph. It is fortunate that those who will watch and wonder about everything are easily satisfied with a reason, and are ever quick in detecting a cause; so Mrs. Dallington Vere was the fact that duly accounted for the Baronet's intimacy with the Dacres. All was right again between them. It was unusual, to be sure, these *rifacimentos*; still she was a charming woman; and it was well known that Lucius had spent twenty thousand on the county. Where was that to come from, they should like to know, but from old Dallington Vere's Yorkshire estates, which he had so wisely left to his pretty wife by the pink paper codicil?

And this lady of so many loves, how felt she? Most agreeably, as all dames do who dote upon a passion which they feel convinced will be returned, but which still waits for a response. Arundel Dacre would yield her a smile from a face more worn by thought than joy; and Arundel Dacre, who was wont to muse alone, was now ever ready to join his cousin and her friends in the ride or the promenade. Miss Dacre, too, had noticed to her a kindly change in her cousin's conduct to her father. He was more cordial to his uncle, sought to pay him deference, and seemed more desirous of gaining his good-will. The experienced eye, too, of this pretty woman allowed her often to observe that her hero's presence was not particularly occasioned, or particularly inspired, by his cousin. In a word, it was to herself that his remarks were addressed, his attentions devoted, and often she caught his dark and liquid eye fixed upon her beaming and refulgent brow.

Sir Lucius Grafton proceeded with that strange mixture of craft and passion which characterised him. Each day his heart yearned more for the being on whom his thoughts should never have pondered. Now exulting in her increased confidence, she seemed already his victim; now awed by her majestic spirit, he despaired even of her being his bride. Now melted by her unsophisticated innocence, he cursed even the least unhallowed of his purposes; and now enchanted by her consummate loveliness, he forgot all but her beauty and his own passion.

Often had he dilated to her, with the skill of an arch deceiver, on the blessings of domestic joy; often, in her presence, had his eye sparkled, when he watched the infantile graces of some playful children. Then he would embrace them with a soft care and gushing fondness, enough to melt the heart of any mother whom he was desirous to seduce, and then, with a half-murmured sigh, he regretted, in broken accents, that he, too, was not a father.

In due time he proceeded even further. Dark hints of domestic infelicity broke unintentionally from his ungoverned lips. Miss Dacre stared. He quelled the tumult of his thoughts, struggled with his outbreaking feelings, and triumphed; yet not without a tear, which forced its way down a face not formed for grief, and quivered upon his fair and downy cheek. Sir Lucius Grafton was well aware of the magic of his beauty, and used his charms to betray, as if he were a woman.

Miss Dacre, whose soul was sympathy, felt in silence for this excellent, this injured, this unhappy, this agreeable man. Ill could even her practised manner check the current of her mind, or conceal from Lady Aphrodite that she possessed her dislike. As for the young Duke, he fell into the lowest abyss of her opinions, and was looked upon as alike frivolous, heartless, and irreclaimable.

But how are the friends with whom we dined yesterday? Frequent were the meetings, deep the consultations, infinite the suggestions, innumerable the expedients. In the morning they met and breakfasted with Annesley; in the afternoon they met and lunched with Lord Squib; in the evening they met and dined with Lord Darrell; and at night they met and supped at the Alhambra. Each council only the more convinced them that the scheme was feasible, and must be glorious. At last their ideas were matured, and Annesley took steps to break a great event to the world, who were on the eve of being astonished.

He repaired to Lady Bloomerly. The world sometimes talked of her Ladyship and Mr. Annesley; the world were quite wrong, as they often are on this subject. Mr. Annesley knew the value of a female friend. By Lady Bloomerly's advice, the plan was entrusted in confidence to about a dozen dames equally influential. Then a few of the most considered male friends heard a strange report. Lord Darrell dropped a rumour at the Treasury; but with his finger on the mouth, and leaving himself out of the list, proceeded to give his favourable opinion of the project, merely as a disinterested and expected guest. Then the Duke promised Peacock Piggott one night at the Alhambra, but swore him to solemn secrecy over a vase of sherbet. Then Squib told his tailor, in consideration that his bill should not be sent in; and finally, the Bird of Paradise betrayed the whole affair to the musical world, who were, of course, all agog. Then, when rumour began to wag its hundred tongues, the twelve peeresses found themselves bound in honour to step into the breach, yielded the plan their decided approbation, and their avowed patronage puzzled the grumblers, silenced the weak, and sneered down the obstinate.

The invitations began to issue, and the outcry against them burst forth. A *fronde* was formed, but they wanted a De Retz; and many kept back, with the hope of being bribed from joining it. The four cavaliers soon found themselves at the head of a strong party, and then, like a faction who have successfully struggled for toleration, they now openly maintained their supremacy. It was too late to cabal. The uninvited could only console themselves by a passive sulk or an active sneer; but this would not do, and their bilious countenances betrayed their chagrin.

The difficulty now was, not to keep the bores away, but to obtain a few of the beauties, who hesitated. A chaperon must be found for one; another must be added on to a party, like a star to the cluster of a constellation. Among those whose presence was most ardently desired, but seemed most doubtful, was Miss Dacre. An invitation had been sent to her father; but he was out of town, and she did not like to join so peculiar a party without him: but it was unanimously agreed that, without her, the affair would be a failure; and Charles Annesley was sent, envoy extraordinary, to arrange. With the good aid of his friend Mrs. Dallington all was at length settled; and fervid prayers that the important day might be ushered in by a smiling sun were offered up during the next fortnight, at half-past six every morning, by all civilised society, who then hurried to their night's rest.

CHAPTER X.

Sir Lucius Drops the Mask

THE fÃªte at 'the Pavilion,' such was the title of the Twickenham Villa, though the subject of universal interest, was anticipated by no one with more eager anxiety than by Sir Lucius Grafton; for that day, he determined, should decide the fate of the Duke of St. James. He was sanguine as to the result, nor without reason. For the last month he had, by his dark machinery, played desperately upon the feelings of Lady Aphrodite; and more than once had she despatched rapid notes to her admirer for counsel and for consolation. The Duke was more skilful in soothing her griefs than in devising expedients for their removal. He treated the threatened as a distant evil! and wiped away her tears in a manner which is almost an encouragement to weep.

At last the eventful morn arrived, and a scorching sun made those exult to whom the barge and the awning promised a progress equally calm and cool. Woe to the dusty britzska! woe to the molten furnace of the crimson cabriolet!

They came, as the stars come out from the heavens, what time the sun is in his first repose: now a single hero, brilliant as a planet; now a splendid party, clustering like a constellation. Music is on the waters and perfume on the land; each moment a barque glides up with its cymbals, each moment a cavalcade bright with bouquets!

Ah, gathering of brightness! ah, meeting of lustre! why, why are you to be celebrated by one so obscure and dull as I am? Ye Lady Carolines and ye Lady Franceses, ye Lady Barbaras and ye Lady Blanches, is it my fault?

O, graceful Lord Francis, why, why have you left us; why, why have you exchanged your Ionian lyre for an Irish harp? You were not made for politics; leave them to clerks. Fly, fly back to pleasure, to frolic, and fun! Confess, now, that you sometimes do feel a little queer. We say nothing of the difference between May Fair and Donnybrook.

And thou, too, Luttrell, gayest bard that ever threw off a triplet amid the clattering of cabs and the chattering of clubs, art thou, too, mute? Where, where dost thou linger? Is our Druid among the oaks of Ampthill; or, like a truant Etonian, is he lurking among the beeches of Burnham? What! has the immortal letter, unlike all other good advice, absolutely not been thrown away? or is the jade incorrigible? Whichever be the case, you need not be silent. There is yet enough to do, and yet enough to instruct. Teach us that wealth is not elegance; that profusion is not magnificence; and that splendour is not beauty. Teach us that taste is a talisman which can do greater wonders than the millions of the loanmonger. Teach us that to vie is not to rival, and

- 153 -

to imitate not to invent. Teach us that pretension is a bore. Teach us that wit is excessively good-natured, and, like champagne, not only sparkles, but is sweet. Teach us the vulgarity of malignity. Teach us that envy spoils our complexions, and that anxiety destroys our figure. Catch the fleeting colours of that sly chameleon, Cant, and show what excessive trouble we are ever taking to make ourselves miserable and silly. Teach us all this, and Aglaia shall stop a crow in its course and present you with a pen, Thalia hold the golden fluid in a SÃ¨vres vase, and Euphrosyne support the violet-coloured scroll.

The four hosts greeted the arrivals and assisted the disembarkations, like the famous four sons of Aymon.

They were all dressed alike, and their costume excited great attention. At first it was to have been very plain, black and white and a single rose; but it was settled that simplicity had been overdone, and, like a country girl after her first season, had turned into a most affected baggage, so they agreed to be regal; and fancy uniforms, worthy of the court of Oberon, were the order of the day. We shall not describe them, for the description of costume is the most inventive province of our historical novelists, and we never like to be unfair, or trench upon our neighbour's lands or rights; but the Alhambra button indicated a mystical confederacy, and made the women quite frantic with curiosity.

The guests wandered through the gardens, always various, and now a paradise of novelty. There were four brothers, fresh from the wildest recesses of the Carpathian Mount, who threw out such woodnotes wild that all the artists stared; and it was universally agreed that, had they not been French chorus-singers, they would have been quite a miracle. But the Lapland sisters were the true prodigy, who danced the Mazurka in the national style. There was also a fire-eater; but some said he would never set the river in flames, though he had an antidote against all poisons! But then our Mithridates always tried its virtues on a stuffed poodle, whose bark evinced its vitality. There also was a giant in the wildest part of the shrubbery, and a dwarf, on whom the ladies showered their sugarplums, and who, in return, offered them tobacco. But it was not true that the giant sported stilts, or that the dwarf was a sucking-babe. Some people are so suspicious. Then a bell rang, and assembled them in the concert-room; and the Bird of Paradise who to-day was consigned to the cavaliership of Peacock Piggott, condescended to favour them with a new song, which no one had ever heard, and which, consequently, made them feel more intensely all the sublimity of exclusiveness. Shall we forget the panniers of shoes which Melnotte had placed in every quarter of the gardens? We will say nothing of Maradan's cases of caps, because, for this incident, Lord Bagshot is our authority.

On a sudden, it seemed that a thousand bugles broke the blue air, and they were summoned to a déjeûner in four crimson tents worthy of Sardanapalus.

Over each waved the scutcheon of the president. Glittering were the glories of the hundred quarterings of the house of Darrell. '*Si non Â¨ vero Â¨ ben trovato,*' was the motto. Lord Darrell's grandfather had been a successful lawyer. Lord Squib's emblazonry was a satire on its owner. '*Holdfast*' was the motto of a man who had let loose. Annesley's simple shield spoke of the Conquest; but all paled before the banner of the house of Hauteville, for it indicated an alliance with royalty. The attendants of each pavilion wore the livery of its lord.

Shall we attempt to describe the delicacy of this banquet, where imagination had been racked for novel luxury? Through the centre of each table ran a rivulet of rose-water, and gold and silver fish glanced in its unrivalled course. The bouquets were exchanged every half-hour, and music soft and subdued, but constant and thrilling, wound them up by exquisite gradations to that pitch of refined excitement which is so strange a union of delicacy and voluptuousness, when the soul, as it were, becomes sensual, and the body, as it were, dissolves into spirit. And in this choice assembly, where all was youth, and elegance, and beauty, was it not right that every sound should be melody, every sight a sight of loveliness, and every thought a thought of pleasure?

They arose and re-assembled on the lawn, where they found, to their surprise, had arisen in their absence a Dutch Fair. Numerous were the booths, innumerable were the contents. The first artists had arranged the picture and the costumes; the first artists had made the trinkets and the toys. And what a very agreeable fair, where all might suit their fancy without the permission of that sulky tyrant, a purse! All were in excellent humour, and no false shame prevented them from plundering the stalls. The noble proprietors set the example. Annesley offered a bouquet of precious stones to Charlotte Bloomerly, and it was accepted, and the Duke of St. James showered a sack of whimsical breloques among a scrambling crowd of laughing beauties. Among them was Miss Dacre. He had not observed her. Their eyes met, and she smiled. It seemed that he had never felt happiness before.

Ere the humours of the fair could be exhausted they were summoned to the margin of the river, where four painted and gilded galleys, which might have sailed down the Cydmus, and each owning its peculiar chief, prepared to struggle for pre-eminence in speed. All betted; and the Duke, encouraged by the smile, hastened to Miss Dacre to try to win back some of his Doncaster losses, but Arundel Dacre had her arm in his, and she was evidently delighted with his discourse. His Grace's blood turned, and he walked away.

It was sunset when they returned to the lawn, and then the ball-room presented itself; but the twilight was long, and the night was warm; there were no hateful dews, no odious mists, and therefore a great number danced on the lawn. The fair was illuminated, and all the little *marchandes* and their lusty porters walked about in their costume.

The Duke again rallied his courage, and seeing Arundel Dacre with Mrs. Dallington Vere, he absolutely asked Miss Dacre to dance. She was engaged. He doubted, and walked into the house disconsolate; yet, if he had waited one moment, he would have seen Sir Lucius Grafton rejoin her, and lead her to the cotillon that was forming on the turf. The Duke sauntered to Lady Aphrodite, but she would not dance; yet she did not yield his arm, and proposed a stroll. They wandered away to the extremity of the grounds. Fainter and fainter grew the bursts of the revellers, yet neither of them spoke much, for both were dull.

Yet at length her Ladyship did speak, and amply made up for her previous silence. All former scenes, to this, were but as the preface to the book. All she knew and all she dreaded, all her suspicions, all her certainties, all her fears, were poured forth in painful profusion. This night was to decide her fate. She threw herself on his mercy, if he had forgotten his love. Out dashed all those arguments, all those appeals, all those assertions, which they say are usual under these circumstances. She was a woman; he was a man. She had staked her happiness on this venture; he had a thousand cards to play. Love, and first love, with her, as with all women, was everything; he and all men, at the worst, had a thousand resources. He might plunge into politics, he might game, he might fight, he might ruin himself in innumerable ways, but she could only ruin herself in one. Miserable woman! Miserable sex! She had given him her all. She knew it was little: would she had more! She knew she was unworthy of him: would she were not! She did not ask him to sacrifice himself to her: she could not expect it; she did not even desire it. Only, she thought he ought to know exactly the state of affairs and of consequences, and that certainly if they were parted, which assuredly they would be, most decidedly she would droop, and fade, and die. She wept, she sobbed; his entreaties alone seemed to prevent hysterics.

These scenes are painful at all times, and even the callous, they say, have a twinge; but when the actress is really beautiful and pure, as this lady was, and the actor young and inexperienced and amiable, as this actor was, the consequences are more serious than is usual. The Duke of St. James was unhappy, he was discontented, he was dissatisfied with himself. He did not love this lady, if love were the passion which he entertained for Miss Dacre, but she loved him. He knew that she was beautiful, and he was convinced that she was excellent. The world is malicious, but the world had agreed that Lady Aphrodite was an unblemished pearl: yet this jewel was reserved for him! Intense gratitude almost amounted to love. In short, he had no idea at this moment that feelings are not in our power. His were captive, even if entrapped. It was a great responsibility to desert this creature, the only one from whom he had experienced devotion. To conclude: a season of extraordinary dissipation, to use no harsher phrase, had somewhat exhausted the nervous powers of our hero; his energies were deserting him; he had not heart or heartlessness enough to extricate himself from this dilemma. It seemed that if this being to whom he was indebted for so much joy were miserable, he must be unhappy; that if she died, life ought to have, could have, no charms for him. He kissed away her tears, he pledged his faith, and Lady Aphrodite Grafton was his betrothed!

She wonderfully recovered. Her deep but silent joy seemed to repay him even for this bitter sacrifice. Compared with the late racking of his feelings, the present calm, which was merely the result of suspense being destroyed, seemed happiness. His conscience whispered approbation, and he felt that, for once, he had sacrificed himself to another.

They re-entered the villa, and he took the first opportunity of wandering alone to the least frequented parts of the grounds: his mind demanded solitude, and his soul required soliloquy.

'So the game is up! truly a most lame and impotent conclusion! And this, then, is the result of all my high fancies and indefinite aspirations! Verily, I am a very distinguished hero, and have not abused my unrivalled advantages in the least. What! am I bitter on myself? There will be enough to sing my praises without myself joining in this chorus of congratulation. O! fool! fool! Now I know what folly is. But barely fifteen months since I stepped upon these shores, full of hope and full of pride; and now I leave them; how? O! my dishonoured fathers! Even my posterity, which God grant I may not have, will look on my memory with hatred, and on hers with scorn!

'Well, I suppose we must live for ourselves. We both of us know the world; and Heaven can bear witness that we should not be haunted by any uneasy hankering after what has brought us such a heartache. If it were for love, if it were for—but away! I will not profane her name; if it were for her that I was thus sacrificing myself. I could bear it, I could welcome it. I can imagine perfect and everlasting bliss in the sole society of one single being, but she is not that being. Let me not conceal it; let me wrestle with this bitter conviction!

'And am I, indeed, bound to close my career thus; to throw away all hope, all chance of felicity, at my age, for a point of honour? No, no; it is not that. After all, I have experienced that with her, and from her, which I have with no other woman; and she is so good, so gentle, and, all agree, so lovely! How infinitely worse would her situation be if deserted, than mine is as her perpetual companion! The very thought makes my heart bleed. Yes! amiable, devoted, dearest Afy, I throw aside these morbid feelings; you shall never repent having placed your trust in me. I will be proud and happy of such a friend, and you shall be mine for ever!'

A shriek broke on the air: he started. It was near: he hastened after the sound. He entered into a small green glade surrounded by shrubs, where had been erected a fanciful hermitage. There he found Sir Lucius Grafton on his knees, grasping the hand of the indignant but terrified Miss Dacre. The Duke rushed forward; Miss Dacre ran to meet him; Sir Lucius rose.

'This lady, Sir Lucius Grafton, is under my protection,' said the young Duke, with a flashing eye but a calm voice. She clung to his arm; he bore her away. The whole was the affair of an instant.

The Duke and his companion proceeded in silence. She tried to hasten, but he felt her limbs shake upon his arm. He stopped: no one, not even a servant, was near. He could not leave her for an instant. There she stood trembling, her head bent down, and one hand clasping the other, which rested on his arm. Terrible was her struggle, but she would not faint, and at length succeeded in repressing her emotions. They were yet a considerable way from the house. She motioned with her left hand to advance; but still she did not speak. On they walked, though more slowly, for she was exhausted, and occasionally stopped for breath or strength.

At length she said, in a faint voice, 'I cannot join the party. I must go home directly. How can it be done?'

'Your companions?' said the Duke.

'Are of course engaged, or not to be found; but surely somebody I know is departing. Manage it: say I am ill.'

'O, Miss Dacre! if you knew the agony of my mind!'

'Do not speak; for Heaven's sake, do not speak!'

He turned off from the lawn, and approached by a small circuit the gate of the ground. Suddenly he perceived a carriage on the point of going off. It was the Duchess of Shropshire's.

'There is the Duchess of Shropshire! You know her; but not a minute is to be lost. There is such a noise, they will not hear. Are you afraid to stop here one instant by yourself? I shall not be out of sight, and not away a second. I run very quick.'

'No, no, I am not afraid. Go, go!'

Away rushed the Duke of St. James as if his life were on his speed. He stopped the carriage, spoke, and was back in an instant.

'Lean, lean on me with all your strength. I have told everything necessary to Lady Shropshire. Nobody will speak a word, because they believe you have a terrible headache. I will say everything necessary to Mrs. Dallington and your cousin. Do not give yourself a moment's uneasiness. And, oh! Miss Dacre! if I might say one word!'

She did not stop him.

'If,' continued he, 'it be your wish that the outrage of to-night should be known only to myself and him, I pledge my word it shall be so; though willingly, if I were authorised, I would act a different part in this affair.'

'It is my wish.' She spoke in a low voice, with her eyes still upon the ground. 'And I thank you for this, and for all.'

They had now joined the Shropshires; but it was now discovered Miss Dacre had no shawl: and sundry other articles were wanting, to the evident dismay of the Ladies Wrekin. They offered theirs, but their visitor refused, and would not allow the Duke to fetch her own. Off they drove; but when they had

- 159 -

proceeded above half a mile, a continued shout on the road, which the fat coachman for a long time would not hear, stopped them, and up came the Duke of St. James, covered with dust, and panting like a racer, with Miss Dacre's shawl.

CHAPTER XI.

Grim Preparations

SO MUCH time was occupied by this adventure of the shawl, and by making requisite explanations to Mrs. Dallington Vere, that almost the whole of the guests had retired, when the Duke found himself again in the saloon. His brother-hosts, too, were off with various parties, to which they had attached themselves. He found the Fitz-pompeys and a few still lingering for their carriages, and Arundel Dacre and his fair admirer. His Grace had promised to return with Lady Afy, and was devising some scheme by which he might free himself from this, now not very suitable, engagement, when she claimed his arm. She was leaning on it, and talking to Lady Fitz-pompey, when Sir Lucius approached, and, with his usual tone, put a note into the Duke's hand, saying at the same time, 'This appears to belong to you. I shall go to town with Piggott;' and then he walked away.

With the wife leaning on his arm, the young Duke had the pleasure of reading the following lines, written with the pencil of the husband:—

'After what has just occurred, only one more meeting can take place between us, and the sooner that takes place the better for all parties. This is no time for etiquette. I shall be in Kensington Gardens, in the grove on the right side of the summer-house, at half-past six to-morrow morning, and shall doubtless find you there.'

Sir Lucius was not out of sight when the Duke had finished reading his cartel. Making some confused excuse to Lady Afy, which was not expected, he ran after the Baronet, and soon reached him.

'Grafton, I shall be punctual: but there is one point on which I wish to speak to you at once. The cause of this meeting may be kept, I hope, a secret?'

'So far as I am concerned, an inviolable one,' bowed the Baronet, stiffly; and they parted.

The Duke returned satisfied, for Sir Lucius Grafton ever observed his word, to say nothing of the great interest which he surely had this time in maintaining his pledge.

Our hero thought that he never should reach London. The journey seemed a day; and the effort to amuse Lady Afy, and to prevent her from suspecting, by his conduct, that anything had occurred, was most painful. Silent, however, he at last became; but her mind, too, was engaged, and she supposed that her admirer was quiet only because, like herself, he was happy. At length they reached her house, but he excused himself from entering, and drove on immediately to Annesley. He was at Lady Bloomerly's. Lord Darrell

- 161 -

had not returned, and his servant did not expect him. Lord Squib was never to be found.

The Duke put on a great coat over his uniform and drove to White's; it was really a wilderness. Never had he seen fewer men there in his life, and there were none of his set. The only young-looking man was old Colonel Carlisle, who, with his skilfully enamelled cheek, flowing auburn locks, shining teeth, and tinted whiskers, might have been mistaken for gay twenty-seven, instead of grey seventy-two; but the Colonel had the gout, to say nothing of any other objections.

The Duke took up the 'Courier' and read three or four advertisements of quack medicines, but nobody entered. It was nearly midnight: he got nervous. Somebody came in; Lord Hounslow for his rubber. Even his favoured child, Bagshot, would be better than nobody. The Duke protested that the next acquaintance who entered should be his second, old or young. His vow had scarcely been registered when Arundel Dacre came in alone. He was the last man to whom the Duke wished to address himself, but Fate seemed to have decided it, and the Duke walked up to him.

'Mr. Dacre, I am about to ask of you a favour to which I have no claim.'

Mr. Dacre looked a little confused, and murmured his willingness to do anything.

'To be explicit, I am engaged in an affair of honour of an urgent nature. Will you be my friend?'

'Willingly.' He spoke with more ease. 'May I ask the name of the other party, the—the cause of the meeting?'

'The other party is Sir Lucius Grafton.'

'Hum!' said Arundel Dacre, as if he were no longer curious about the cause. 'When do you meet?'

'At half-past six, in Kensington Gardens, to-morrow; I believe I should say this morning.'

'Your Grace must be wearied,' said Arundel, with unusual ease and animation. 'Now, follow my advice. Go home at once and get some rest. Give yourself no trouble about preparations; leave everything to me. I will call upon you at half-past five precisely, with a chaise and post-horses, which will divert suspicion. Now, good night!'

'But really, your rest must be considered; and then all this trouble!'

- 162 -

'Oh! I have been in the habit of sitting up all night. Do not think of me; nor am I quite inexperienced in these matters, in too many of which I have unfortunately been engaged in Germany.'

The young men shook hands, and the Duke hastened home. Fortunately the Bird of Paradise was at her own establishment in Baker Street, a bureau where her secretary, in her behalf, transacted business with the various courts of Europe and the numerous cities of Great Britain. Here many a negotiation was carried on for opera engagements at Vienna, or Paris, or Berlin, or St. Petersburg. Here many a diplomatic correspondence conducted the fate of the musical festivals of York, or Norwich, or Exeter.

CHAPTER XII.

An Affair of Honour.

LET us return to Sir Lucius Grafton. He is as mad as any man must be who feels that the imprudence of a moment has dashed the ground all the plans, and all the hopes, and all the great results, over which he had so often pondered. The great day from which he had expected so much had passed, nor was it possible for four-and-twenty hours more completely to have reversed all his feelings and all his prospects. Miss Dacre had shared the innocent but unusual and excessive gaiety which had properly become a scene of festivity at once so agreeable, so various, and so novel. Sir Lucius Grafton had not been insensible to the excitement. On the contrary his impetuous passions seemed to recall the former and more fervent days of his career, and his voluptuous mind dangerously sympathised with the beautiful and luxurious scene. He was elated, too, with the thought that his freedom would perhaps be sealed this evening, and still more by his almost constant attendance on his fascinating companion. As the particular friend of the Dacre family, and as the secret ally of Mrs. Dallington Vere, he in some manner contrived always to be at Miss Dacre's side. With the laughing but insidious pretence that he was now almost too grave and staid a personage for such scenes, he conversed with few others, and humourously maintaining that his 'dancing days were over,' danced with none but her. Even when her attention was engaged by a third person, he lingered about, and with his consummate knowledge of the world, easy wit, and constant resources, generally succeeded in not only sliding into the conversation, but engrossing it. Arundel Dacre, too, although that young gentleman had not departed from his usual coldness in favour of Sir Lucius Grafton, the Baronet would most provokingly consider as his particular friend; never seemed to be conscious that his reserved companion was most punctilious in his address to him; but on the contrary, called him in return 'Dacre,' and sometimes 'Arundel.' In vain young Dacre struggled to maintain his position. His manner was no match for that of Sir Lucius Grafton. Annoyed with himself, he felt confused, and often quitted his cousin that he might be free of his friend. Thus Sir Lucius Grafton contrived never to permit Miss Dacre to be alone with Arundel, and to her he was so courteous, so agreeable, and so useful, that his absence seemed always a blank, or a period in which something ever went wrong.

The triumphant day rolled on, and each moment Sir Lucius felt more sanguine and more excited. We will not dwell upon the advancing confidence of his desperate mind. Hope expanded into certainty, certainty burst into impatience. In a desperate moment he breathed his passion.

May Dacre was the last girl to feel at a loss in such a situation. No one would have rung him out of a saloon with an air of more contemptuous majesty. But the shock, the solitary strangeness of the scene, the fear, for the first time, that none were near, and perhaps, also, her exhausted energy, frightened her, and she shrieked. One only had heard that shriek, yet that one was legion. Sooner might the whole world know the worst than this person suspect the least. Sir Lucius was left silent with rage, mad with passion, desperate with hate.

He gasped for breath. Now his brow burnt, now the cold dew ran off his countenance in streams. He clenched his fist, he stamped with agony, he found at length his voice, and he blasphemed to the unconscious woods.

His quick brain flew to the results like lightning. The Duke had escaped from his mesh; his madness had done more to win this boy Miss Dacre's heart than an age of courtship. He had lost the idol of his passion; he was fixed for ever with the creature of his hate. He loathed the idea. He tottered into the hermitage, and buried his face in his hands.

Something must be done. Some monstrous act of energy must repair this fatal blunder. He appealed to the mind which had never deserted him. The oracle was mute. Yet vengeance might even slightly redeem the bitterness of despair. This fellow should die; and his girl, for already he hated Miss Dacre, should not triumph in her minion. He tore a leaf from his tablets, and wrote the lines we have already read.

The young Duke reached home. You expect, of course, that he sat up all night making his will and answering letters. By no means. The first object that caught his eye was an enormous ottoman. He threw himself upon it without undressing, and without speaking a word to Luigi, and in a moment was fast asleep. He was fairly exhausted. Luigi stared, and called Spiridion to consult. They agreed that they dare not go to bed, and must not leave their lord; so they played écarté, till at last they quarrelled and fought with the candles over the table. But even this did not wake their unreasonable master; so Spiridion threw down a few chairs by accident; but all in vain. At half-past five there was a knocking at the gate, and they hurried away.

Arundel Dacre entered with them, woke the Duke, and praised him for his punctuality. His Grace thought that he had only dozed a few minutes; but time pressed; five minutes arranged his toilet, and they were first on the field.

In a moment Sir Lucius and Mr. Piggott appeared. Arundel Dacre, on the way, had anxiously enquired as to the probability of reconciliation, but was told at once it was impossible, so now he measured the ground and loaded the pistols with a calmness which was admirable. They fired at once; the Duke in the air, and the Baronet in his friend's side. When Sir Lucius saw his

- 165 -

Grace fall his hate vanished. He ran up with real anxiety and unfeigned anguish.

'Have I hit you? by h-ll!'

His Grace was magnanimous, but the case was urgent. A surgeon gave a favourable report, and extracted the ball on the spot. The Duke was carried back to his chaise, and in an hour was in the state bed, not of the Alhambra, but of his neglected mansion.

Arundel Dacre retired when he had seen his friend home, but gave urgent commands that he should be kept quiet. No sooner was the second out of sight than the principal ordered the room to be cleared, with the exception of Spiridion, and then, rising in his bed, wrote this note, which the page was secretly to deliver.

'——House, ——, 182-.

'Dear Miss Dacre,

'A very unimportant but somewhat disagreeable incident has occurred. I have been obliged to meet Sir Lucius Grafton, and our meeting has fortunately terminated without any serious consequences. Yet I wish that you should hear of this first from me, lest you might imagine that I had not redeemed my pledge of last night, and that I had placed for a moment my own feelings in competition with yours. This is not the case, and never shall be, dear Miss Dacre, with one whose greatest pride is to subscribe himself

'Your most obedient and faithful servant,

'St. James.'

CHAPTER XIII.

A Mind Distraught

THE world talked of nothing but the duel between the Duke of St. James and Sir Lucius Grafton.

It was a thunderbolt; and the phenomenon was accounted for by every cause but the right one. Yet even those who most confidently solved the riddle were the most eagerly employed in investigating its true meaning. The seconds were of course applied to. Arundel Dacre was proverbially unpumpable; but Peacock Piggott, whose communicative temper was an adage, how came he on a sudden so diplomatic? Not a syllable oozed from a mouth which was ever open; not a hint from a countenance which never could conceal its mind. He was not even mysterious, but really looked just as astonished and was just as curious as themselves. Fine times these for 'The Universe' and 'The New World!' All came out about Lady Afy; and they made up for their long and previous ignorance, or, as they now boldly blustered, their long and considerate forbearance. Sheets given away gratis, edition on Saturday night for the country, and woodcuts of the Pavilion fÃªte: the when, the how, and the wherefore. A. The summer-house, and Lady Aphrodite meeting the young Duke. B. The hedge behind which Sir Lucius Grafton was concealed. C. Kensington Gardens, and a cloudy morning; and so on. Cruikshank did wonders.

But let us endeavour to ascertain the feelings of the principal agents in this odd affair. Sir Lucius now was cool, and, the mischief being done, took a calm review of the late mad hours. As was his custom, he began to enquire whether any good could be elicited from all this evil. He owed his late adversary sundry moneys, which he had never contemplated the possibility of repaying to the person who had eloped with his wife. Had he shot his creditor the account would equally have been cleared; and this consideration, although it did not prompt, had not dissuaded, the late desperate deed. As it was, he now appeared still to enjoy the possession both of his wife and his debts, and had lost his friend. Bad generalship, Sir Lucy! Reconciliation was out of the question. The Duke's position was a good one. Strongly entrenched with a flesh wound, he had all the sympathy of society on his side; and, after having been confined for a few weeks, he could go to Paris for a few months, and then return, as if the Graftons had never crossed his eye, rid of a troublesome mistress and a troublesome friend. His position was certainly a good one; but Sir Lucius was astute, and he determined to turn this Shumla of his Grace. The quarrel must have been about her Ladyship. Who could assign any other cause for it? And the Duke must now be weak with loss of blood and anxiety, and totally unable to resist any appeal,

- 167 -

particularly a personal one, to his feelings. He determined, therefore, to drive Lady Afy into his Grace's arms. If he could only get her into the house for an hour, the business would be settled.

These cunning plans were, however, nearly being crossed by a very simple incident. Annoyed at finding that her feelings could be consulted only by sacrificing those of another woman, Miss Dacre, quite confident that, as Lady Aphrodite was innocent in the present instance, she must be immaculate, told everything to her father, and, stifling her tears, begged him to make all public; but Mr. Dacre, after due consideration, enjoined silence.

In the meantime the young Duke was not in so calm a mood as Sir Lucius. Rapidly the late extraordinary events dashed through his mind, and already those feelings which had prompted his soliloquy in the garden were no longer his. All forms, all images, all ideas, all memory, melted into Miss Dacre. He felt that he loved her with a perfect love: that she was to him what no other woman had been, even in the factitious delirium of early passion. A thought of her seemed to bring an entirely novel train of feelings, impressions, wishes, hopes. The world with her must be a totally different system, and his existence in her society a new and another life. Her very purity refined the passion which raged even in his exhausted mind. Gleams of virtue, morning streaks of duty, broke upon the horizon of his hitherto clouded soul; an obscure suspicion of the utter worthlessness of his life whispered in his hollow ear; he darkly felt that happiness was too philosophical a system to be the result or the reward of impulse, however unbounded, and that principle alone could create and could support that bliss which is our being's end and aim.

But when he turned to himself, he viewed his situation with horror, and yielded almost to despair. What, what could she think of the impure libertine who dared to adore her? If ever time could bleach his own soul and conciliate hers, what, what was to become of Aphrodite? Was his new career to commence by a new crime? Was he to desert this creature of his affections, and break a heart which beat only for him? It seemed that the only compensation he could offer for a life which had achieved no good would be to establish the felicity of the only being whose happiness seemed in his power. Yet what a prospect! If before he had trembled, now——

But his harrowed mind and exhausted body no longer allowed him even anxiety. Weak, yet excited, his senses fled; and when Arundel Dacre returned in the evening he found his friend delirious. He sat by his bed for hours. Suddenly the Duke speaks. Arundel Dacre rises: he leans over the sufferer's couch.

Ah! why turns the face of the listener so pale, and why gleam those eyes with terrible fire? The perspiration courses down his clear but sallow cheek: he throws his dark and clustering curls aside, and passes his hand over his damp brow, as if to ask whether he, too, had lost his senses from this fray.

The Duke is agitated. He waves his arm in the air, and calls out in a tone of defiance and of hate. His voice sinks: it seems that he breathes a milder language, and speaks to some softer being. There is no sound, save the long-drawn breath of one on whose countenance is stamped infinite amazement. Arundel Dacre walks the room disturbed; often he pauses, plunged in deep thought. 'Tis an hour past midnight, and he quits the bedside of the young Duke.

He pauses at the threshold, and seems to respire even the noisome air of the metropolis as if it were Eden. As he proceeds down Hill Street he stops, and gazes for a moment on the opposite house. What passes in his mind we know not. Perhaps he is reminded that in that mansion dwell beauty, wealth, and influence, and that all might be his. Perhaps love prompts that gaze, perhaps ambition. Is it passion, or is it power? or does one struggle with the other?

As he gazes the door opens, but without servants; and a man, deeply shrouded in his cloak, comes out. It was night, and the individual was disguised; but there are eyes which can pierce at all seasons and through all concealments, and Arundel Dacre marked with astonishment Sir Lucius Grafton.

CHAPTER XIV.

Reconciliation

WHEN it was understood that the Duke of St. James had been delirious, public feeling reached what is called its height; that is to say, the curiosity and the ignorance of the world were about equal. Everybody was indignant, not so much because the young Duke had been shot, but because they did not know why. If the sympathy of the women could have consoled him, our hero might have been reconciled to his fate. Among these, no one appeared more anxious as to the result, and more ignorant as to the cause, than Mrs. Dallington Vere. Arundel Dacre called on her the morning ensuing his midnight observation, but understood that she had not seen Sir Lucius Grafton, who, they said, had quitted London, which she thought probable. Nevertheless Arundel thought proper to walk down Hill Street at the same hour, and, if not at the same minute, yet in due course of time, he discovered the absent man.

In two or three days the young Duke was declared out of immediate danger, though his attendants must say he remained exceedingly restless, and by no means in a satisfactory state; yet, with their aid, they had a right to hope the best. At any rate, if he were to go off, his friends would have the satisfaction of remembering that all had been done that could be; so saying, Dr. X. took his fee, and Surgeons Y. and Z. prevented his conduct from being singular.

Now began the operations on the Grafton side. A letter from Lady Aphrodite full of distraction. She was fairly mystified. What could have induced Lucy suddenly to act so, puzzled her, as well it might. Her despair, and yet her confidence in his Grace, seemed equally great. Some talk there was of going off to Cleve at once. Her husband, on the whole, maintained a rigid silence and studied coolness. Yet he had talked of Vienna and Florence, and even murmured something about public disgrace and public ridicule. In short, the poor lady was fairly worn out, and wished to terminate her harassing career at once by cutting the Gordian knot. In a word, she proposed coming on to her admirer and, as she supposed, her victim, and having the satisfaction of giving him his cooling draughts and arranging his bandages.

If the meeting between the young Duke and Sir Lucius Grafton had been occasioned by any other cause than the real one, it is difficult to say what might have been the fate of this proposition. Our own opinion is, that this work would have been only in one volume; for the requisite morality would have made out the present one; but, as it was, the image of Miss Dacre hovered above our hero as his guardian genius. He despaired of ever obtaining her; but yet he determined not wilfully to crush all hope. Some great effort must be made to right his position. Lady Aphrodite must not be deserted: the very thought increased his fever. He wrote, to gain time; but another billet, in immediate answer, only painted increased terrors, and described the growing urgency of her persecuted situation. He was driven into a corner, but even a stag at bay is awful: what, then, must be a young Duke, the most noble animal in existence?

Ill as he was, he wrote these lines, not to Lady Aphrodite, but to her husband:—

'My Dear Grafton,

'You will be surprised at hearing from me. Is it necessary for me to assure you that my interference on a late occasion was accidental? And can you, for a moment, maintain that, under the circumstances, I could have acted in a different manner? I regret the whole business; but most I regret that we were placed in collision.

'I am ready to cast all memory of it into oblivion; and, as I unintentionally offended, I indulge the hope that, in this conduct, you will bear me company.

'Surely, men like us are not to be dissuaded from following our inclinations by any fear of the opinion of the world. The whole affair is, at present, a mystery; and I think, with our united fancies, some explanation may be hit upon which will render the mystery quite impenetrable, while it professes to offer a satisfactory solution.

'I do not know whether this letter expresses my meaning, for my mind is somewhat agitated and my head not very clear; but, if you be inclined to understand it in the right spirit, it is sufficiently lucid. At any rate, my dear Grafton, I have once more the pleasure of subscribing myself, faithfully yours,

'St. James.'

This letter was marked 'Immediate,' consigned to the custody of Luigi, with positive orders to deliver it personally to Sir Lucius; and, if not at home, to follow till he found him.

He was not at home, and he was found at——'s Clubhouse. Sullen, dissatisfied with himself, doubtful as to the result of his fresh manouvres, and brooding over his infernal debts, Sir Lucius had stepped into——, and passed the whole morning playing desperately with Lord Hounslow and Baron de Berghem. Never had he experienced such a smashing morning. He had long far exceeded his resources, and was proceeding with a vague idea that he should find money somehow or other, when this note was put into his hand, as it seemed to him by Providence. The signature of Semiramis could not have imparted more exquisite delight to a collector of autographs. Were his long views, his complicated objects, and doubtful results to be put

- 171 -

in competition a moment with so decided, so simple, and so certain a benefit? certainly not, by a gamester. He rose from the table, and with strange elation wrote these lines:—

'My Dearest Friend,

'You forgive me, but can I forgive myself? I am plunged in overwhelming grief. Shall I come on? Your mad but devoted friend,

'Lucius Grafton.

'The Duke of St. James.'

They met the same day. After a long consultation, it was settled that Peacock Piggott should be entrusted, in confidence, with the secret of the affair: merely a drunken squabble, 'growing out' of the Bird of Paradise. Wine, jealousy, an artful woman, and headstrong youth will account for anything; they accounted for the present affair. The story was believed, because the world were always puzzled at Lady Aphrodite being the cause. The Baronet proceeded with promptitude to make the version pass current: he indicted 'The Universe' and 'The New World;' he prosecuted the caricaturists; and was seen everywhere with his wife. 'The Universe' and 'The New World' revenged themselves on the Signora; and then she indicted them. They could not now even libel an opera singer with impunity; where was the boasted liberty of the press?

In the meantime the young Duke, once more easy in his mind, wonderfully recovered; and on the eighth day after the Ball of Beauty he returned to the Pavilion, which had now resumed its usual calm character, for fresh air and soothing quiet.

CHAPTER XV.

Arundel's Warning

IN THE morning of the young Duke's departure for Twickenham, as Miss Dacre and Lady Caroline St. Maurice were sitting together at the house of the former, and moralising over the last night's ball, Mr. Arundel Dacre was announced.

'You have just arrived in time to offer your congratulations, Arundel, on an agreeable event,' said Miss Dacre. 'Lord St. Maurice is about to lead to the hymeneal altar——'

'Lady Sophy Wrekin; I know it.'

'How extremely diplomatic! The *attachÃ©* in your very air. I thought, of course, I was to surprise you; but future ambassadors have such extraordinary sources of information.'

'Mine is a simple one. The Duchess, imagining, I suppose, that my attentions were directed to the wrong lady, warned me some weeks past. However, my congratulations shall be duly paid. Lady Caroline St. Maurice, allow me to express——'

'All that you ought to feel,' said Miss Dacre. 'But men at the present day pride themselves on insensibility.'

'Do you think I am insensible, Lady Caroline?' asked Arundel.

'I must protest against unfair questions,' said her Ladyship.

'But it is not unfair. You are a person who have now seen me more than once, and therefore, according to May, you ought to have a perfect knowledge of my character. Moreover, you do not share the prejudices of my family. I ask you, then, do you think I am so heartless as May would insinuate?'

'Does she insinuate so much?'

'Does she not call me insensible, because I am not in raptures that your brother is about to marry a young lady, who, for aught she knows, may be the object of my secret adoration?'

'Arundel, you are perverse,' said Miss Dacre.

'No, May; I am logical.'

'I have always heard that logic is much worse than wilfulness,' said Lady Caroline.

- 173 -

'But Arundel always was both,' said Miss Dacre. 'He is not only unreasonable, but he will always prove that he is right. Here is your purse, sir!' she added with a smile, presenting him with the result of her week's labour.

'This is the way she always bribes me, Lady Caroline. Do you approve of this corruption?'

'I must confess, I have a slight though secret kindness for a little bribery. Mamma is now on her way to Mortimer's, on a corrupt embassy. The *nouvelle mariÂ©e*, you know, must be reconciled to her change of lot by quite a new set of playthings. I can give you no idea of the necklace that our magnificent cousin, in spite of his wound, has sent Sophy.'

'But then, such a cousin!' said Miss Dacre. 'A young Duke, like the young lady in the fairy tale, should scarcely ever speak without producing brilliants.'

'Sophy is highly sensible of the attention. As she amusingly observed, except himself marrying her, he could scarcely do more. I hear the carriage. Adieu, love! Good morning, Mr. Dacre.'

'Allow me to see you to your carriage. I am to dine at Fitz-pompey House to-day, I believe.'

Arundel Dacre returned to his cousin, and, seating himself at the table, took up a book, and began reading it the wrong side upwards; then he threw down a ball of silk, then he cracked a knitting-needle, and then with a husky sort of voice and a half blush, and altogether an air of infinite confusion, he said, 'This has been an odd affair, May, of the Duke of St. James and Sir Lucius Grafton?'

'A very distressing affair, Arundel.'

'How singular that I should have been his second, May?'

'Could he have found anyone more fit for that office, Arundel?'

'I think he might. I must say this: that, had I known at the time the cause of the fray, I should have refused to accompany him.'

She was silent, and he resumed:

'An opera singer, at the best! Sir Lucius Grafton showed more discrimination. Peacock Piggott was just the character for his place, and I think my principal, too, might have found a more congenial spirit. What do you think, May?'

'Really, Arundel, this is a subject of which I know nothing.'

'Indeed! Well, it is odd, May; but do you know I have a queer suspicion that you know more about it than anybody else.'

'I! Arundel?' she exclaimed, with marked confusion.

'Yes, you, May,' he repeated with firmness, and looked her in the face with a glance which would read her soul. 'Ay! I am sure you do.'

'Who says so?'

'Oh! do not fear that you have been betrayed. No one says it; but I know it. We future ambassadors, you know, have such extraordinary sources of information.'

'You jest, Arundel, on a grave subject.'

'Grave! yes, it is grave, May Dacre. It is grave that there should be secrets between us; it is grave that our house should have been insulted; it is grave that you, of all others, should have been outraged; but oh! it is much more grave, it is bitter, that any other arm than this should have avenged the wrong.' He rose from his chair, he paced the room in agitation, and gnashed his teeth with a vindictive expression that he tried not to suppress.

'O! my cousin, my dear, dear cousin! spare me!' She hid her face in her hands, yet she continued speaking in a broken voice: 'I did it for the best. It was to suppress strife, to prevent bloodshed. I knew your temper, and I feared for your life; yet I told my father; I told him all: and it was by his advice that I have maintained throughout the silence which I, perhaps too hastily, at first adopted.'

'My own dear May! spare me! I cannot mark a tear from you without a pang. How I came to know this you wonder. It was the delirium of that person who should not have played so proud a part in this affair, and who is yet our friend; it was his delirium that betrayed all. In the madness of his excited brain he reacted the frightful scene, declared the outrage, and again avenged it. Yet, believe me, I am not tempted by any petty feeling of showing I am not ignorant of what is considered a secret to declare all this. I know, I feel your silence was for the best; that it was prompted by sweet and holy feelings for my sake. Believe me, my dear cousin, if anything could increase the infinite affection with which I love you, it would be the consciousness that at all times, whenever my image crosses your mind, it is to muse for my benefit, or to extenuate my errors.

'Dear May, you, who know me better than the world, know well my heart is not a mass of ice; and you, who are ever so ready to find a good reason even for my most wilful conduct, and an excuse for my most irrational, will easily credit that, in interfering in an affair in which you are concerned, I am not influenced by an unworthy, an officious, or a meddling spirit. No, dear May! it is because I think it better for you that we should speak upon this subject that I have ventured to treat upon it. Perhaps I broke it in a crude, but, credit me, not in an unkind, spirit. I am well conscious I have a somewhat ungracious manner; but you, who have pardoned it so often, will excuse it now. To be brief, it is of your companion to that accursed fête that I would speak.'

'Mrs. Dallington?'

'Surely she. Avoid her, May. I do not like that woman. You know I seldom speak at hazard; if I do not speak more distinctly now, it is because I will never magnify suspicions into certainties, which we must do even if we mention them. But I suspect, greatly suspect. An open rupture would be disagreeable, would be unwarrantable, would be impolitic. The season draws to a close. Quit town somewhat earlier than usual, and, in the meantime, receive her, if necessary; but, if possible, never alone. You have many friends; and, if no other, Lady Caroline St. Maurice is worthy of your society.'

He bent down his head and kissed her forehead: she pressed his faithful hand.

'And now, dear May, let me speak of a less important object, of myself. I find this borough a mere delusion. Every day new difficulties arise; and every day my chance seems weaker. I am wasting precious time for one who should be in action. I think, then, of returning to Vienna, and at once. I have some chance of being appointed Secretary of Embassy, and I then shall have achieved what was the great object of my life, independence.'

'This is always a sorrowful subject to me, Arundel. You have cherished such strange, do not be offended if I say such erroneous, ideas on the subject of what you call independence, that I feel that upon it we can consult neither with profit to you nor satisfaction to myself. Independence! Who is independent, if the heir of Dacre bow to anyone? Independence! Who can be independent, if the future head of one of the first families in this great country, will condescend to be the secretary even of a king?'

'We have often talked of this, May, and perhaps I have carried a morbid feeling to some excess; but my paternal blood flows in these veins, and it is too late to change. I know not how it is, but I seem misplaced in life. My existence is a long blunder.'

'Too late to change, dearest Arundel! Oh! thank you for those words. Can it, can it ever be too late to acknowledge error? Particularly if, by that very acknowledgment, we not only secure our own happiness, but that of those we love and those who love us?'

'Dear May! when I talk with you, I talk with my good genius; but I am in closer and more constant converse with another mind, and of that I am the slave. It is my own. I will not conceal from you, from whom I have concealed nothing, that doubts and dark misgivings of the truth and wisdom of my past feelings and my past career will ever and anon flit across my fancy, and obtrude themselves upon my consciousness. Your father—yes! I feel that I have not been to him what nature intended, and what he deserved.'

'O Arundel!' she said, with streaming eyes, 'he loves you like a son. Yet, yet be one!'

He seated himself on the sofa by her side, and took her small hand and bathed it with his kisses.

'My sweet and faithful friend, my very sister! I am overpowered with feelings to which I have hitherto been a stranger. There is a cause for all this contest of my passions. It must out. My being has changed. The scales have fallen from my sealed eyes, and the fountain of my heart o'erflows. Life seems to have a new purpose, and existence a new cause. Listen to me, listen; and if you can, May, comfort me!'

CHAPTER XVI.

Three Graces

AT TWICKENHAM the young Duke recovered rapidly. Not altogether displeased with his recent conduct, his self-complacency assisted his convalescence. Sir Lucius Grafton visited him daily. Regularly, about four or five o'clock, he galloped down to the Pavilion with the last *on dit*: some gay message from White's, a *mot* of Lord Squib, or a trait of Charles Annesley. But while he studied to amuse the wearisome hours of his imprisoned friend, in the midst of all his gaiety an interesting contrition was ever breaking forth, not so much by words as looks. It was evident that Sir Lucius, although he dissembled his affliction, was seriously affected by the consequence of his rash passion; and his amiable victim, whose magnanimous mind was incapable of harbouring an inimical feeling, and ever respondent to a soft and generous sentiment, felt actually more aggrieved for his unhappy friend than for himself. Of Arundel Dacre the Duke had not seen much. That gentleman never particularly sympathised with Sir Lucius Grafton, and now he scarcely endeavoured to conceal the little pleasure which he received from the Baronet's society. Sir Lucius was the last man not to detect this mood; but, as he was confident that the Duke had not betrayed him, he could only suppose that Miss Dacre had confided the affair to her family, and therefore, under all circumstances, he thought it best to be unconscious of any alteration in Arundel Dacre's intercourse with him. Civil, therefore, they were when they met; the Baronet was even courteous; but they both mutually avoided each other.

At the end of three weeks the Duke of St. James returned to town in perfect condition, and received the congratulations of his friends. Mr. Dacre had been of the few who had been permitted to visit him at Twickenham. Nothing had then passed between them on the cause of his illness; but his Grace could not but observe that the manner of his valued friend was more than commonly cordial. And Miss Dacre, with her father, was among the first to hail his return to health and the metropolis.

The Bird of Paradise, who, since the incident, had been several times in hysterics, and had written various notes, of three or four lines each, of enquiries and entreaties to join her noble friend, had been kept off from Twickenham by the masterly tactics of Lord Squib. She, however, would drive to the Duke's house the day after his arrival in town, and was with him when sundry loud knocks, in quick succession, announced an approaching levÃ©e. He locked her up in his private room, and hastened to receive the compliments of his visitors. In the same apartment, among many others, he had the pleasure of meeting, for the first time, Lady Aphrodite Grafton, Lady

- 178 -

Caroline St. Maurice, and Miss Dacre, all women whom he had either promised, intended, or offered to marry. A curious situation this! And really, when our hero looked upon them once more, and viewed them, in delightful rivalry, advancing with their congratulations, he was not surprised at the feelings with which they had inspired him. Far, far exceeding the *bonhomie* of Macheath, the Duke could not resist remembering that, had it been his fortune to have lived in the land in which his historiographer will soon be wandering; in short, to have been a pacha instead of a peer, he might have married all three.

A prettier fellow and three prettier women had never met since the immortal incident of Ida.

It required the thorough breeding of Lady Afy to conceal the anxiety of her passion; Miss Dacre's eyes showered triple sunshine, as she extended a hand not too often offered; but Lady Caroline was a cousin, and consanguinity, therefore, authorised as well as accounted for the warmth of her greeting.

CHAPTER XVII.

A Second Refusal

A VERY few days after his return the Duke of St. James dined with Mr. Dacre. It was the first time that he had dined with him during the season. The Fitz-pompeys were there; and, among others, his Grace had the pleasure of again meeting a few of his Yorkshire friends.

Once more he found himself at the right hand of Miss Dacre. All his career, since his arrival in England, flitted across his mind. Doncaster, dear Doncaster, where he had first seen her, teemed only with delightful reminiscences to a man whose favourite had bolted. Such is the magic of love! Then came Castle Dacre and the orange terrace, and their airy romps, and the delightful party to Hauteville; and then Dacre Abbey. An involuntary shudder seemed to damp all the ardour of his soul; but when he turned and looked upon her beaming face, he could not feel miserable.

He thought that he had never been at so agreeable a party in his life: yet it was chiefly composed of the very beings whom he daily execrated for their powers of boredom. And he himself was not very entertaining. He was certainly more silent than loquacious, and found himself often gazing with mute admiration on the little mouth, every word breathed forth from which seemed inspiration. Yet he was happy. Oh! what happiness is his who dotes upon a woman! Few could observe from his conduct what was passing in his mind; yet the quivering of his softened tones and the mild lustre of his mellowed gaze; his subdued and quiet manner; his un-perceived yet infinite attentions; his memory of little incidents that all but lovers would have forgotten; the total absence of all compliment, and gallantry, and repartee; all these, to a fine observer, might have been gentle indications of a strong passion; and to her to whom they were addressed sufficiently intimated that no change had taken place in his feelings since the warm hour in which he first whispered his o'erpowering love.

The ladies retired, and the Duke of St. James fell into a reverie. A political discourse of elaborate genius now arose. Lord Fitz-pompey got parliamentary. Young Faulcon made his escape, having previously whispered to another youth, not unheard by the Duke of St. James, that his mother was about to depart, and he was convoy. His Grace, too, had heard Lady Fitz-pompey say that she was going early to the opera. Shortly afterwards parties evidently retired. But the debate still raged. Lord Fitz-pompey had caught a stout Yorkshire squire, and was delightedly astounding with official graces his stern opponent. A sudden thought occurred to the Duke; he stole out of the room, and gained the saloon.

- 180 -

He found it almost empty. With sincere pleasure he bid Lady Balmont, who was on the point of departure, farewell, and promised to look in at her box. He seated himself by Lady Greville Nugent, and dexterously made her follow Lady Balmont's example. She withdrew with the conviction that his Grace would not be a moment behind her. There were only old Mrs. Hungerford and her rich daughter remaining. They were in such raptures with Miss Dacre's singing that his Grace was quite in despair; but chance favoured him. Even old Mrs. Hungerford this night broke through her rule of not going to more than one house, and she drove off to Lady de Courcy's.

They were alone. It is sometimes an awful thing to be alone with those we love.

'Sing that again!' asked the Duke, imploringly. 'It is my favourite air; it always reminds me of Dacre.'

She sang, she ceased; she sang with beauty, and she ceased with grace; but all unnoticed by the tumultuous soul of her adoring guest. His thoughts were intent upon a greater object. The opportunity was sweet; and yet those boisterous wassailers, they might spoil all.

'Do you know that this is the first time that I have seen your rooms lit up?' said the Duke.

'Is it possible! I hope they gain the approbation of so distinguished a judge.'

'I admire them exceedingly. By-the-bye, I see a new cabinet in the next room. Swaby told me, the other day, that you were one of his lady-patronesses. I wish you would show it me. I am very curious in cabinets.'

She rose, and they advanced to the end of another and a longer room.

'This is a beautiful saloon,' said the Duke. 'How long is it?'

'I really do not know; but I think between forty and fifty feet.'

'Oh! you must be mistaken. Forty or fifty feet! I am an excellent judge of distances. I will try. Forty or fifty feet! Ah! the next room included. Let us walk to the end of the next room. Each of my paces shall be one foot and a half.'

They had now arrived at the end of the third room.

'Let me see,' resumed the Duke; 'you have a small room to the right. Oh! did I not hear that you had made a conservatory? I see, I see it; lit up, too! Let us go in. I want to gain some hints about London conservatories.'

It was not exactly a conservatory; but a balcony of large dimensions had been fitted up on each side with coloured glass, and was open to the gardens. It was a rich night of fragrant June. The moon and stars were as bright as if they had shone over the terrace of Dacre, and the perfume of the flowers reminded him of his favourite orange-trees. The mild, cool scene was such a contrast to the hot and noisy chamber they had recently quitted, that for a moment they were silent.

'You are not afraid of this delicious air?' asked his Grace.

'Midsummer air,' said Miss Dacre, 'must surely be harmless.'

Again there was silence; and Miss Dacre, after having plucked a flower and tended a plant, seemed to express an intention of withdrawing. Suddenly he spoke, and in a gushing voice of heartfelt words:

'Miss Dacre, you are too kind, too excellent to be offended, if I dare to ask whether anything could induce you to view with more indulgence one who sensibly feels how utterly he is unworthy of you.'

'You are the last person whose feelings I should wish to hurt. Let us not revive a conversation to which, I can assure you, neither of us looks back with satisfaction.'

'Is there, then, no hope? Must I ever live with the consciousness of being the object of your scorn?'

'Oh, no, no! As you will speak, let us understand each other. However I may approve of my decision, I have lived quite long enough to repent the manner in which it was conveyed. I cannot, without the most unfeigned regret, I cannot for a moment remember that I have addressed a bitter word to one to whom I am under the greatest obligations. If my apologies——'

'Pray, pray be silent!'

'I must speak. If my apologies, my complete, my most humble apologies, can be any compensation for treating with such lightness feelings which I now respect, and offers by which I now consider myself honoured, accept them!'

'O, Miss Dacre! that fatal word, respect!'

'We have warmer words in this house for you. You are now our friend.'

'I dare not urge a suit which may offend you; yet, if you could read my heart, I sometimes think that we might be happy. Let me hope!'

'My dear Duke of St. James, I am sure you will not ever offend me, because I am sure you will not ever wish to do it. There are few people in this world for whom I entertain a more sincere regard than yourself. I am convinced, I am conscious, that when we met I did sufficient justice neither to your virtues nor your talents. It is impossible for me to express with what satisfaction I now feel that you have resumed that place in the affections of this family to which you have an hereditary right. I am grateful, truly, sincerely grateful, for all that you feel with regard to me individually; and believe me, in again expressing my regret that it is not in my power to view you in any other light than as a valued friend, I feel that I am pursuing that conduct which will conduce as much to your happiness as my own.'

'My happiness, Miss Dacre!'

'Indeed, such is my opinion. I will not again endeavour to depreciate the feelings which you entertain for me, and by which, ever remember, I feel honoured; but these very feelings prevent you from viewing their object so dispassionately as I do.'

'I am at a loss for your meaning; at least, favour me by speaking explicitly: you see I respect your sentiments, and do not presume to urge that on which my very happiness depends.'

'To be brief, then, I will not affect to conceal that marriage is a state which has often been the object of my meditations. I think it the duty of all women that so important a change in their destiny should be well considered. If I know anything of myself, I am convinced that I should never survive an unhappy marriage.'

'But why dream of anything so utterly impossible?'

'So very probable, so very certain, you mean. Ay! I repeat my words, for they are truth. If I ever marry, it is to devote every feeling and every thought, each hour, each instant of existence, to a single being for whom I alone live. Such devotion I expect in return; without it I should die, or wish to die; but such devotion can never be returned by you.'

'You amaze me! I! who live only on your image.'

'Your education, the habits in which you are brought up, the maxims which have been instilled into you from your infancy, the system which each year of your life has more matured, the worldly levity with which everything connected with woman is viewed by you and your companions; whatever may be your natural dispositions, all this would prevent you, all this would render it a perfect impossibility, all this will ever make you utterly unconscious of the importance of the subject on which we are now conversing. Pardon me for saying it, you know not of what you speak. Yes! however sincere may be the expression of your feelings to me this moment, I shudder to think on whom your memory dwelt even this hour but yesterday. I never will peril my happiness on such a chance; but there are others who do not think as I do.'

'Miss Dacre! save me! If you knew all, you would not doubt. This moment is my destiny.'

'My dear Duke of St. James, save yourself. There is yet time. You have my prayers.'

'Let me then hope——'

'Indeed, indeed, it cannot be. Here our conversation on this subject ends for ever.'

'Yet we part friends!' He spoke in a broken voice.

'The best and truest!' She extended her arm; he pressed her hand to his impassioned lips, and quitted the house, mad with love and misery.

CHAPTER XVIII.

Joys of the Alhambra

THE Duke threw himself into his carriage in that mood which fits us for desperate deeds. What he intended to do, indeed, was doubtful, but something very vigorous, very decided, perhaps very terrible. An indefinite great effort danced, in misty magnificence, before the vision of his mind. His whole being was to be changed, his life was to be revolutionised. Such an alteration was to take place that even she could not doubt the immense yet incredible result. Then despair whispered its cold-blooded taunts, and her last hopeless words echoed in his ear. But he was too agitated to be calmly miserable, and, in the poignancy of his feelings, he even meditated death. One thing, however, he could obtain; one instant relief was yet in his power, solitude. He panted for the loneliness of his own chamber, broken only by his agitated musings.

The carriage stopped; the lights and noise called him to life. This, surely, could not be home? Whirled open the door, down dashed the steps, with all that prompt precision which denotes the practised hand of an aristocratic retainer. (284)

'What is all this, Symmons? Why did you not drive home?'

'Your Grace forgets that Mr. Annesley and some gentlemen sup with your Grace to-night at the Alhambra.'

'Impossible! Drive home.'

'Your Grace perhaps forgets that your Grace is expected?' said the experienced servant, who knew when to urge a master, who, to-morrow, might blame him for permitting his caprice.

'What am I to do? Stay here. I will run upstairs, and put them off.'

He ran up into the crush-room. The opera was just over, and some parties who were not staying the ballet, had already assembled there. As he passed along he was stopped by Lady Fitz-pompey, who would not let such a capital opportunity escape of exhibiting Caroline and the young Duke together.

'Mr. Bulkley,' said her Ladyship, 'there must be something wrong about the carriage.' An experienced, middle-aged gentleman, who jobbed on in society by being always ready and knowing his cue, resigned the arm of Lady Caroline St. Maurice and disappeared.

'George,' said Lady Fitz-pompey, 'give your arm to Carry just for one moment.'

- 185 -

If it had been anybody but his cousin, the Duke would easily have escaped; but Caroline he invariably treated with marked regard; perhaps because his conscience occasionally reproached him that he had not treated her with a stronger feeling. At this moment, too, she was the only being in the world, save one, whom he could remember with satisfaction: he felt that he loved her most affectionately, but somehow she did not inspire him with those peculiar feelings which thrilled his heart at the recollection of May Dacre.

In this mood he offered an arm, which was accepted; but he could not in a moment assume the tone of mind befitting his situation and the scene. He was silent; for him a remarkable circumstance.

'Do not stay here,' said Lady Caroline is a soft voice, which her mother could not overhear. 'I know you want to be away. Steal off.'

'Where can I be better than with you, Carry?' said the young Duke, determined not to leave her, and loving her still more for her modest kindness; and thereon he turned round, and, to show that he was sincere, began talking with his usual spirit. Mr. Bulkley of course never returned, and Lady Fitz-pompey felt as satisfied with her diplomatic talents as a plenipotentiary who has just arranged an advantageous treaty.

Arundel Dacre came up and spoke to Lady Fitz-pompey. Never did two persons converse together who were more dissimilar in their manner and their feelings; and yet Arundel Dacre did contrive to talk; a result which he could not always accomplish, even with those who could sympathise with him. Lady Fitz-pompey listened to him with attention; for Arundel Dacre, in spite of his odd manner, or perhaps in some degree in consequence of it, had obtained a distinguished reputation both among men and women; and it was the great principle of Lady Fitz-pompey to attach to her the distinguished youth of both sexes. She was pleased with this public homage of Arundel Dacre; because he was one who, with the reputation of talents, family, and fashion, seldom spoke to anyone, and his attentions elevated their object. Thus she maintained her empire.

St. Maurice now came up to excuse himself to the young Duke for not attending at the Alhambra to-night. 'Sophy could not bear it,' he whispered: 'she had got her head full of the most ridiculous fancies, and it was in vain to speak: so he had promised to give up that, as well as Crockford's.'

This reminded our hero of his party, and the purpose of his entering the opera. He determined not to leave Caroline till her carriage was called; and he began to think that he really must go to the Alhambra, after all. He resolved to send them off at an early hour.

'Anything new to-night, Henry?' asked his Grace, of Lord St. Maurice. 'I have just come in.'

'Oh! then you have seen them?'

'Seen whom?'

'The most knowing *forestieri* we ever had. We have been speaking of nothing else the whole evening. Has not Caroline told you? Arundel Dacre introduced me to them.'

'Who are they?'

'I forget their names. Dacre, how do you call the heroes of the night? Dacre never answers. Did you ever observe that? But, see! there they come.'

The Duke turned, and observed Lord Darrell advancing with two gentlemen with whom his Grace was well acquainted. These were Prince Charles de Whiskerburg and Count Frill.

M. de Whiskerburg was the eldest son of a prince, who, besides being the premier noble of the empire, possessed, in his own country, a very pretty park of two or three hundred miles in circumference, in the boundaries of which the imperial mandate was not current, but hid its diminished head before the supremacy of a subject worshipped under the title of John the Twenty-fourth. M. de Whiskerburg was a young man, tall, with a fine figure, and fine features. In short, a sort of Hungarian Apollo; only his beard, his mustachios, his whiskers, his *favoris*, his *padishas*, his sultanas, his mignonettas, his dulcibellas, did not certainly entitle him to the epithet of *imberbis*, and made him rather an apter representative of the Hungarian Hercules.

Count Frill was a different sort of personage. He was all rings and ringlets, ruffles, and a little rouge. Much older than his companion, short in stature, plump in figure, but with a most defined waist, fair, blooming, with a multiplicity of long light curls, and a perpetual smile playing upon his round countenance, he looked like the Cupid of an opera Olympus.

The Duke of St. James had been intimate with these distinguished gentlemen in their own country, and had received from them many and distinguished attentions. Often had he expressed to them his sincere desire to greet them in his native land. Their mutual anxiety of never again meeting was now removed. If his heart, instead of being bruised, had been absolutely broken, still honour, conscience, the glory of his house, his individual reputation, alike urged him not to be cold or backward at such a moment. He advanced, therefore, with a due mixture of grace and warmth, and congratulated them on their arrival. At this moment, Lady Fitz-pompey's carriage was announced. Promising to return to them in an instant, he hastened to his cousin; but Mr. Arundel Dacre had already offered his arm, which, for Arundel Dacre, was really pretty well.

- 187 -

The Duke was now glad that he had a small reunion this evening, as he could at once pay a courtesy to his foreign friends. He ran into the Signora's dressing-room, to assure her of his presence. He stumbled upon Peacock Piggott as he came out, and summoned him to fill the vacant place of St. Maurice, and then sent him with a message to some friends who yet lingered in their box, and whose presence, he thought, might be an agreeable addition to the party.

You entered the Alhambra by a Saracenic cloister, from the ceiling of which an occasional lamp threw a gleam upon some Eastern arms hung up against the wall. This passage led to the armoury, a room of moderate dimensions, but hung with rich contents. Many an inlaid breastplate, many a Mameluke scimitar and Damascus blade, many a gemmed pistol and pearl-embroidered saddle, might there be seen, though viewed in a subdued and quiet light. All seemed hushed, and still, and shrouded in what had the reputation of being a palace of pleasure.

In this chamber assembled the expected guests. And having all arrived, they proceeded down a small gallery to the banqueting-room. The room was large and lofty. It was fitted up as an Eastern tent. The walls were hung with scarlet cloth, tied up with ropes of gold. Round the room crouched recumbent lions richly gilt, who grasped in their paws a lance, the top of which was a coloured lamp. The ceiling was emblazoned with the Hauteville arms, and was radiant with burnished gold. A cresset lamp was suspended from the centre of the shield, and not only emitted an equable flow of soft though brilliant light, but also, as the aromatic oil wasted away, distilled an exquisite perfume.

The table blazed with golden plate, for the Bird of Paradise loved splendour. At the end of the room, under a canopy and upon a throne, the shield and vases lately executed for his Grace now appeared. Everything was gorgeous, costly, and imposing; but there was no pretence, save in the original outline, at maintaining the Oriental character. The furniture was French; and opposite the throne Canova's Hebe, bounded with a golden cup from a pedestal of ormolu.

The guests are seated; but after a few minutes the servants withdraw. Small tables of ebony and silver, and dumb waiters of ivory and gold, conveniently stored, are at hand, and Spiridion never leaves the room. The repast was refined, exquisite, various. It was one of those meetings where all eat. When a few persons, easy and unconstrained, unencumbered with cares, and of dispositions addicted to enjoyment, get together at past midnight, it is extraordinary what an appetite they evince. Singers also are proverbially prone to gourmandise; and though the Bird of Paradise unfortunately possessed the smallest mouth in all Singingland, it is astonishing how she pecked! But they talked as well as feasted, and were really gay.

'Prince,' said the Duke, 'I hope Madame de Harestein approves of your trip to England?'

The Prince only smiled, for he was of a silent disposition, and therefore wonderfully well suited his travelling companion.

'Poor Madame de Harestein!' exclaimed Count Frill. 'What despair she was in, when you left Vienna, my dear Duke. I did what I could to amuse her. I used to take my guitar, and sing to her morning and night, but without effect. She certainly would have died of a broken heart, if it had not been for the dancing-dogs.'

'Did they bite her?' asked a lady who affected the wit of Lord Squib, 'and so inoculate her with gaiety.'

'Everybody was mad about the dancing-dogs. They came from Peru, and danced the mazurka in green jackets with a *jabot*. Oh! what a *jabot!*'

'I dislike animals excessively,' remarked another lady, who was as refined as Mr. Annesley, her model.

'Dislike the dancing-dogs!' said Count Frill. 'Ah! my good lady, you would have been enchanted. Even the Kaiser fed them with pistachio nuts. Oh! so pretty! Delicate leetle things, soft shining little legs, and pretty little faces! so sensible, and with such *jabots!*'

'I assure you they were excessively amusing,' said the Prince, in a soft, confidential undertone to his neighbour, Mrs. Montfort, who was as dignified as she was beautiful, and who, admiring his silence, which she took for state, smiled and bowed with fascinating condescension.

'And what else has happened very remarkable, Count, since I left you?' asked Lord Darrell.

'Nothing, nothing, my dear Darrell. This *bÃ"tise* of a war has made us all serious. If old Clamstandt had not married that gipsy, little Dugiria, I really think I should have taken a turn to Belgrade.'

'You should not eat so much, Poppet!' drawled Charles Annesley to a Spanish danseuse, tall, dusky and lithe, glancing like a lynx and graceful as a jennet. She was very silent, but no doubt indicated the possession of Cervantic humour by the sly calmness with which she exhausted her own waiter, and pillaged her neighbours.

'Why not?' said a little French actress, highly finished like a miniature, who scarcely ate anything, but drank champagne and chatted with equal rapidity and composure, and who was always ready to fight anybody's battle, provided she could get an opportunity to talk. 'Why not, Mr. Annesley? You never will let anybody eat. I never eat myself, because every night, having to talk so much, I am dry, dry, dry; so I drink, drink, drink. It is an extraordinary thing that there is no language which makes you so thirsty as French.'

'What can be the reason?' asked a sister of Mrs. Montfort, a tall fair girl, who looked sentimental, but was only silly.

'Because there is so much salt in it,' said Lord Squib.

'Delia,' drawled Mr. Annesley, 'you look very pretty to-night!'

'I am charmed to charm you, Mr. Annesley. Shall I tell you what Lord Bon Mot said of you?'

'No, *ma mignonne!* I never wish to hear my own good things.'

'Spoiled, you should add,' said the fair rival of Lord Squib, 'if Bon Mot be in the case.'

'Lord Bon Mot is a most gentlemanlike man,' said Delia, indignant at an admirer being attacked. 'He always wants to be amusing. Whenever he dines out, he comes and sits with me for half an hour to catch the air of the Parisian badinage.'

'And you tell him a variety of little things?' asked Lord Squib, insidiously drawing out the secret tactics of Bon Mot.

'*Beaucoup, beaucoup,*' said Delia, extending two little white hands sparkling with gems. 'If he come in ever so, how do you call it? heavy, not that: in the domps. Ah! it is that. If ever he come in the domps, he goes out always like a *soufflÃ©e.*'

'As empty, I have no doubt,' said the witty lady.

'And as sweet, I have no doubt,' said Lord Squib; 'for Delcroix complains sadly of your excesses, Delia.'

'Mr. Delcroix complain of me! That, indeed, is too bad. Just because I recommend Montmorency de Versailles to him for an excellent customer, ever since he abuses me, merely because Montmorency has forgot, in the hurry of going off, to pay his little account.'

'But he says you have got all the things,' said Lord Squib, whose great amusement was to put Delia in a passion.

'What of that?' screamed the little lady. 'Montmorency gave them me.'

'Don't make such a noise,' said the Bird of Paradise. 'I never can eat when there is a noise. Duke,' continued she in a fretful tone, 'they make such a noise!'

'Annesley, keep Squib quiet.'

'Delia, leave that young man alone. If Isidora would talk a little more, and you eat a little more, I think you would be the most agreeable little ladies I know. Poppet! put those bonbons in your pocket. You should never eat sugarplums in company.'

Thus, talking agreeable nonsense, tasting agreeable dishes, and sipping agreeable wines, an hour ran on. Sweetest music from an unseen source ever and anon sounded, and Spiridion swung a censer full of perfumes round the chamber. At length the Duke requested Count Frill to give them a song. The Bird of Paradise would never sing for pleasure, only for fame and a slight cheque. The Count begged to decline, and at the same time asked for a guitar. The Signora sent for hers; and his Excellency, preluding with a beautiful simper, gave them some slight thing to this effect.

I.

Charming Bignetta! charming Bignetta!
What a gay little girl is charming Bignetta!
She dances, she prattles,
She rides and she rattles;
But she always is charming, that charming Bignetta!
II

Charming Bignetta! charming Bignetta!
What a wild little witch is charming Bignetta!
When she smiles, I'm all madness;
When she frowns, I'm all sadness;
But she always is smiling, that charming Bignetta!
III.

Charming Bignetta! charming Bignetta!
What a wicked young rogue is charming Bignetta!
She laughs at my shyness,
And flirts with his Highness;

Yet still she is charming, that charming Bignetta!

IV.

Charming Bignetta! charming Bignetta!

What a dear little girl is charming Bignetta!

'Think me only a sister,'

Said she trembling: I kissed her.

What a charming young sister is charming Bignetta!

To choicer music chimed his gay guitar 'In Este's Halls,' yet still his song served its purpose, for it raised a smile.

'I wrote that for Madame Sapiepha, at the Congress of Verona,' said Count Frill. 'It has been thought amusing.'

'Madame Sapiepha!' exclaimed the Bird of Paradise. 'What! that pretty little woman, who has such pretty caps?'

'The same! Ah! what caps! what taste!'

'You like caps, then?' asked the Bird of Paradise, with a sparkling eye.

'Oh! if there be anything more than another that I know most, it is the cap. Here,' said he, rather oddly unbuttoning his waistcoat, 'you see what lace I have got.'

'Ah me! what lace!' exclaimed the Bird, in rapture. 'Duke, look at his lace. Come here, sit next to me. Let me look at that lace.' She examined it with great attention, then turned up her beautiful eyes with a fascinating smile. '*Ah! c'est jolie, n'est-ce pas?* But you like caps. I tell you what, you shall see my caps. Spiridion, go, *mon cher*, and tell Ma'amselle to bring my caps, all my caps, one of each set.'

In due time entered the Swiss, with the caps, all the caps, one of each set. As she handed them in turn to her mistress, the Bird chirped a panegyric upon each.

'That is pretty, is it not, and this also? but this is my favourite. What do you think of this border? *c'est belle cette garniture? et ce jabot, c'est trÂ¨s-sÂ©duisant, n'est-ce pas? Mais voici*, the cap of Princess Lichtenstein. *C'est superb, c'est mon favori.* But I also love very much this of the Duchess de Berri. She gave me the pattern herself. And, after, all, this *cornette Â petite santÂ©* of Lady Blaze is a dear little thing; then, again, this *coiffe Â dentelle* of Lady Macaroni is quite a pet.'

'Pass them down,' said Lord Squib; 'we want to look at them.' Accordingly they were passed down. Lord Squib put one on.

'Do I look superb, sentimental, or only pretty?' asked his Lordship. The example was contagious, and most of the caps were appropriated. No one laughed more than their mistress, who, not having the slightest idea of the value of money, would have given them all away on the spot; not from any good-natured feeling, but from the remembrance that tomorrow she might amuse half an hour in buying others.

Whilst some were stealing, and she remonstrating, the Duke clapped his hands like a caliph. The curtain at the end of the apartment was immediately withdrawn, and the ball-room stood revealed.

It was the same size as the banqueting-hall. Its walls exhibited a long perspective of golden pilasters, the frequent piers of which were of looking-glass, save where, occasionally, a picture had been, as it were, inlaid in its rich frame. Here was the Titian Venus of the Tribune, deliciously copied by a French artist: there, the Roman Fornarina, with her delicate grace, beamed like the personification of Raf-faelle's genius. Here, Zuleikha, living in the light and shade of that magician Guercino, in vain summoned the passions of the blooming Hebrew: and there, Cleopatra, preparing for her last immortal hour, proved by what we saw that Guido had been a lover.

The ceiling of this apartment was richly painted, and richly gilt: from it were suspended three lustres by golden cords, which threw a softened light upon the floor of polished and curiously inlaid woods. At the end of the apartment was an orchestra.

Round the room waltzed the elegant revellers. Softly and slowly, led by their host, they glided along like spirits of air; but each time that the Duke passed the musicians, the music became livelier, and the motion more brisk, till at length you might have mistaken them for a college of spinning dervishes. One by one, an exhausted couple retreated from the lists. Some threw themselves on a sofa, some monopolised an easy chair; but in twenty minutes the whirl had ceased. At length Peacock Piggott gave a groan, which denoted returning energy, and raised a stretching leg in air, bringing up, though most unwittingly, upon his foot, one of the Bird's sublime and beautiful caps.

'Halloa! Piggott, armed *cap-au-pied*, I see,' said Lord Squib. This joke was a signal for general resuscitation.

The Alhambra formed a quadrangle: all the chambers were on the basement story. In the middle of the court of the quadrangle was a beautiful fountain; and the court was formed by a conservatory, which was built along each side of the interior square, and served, like a cloister or covered way, for a communication between the different parts of the building. To this conservatory they now repaired. It was broad, full of rare and delicious plants and flowers, and brilliantly illuminated. Busts and statues were intermingled with the fairy grove; and a rich, warm hue, by a skilful arrangement of coloured lights, was thrown over many a nymph and fair divinity, many a blooming hero and beardless god. Here they lounged in different parties, talking on such subjects as idlers ever fall upon; now and then plucking a flower, now and then listening to the fountain, now and then lingering over the distant music, and now and then strolling through a small apartment which opened to their walks, and which bore the title of the Temple of Gnidus. Here, Canova's Venus breathed an atmosphere of perfume and of light; that wonderful statue, whose full-charged eye is not very classical, to be sure; but then, how true!

While they were thus whiling away their time, Lord Squib proposed a visit to the theatre, which he had ordered to be lit up. To the theatre they repaired. They rambled over every part of the house, amused themselves with a visit to the gallery, and then collected behind the scenes. They were excessively amused with the properties; and Lord Squib proposed they should dress themselves. In a few minutes they were all in costume. A crowd of queens and chambermaids, Jews and chimney-sweeps, lawyers and Charleys, Spanish Dons, and Irish officers, rushed upon the stage. The little Spaniard was Almaviva, and fell into magnificent attitudes, with her sword and plume. Lord Squib was the old woman of Brentford, and very funny. Sir Lucius Grafton, Harlequin; and Darrell, Grimaldi. The Prince, and the Count without knowing it, figured as watchmen. Squib whispered Annesley, that Sir Lucius O'Trigger might appear in character, but was prudent enough to suppress the joke.

The band was summoned, and they danced quadrilles with infinite spirit, and finished the night, at the suggestion of Lord Squib, by breakfasting on the stage. By the time this meal was despatched the purple light of morn had broken into the building, and the ladies proposed an immediate departure.

BOOK IV.

CHAPTER I.

Pen Bronnock Palace

THE arrival of the two distinguished foreigners reanimated the dying season. All vied in testifying their consideration, and the Duke of St. James exceeded all. He took them to see the alterations at Hauteville House, which no one had yet witnessed; and he asked their opinion of his furniture, which no one had yet decided on. Two fÃªtes in the same week established, as well as maintained, his character as the Archduke of fashion. Remembering, however, the agreeable month which he had spent in the kingdom of John the Twenty-fourth, he was reminded, with annoyance, that his confusion at Hauteville prevented him from receiving his friends *en grand seigneur* in his hereditary castle. Metropolitan magnificence, which, if the parvenu could not equal, he at least could imitate, seemed a poor return for the feudal splendour and impartial festivity of an Hungarian magnate. While he was brooding over these reminiscences, it suddenly occurred to him that he had never made a progress into his western territories. Pen Bronnock Palace was the boast of Cornwall, though its lord had never paid it a visit. The Duke of St. James sent for Sir Carte Blanche.

Besides entertaining the foreign nobles, the young Duke could no longer keep off the constantly-recurring idea that something must be done to entertain himself. He shuddered to think where and what he should have been been, had not these gentlemen so providentially arrived. As for again repeating the farce of last year, he felt that it would no longer raise a smile. Yorkshire he shunned. Doncaster made him tremble. A week with the Duke of Burlington at Marringworth; a fortnight with the Fitz-pompeys at Malthorpe; a month with the Graftons at Cleve; and so on: he shuddered at the very idea. Who can see a pantomime more than once? Who could survive a pantomime the twentieth time? All the shifting scenes, and flitting splendour; all the motley crowds of sparkling characters; all the quick changes, and full variety, are, once, enchantment. But when the splendour is discovered to be monotony; the change, order, and the caprice a system; when the characters play ever the same part, and the variety never varies; how dull, how weary, how infinitely flat, is such a world to that man who requires from its converse, not occasional relaxation, but constant excitement!

Pen Bronnock was a new object. At this moment in his life, novelty was indeed a treasure. If he could cater for a month, no expense should be grudged; as for the future, he thrust it from his mind. By taking up his residence, too, at Pen Bronnock, he escaped from all invitations; and so, in a word, the worthy Knight received orders to make all preparations at the palace for the reception of a large party in the course of three weeks.

Sir Carte, as usual, did wonders. There was, fortunately for his employer, no time to build or paint, but some dingy rooms were hung with scarlet cloth; cart-loads of new furniture were sent down; the theatre was re-burnished; the stables put in order; and, what was of infinitely more importance in the estimation of all Englishmen, the neglected pile was 'well aired.'

CHAPTER II.

A Dandy From Vienna

WE ARE in the country, and such a country, that even in Italy we think of thee, native Hesperia! Here, myrtles grow, and fear no blasting north, or blighting east. Here, the south wind blows with that soft breath which brings the bloom to flesh. Here, the land breaks in gentle undulations; and here, blue waters kiss a verdant shore. Hail! to thy thousand bays, and deep-red earth, thy marble quarries, and thy silver veins! Hail! to thy far-extending landscape, whose sparkling villages and streaky fields no clime can match!

Some gales we owe to thee of balmy breath, some gentle hours when life had fewest charms. And we are grateful for all this, to say nothing of your cider and your junkets.

The Duke arrived just as the setting sun crowned the proud palace with his gleamy rays. It was a pile which the immortal Inigo had raised in sympathy with the taste of a noble employer, who had passed his earliest years in Lombardy. Of stone, and sometimes even of marble, with pediments and balustrades, and ornamental windows, and richly-chased keystones, and flights of steps, and here and there a statue, the structure was quite Palladian, though a little dingy, and, on the whole, very imposing.

There were suites of rooms which had no end, and staircases which had no beginning. In this vast pile, nothing was more natural than to lose your way, an agreeable amusement on a rainy morning. There was a collection of pictures, very various, by which phrase we understand not select. Yet they were amusing; and the Canalettis were unrivalled. There was a regular ball-room, and a theatre; so resources were at hand. The scenes, though dusty, were numerous; and the Duke had provided new dresses. The park was not a park; by which we mean, that it was rather a chase than the highly-finished enclosure which we associate with the first title. In fact, Pen Bronnock Chase was the right name of the settlement; but some monarch travelling, having been seized with a spasm, recruited his strength under the roof of his loyal subject, then the chief seat of the House of Hauteville, and having in his urgency been obliged to hold a privy council there, the supreme title of palace was assumed by right.

The domain was bounded on one side by the sea; and here a yacht and some slight craft rode at anchor in a small green bay, and offered an opportunity for the adventurous, and a refuge for the wearied. When you have been bored for an hour or two on earth, it sometimes is a change to be bored for an hour or two on water.

The house was soon full, and soon gay. The guests, and the means of amusing them, were equally numerous. But this was no common *villeggiatura*, no visit to a family with their regular pursuits and matured avocations. The host was as much a guest as any other. The young Duke appointed Lord Squib master of the ceremonies, and gave orders for nothing but constant excitement. Constant excitement his Lordship managed to maintain, for he was experienced, clever, careless and gay, and, for once in his life, had the command of unbounded resources. He ordered, he invented, he prepared, and he expended. They acted, they danced, they sported, they sailed, they feasted, they masqueraded; and when they began to get a little wearied of themselves, and their own powers of diversion gradually vanished, then a public ball was given twice a week at the palace, and all the West of England invited. New faces brought new ideas; new figures brought new fancies. All were delighted with the young Duke, and flattery from novel quarters will for a moment whet even the appetite of the satiated. Simplicity, too, can interest. There were some Misses Gay-weather who got unearthed, who never had been in London, though nature had given them sparkling eyes and springing persons. This tyranny was too bad. Papa was quizzed, mamma flattered, and the daughters' simplicity amused these young lordlings. Rebellion was whispered in the small ears of the Gay weathers. The little heads, too, of the Gay-weathers were turned. They were the constant butt, and the constant resource, of every lounging dandy.

The Bird of Paradise also arranged her professional engagements so as to account with all possible propriety for her professional visit at Pen Bronnock. The musical meeting at Exeter over, she made her appearance, and some concerts were given, which electrified all Cornwall. Count Frill was very strong here; though, to be sure, he also danced, and acted, in all varieties. He was the soul, too, of a masqued ball; but when complimented on his accomplishments, and thanked for his exertions, he modestly depreciated his worth, and panegyrised the dancing-dogs.

As for the Prince, on the whole, he maintained his silence; but it was at length discovered by the fair sex that he was not stupid, but sentimental. When this was made known he rather lost ground with the dark sex, who, before thinking him thick, had vowed that he was a devilish good fellow; but now, being really envious, had their tale and hint, their sneer and sly joke. M. de Whiskerburg had one active accomplishment; this was his dancing. His gallopade was declared to be divine: he absolutely sailed in air. His waltz, at his will, either melted his partner into a dream, or whirled her into a frenzy! Dangerous M. de Whiskerburg!

CHAPTER III.

'A Little Rift.'

IT IS said that the conduct of refined society, in a literary point of view, is, on the whole, productive but of slight interest; that all we can aspire to is, to trace a brilliant picture of brilliant manners; and that when the dance and the festival have been duly inspired by the repartee and the sarcasm, and the gem, the robe, and the plume adroitly lighted up by the lamp and the lustre, our cunning is exhausted. And so your novelist generally twists this golden thread with some substantial silken cord, for use, and works up, with the light dance, and with the heavy dinner, some secret marriage, and some shrouded murder. And thus, by English plots and German mysteries, the page trots on, or jolts, till, in the end, Justice will have her way, and the three volumes are completed.

A plan both good and antique, and also popular, but not our way. We prefer trusting to the slender incidents which spring from out our common intercourse. There is no doubt that that great pumice-stone, Society, smooths down the edges of your thoughts and manners. Bodies of men who pursue the same object must ever resemble each other: the life of the majority must ever be imitation. Thought is a labour to which few are competent; and truth requires for its development as much courage as acuteness. So conduct becomes conventional, and opinion is a legend; and thus all men act and think alike.

But this is not peculiar to what is called fashionable life, it is peculiar to civilisation, which gives the passions less to work upon. Mankind are not more heartless because they are clothed in ermine; it is that their costume attracts us to their characters, and we stare because we find the prince or the peeress neither a conqueror nor a heroine. The great majority of human beings in a country like England glides through existence in perfect ignorance of their natures, so complicated and so controlling is the machinery of our social life! Few can break the bonds that tie them down, and struggle for self-knowledge; fewer, when the talisman is gained, can direct their illuminated energies to the purposes with which they sympathise.

A mode of life which encloses in its circle all the dark and deep results of unbounded indulgence, however it may appear to some who glance over the sparkling surface, does not exactly seem to us one either insipid or uninteresting to the moral speculator; and, indeed, we have long been induced to suspect that the seeds of true sublimity lurk in a life which, like this book, is half fashion and half passion.

We know not how it was, but about this time an unaccountable, almost an imperceptible, coolness seemed to spring up between our hero and the Lady

Aphrodite. If we were to puzzle our brains for ever, we could not give you the reason. Nothing happened, nothing had been said or done, which could indicate its origin. Perhaps this *was* the origin; perhaps the Duke's conduct had become, though unexceptionable, too negative. But here we only throw up a straw. Perhaps, if we must go on suggesting, anxiety ends in callousness.

His Grace had thought so much of her feelings, that he had quite forgotten his own, or worn them out. Her Ladyship, too, was perhaps a little disappointed at the unexpected reconciliation. When we have screwed our courage up to the sticking point, we like not to be baulked. Both, too, perhaps—we go on *perhapsing*—both, too, we repeat, perhaps, could not help mutually viewing each other as the cause of much mutual care and mutual anxiousness. Both, too, perhaps, were a little tired, but without knowing it. The most curious thing, and which would have augured worst to a calm judge, was, that they silently seemed to agree not to understand that any alteration had really taken place between them, which, we think, was a bad sign: because a lover's quarrel, we all know, like a storm in summer, portends a renewal of warm weather or ardent feelings; and a lady is never so well seated in her admirer's heart as when those betters are interchanged which express so much, and those explanations entered upon which explain so little.

And here we would dilate on greater things than some imagine; but, unfortunately, we are engaged. For Newmarket calls Sir Lucius and his friends. We will not join them, having lost enough. His Grace half promised to be one of the party; but when the day came, just remembered the Shropshires were expected, and so was very sorry, and the rest. Lady Aphrodite and himself parted with warmth which remarkably contrasted with their late intercourse, and which neither of them could decide whether it were reviving affection or factitious effort. M. de Whiskerburg and Count Frill departed with Sir Lucius, being extremely desirous to be initiated in the mysteries of the turf, and, above all, to see a real English jockey.

CHAPTER IV.

Satiety.

THE newspapers continued to announce the departures of new visitors to the Duke of St. James, and to dilate upon the protracted and princely festivity of Pen Bron-nock. But while thousands were envying his lot, and hundreds aspiring to share it, what indeed was the condition of our hero?

A month or two had rolled on and if he had not absolutely tasted enjoyment, at least he had thrown off reflection; but as the autumn wore away, and as each day he derived less diversion or distraction from the repetition of the same routine, carried on by different actors, he could no longer control feelings which would be predominant, and those feelings were not such as perhaps might have been expected from one who was receiving the homage of an admiring world. In a word, the Duke of St. James was the most miserable wretch that ever lived.

'Where is this to end?' he asked himself. 'Is this year to close, to bring only a repetition of the past? Well, I have had it all, and what is it? My restless feelings are at last laid, my indefinite appetites are at length exhausted. I have known this mighty world, and where am I? Once, all prospects, all reflections merged in the agitating, the tremulous and panting lust with which I sighed for it. Have I been deceived? Have I been disappointed? Is it different from what I expected? Has it fallen short of my fancy? Has the dexterity of my musings deserted me? Have I under-acted the hero of my reveries? Have I, in short, mismanaged my dÃ©but? Have I blundered? No, no, no! Far, far has it gone beyond even my imagination, and *my* life has, if no other, realised its ideas!

'Who laughs at me? Who does not burn incense before my shrine? What appetite have I not gratified? What gratification has proved bitter? My vanity! Has it been, for an instant, mortified? Am I not acknowledged the most brilliant hero of the most brilliant society in Europe? Intense as is my self-love, has it not been gorged? Luxury and splendour were my youthful dreams, and have I not realised the very romance of indulgence and magnificence? My career has been one long triumph. My palaces, and my gardens, and my jewels, my dress, my furniture, my equipages, my horses, and my festivals, these used to occupy my meditations, when I could only meditate; and have my determinations proved a delusion? Ask the admiring world.

'And now for the great point to which all this was to tend, which all this was to fascinate and subdue, to adorn, to embellish, to delight, to honour. Woman! Oh! when I first dared, among the fields of Eton, to dwell upon the soft yet agitating fancy, that some day my existence might perhaps be rendered more intense, by the admiration of these maddening but then mysterious creatures; could, could I have dreamt of what has happened? Is not this the very point in which my career has most out-topped my lofty hopes?

'I have read, and sometimes heard, of *satiety*. It must then be satiety that I feel; for I do feel more like a doomed man, than a young noble full of blood and youth. And yet, satiety; it is a word. What then? A word is breath, and am I wiser? Satiety! Satiety! Satiety! Oh! give me happiness! Oh! give me love!

'Ay! there it is, I feel it now. Too well I feel that happiness must spring from purer fountains than self-love. We are not born merely for ourselves, and they who, full of pride, make the trial, as I have done, and think that the world is made for them, and not for mankind, must come to as bitter results, perhaps as bitter a fate; for, by Heavens! I am half tempted at this moment to fling myself from off this cliff, and so end all.

'Why should I live? For virtue, and for duty; to compensate for all my folly, and to achieve some slight good end with my abused and unparalleled means. Ay! it is all vastly rational, and vastly sublime, but it is too late. I feel the exertion above me. I am a lost man.

'We cannot work without a purpose and an aim. I had mine, although it was a false one, and I succeeded. Had I one now I might succeed again, but my heart is a dull void. And Caroline, that gentle girl, will not give me what I want; and to offer her but half a heart may break hers, and I would not bruise that delicate bosom to save my dukedom. Those sad, silly parents of hers have already done mischief enough; but I will see Darrell, and will at least arrange that. I like him, and will make him my friend for her sake. God! God! why am I not loved! A word from her, and all would change. I feel a something in me which could put all right. I have the will, and she could give the power.

'Now see what a farce life is! I shall go on, Heaven knows how! I cannot live long. Men like me soon bloom and fade. What I may come to, I dread to think. There is a dangerous facility in my temper; I know it well, for I know more of myself than people think; there is a dangerous facility which, with May Dacre, might be the best guaranty of virtue; but with all others, for all others are at the best weak things, will as certainly render me despicable, perhaps degraded. I hear the busy devil whispering even now. It is my demon. Now, I say, see what a farce life is! I shall die like a dog, as I have lived like a fool; and then my epitaph will be in everybody's mouth. Here are the consequences of self-indulgence: here is a fellow, forsooth, who thought only of the gratification of his vile appetites; and by the living Heaven, am I not standing here among my hereditary rocks, and sighing to the ocean, to be virtuous!

'She knew me well, she read me in a minute, and spoke more truth at that last meeting than is in a thousand sermons. It is out of our power to redeem ourselves. Our whole existence is a false, foul state, totally inimical to love and purity, and domestic gentleness, and calm delight. Yet are we envied! Oh! could these fools see us at any other time except surrounded by our glitter, and hear of us at any other moment save in the first bloom of youth, which is, even then, often wasted; could they but mark our manhood, and view our hollow marriages, and disappointed passions; could they but see the traitors that we have for sons, the daughters that own no duty; could they but watch us even to our grave, tottering after some fresh bauble, some vain delusion, which, to the last, we hope may prove a substitute for what we have never found through life, a contented mind, they would do something else but envy us.

'But I stand prating when I am wanted. I must home. Home! O sacred word! and then comes night! Horrible night! Horrible day! It seems to me I am upon the eve of some monstrous folly, too ridiculous to be a crime, and yet as fatal. I have half a mind to go and marry the Bird of Paradise, out of pure pique with myself, and with the world.'

CHAPTER V.

A Startling Letter

SOUTHEY, that virtuous man, whom Wisdom calls her own, somewhere thanks God that he was not born to a great estate. We quite agree with the seer of Keswick; it is a bore. Provided a man can enjoy every personal luxury, what profits it that your flag waves on castles you never visit, and that you count rents which you never receive? And yet there are some things which your miserable, moderate incomes cannot command, and which one might like to have; for instance, a band.

A complete, a consummate band, in uniforms of uncut white velvet, with a highly-wrought gold button, just tipped with a single pink topaz, appears to me [Greek phrase]. When we die, 'Band' will be found impressed upon our heart, like 'Frigate' on the core of Nelson. The negroes should have their noses bored, as well as their ears, and hung with rings of rubies. The kettle-drums should be of silver. And with regard to a great estate, no doubt it brings great cares; or, to get free of them, the estate must be neglected, and then it is even worse.

Elections come on, and all your members are thrown out; so much for neglected influence. Agricultural distress prevails, and all your farms are thrown up; so much for neglected tenants. Harassed by leases, renewals, railroads, fines, and mines, you are determined that life shall not be worn out by these continual and petty cares. Thinking it somewhat hard, that, because you have two hundred thousand a-year, you have neither ease nor enjoyment, you find a remarkably clever man, who manages everything for you. Enchanted with his energy, his acuteness, and his foresight, fascinated by your increasing rent-roll, and the total disappearance of arrears, you dub him your right hand, introduce him to all your friends, and put him into Parliament; and then, fired by the ambition of rivalling his patron, he disburses, embezzles, and decamps.

But where is our hero? Is he forgotten? Never! But in the dumps, blue devils, and so on. A little bilious, it may be, and dull. He scarcely would amuse you at this moment. So we come forward with a graceful bow; the Jack Pudding of our doctor, who is behind.

In short, that is to say, in long—for what is true use of this affected brevity? When this tale is done, what have you got? So let us make it last. We quite repent of having intimated so much: in future, it is our intention to develop more, and to describe, and to delineate, and to define, and, in short, to bore. You know the model of this kind of writing, Richardson, whom we shall revive. In future, we shall, as a novelist, take Clarendon's Rebellion for our guide, and write our hero's notes, or heroine's letters, like a state paper, or a broken treaty.

The Duke, and the young Duke—oh! to be a Duke, and to be young, it is too much—was seldom seen by the gay crowd who feasted in his hall. His mornings now were lonely, and if, at night, his eye still sparkled, and his step still sprang, why, between us, wine gave him beauty, and wine gave him grace.

It was the dreary end of dull November, and the last company were breaking off. The Bird of Paradise, according to her desire, had gone to Brighton, where his Grace had presented her with a tenement, neat, light, and finished; and though situated amid the wilds of Kemp Town, not more than one hyÃ¦na on a night ventured to come down from the adjacent heights. He had half promised to join her, because he thought he might as well be there as here, and consequently he had not invited a fresh supply of visitors from town, or rather from the country. As he was hesitating about what he should do, he received a letter from his bankers, which made him stare. He sent for the groom of the chambers, and was informed the house was clear, save that some single men still lingered, as is their wont. They never take a hint. His Grace ordered his carriage; and, more alive than he had been for the last two months, dashed off to town.

CHAPTER VI.

The Cost of Pleasure

THE letter from his bankers informed the Duke of St. James that not only was the half-million exhausted, but, in pursuance of their powers, they had sold out all his stock, and, in reliance on his credit, had advanced even beyond it. They were ready to accommodate him in every possible way, and to advance as much more as he could desire, at five per cent.! Sweet five per cent.! Oh! magical five per cent.! Lucky the rogue now who gets three. Nevertheless, they thought it but proper to call his Grace's attention to the circumstance, and to put him in possession of the facts. Something unpleasant is coming when men are anxious to tell the truth.

The Duke of St. James had never affected to be a man of business; still, he had taken it for granted that pecuniary embarrassment was not ever to be counted among his annoyances. He wanted something to do, and determined to look into his affairs, merely to amuse himself.

The bankers were most polite. They brought their books, also several packets of papers neatly tied up, and were ready to give every information. The Duke asked for results. He found that the turf, the Alhambra, the expenses of his outfit in purchasing the lease and furniture of his mansion, and the rest, had, with his expenditure, exhausted his first year's income; but he reconciled himself to this, because he chose to consider them extraordinary expenses. Then the festivities of Pen Bronnock counterbalanced the economy of his more scrambling life the preceding year; yet he had not exceeded his income much. Then he came to Sir Carte's account. He began to get a little frightened. Two hundred and fifty thousand had been swallowed by Hauteville Castle: one hundred and twenty thousand by Hauteville House. Ninety-six thousand had been paid for furniture. There were also some awkward miscellanies which, in addition, exceeded the half-million.

This was smashing work; but castles and palaces, particularly of the correctest style of architecture, are not to be had for nothing. The Duke had always devoted the half-million to this object; but he had intended that sum to be sufficient. What puzzled and what annoyed him was a queer suspicion that his resources had been exhausted without his result being obtained. He sent for Sir Carte, who gave every information, and assured him that, had he had the least idea that a limit was an object, he would have made his arrangements accordingly. As it was, he assured the young Duke that he would be the Lord of the most sumptuous and accurate castle, and of the most gorgeous and tasteful palace, in Europe. He was proceeding with a cloud of words, when his employer cut him short by a peremptory demand of the exact sum requisite for the completion of his plans. Sir Carte was confused, and requested time. The estimates should be sent in as quickly as possible. The clerks should sit up all night, and even his own rest should not be an object, any more than the Duke's purse. So they parted.

The Duke determined to run down to Brighton for change of scene. He promised his bankers to examine everything on his return; in the meantime, they were to make all necessary advances, and honour his drafts to any amount.

He found the city of chalk and shingles not quite so agreeable as last year. He discovered that it had no trees. There was there, also, just everybody that he did not wish to see. It was one great St. James' Street, and seemed only an anticipation of that very season which he dreaded. He was half inclined to go somewhere else, but could not fix upon any spot. London might be agreeable, as it was empty; but then those confounded accounts awaited him. The Bird of Paradise was a sad bore. He really began to suspect that she was little better than an idiot: then, she ate so much, and he hated your eating women. He gladly shuffled her off on that fool Count Frill, who daily brought his guitar to Kemp Town. They just suited each other. What a madman he had been, to have embarrassed himself with this creature! It would cost him a pretty ransom now before he could obtain his freedom. How we change! Already the Duke of St. James began to think of pounds, shillings, and pence. A year ago, so long as he could extricate himself from a scrape by force of cash, he thought himself a lucky fellow.

The Graftons had not arrived, but were daily expected. He really could not stand them. As for Lady Afy, he execrated the greenhornism which had made him feign a passion, and then get caught where he meant to capture. As for Sir Lucius, he wished to Heaven he would just take it into his head to repay him the fifteen thousand he had lent him at that confounded election, to say nothing of anything else.

Then there was Burlington, with his old loves and his new dances. He wondered how the deuce that fellow could be amused with such frivolity, and always look so serene and calm. Then there was Squib: that man never knew when to leave off joking; and Annesley, with his false refinement; and Darrell, with his petty ambition. He felt quite sick, and took a solitary ride: but he flew from Scylla to Charybdis. Mrs. Montfort could not forget their many delightful canters last season to Rottingdean, and, lo! she was at his side. He wished her down the cliff.

In this fit of the spleen he went to the theatre: there were eleven people in the boxes. He listened to the 'School for Scandal.' Never was slander more harmless. He sat it all out, and was sorry when it was over, but was consoled by the devils of 'Der Freischutz.' How sincerely, how ardently did he long to sell himself to the demon! It was eleven o'clock, and he dreaded the play to be over as if he were a child. What to do with himself, or where to go, he was equally at a loss. The door of the box opened, and entered Lord Bagshot. If it must be an acquaintance, this cub was better than any of his refined and lately cherished companions.

'Well, Bag, what are you doing with yourself?'

'Oh! I don't know; just looking in for a lark. Any game?'

'On my honour, I can't say.'

'What's that girl? Oh! I see; that's little Wilkins. There's Moll Otway. Nothing new. I shall go and rattle the bones a little; eh! my boy?'

'Rattle the bones? what is that?'

'Don't you know?' and here this promising young peer manually explained his meaning.

'What do you play at?' asked the Duke.

'Hazard, for my money; but what you like.'

'Where?'

'We meet at De Berghem's. There is a jolly set of us. All crack men. When my governor is here, I never go. He is so jealous. I suppose there must be only one gamester in the family; eh! my covey?' Lord Bagshot, excited by the unusual affability of the young Duke, grew quite familiar.

'I have half a mind to look in with you,' said his Grace with a careless air.

'Oh! come along, by all means. They'll be devilish glad to see you. De Berghem was saying the other day what a nice fellow you were, and how he should like to know you. You don't know De Berghem, do you?'

'I have seen him. I know enough of him.'

They quitted the theatre together, and under the guidance of Lord Bagshot, stopped at a door in Brunswick Terrace. There they found collected a numerous party, but all persons of consideration. The Baron, who had once been a member of the diplomatic corps, and now lived in England, by choice, on his pension and private fortune, received them with marked courtesy. Proud of his companion, Lord Bagshot's hoarse, coarse, idiot voice seemed ever braying. His frequent introductions of the Duke of St. James were excruciating, and it required all the freezing of a finished manner to pass through this fiery ordeal. His Grace was acquainted with most of the guests by sight, and to some he even bowed. They were chiefly men of a certain age, with the exception of two or three young peers like himself.

There was the Earl of Castlefort, plump and luxurious, with a youthful wig, who, though a sexagenarian, liked no companion better than a minor. His Lordship was the most amiable man in the world, and the most lucky; but the first was his merit, and the second was not his fault. There was the juvenile Lord Dice, who boasted of having done his brothers out of their miserable 5,000L. patrimony, and all in one night. But the wrinkle that had already ruffled his once clear brow, his sunken eye, and his convulsive lip, had been thrown, we suppose, into the bargain, and, in our opinion, made it a dear one. There was Temple Grace, who had run through four fortunes, and ruined four sisters. Withered, though only thirty, one thing alone remained to be lost, what he called his honour, which was already on the scent to play booty. There was Cogit, who, when he was drunk, swore that he had had a father; but this was deemed the only exception to *in vino Veritas.* Who he was, the Goddess of Chance alone could decide; and we have often thought that he might bear the same relation to her as Ã†neas to the Goddess of Beauty. His age was as great a mystery as anything else. He dressed still like a boy, yet some vowed he was eighty. He must have been Salathiel. Property he never had, and yet he contrived to live; connection he was not born with, yet he was upheld by a set. He never played, yet he was the most skilful dealer going. He did the honours of a *rouge et noir* table to a miracle; and looking, as he thought, most genteel in a crimson waistcoat and a gold chain, raked up the spoils, or complacently announced aprÃ¨s. Lord Castlefort had few secrets from him: he was the jackal to these prowling beasts of prey; looked out for pigeons, got up little parties to Richmond or Brighton, sang a song when the rest were too anxious to make a noise, and yet desired a little life, and perhaps could cog a die, arrange a looking-glass, or mix a tumbler.

Unless the loss of an occasional napoleon at a German watering-place is to be so stigmatised, gaming had never formed one of the numerous follies of the Duke of St. James. Rich, and gifted with a generous, sanguine, and luxurious disposition, he had never been tempted by the desire of gain, or as some may perhaps maintain, by the desire of excitement, to seek assistance or enjoyment in a mode of life which stultifies all our fine fancies, deadens all our noble emotions, and mortifies all our beautiful aspirations.

We know that we are broaching a doctrine which many will start at, and which some will protest against, when we declare our belief that no person, whatever his apparent wealth, ever yet gamed except from the prospect of immediate gain. We hear much of want of excitement, of ennui, of satiety; and then the gaming-table is announced as a sort of substitute for opium, wine, or any other mode of obtaining a more intense vitality at the cost of reason. Gaming is too active, too anxious, too complicated, too troublesome;

in a word, *too sensible* an affair for such spirits, who fly only to a sort of dreamy and indefinite distraction.

The fact is, gaming is a matter of business. Its object is tangible, clear, and evident. There is nothing high, or inflammatory, or exciting; no false magnificence, no visionary elevation, in the affair at all. It is the very antipodes to enthusiasm of any kind. It pre-supposes in its votary a mind essentially mercantile. All the feelings that are in its train are the most mean, the most commonplace, and the most annoying of daily life, and nothing would tempt the gamester to experience them except the great object which, as a matter of calculation, he is willing to aim at on such terms. No man flies to the gaming-table in a paroxysm. The first visit requires the courage of a forlorn hope. The first stake will make the lightest mind anxious, the firmest hand tremble, and the stoutest heart falter. After the first stake, it is all a matter of calculation and management, even in games of chance. Night after night will men play at *rouge et noir*, upon what they call a system, and for hours their attention never ceases, any more than it would if they were in the shop or oh the wharf. No manual labour is more fatiguing, and more degrading to the labourer, than gaming. Every gamester feels ashamed. And this vice, this worst vice, from whose embrace, moralists daily inform us, man can never escape, is just the one from which the majority of men most completely, and most often, free themselves. Infinite is the number of men who have lost thousands in their youth, and never dream of chance again. It is this pursuit which, oftener than any other, leads man to self-knowledge. Appalled by the absolute destruction on the verge of which he finds his early youth just stepping; aghast at the shadowy crimes which, under the influence of this life, seem, as it were, to rise upon his soul; often he hurries to emancipate himself from this fatal thraldom, and with a ruined fortune, and marred prospects, yet thanks his Creator that his soul is still white, his conscience clear, and that, once more, he breathes the sweet air of heaven.

And our young Duke, we must confess, gamed, as all other men have gamed, for money. His satiety had fled the moment that his affairs were embarrassed. The thought suddenly came into his head while Bag-shot was speaking. He determined to make an effort to recover; and so completely was it a matter of business with him, that he reasoned that, in the present state of his affairs, a few thousands more would not signify; that these few thousands might lead to vast results, and that, if they did, he would bid adieu to the gaming-table with the same coolness with which he had saluted it.

Yet he felt a little odd when he first 'rattled the bones;' and his affected nonchalance made him constrained. He fancied every one was watching him; while, on the contrary, all were too much interested in their own different parties. This feeling, however, wore off.

According to every novelist, and the moralists 'our betters,' the Duke of St. James should have been fortunate at least to-night. You always win at first, you know. If so, we advise said children of fancy and of fact to pocket their gains, and not play again. The young Duke had not the opportunity of thus acting. He lost fifteen hundred pounds, and at half-past five he quitted the Baron's.

Hot, bilious, with a confounded twang in his mouth, and a cracking pain in his head, he stood one moment and sniffed in the salt sea breeze. The moon was unfortunately on the waters, and her cool, beneficent light reminded him, with disgust, of the hot, burning glare of the Baron's saloon. He thought of May Dacre, but clenched his fist, and drove her image from his mind.

CHAPTER VII.

Dangerous Friends

HE ROSE late, and as he was lounging over his breakfast, entered Lord Bagshot and the Baron. Already the young Duke began to experience one of the gamester's curses, the intrusive society of those of whom you are ashamed. Eight-and-forty hours ago, Lord Bagshot would no more have dared to call on the Duke of St. James than to call at the Pavilion; and now, with that reckless want of tact which marks the innately vulgar, he seemed to triumph in their unhallowed intimacy, and lounging into his Grace's apartment with that half-shuffling, hair-swaggering air indicative of the 'cove,' hat cocked, and thumbs in his great-coat pockets, cast his complacent eye around, and praised his Grace's 'rooms.' Lord Bagshot, who for the occasional notice of the Duke of St. James had been so long a ready and patient butt, now appeared to assume a higher character, and addressed his friend in a tone and manner which were authorised by the equality of their rank and the sympathy of their tastes. If this change had taken place in the conduct of the Viscount, it was not a singular one. The Duke also, to his surprise, found himself addressing his former butt in a very different style from that which he had assumed in the ballroom of Doncaster. In vain he tried to rally, in vain he tried to snub. It was indeed in vain. He no longer possessed any right to express his contempt of his companion. That contempt, indeed, he still felt. He despised Lord Bagshot still, but he also despised himself.

The soft and silky Baron was a different sort of personage; but there was something sinister in all his elaborate courtesy and highly artificial manner, which did not touch the feelings of the Duke, whose courtesy was but the expression of his noble feelings, and whose grace was only the impulse of his rich and costly blood. Baron de Berghem was too attentive, and too deferential. He smiled and bowed too much. He made no allusion to the last night's scene, nor did his tutored companion, but spoke of different and lighter subjects, in a manner which at once proved his experience of society, the liveliness of his talents, and the cultivation of his taste. He told many stories, all short and poignant, and always about princes and princesses. Whatever was broached, he always had his *apropos* of Vienna, and altogether seemed an experienced, mild, tolerant man of the world, not bigoted to any particular opinions upon any subject, but of a truly liberal and philosophic mind.

When they had sat chatting for half-an-hour, the Baron developed the object of his visit, which was to endeavour to obtain the pleasure of his Grace's company at dinner, to taste some wild boar and try some tokay. The Duke, who longed again for action, accepted the invitation; and then they parted.

Our hero was quite surprised at the feverish anxiety with which he awaited the hour of union. He thought that seven o'clock would never come. He had no appetite at breakfast, and after that he rode, but luncheon was a blank. In the midst of the operation, he found himself in a brown study, calculating chances. All day long his imagination had been playing hazard, or *rouge et noir*. Once he thought that he had discovered an infallible way of winning at the latter. On the long run, he was convinced it must answer, and he panted to prove it.

Seven o'clock at last arrived, and he departed to Brunswick Terrace. There was a brilliant party to meet him: the same set as last night, but select. He was faint, and did justice to the *cuisine* of his host, which was indeed remarkable. When we are drinking a man's good wine, it is difficult to dislike him. Prejudice decreases with every draught. His Grace began to think the Baron as good-hearted as agreeable. He was grateful for the continued attentions of old Castlefort, who, he now found out, had been very well acquainted with his father, and once even made a trip to Spa with him. Lord Dice he could not manage to endure, though that worthy was, for him, remarkably courteous, and grinned with his parchment face, like a good-humoured ghoul. Temple Grace and the Duke became almost intimate. There was an amiable candour in that gentleman's address, a softness in his tones, and an unstudied and extremely interesting delicacy in his manner, which in this society was remarkable. Tom Cogit never presumed to come near the young Duke, but paid him constant attention. He sat at the bottom of the table, and was ever sending a servant with some choice wine, or recommending him, through some third person, some choice dish. It is pleasant to be 'made much of,' as Shakspeare says, even by scoundrels. To be king of your company is a poor ambition, yet homage is homage, and smoke is smoke, whether it come out of the chimney of a palace or of a workhouse.

The banquet was not hurried. Though all wished it finished, no one liked to appear urgent. It was over at last, and they walked up-stairs, where the tables were arranged for all parties, and all play. Tom Cogit went up a few minutes before them, like the lady of the mansion, to review the lights, and arrange the cards. Feminine Tom Cogit!

The events of to-night were much the same as of the preceding one. The Duke was a loser, but his losses were not considerable. He retired about the same hour, with a head not so hot, or heavy: and he never looked at the moon, or thought of May Dacre. The only wish that reigned in his soul was a longing for another opportunity, and he had agreed to dine with the Baron, before he left Brunswick Terrace.

- 215 -

Thus passed a week, one night the Duke of St. James redeeming himself, another falling back to his old position, now pushing on to Madrid, now re-crossing the Tagus. On the whole, he had lost four or five thousand pounds, a mere trifle to what, as he had heard, had been lost and gained by many of his companions during only the present season. On the whole, he was one of the most moderate of these speculators, generally played at the large table, and never joined any of those private coteries, some of which he had observed, and of some of which he had heard. Yet this was from no prudential resolve or temperate resolution. The young Duke was heartily tired of the slight results of all his anxiety, hopes, and plans, and ardently wished for some opportunity of coming to closer and more decided action. The Baron also had resolved that an end should be put to this skirmishing; but he was a calm head, and never hurried anything.

'I hope your Grace has been lucky to-night!' said the Baron one evening, strolling up to the Duke: 'as for myself, really, if Dice goes on playing, I shall give up banking. That fellow must have a talisman. I think he has broken more banks than any man living. The best thing he did of that kind was the roulette story at Paris. You have heard of that?'

'Was that Lord Dice?'

'Oh yes! he does everything. He must have cleared his hundred thousand last year. I have suffered a good deal since I have been in England. Castlefort has pulled in a great deal of my money. I wonder to whom he will leave his property?'

'You think him rich?'

'Oh! he will cut up large!' said the Baron, elevating his eyebrows. 'A pleasant man too! I do not know any man that I would sooner play with than Castlefort; no one who loses his money with better temper.'

'Or wins it,' said his Grace.

'That we all do,' said the Baron, faintly laughing. 'Your Grace has lost, and you do not seem particularly dull. You will have your revenge. Those who lose at first are always the children of fortune. I always dread a man who loses at first. All I beg is, that you will not break my bank.'

'Why! you see I am not playing now.' 'I am not surprised. There is too much heat and noise here,' said he. 'We will have a quiet dinner some day, and play at our ease. Come to-morrow, and I will ask Castlefort and Dice. I should uncommonly like, *entre nous*, to win some of their money. I will take care that nobody shall be here whom you would not like to meet. By-the-bye, whom were you riding with this morning? Fine woman!'

CHAPTER VIII.

Birds of Prey

THE young Duke had accepted the invitation of the Baron de Berg-hem for to-morrow, and accordingly, himself, Lords Castlefort and Dice, and Temple Grace assembled in Brunswick Terrace at the usual hour. The dinner was studiously plain, and very little wine was drunk; yet everything was perfect. Tom Cogit stepped in to carve in his usual silent manner. He always came in and went out of a room without anyone observing him. He winked familiarly to Temple Grace, but scarcely presumed to bow to the Duke. He was very busy about the wine, and dressed the wild fowl in a manner quite unparalleled. Tom Cogit was the man for a sauce for a brown bird. What a mystery he made of it! Cayenne and Burgundy and limes were ingredients, but there was a magic in the incantation with which he alone was acquainted. He took particular care to send a most perfect portion to the young Duke, and he did this, as he paid all attentions to influential strangers, with the most marked consciousness of the sufferance which permitted his presence: never addressing his Grace, but audibly whispering to the servant, 'Take this to the Duke;' or asking the attendant, 'whether his Grace would try the Hermitage?'

After dinner, with the exception of Cogit, who was busied in compounding some wonderful liquid for the future refreshment, they sat down to Â©cartÂ©. Without having exchanged a word upon the subject, there seemed a general understanding among all the parties that to-night was to be a pitched battle, and they began at once, briskly. Yet, in spite of their universal determination, midnight arrived without anything decisive. Another hour passed over, and then Tom Cogit kept touching the Baron's elbow and whispering in a voice which everybody could understand. All this meant that supper was ready. It was brought into the room.

Gaming has one advantage, it gives you an appetite; that is to say, so long as you have a chance remaining. The Duke had thousands; for at present his resources were unimpaired, and he was exhausted by the constant attention and anxiety of five hours. He passed over the delicacies and went to the side-table, and began cutting himself some cold roast beef. Tom Cogit ran up, not to his Grace, but to the Baron, to announce the shocking fact that the Duke of St. James was enduring great trouble; and then the Baron asked his Grace to permit Mr. Cogit to serve him. Our hero devoured—we use the word advisedly, as fools say in the House of Commons—he devoured the roast beef, and rejecting the Hermitage with disgust, asked for porter.

They set to again fresh as eagles. At six o'clock accounts were so complicated that they stopped to make up their books. Each played with his memoranda and pencil at his side. Nothing fatal had yet happened. The Duke owed Lord

Dice about five thousand pounds, and Temple Grace owed him as many hundreds. Lord Castlefort also was his debtor to the tune of seven hundred and fifty, and the Baron was in his books, but slightly. Every half-hour they had a new pack of cards, and threw the used one on the floor. All this time Tom Cogit did nothing but snuff the candles, stir the fire, bring them a new pack, and occasionally make a tumbler for them. At eight o'clock the Duke's situation was worsened. The run was greatly against him, and perhaps his losses were doubled. He pulled up again the next hour or two; but nevertheless, at ten o'clock, owed everyone something. No one offered to give over; and everyone, perhaps, felt that his object was not obtained. They made their toilets and went down-stairs to breakfast. In the meantime the shutters were opened, the room aired, and in less than an hour they were at it again.

They played till dinner-time without intermission; and though the Duke made some desperate efforts, and some successful ones, his losses were, nevertheless, trebled. Yet he ate an excellent dinner and was not at all depressed; because the more he lost, the more his courage and his resources seemed to expand. At first he had limited himself to ten thousand; after breakfast it was to have been twenty thousand; then thirty thousand was the ultimatum; and now he dismissed all thoughts of limits from his mind, and was determined to risk or gain everything.

At midnight, he had lost forty-eight thousand pounds. Affairs now began to be serious. His supper was not so hearty. While the rest were eating, he walked about the room, and began to limit his ambition to recovery, and not to gain. When you play to win back, the fun is over: there is nothing to recompense you for your bodily tortures and your degraded feelings; and the very best result that can happen, while it has no charms, seems to your cowed mind impossible.

On they played, and the Duke lost more. His mind was jaded. He floundered, he made desperate efforts, but plunged deeper in the slough. Feeling that, to regain his ground, each card must tell, he acted on each as if it must win, and the consequences of this insanity (for a gamester at such a crisis is really insane) were, that his losses were prodigious.

Another morning came, and there they sat, ankle-deep in cards. No attempt at breakfast now, no affectation of making a toilet or airing the room. The atmosphere was hot, to be sure, but it well became such a Hell. There they sat, in total, in positive forgetfulness of everything but the hot game they were hunting down. There was not a man in the room, except Tom Cogit, who could have told you the name of the town in which they were living. There they sat, almost breathless, watching every turn with the fell look in their cannibal eyes which showed their total inability to sympathise with their fellow-beings. All forms of society had been long forgotten. There was no snuff-box handed about now, for courtesy, admiration, or a pinch; no affectation of occasionally making a remark upon any other topic but the all-engrossing one. Lord Castlefort rested with his arms on the table: a false tooth had got unhinged. His Lordship, who, at any other time, would have been most annoyed, coolly put it in his pocket. His cheeks had fallen, and he looked twenty years older. Lord Dice had torn off his cravat, and his hair hung down over his callous, bloodless cheeks, straight as silk. Temple Grace looked as if he were blighted by lightning; and his deep blue eyes gleamed like a hyaena's. The Baron was least changed. Tom Cogit, who smelt that the crisis was at hand, was as quiet as a bribed rat.

On they played till six o'clock in the evening, and then they agreed to desist till after dinner. Lord Dice threw himself on a sofa. Lord Castlefort breathed with difficulty. The rest walked about. While they were resting on their oars, the young Duke roughly made up his accounts. He found that he was minus about one hundred thousand pounds.

Immense as this loss was, he was more struck, more appalled, let us say, at the strangeness of the surrounding scene, than even by his own ruin. As he looked upon his fellow gamesters, he seemed, for the first time in his life, to gaze upon some of those hideous demons of whom he had read. He looked in the mirror at himself. A blight seemed to have fallen over his beauty, and his presence seemed accursed. He had pursued a dissipated, even more than a dissipated career. Many were the nights that had been spent by him not on his couch; great had been the exhaustion that he had often experienced; haggard had sometimes even been the lustre of his youth. But when had been marked upon his brow this harrowing care? when had his features before been stamped with this anxiety, this anguish, this baffled desire, this strange unearthly scowl, which made him even tremble? What! was it possible? it could not be, that in time he was to be like those awful, those unearthly, those unhallowed things that were around him. He felt as if he had fallen from his state, as if he had dishonoured his ancestry, as if he had betrayed his trust.

He felt a criminal. In the darkness of his meditations a flash burst from his lurid mind, a celestial light appeared to dissipate this thickening gloom, and his soul felt as if it were bathed with the softening radiancy. He thought of May Dacre, he thought of everything that was pure, and holy, and beautiful, and luminous, and calm. It was the innate virtue of the man that made this appeal to his corrupted nature. His losses seemed nothing; his dukedom would be too slight a ransom for freedom from these ghouls, and for the breath of the sweet air.

He advanced to the Baron, and expressed his desire to play no more. There was an immediate stir. All jumped up, and now the deed was done. Cant, in spite of their exhaustion, assumed her reign. They begged him to have his revenge, were quite annoyed at the result, had no doubt he would recover if he proceeded. Without noticing their remarks, he seated himself at the table, and wrote cheques for their respective amounts, Tom Cogit jumping up and bringing him the inkstand. Lord Castlefort, in the most affectionate manner, pocketed the draft; at the same time recommending the Duke not to be in a hurry, but to send it when he was cool. Lord Dice received his with a bow, Temple Grace with a sigh, the Baron with an avowal of his readiness always to give him his revenge.

The Duke, though sick at heart, would not leave the room with any evidence of a broken spirit; and when Lord Castlefort again repeated, 'Pay us when we meet again,' he said, 'I think it very improbable that we shall meet again, my Lord. I wished to know what gaming was. I had heard a great deal about it. It is not so very disgusting; but I am a young man, and cannot play tricks with my complexion.'

He reached his house. The Bird was out. He gave orders for himself not to be disturbed, and he went to bed; but in vain he tried to sleep. What rack exceeds the torture of an excited brain and an exhausted body? His hands and feet were like ice, his brow like fire; his ears rung with supernatural roaring; a nausea had seized upon him, and death he would have welcomed. In vain, in vain he courted repose; in vain, in vain he had recourse to every expedient to wile himself to slumber. Each minute he started from his pillow with some phrase which reminded him of his late fearful society. Hour after hour moved on with its leaden pace; each hour he heard strike, and each hour seemed an age. Each hour was only a signal to cast off some covering, or shift his position. It was, at length, morning. With a feeling that he should go mad if he remained any longer in bed, he rose, and paced his chamber. The air refreshed him. He threw himself on the floor; the cold crept over his senses, and he slept.

CHAPTER IX.

A Duke Without A Friend

O YE immortal Gods! ye are still immortal, although no longer ye hover o'er Olympus. The Crescent glitters on your mountain's base, and Crosses spring from out its toppling crags. But in vain the Mufti, and the Patriarch, and the Pope flout at your past traditions. They are married to man's memory by the sweetest chain that ever Fancy wove for Love. The poet is a priest, who does not doubt the inspiration of his oracles; and your shrines are still served by a faithful band, who love the beautiful and adore the glorious! In vain, in vain they tell us your divinity is a dream. From the cradle to the grave, our thoughts and feelings take their colour from you! O! Ã†giochus, the birch has often proved thou art still a thunderer; and, although thy twanging bow murmur no longer through the avenging air, many an apple twig still vindicates thy outraged dignity, *pulcher* Apollo.

O, ye immortal Gods! nothing so difficult as to begin a chapter, and therefore have we flown to you. In literature, as in life, it is the first step; you know the rest. After a paragraph or so our blood Is up, and even our jaded hackneys scud along, and warm up into friskiness.

The Duke awoke: another day of his eventful life is now to run its course. He found that the Bird of Paradise had not returned from an excursion to a neighbouring park: he left a note for her, apprising her of his departure to London, and he despatched an affectionate letter to Lady Aphrodite, which was the least that he could do, considering that he perhaps quitted Brighton the day of her arrival. And having done all this, he ordered his horses, and before noon was on his first stage.

It was his birthday. He had completed his twenty-third year. This was sufficient, even if he had no other inducement, to make him indulge in some slight reflection. These annual summings up are awkward things, even to the prosperous and the happy, but to those who are the reverse, who are discontented with themselves, and find that youth melting away which they believe can alone achieve anything, I think a birthday is about the most gloomy four-and-twenty hours that ever flap their damp dull wings over melancholy man.

Yet the Duke of St. James was rather thoughtful than melancholy. His life had been too active of late to allow him to indulge much in that passive mood. 'I may never know what happiness is,' thought his Grace, as he leaned back in his whirling britzska, 'but I think I know what happiness is not. It is not the career which I have hitherto pursued. All this excitement which they talk of so much wears out the mind, and, I begin to believe, even the body, for certainly my energies seem deserting me. But two years, two miserable years, four-and-twenty months, eight-and-forty times the hours, the few hours, that I have been worse than wasting here, and I am shipwrecked, fairly bulged. Yet I have done everything, tried everything, and my career has been an eminent career. Woe to the wretch who trusts to his pampered senses for felicity! Woe to the wretch who flies from the bright goddess Sympathy, to sacrifice before the dark idol Self-love! Ah! I see too late, we were made for each other. Too late, I discover the beautiful results of this great principle of creation. Oh! the blunders of an unformed character! Oh! the torture of an ill-regulated mind!

'Give me a life with no fierce alternations of rapture and anguish, no impossible hopes, no mad depression. Free me from the delusions which succeed each other like scentless roses, that are ever blooming. Save me from the excitement which brings exhaustion, and from the passion that procreates remorse. Give me the luminous mind, where recognised and paramount duty dispels the harassing, ascertains the doubtful, confirms the wavering, sweetens the bitter. Give me content. Oh! give me love!

'How is it to end? What is to become of me? Can nothing rescue me? Is there no mode of relief, no place of succour, no quarter of refuge, no hope of salvation? I cannot right myself, and there is an end of it. Society, society, society! I owe thee much; and perhaps in working in thy service, those feelings might be developed which I am now convinced are the only source of happiness; but I am plunged too deep in the quag. I have no impulse, no call. I know not how it is, but my energies, good and evil, seem alike vanishing. There stares that fellow at my carriage! God! willingly would I break the stones upon the road for a year, to clear my mind of all the past!'

A carriage dashed by, and a lady bowed. It was Mrs. Dallington Vere.

The Duke had appointed his banker to dine with him, as not a moment must be lost in preparing for the reception of his Brighton drafts. He was also to receive, this evening, a complete report of all his affairs. The first thing that struck his eye on his table was a packet from Sir Carte Blanche. He opened it eagerly, stared, started, nearly shrieked. It fell from his hands. He was fortunately alone. The estimates for the completion of his works, and the purchase of the rest of the furniture, exactly equalled the sum already expended. Sir Carte added, that the works might of course be stopped, but that there was no possible way of reducing them, with any deference to the original design, scale, and style; that he had already given instructions not to proceed with the furniture until further notice, but regretted to observe that the orders were so advanced that he feared it was too late to make any sensible reduction. It might in some degree reconcile his Grace to this report when he concluded by observing that the advanced state of the works could permit him to guarantee that the present estimates would not be exceeded.

The Duke had sufficiently recovered before the arrival of his confidential agent not to appear agitated, only serious. The awful catastrophe at Brighton was announced, and his report of affairs was received. It was a very gloomy one. Great agricultural distress prevailed, and the rents could not be got in. Five-and-twenty per cent, was the least that must be taken off his income, and with no prospect of being speedily added on. There was a projected railroad which would entirely knock up his canal, and even if crushed must be expensively opposed. Coals were falling also, and the duties in town increasing. There was sad confusion in the Irish estates. The missionaries, who were patronised on the neighbouring lands of one of the City Companies, had been exciting fatal confusion. Chapels were burnt, crops destroyed, stock butchered, and rents all in arrear. Mr. Dacre had contrived with great prudence to repress the efforts of the new reformation, and had succeeded in preventing any great mischief. His plans for the pursual of his ideas and feelings upon this subject had been communicated to his late ward in an urgent and important paper, which his Grace had never seen, but one day, unread, pushed into a certain black cabinet, which perhaps the reader may remember. His Grace's miscellaneous debts had also been called in, and amounted to a greater sum than they had anticipated, which debts always do. One hundred and forty thousand pounds had crumbled away in the most imperceptible manner. A great slice of this was the portion of the jeweller. His shield and his vases would at least be evidence to his posterity of the splendour and the taste of their imprudent ancestor; but he observed the other items with less satisfaction. He discovered that in the course of two years he had given away one hundred and thirty-seven necklaces and bracelets; and as for rings, they must be counted by the bushel. The result of this gloomy interview was, that the Duke had not only managed to get rid of the immortal half-million, but had incurred debts or engagements to the amount of nearly eight hundred thousand pounds, incumbrances which were to be borne by a decreased and perhaps decreasing income. His Grace was once more alone. 'Well! my brain is not turned; and yet I think it has been pretty well worked these last few days. It cannot be true: it must all be a dream. He never could have dined here, and said all this. Have I, indeed, been at Brighton? No, no, no; I have been sleeping after dinner. I have a good mind to ring and ask whether he really was here. It must be one great delusion. But no! there are those cursed accounts. Well! what does it signify? I was miserable before, and now I am only contemptible in addition. How the world will laugh! They were made forsooth for my diversion. O, idiot! you will be the butt of everyone! Talk of Bagshot, indeed! Why, he will scarcely speak to me!

'Away with this! Let me turn these things in my mind. Take it at one hundred and fifty thousand. It is more, it must be more, but we will take it at that. Now, suppose one hundred thousand is allotted every year to meet my debts; I suppose, in nine or ten years I shall be free. Not that freedom will be worth much then; but still I am thinking of the glory of the House I have betrayed. Well, then, there is fifty thousand a-year left. Let me see; twenty thousand have always been spent in Ireland, and ten at Pen Bronnock, and they must not be cut down. The only thing I can do now is, not to spare myself. I am the cause, and let me meet the consequences. Well, then, perhaps twenty thousand a-year remain to keep Hauteville Castle and Hauteville House; to maintain the splendour of the Duke of St. James. Why, my hereditary charities alone amount to a quarter of my income, to say nothing of incidental charges: I too, who should and who would wish to rebuild, at my own cost, every bridge that is swept away, and every steeple that is burnt, in my county.

'And now for the great point. Shall I proceed with my buildings? My own personal convenience whispers no! But I have a strong conviction that the advice is treasonable. What! the young Duke's folly for every gazer in town and country to sneer at! Oh! my fathers, am I indeed your child, or am I bastard? Never, never shall your shield be sullied while I bear it! Never shall your proud banner veil while I am chieftain! They shall be finished; certainly, they shall be finished, if I die an exile! There can be no doubt about this; I feel the deep propriety.

'This girl, too, something must be done for her. I must get Squib to run down to Brighton for me: and Afy, poor dear Afy, I think she will be sorry when she hears it all!

'My head is weak: I want a counsellor. This man cannot enter into my feelings. Then there is my family lawyer; if I ask him for advice, he will ask me for instructions. Besides, this is not a matter of pounds, shillings, and pence; it is an affair as much of sentiment as economy; it involves the honour of my family, and I want one to unburden myself to, who can sympathise with the tortured feelings of a noble, of a Duke without a dukedom, for it has come to that. But I will leave sneers to the world.

'There is Annesley. He is clever, but so coldblooded. He has no heart. There is Squib; he is a good fellow, and has heart enough; and I suppose, if I wanted to pension off a mistress, or compound with a few rascally tradesmen, he would manage the affair to a miracle. There is Darrell; but he will be so fussy, and confidential, and official. Every meeting will be a cabinet council, every discussion a debate, every memorandum a state paper. There is Burlington; he is experienced, and clever, and kind-hearted, and, I really think, likes me; but, no, no, it is too ridiculous. We who have only met for enjoyment, whose countenance was a smile, and whose conversation was badinage; we to meet,

- 224 -

and meditate on my broken fortunes! Impossible! Besides, what right have I to compel a man, the study of whose life is to banish care, to take all my anxieties on his back, or refuse the duty at the cost of my acquaintance and the trouble of his conscience. Ah! I once had a friend, the best, the wisest; but no more of that. What is even the loss of fortune and of consideration to the loss of his—his daughter's love?'

His voice faltered, yet it was long before he retired; and he rose on the morrow only to meditate over his harassing embarrassments. As if the cup of his misery were not o'erflowing, a new incident occurred about this time, which rendered his sense of them even keener. But this is important enough to commence a new chapter.

CHAPTER X.

A New Star Rises

WILLIAM HENRY, MARQUESS OF MARYLEBONE, completed his twenty-first year: an event which created a greater sensation among the aristocracy of England, even, than the majority of George Augustus Frederick, Duke of St. James. The rent-roll of his Grace was great: but that of his Lordship was incalculable. He had not indeed so many castles as our hero; but then, in the metropolis, a whole parish owned him as Lord, and it was whispered that, when a few miles of leases fell in, the very Civil List must give him the wall. Even in the duration of his minority, he had the superiority over the young Duke, for the Marquess was a posthumous son.

Lord Marylebone was a short, thick, swarthy young gentleman, with wiry black hair, a nose somewhat flat, sharp eyes, and tusky mouth; altogether not very unlike a terrier. His tastes were unknown: he had not travelled, nor done anything very particular, except, with a few congenial spirits, beat the Guards in a rowing-match, a pretty diversion, and almost as conducive to a small white hand as almond-paste.

But his Lordship was now of age, and might be seen every day at a certain hour rattling up Bond Street in a red drag, in which he drove four or five particular friends who lived at Stevens' Hotel, and therefore, we suppose, were the partners of his glory in his victory over his Majesty's household troops. Lord Marylebone was the universal subject of conversation. Pursuits which would have devoted a shabby Earl of twelve or fifteen thousand a year to universal reprobation, or, what is much worse, to universal sneers, assumed quite a different character when they constituted the course of life of this fortunate youth. He was a delightful young man. So unaffected! No super-refinement, no false delicacy. Everyone, each sex, everything, extended his, her, or its hand to this cub, who, quite puzzled, but too brutal to be confused, kept driving on the red van, and each day perpetrating some new act of profligacy, some new instance of coarse profusion, tasteless extravagance, and inelegant eccentricity.

But, nevertheless, he was the hero of the town. He was the great point of interest in 'The Universe,' and 'The New World' favoured the old one with weekly articles on his character and conduct. The young Duke was quite forgotten, if really young he could be longer called. Lord Marylebone was in the mouth of every tradesman, who authenticated his own vile inventions by foisting them on his Lordship. The most grotesque fashions suddenly inundated the metropolis; and when the Duke of St. James ventured to express his disapprobation, he found his empire was over. 'They were sorry that it did not meet his Grace's taste, but really what his Grace had suggested was quite gone by. This was the only hat, or cane, or coat which any civilised being could be seen with. Lord Marylebone wore, or bore, no other.'

In higher circles, it was much the same. Although the dandies would not bate an inch, and certainly would not elect the young Marquess for their leader, they found, to their dismay, that the empire which they were meditating to defend, had already slipped away from their grasp. A new race of adventurous youths appeared upon the stage. Beards, and greatcoats even rougher, bull-dogs instead of poodles, clubs instead of canes, cigars instead of perfumes, were the order of the day. There was no end to boat-racing; Crockford's sneered at White's; and there was even a talk of reviving the ring. Even the women patronised the young Marquess, and those who could not be blind to his real character, were sure, that, if well managed, he would not turn out ill.

Assuredly our hero, though shelved, did not envy his successful rival. Had he been, instead of one for whom he felt a sovereign contempt, a being even more accomplished than himself, pity and not envy would have been the sentiment he would have yielded to his ascendant star. But, nevertheless, he could not be insensible to the results of this incident; and the advent of the young Marquess seemed like the sting in the epigram of his life. After all his ruinous magnificence, after all the profuse indulgence of his fantastic tastes, he had sometimes consoled himself, even in the bitterness of satiety, by reminding himself, that he at least commanded the admiration of his fellow-creatures, although it had been purchased at a costly price. Not insensible to the power of his wealth, the magic of his station, he had, however, ventured to indulge in the sweet belief that these qualities were less concerned in the triumphs of his career than his splendid person, his accomplished mind, his amiable disposition, and his finished manner; his beauty, his wit, his goodness, and his grace. Even from this delusion, too, was he to waken, and, for the first time in his life, he gauged the depth and strength of that popularity which had been so dear to him, and which he now found to be so shallow and so weak.

'What will they think of me when they know all? What they will: I care not. I would sooner live in a cottage with May Dacre, and work for our daily bread, than be worshipped by all the beauty of this Babylon.'

Gloomy, yet sedate, he returned home. His letters announced two extraordinary events. M. de Whiskerburg had galloped off with Lady Aphrodite, and Count Frill had flown away with the Bird of Paradise.

CHAPTER XI.

'Lovely Woman Stoops to Folly.'

THE last piece of information was a relief; but the announcement of the elopement cost him a pang. Both surprised, and the first shocked him. We are unreasonable in love, and do not like to be anticipated even in neglect. An hour ago Lady Aphrodite Grafton was to him only an object of anxiety and a cause of embarrassment. She was now a being to whom he was indebted for some of the most pleasing hours of his existence, and who could no longer contribute to his felicity. Everybody appeared deserting him.

He had neglected her, to be sure; and they must have parted, it was certain. Yet, although the present event saved him from the most harrowing of scenes, he could not refrain shedding a tear. So good! and so beautiful! and was this her end? He who knew all knew how bitter had been the lot of her life.

It is certain that when one of your very virtuous women ventures to be a little indiscreet, we say it is certain, though we regret it, that sooner or later there is an explosion. And the reason is this, that they are always in a hurry to make up for lost time, and so love with them becomes a business instead of being a pleasure. Nature had intended Lady Aphrodite Grafton for a Psyche, so spiritual was her soul, so pure her blood! Art—that is, education, which at least should be an art, though it is not—art had exquisitely sculptured the precious gem that Nature had developed, and all that was wanting was love to stamp an impression. Lady Aphrodite Grafton might have been as perfect a character as was ever the heroine of a novel. And to whose account shall we place her blighted fame and sullied lustre? To that animal who seems formed only to betray woman. Her husband was a traitor in disguise. She found herself betrayed; but like a noble chieftain, when her capital was lost, maintained herself among the ruins of her happiness, in the citadel of her virtue. She surrendered, she thought, on terms; and in yielding her heart to the young Duke, though never for a moment blind to her conduct, yet memory whispered extenuation, and love added all that was necessary.

Our hero (we are for none of your perfect heroes) did not behave much better than her husband. The difference between them was, Sir Lucius Grafton's character was formed, and formed for evil; while the Duke of St. James, when he became acquainted with Lady Aphrodite, possessed none. Gallantry was a habit, in which he had been brought up. To protest to woman what he did not believe, and to feign what he did not feel, were, as he supposed, parts in the character of an accomplished gentleman; and as hitherto he had not found his career productive of any misery, we may perhaps view his conduct with less severity. But at length he approaches, not a mere woman of the world, who tries to delude him into the idea that he is the first hero of a romance that has been a hundred times repeated. He trembles at the responsibility which he has incurred by engaging the feelings of another. In the conflict of his emotions, some rays of moral light break upon his darkened soul. Profligacy brings its own punishment, and he feels keenly that man is the subject of sympathy, and not the slave of self-love.

This remorse protracts a connection which each day is productive of more painful feelings; but the heart cannot be overstrung, and anxiety ends in callousness. Then come neglect, remonstrance, explanations, protestations, and, sooner or later, a catastrophe.

But love is a dangerous habit, and when once indulged, is not easily thrown off, unless you become devout, which is, in a manner, giving the passion a new direction. In Catholic countries, it is surprising how many adventures end in a convent. A dame, in her desperation, flies to the grate, which never reopens; but in Protestant regions she has time to cool, and that's the deuce; so, instead of taking the veil, she takes a new lover.

Lady Aphrodite had worked up her mind and the young Duke to a step the very mention of which a year before would have made him shudder. What an enchanter is Passion! No wonder Ovid, who was a judge, made love so much connected with his Metamorphoses. With infinite difficulty she had dared to admit the idea of flying with his Grace; but when the idea was once admitted, when she really had, once or twice, constantly dwelt on the idea of at length being free from her tyrant, and perhaps about to indulge in those beautiful affections for which she was formed, and of which she had been rifled; when, I say, all this occurred, and her hero diplomatised, and, in short, kept back; why, she had advanced one step, without knowing it, to running away with another man.

It was unlucky that De Whiskerburg stepped in. An Englishman would not have done. She knew them well, and despised them all; but he was new (dangerous novelty), with a cast of feelings which, because they were strange, she believed to be unhackneyed; and he was impassioned. We need not go on.

So this star has dropped from out the heaven; so this precious pearl no longer gleams among the jewels of society, and there she breathes in a foreign land, among strange faces and stranger customs, and, when she thinks of what is past, laughs at some present emptiness, and tries to persuade her withering heart that the mind is independent of country, and blood, and opinion. And her father's face no longer shines with its proud love, and her mother's voice no longer whispers to her with sweet anxiety. Clouded is the brow of her bold brother, and dimmed is the radiancy of her budding sister's bloom.

Poor creature! that is to say, wicked woman! for we are not of those who set themselves against the verdict of society, or ever omit to expedite, by a gentle kick, a falling friend. And yet, when we just remember beauty is beauty, and grace is grace, and kindness is kindness, although the beautiful, the graceful, and the amiable do get in a scrape, we don't know how it is, we confess it is a weakness, but, under these circumstances, we do not feel quite inclined to sneer.

But this is wrong. We should not pity or pardon those who have yielded to great temptation, or perchance great provocation. Besides, it is right that our sympathy should be kept for the injured.

To stand amid the cold ashes of your desolate hearth, with all your Penates shivered at your feet; to find no smiling face meet your return, no brow look gloomy when you leave your door; to eat and sleep alone; to be bored with grumbling servants and with weekly bills; to have your children asking after mamma; and no one to nurse your gout, or cure the influenza that rages in your household: all this is doubtless hard to digest, and would tell in a novel, particularly if written by my friends Mr. Ward or Mr. Bulwer.

CHAPTER XII.

Kindly Words

THE Duke had passed a stormy morning with his solicitor, who wished him to sell the Pen Bronnock property, which, being parliamentary, would command a price infinitely greater than might be expected from its relative income. The very idea of stripping his coronet of this brightest jewel, and thus sacrificing for wealth the ends of riches, greatly disordered him, and he more and more felt the want of a counsellor who could sympathise with his feelings as well as arrange his fortunes. In this mood he suddenly seized a pen, and wrote the following letter:—

'——House, Feb. 5, 182—.

'My dear Mr. Dacre,

'I keenly feel that you are the last person to whom I should apply for the counsels or the consolation of friendship. I have long ago forfeited all claims to your regard, and your esteem I never possessed. Yet, if only because my career ought to end by my being an unsuccessful suppliant to the individual whom both virtue and nature pointed out to me as my best friend, and whose proffered and parental support I have so wantonly, however thoughtlessly, rejected, I do not regret that this is written. No feeling of false delicacy can prevent me from applying to one to whom I have long ago incurred incalculable obligations, and no feeling of false delicacy will, I hope, for a moment, prevent you from refusing the application of one who has acknowledged those obligations only by incalculable ingratitude.

'In a word, my affairs, are, I fear, inextricably involved. I will not dwell upon the madness of my life; suffice that its consequences appall me. I have really endeavoured to examine into all details, and am prepared to meet the evil as becomes me; but, indeed, my head turns with the complicated interests which solicit my consideration, and I tremble lest, in the distraction of my mind, I may adopt measures which may baffle the very results I would attain. For myself, I am ready to pay the penalty of my silly profligacy; and if exile, or any other personal infliction, can redeem the fortunes of the House that I have betrayed, I shall cheerfully submit to my destiny. My career has been productive of too little happiness to make me regret its termination.

'But I want advice: I want the counsel of one who can sympathise with my distracted feelings, who will look as much, or rather more, to the honour of my family than to the convenience of myself. I cannot obtain this from what are called men of business, and, with a blush I confess, I have no friend. In this situation my thoughts recur to one on whom, believe me, they have often dwelt; and although I have no right to appeal to your heart, for my father's sake you will perhaps pardon this address. Whatever you may resolve, my dearest sir, rest assured that you and your family will always command the liveliest gratitude of one who regrets he may not subscribe himself

'Your obliged and devoted friend,

'St. James.

'I beg that you will not answer this, if your determination be what I anticipate and what I deserve. 'Dacre Dacre, Esq., &c, &c, &c.'

It was signed, sealed, and sent. He repented its transmission when it was gone. He almost resolved to send a courier to stop the post. He continued walking up and down his room for the rest of the day; he could not eat, or read, or talk. He was plunged in a nervous reverie. He passed the next day in the same state. Unable to leave his house, and unseen by visitors, he retired to his bed feverish and dispirited. The morning came, and he woke from his hot and broken sleep at an early hour; yet he had not energy to rise. At last the post arrived, and his letters were brought up to him. With a trembling hand and sinking breath he read these lines:—

'Castle Dacre, February 6, 182—.

'My dear young Friend,

'Not only for your father's sake, but your own, are my services ever at your command. I have long been sensible of your amiable disposition, and there are circumstances which will ever make me your debtor.

'The announcement of the embarrassed state of your affairs fills me with sorrow and anxiety, yet I will hope the best. Young men, unconsciously, exaggerate adversity as well as prosperity. If you are not an habitual gamester, and I hope you have not been even an occasional one, unbounded extravagance could scarcely in two years have permanently injured your resources. However, bring down with you all papers, and be careful to make no arrangement, even of the slightest nature, until we meet.

'We expect you hourly. May desires her kindest regards, and begs me to express the great pleasure which she will feel at again finding you our guest. It is unnecessary for me to repeat how very sincerely

'I am your friend,

'Dacre Dacre.'

He read the letter three times to be sure he did not mistake the delightful import. Then he rang the bell with a vivacity which had not characterised him for many a month.

'Luigi! prepare to leave town to-morrow morning for an indefinite period. I shall only take you. I must dress immediately, and order breakfast and my horses.'

The Duke of St. James had communicated the state of his affairs to Lord Fitz-pompey, who was very shocked, offered his best services, and also asked him to dinner, to meet the Marquess of Marylebone. The young Duke had also announced to his relatives, and to some of his particular friends, that he intended to travel for some time, and he well knew that their charitable experience would understand the rest. They understood everything. The Marquess's party daily increased, and 'The Universe' and 'The New World' announced that the young Duke was 'done up.'

There was one person to whom our hero would pay a farewell visit before he left London. This was Lady Caroline St. Maurice. He had called at Fitz-pompey House one or two mornings in the hope of finding her alone, and to-day he determined to be more successful. As he stopped his horse for the last time before his uncle's mansion, he could not help calling to mind the first visit which he had paid after his arrival. But the door opens, he enters, he is announced, and finds Lady Caroline alone.

Ten minutes passed away, as if the morning ride or evening ball were again to bring them together. The young Duke was still gay and still amusing. At last he said with a smile,

'Do you know, Caroline, this is a farewell visit, and to you?'

She did not speak, but bent her head as if she were intent upon some work, and so seated herself that her countenance was almost hid.

'You have heard from my uncle,' continued he, laughing; 'and if you have not heard from him, you have heard from somebody else, of my little scrape. A fool and his money, you know, Caroline, and a short reign and a merry one. When we get prudent we are wondrous fond of proverbs. My reign has certainly been brief enough; with regard to the merriment, that is not quite so certain. I have little to regret except your society, sweet coz!'

'Dear George, how can you talk so of such serious affairs! If you knew how unhappy, how miserable I am, when I hear the cold, callous world speak of such things with indifference, you would at least not imitate their heartlessness.'

'Dear Caroline!' said he, seating himself at her side.

'I cannot help thinking,' she continued, 'that you have not sufficiently exerted yourself about these embarrassments. You are, of course, too harassed, too much annoyed, too little accustomed to the energy and the detail of business, to interfere with any effect; but surely a friend might. You will not speak to

- 233 -

my father, and perhaps you have your reasons; but is there no one else? St. Maurice, I know, has no head. Ah! George, I often feel that if your relations had been different people, your fate might have been different. We are the fault.'

He kissed her hand.

'Among all your intimates,' she continued, 'is there no one fit to be your counsellor, no one worthy of your confidence?'

'None,' said the Duke, bitterly, 'none, none. I have no friend among those intimates: there is not a man of them who cares to serve or is capable of serving me.'

'You have well considered?' asked Lady Caroline.

'Well, dear, well. I know them all by rote, head and heart. Ah! my dear, dear Carry, if you were a man, what a nice little friend you would be!'

'You will always laugh, George. But I—I have no heart to laugh. This breaking up of your affairs, this exile, this losing you whom we all love, love so dearly, makes me quite miserable.'

He kissed her hand again.

'I dare say,' she continued, 'you have thought me as heartless as the rest, because I never spoke. But I knew; that is, I feared; or, rather, hoped that a great part of what I heard was false; and so I thought notice was unnecessary, and might be painful. Yet, heaven knows, there are few subjects that have been oftener in my thoughts, or cost me more anxiety. Are you sure you have no friend?'

'I have you, Caroline. I did not say I had no friends: I said I had none among those intimates you talked of; that there was no man among them capable of the necessary interference, even if he were willing to undertake it. But I am not friendless, not quite forlorn, dear! My fate has given me a friend that I but little deserve: one whom, if I had prized better, I should not perhaps have been obliged to put his friendship to so severe a trial. To-morrow, Caroline, I depart for Castle Dacre; there is my friend. Alas! how little have I deserved such a boon!'

'Dacre!' exclaimed Lady Caroline, 'Mr. Dacre! Oh! you have made me so happy, George! Mr. Dacre is the very, very person; that is, the very best person you could possibly have applied to.'

'Good-bye, Caroline,' said his Grace, rising.

She burst into tears.

Never, never had she looked so lovely: never, never had he loved her so entirely! Tears! tears shed for him! Oh! what, what is grief when a lovely woman remains to weep over our misfortunes! Could he be miserable, could his career indeed be unfortunate, when this was reserved for him? He was on the point of pledging his affection, but to leave her under such circumstances was impossible: to neglect Mr. Dacre was equally so. He determined to arrange his affairs with all possible promptitude, and then to hasten up, and entreat her to share his diminished fortunes. But he would not go without whispering hope, without leaving some soft thought to lighten her lonely hours. He caught her in his arms; he covered her sweet small mouth with kisses, and whispered, in the midst of their pure embrace,

'Dearest Carry! I shall soon return, and we will yet be happy.'

BOOK V.

- 238 -

CHAPTER I.

Once More at Dacre

MISS DACRE, although she was prepared to greet the Duke of St. James with cordiality, did not anticipate with equal pleasure the arrival of the page and the jÃ¤ger. Infinite had been the disturbances they had occasioned during their first visit, and endless the complaints of the steward and the housekeeper. The men-servants were initiated in the mysteries of dominoes, and the maid-servants in the tactics of flirtation. Karlstein was the hero of the under-butlers, and even the trusty guardian of the cellar himself was too often on the point of obtaining the German's opinion of his master's German wines. Gaming, and drunkenness, and love, the most productive of all the teeming causes of human sorrow, had in a week sadly disordered the well-regulated household of Castle Dacre, and nothing but the impetuosity of our hero would have saved his host's establishment from utter perdition. Miss Dacre was, therefore, not less pleased than surprised when the britzska of the Duke of St. James discharged on a fine afternoon, its noble master, attended only by the faithful Luigi, at the terrace of the Castle.

A few country cousins, fresh from Cumberland, who knew nothing of the Duke of St. James except from a stray number of 'The Universe,' which occasionally stole down to corrupt the pure waters of their lakes, were the only guests. Mr. Dacre grasped our hero's hand with a warmth and expression which were unusual with him, but which conveyed, better than words, the depth of his friendship; and his daughter, who looked more beautiful than ever, advanced with a beaming face and joyous tone, which quite reconciled the Duke of St. James to being a ruined man.

The presence of strangers limited their conversation to subjects of general interest. At dinner, the Duke took care to be agreeable: he talked in an unaffected manner, and particularly to the cousins, who were all delighted with him, and found him 'quite a different person from what they had fancied.' The evening passed over, and even lightly, without the aid of Ã©cartÃ©, romances, or gallops. Mr. Dacre chatted with old Mr. Montingford, and old Mrs. Montingford sat still admiring her 'girls,' who stood still admiring May Dacre singing or talking, and occasionally reconciled us to their occasional silence by a frequent and extremely hearty laugh; that Cumberland laugh which never outlives a single season in London.

And the Duke of St. James, what did he do? It must be confessed that in some points he greatly resembled the Misses Montingford, for he was both silent and admiring; but he never laughed. Yet he was not dull, and was careful not to show that he had cares, which is vulgar. If a man be gloomy, let him keep to himself. No one has a right to go croaking about society, or,

- 239 -

what is worse, looking as if he stifled grief. These fellows should be put in the pound. We like a good broken heart or so now and then; but then one should retire to the Sierra Morena mountains, and live upon locusts and wild honey, not 'dine out' with our cracked cores, and, while we are meditating suicide, the Gazette, or the Chiltern Hundreds, damn a vintage or eulogise an *entrÃ©e*.

And as for cares, what are cares when a man is in love? Once more they had met; once more he gazed upon that sunny and sparkling face; once more he listened to that sweet and thrilling voice, which sounded like a bird-like burst of music upon a summer morning. She moved, and each attitude was fascination. She was still, and he regretted that she moved. Now her neck, now her hair, now her round arm, now her tapering waist, ravished his attention; now he is in ecstasies with her twinkling foot; now he is dazzled with her glancing hand.

Once more he was at Dacre! How different was this meeting to their first! Then, she was cold, almost cutting; then she was disregardful, almost contemptuous; but then he had hoped; ah! madman, he had more than hoped. Now she was warm, almost affectionate; now she listened to him with readiness, ay! almost courted his conversation. And now he could only despair. As he stood alone before the fire, chewing this bitter cud, she approached him.

'How good you were to come directly!' she said with a smile, which melted his heart. 'I fear, however, you will not find us so merry as before. But you can make anything amusing. Come, then, and sing to these damsels. Do you know they are half afraid of you? and I cannot persuade them that a terrible magician has not assumed, for the nonce, the air and appearance of a young gentleman of distinction.'

He smiled, but could not speak. Repartee sadly deserts the lover; yet smiles, under those circumstances, are eloquent; and the eye, after all, speaks much more to the purpose than the tongue. Forgetting everything except the person who addressed him, he offered her his hand, and advanced to the group which surrounded the piano.

CHAPTER II.

The Moth and the Flame

THE next morning was passed by the Duke of St. James in giving Mr. Dacre his report of the state of his affairs. His banker's accounts, his architect's estimates, his solicitor's statements, were all brought forward and discussed. A ride, generally with Miss Dacre and one of her young friends, dinner, and a short evening, and eleven o'clock, sent them all to repose. Thus glided on a fortnight. The mornings continued to be passed in business. Affairs were more complicated than his Grace had imagined, who had no idea of detail. He gave all the information that he could, and made his friend master of his particular feelings. For the rest, Mr. Dacre was soon involved in much correspondence; and although the young Duke could no longer assist him, he recommended and earnestly begged that he would remain at Dacre; for he could perceive, better than his Grace, that our hero was labouring under a great deal of excitement, and that his health was impaired. A regular course of life was therefore as necessary for his constitution as it was desirable for all other reasons.

Behold, then, our hero domesticated at Dacre; rising at nine, joining a family breakfast, taking a quiet ride, or moderate stroll, sometimes looking into a book, but he was no great reader; sometimes fortunate enough in achieving a stray game at billiards, usually with a Miss Montingford, and retiring to rest about the time that in London his most active existence generally began. Was he dull? was he wearied? He was never lighter-hearted or more contented in his life. Happy he could not allow himself to be styled, because the very cause which breathed this calm over his existence seemed to portend a storm which could not be avoided. It was the thought, the presence, the smile, the voice of May Dacre that imparted this new interest to existence: that being who never could be his. He shuddered to think that all this must end; but although he never indulged again in the great hope, his sanguine temper allowed him to thrust away the future, and to participate in all the joys of the flowing hour.

At the end of February the Montingfords departed, and now the Duke was the only guest at Dacre; nor did he hear that any others were expected. He was alone with her again; often was he alone with her, and never without a strange feeling coming over his frame, which made him tremble. Mr. Dacre, a man of active habits, always found occupation in his public duties and in the various interests of a large estate, and usually requested, or rather required, the Duke of St. James to be his companion. He was desirous that the Duke should not be alone, and ponder too much over the past; nor did he conceal his wishes from his daughter, who on all occasions, as the Duke observed with gratification, seconded the benevolent intentions of her

- 241 -

parent. Nor did our hero indeed wish to be alone, or to ponder over the past. He was quite contented with the present; but he did not want to ride with papa, and took every opportunity to shirk; all of which Mr. Dacre set down to the indolence of exhaustion, and the inertness of a mind without an object.

'I am going to ride over to Doncaster, George,' said Mr. Dacre one morning at breakfast. 'I think that you had better order your horse too. A good ride will rouse you, and you should show yourself there.'

'Oh! very well, sir; but, but I think that——'

'But what?' asked Mr. Dacre, smiling.

The Duke looked to Miss Dacre, who seemed to take pity on his idleness.

'You make him ride too much, papa. Leave him at home with me. I have a long round to-day, and want an escort. I will take him instead of my friend Tom Carter. You must carry a basket though,' said she, turning to the Duke, 'and run for the doctor if he be wanted, and, in short, do any odd message that turns up.'

So Mr. Dacre departed alone, and shortly after his daughter and the Duke of St. James set out on their morning ramble. Many were the cottages at which they called; many the old dames after whose rheumatisms, and many the young damsels after whose fortunes they enquired. Old Dame Rawdon was worse or better; worse last night, but better this morning. She was always better when Miss called. Miss's face always did her good. And Fanny was very comfortable at Squire Wentworth's, and the housekeeper was very kind to her, thanks to Miss saying a word to the great Lady. And old John Selby was quite about again. Miss's stuff had done him a world of good, to say nothing of Mr. Dacre's generous old wine.

'And is this your second son, Dame Rishworth?' 'No; that bees our fourth,' said the old woman, maternally arranging the urchin's thin, white, flat, straight, unmanageable hair. 'We are thinking what to do with him, Miss. He wants to go out to service. Since Jem Eustace got on so, I don't know what the matter is with the lads; but I think we shall have none of them in the fields soon. He can clean knives and shoes very well, Miss. Mr. Bradford, at the Castle, was saying t'other day that perhaps he might want a young hand. You haven't heard anything, I suppose, Miss?'

'And what is your name, sir?' asked Miss Dacre. 'Bobby Rishworth, Miss!' 'Well, Bobby, I must consult Mr. Bradford.' 'We be in great trouble, Miss,' said the next cottager. 'We be in great trouble. Tom, poor Tom, was out last night, and the keepers will give him up. The good man has done all he can, we have all done all we can, Miss, and you see how it ends. He is the first of the family that ever went out. I hope that will be considered, Miss. Seventy years, our fathers before us, have we been on the 'state, and nothing ever sworn agin us. I hope that will be considered, Miss. I am sure if Tom had been an underkeeper, as Mr. Roberts once talked of, this would never have happened. I hope that will be considered, Miss. We are in great trouble surely. Tom, you see, was our first, Miss.'

'I never interfere about poaching, you know, Mrs. Jones. Mr. Dacre is the best judge of such matters. But you can go to him, and say that I sent you. I am afraid, however, that he has heard of Tom before.'

'Only that night at Milwood, Miss; and then you see he had been drinking with Squire Ridge's people. I hope that will be considered, Miss.'

'Well, well, go up to the Castle.'

'Pray be seated, Miss,' said a neat-looking mistress of a neat little farmhouse. 'Pray be seated, sir. Let me dust it first. Dust will get everywhere, do what we can. And how's Pa, Miss? He has not given me a look-in for many a day, not since he was a-hunting: bless me, if it ayn't a fortnight. This day fortnight he tasted our ale, sure enough. Will you take a glass, sir?'

'You are very good. No, I thank you; not today.'

'Yes, give him a glass, nurse. He is unwell, and it will do him good.'

She brought the sparkling amber fluid, and the Duke did justice by his draught.

'I shall have fine honey for you, Miss, this year,' said the old nurse. 'Are you fond of honey, sir? Our honey is well known about. I don't know how it is, but we do always contrive to manage the bees. How fond some people are of honey, good Lord! Now, when you were a little girl (I knew this young lady, sir, before you did), you always used to be fond of honey. I remember one day: let me see, it must be, ay! truly, that it is, eighteen years ago next Martinmas: I was a-going down the nursery stairs, just to my poor mistress's room, and I had you in my arms (for I knew this young lady, sir, before you did). Well! I was a-going down the stairs, as I just said, to my poor dear mistress's room with you, who was then a little-un indeed (bless your smiling face! you cost me many a weary hour when you were weaned, Miss. That you did! Some thought you would never get through it; but I always said, while there is life there is hope; and so, you see I were right); but, as I was saying, I was a-going down the stairs to my poor dear mistress, and I had a gallipot in my hand, a covered gallipot, with some leeches. And just as I had got to the bottom of the stairs, and was a-going into my poor dear mistress's room, said you (I never shall forget it), said you, "Honey, honey, nurse." She thought it were honey, sir. So you see she were always very fond of honey (for I knew this young lady long before you did, sir).'

- 243 -

'Are you quite sure of that, nurse?' said Miss Dacre; 'I think this is an older friend than you imagine. You remember the little Duke; do not you? This is the little Duke. Do you think he has grown?'

'Now! bless my life! is it so indeed? Well, be sure, he has grown. I always thought he would turn out well, Miss, though Dr. Pretyman were always a-preaching, and talking his prophecycations. I always thought he would turn out well at last. Bless me! how he has grown, indeed! Perhaps he grows too fast, and that makes him weak. Nothing better than a glass of ale for weak people. I remember when Dr. Pretyman ordered it for my poor dear mistress. "Give her ale," said the Doctor, "as strong as it can be brewed;" and sure enough, my poor dear master had it brewed! Have you done growing, sir? You was ever a troublesome child. Often and often have I called George, George, Georgy, Georgy Porgy, and he never would come near me, though he heard all the time as plainly as he does now. Bless me! he has grown indeed!'

'But I have turned out well at last, nurse, eh?' asked the Duke.

'Ay! sure enough; I always said so. Often and often have I said, he will turn out well at last. You be going, Miss? I thank you for looking in. My duty to my master. I was thinking of bringing up one of those cheeses he likes so.'

'Ay! do, nurse. He can eat no cheese but yours.'

As they wandered home, they talked of Lady Caroline, to whom the Duke mentioned that he must write. He had once intended distinctly to have explained his feelings to her in a letter from Dacre; but each day he postponed the close of his destiny, although without hope. He lingered and he lingered round May Dacre, as a bird flutters round the fruit which is already grasped by a boy. Circumstances, which we shall relate, had already occurred, which confirmed the suspicion he had long entertained that Arundel Dacre was his favoured rival. Impressed with the folly of again encouraging hope, yet unable to harden his heart against her continual fascination, the softness of his manner indicated his passion, and his calm and somewhat languid carriage also told her it was hopeless. Perhaps, after all, there is no demeanour more calculated to melt obdurate woman. The gratification he received from her society was evident, yet he never indulged in that gallantry of which he was once so proud. When she approached him, a mild smile lit up his pensive countenance; he adopted her suggestions, but made none; he listened to her remarks with interest, but no longer bandied repartee. Delicately he impressed her with the absolute power which she might exercise over his mind.

'I write myself to Caroline to-morrow,' said Miss Dacre.

'Ah! Then I need not write. I talked of going up sooner. Have the kindness to explain why I do not: peremptory orders from Mr. Dacre; fresh air, and——'

'Arithmetic. I understand you get on admirably.'

'My follies,' said the Duke with a serious air, 'have at least been productive of one good end, they have amused you.'

'Nay! I have done too many foolish things myself any more to laugh at my neighbours. As for yourself, you have only committed those which were inseparable from your situation; and few, like the Duke of St. James, would so soon have opened their eyes to the truth of their conduct.'

'A compliment from you repays me for all.'

'Self-approbation does, which is much better than compliments from anyone. See! there is papa, and Arundel too: let us run up!'

CHAPTER III.

Again the Rival

THE Duke of St. James had, on his arrival at Dacre, soon observed that a constant correspondence was maintained between Miss Dacre and her cousin. There was no attempt to conceal the fact from any of the guests, and, as that young gentleman was now engaged in an affair interesting to all his friends, every letter generally contained some paragraph almost as interesting to the Montingfords as to herself, which was accordingly read aloud. Mr. Arundel Dacre was candidate for the vacant representation of a town in a distant county. He had been disappointed in his views on the borough, about which he had returned to England, but had been nevertheless persuaded by his cousin to remain in his native country. During this period, he had been a great deal at Castle Dacre, and had become much more intimate and unreserved with his uncle, who observed with great satisfaction this change in his character, and lost no opportunity of deserving and increasing the confidence for which he had so long unavailingly yearned, and which was now so unexpectedly proffered.

The borough for which Arundel Dacre was about to stand was in Sussex, a county in which his family had no property, and very slight connection. Yet at the place, the Catholic interest was strong, and on that, and the usual Whig influence, he ventured. His desire to be a member of the Legislature, at all and from early times extreme, was now greatly heightened by the prospect of being present at the impending Catholic debate. After an absence of three weeks, he had hurried to Yorkshire for four-and-twenty hours, to give a report of the state of his canvass, and the probability of his success. In that success all were greatly interested, but none more so than Miss Dacre, whose thoughts indeed seemed to dwell on no other subject, and who expressed herself with a warmth which betrayed her secret feelings. Had the place only been in Yorkshire, she was sure he must have succeeded. She was the best canvasser in the world, and everybody agreed that Harry Grey-stoke owed his election merely to her insinuating tongue and unrivalled powers of scampering, by which she had completely baffled the tactics of Lady Amarantha.

Germain, who thought that a canvass was only a long morning call, and might be achieved in a cashmere and a britzska.

The young Duke, who had seen little of his second since the eventful day, greeted him with warmth, and was welcomed with a frankness which he had never before experienced from his friend. Excited by rapid travel and his present course of life, and not damped by the unexpected presence of any strangers, Arundel Dacre seemed quite a changed man, and talked immensely.

'Come, May, I must have a kiss! I have been kissing as pretty girls as you. There now! You all said I never should be a popular candidate. I get regularly huzzaed every day, so they have been obliged to hire a band of butchers' boys to pelt me. Whereupon I compare myself to CÃ¦sar set upon in the Senate House, and get immense cheering in "The County Chronicle," which I have bribed. If you knew the butts of wine, the Heidelberg tuns of ale, that I have drank during the last fortnight, you would stare indeed. As much as the lake: but then I have to talk so much, that the ardour of my eloquence, like the hot flannels of the Humane Society, save me from the injurious effects of all this liquid.'

'But will you get in; but will you get in?' exclaimed his cousin.

''Tis not in mortals to command success; but——'

'Pooh! pooh! you must command it!' 'Well, then, I have an excellent chance; and the only thing against me is, that my committee are quite sure. But really I think that if the Protestant overseers, whom, by-the-bye, May, I cannot persuade that I am a heretic (it is very hard that a man is not believed when he says he shall be damned), if they do not empty the workhouse, we shall do. But let us go in, for I have travelled all night, and must be off to-morrow morning.'

They entered the house, and the Duke quitted the family group. About an hour afterwards, he sauntered to the music-room. As he opened the door, his eyes lighted upon May Dacre and her cousin. They were standing before the fire, with their backs to the door. His arm was wound carelessly round her waist, and with his other hand he supported, with her, a miniature, at which she was looking.

The Duke could not catch her countenance, which was completely hid; but her companion was not gazing on the picture: his head, a little turned, indicated that there was a living countenance more interesting to him than all the skill of the most cunning artist. Part of his cheek was alone perceptible, and that was burning red.

All this was the work of a moment. The Duke stared, turned pale, closed the door without a sound, and retired unperceived. When he was sure that he could no longer be observed, he gasped for breath, a cold dew covered his frame, his joints loosened, and his sinking heart gave him that sickening sensation when life appears utterly worthless, and ourselves utterly contemptible. Yet what had he witnessed? A confirmation of what he had never doubted. What was this woman to him? Alas! how supreme was the power with which she ruled his spirit! And this Dacre, this Arundel Dacre, how he hated him! Oh! that they were hand to hand, and sword to sword, in some fair field, and there decide it! He must conquer; he felt that. Already his weapon pierced that craven heart, and ripped open that breast which was to be the pillow of——. Hell! hell! He rushed to his room, and began a letter to Caroline St. Maurice; but he could not write; and after scribbling over a quire of paper, he threw the sheets to the flames, and determined to ride up to town to-morrow.

The dinner bell sounded. Could he meet them? Ay! meet them! Defy them! Insult them! He descended to the dining-room. He heard her musical and liquid voice; the scowl upon his brow melted away; but, gloomy and silent, he took his seat, and gloomy and silent he remained. Little he spoke, and that little was scarcely courteous. But Arundel had enough to say. He was the hero of the party. Well he might be. Story after story of old maids and young widows, sturdy butchers and corrupt coal merchants, sparkled away; but a faint smile was all the tribute of the Duke, and a tribute that was seldom paid.

'You are not well!' said Miss Dacre to him, in a low voice.

'I believe I am,' answered he shortly.

'You do not seem quite so,' she replied, with an air of surprise.

'I believe I have got a headache,' he retorted with little more cordiality. She did not again speak, but she was evidently annoyed.

CHAPTER IV.

Bitter is Jealousy

THERE certainly is a dark delight in being miserable, a sort of strange satisfaction in being savage, which is uncommonly fascinating. One of the greatest pests of philosophy is, that one can no longer be sullen, and most sincerely do I regret it. To brood over misery, to flatter yourself that there is not a single being who cares for your existence, and not a single circumstance to make that existence desirable: there is wild witchery in it, which we doubt whether opium can reach, and are sure that wine cannot.

And the Duke! He soon left the uncle and nephew to their miserable speculations about the state of the poll, and took his sullen way, with the air of Ajax, to the terrace. Here he stalked along in a fierce reverie; asked why he had been born; why he did not die; why he should live, and so on. His wounded pride, which had borne so much, fairly got the mastery, and revenged itself for all insults on Love, whom it ejected most scurvily. He blushed to think how he had humiliated himself before her. She was the cause of that humiliation, and of every disagreeable sensation that he was experiencing. He began, therefore, to imprecate vengeance, walked himself into a fair, cold-hearted, malicious passion, and avowed most distinctly that he hated her. As for him, most ardently he hoped that, some day or other, they might again meet at six o'clock in the morning in Kensington Gardens, but in a different relation to each other.

It was dark when he entered the Castle. He was about ascending to his own room, when he determined not to be cowed, and resolved to show himself the regardless witness of their mutual loves: so he repaired to the drawing-room. At one end of this very spacious apartment, Mr. Dacre and Arundel were walking in deep converse; at the other sat Miss Dacre at a table reading. The Duke seized a chair without looking at her, dragged it along to the fireplace, and there seating himself, with his arms folded, his feet on the fender, and his chair tilting, he appeared to be lost in the abstracting contemplation of the consuming fuel.

Some minutes had passed, when a slight sound, like a fluttering bird, made him look up: Miss Dacre was standing at his side.

'Is your head better?' she asked him, in a soft voice.

'Thank you, it is quite well,' he replied, in a sullen one.

There was a moment's pause, and then she again spoke.

'I am sure you are not well.'

'Perfectly, thank you.'

'Something has happened, then,' she said, rather imploringly.

'What should have happened?' he rejoined, pettishly.

'You are very strange; very unlike what you always are.'

'What I always am is of no consequence to myself, or to anyone else; and as for what I am now, I cannot always command my feelings, though I shall take care that they are not again observed.'

'I have offended you?'

'Then you have shown your discretion, for you should always offend the forlorn.'

'I did not think before that you were bitter.'

'That has made me bitter which has made all others so.'

'What?'

'Disappointment.'

Another pause, yet she did not go.

'I will not quarrel, and so you need not try. You are consigned to my care, and I am to amuse you. What shall we do?'

'Do what you like, Miss Dacre; but spare, oh! spare me your pity!'

'You do indeed surprise me. Pity! I was not thinking of pity! But you are indeed serious, and I leave you.'

He turned; he seized her hand.

'Nay! do not go. Forgive me,' he said, 'forgive me, for I am most miserable.'

'Why, why are you?'

'Oh! do not ask; you agonise me.'

'Shall I sing? Shall I charm the evil spirit?'

'Anything?'

She tripped to the piano, and an air, bursting like the spring, and gay as a village feast, filled the room with its delight. He listened, and each instant the chilly weight loosened from his heart. Her balmy voice now came upon his ear, breathing joy and cheerfulness, content and love. Could love be the savage passion which lately subjugated his soul? He rose from his seat; he walked about the room; each minute his heart was lighter, his brow more smooth. A thousand thoughts, beautiful and quivering like the twilight, glanced o'er his mind in indistinct but exquisite tumult, and hope, like the voice of an angel in a storm, was heard above all. He lifted a chair gently from the ground, and, stealing to the enchantress, seated himself at her side. So softly he reached her, that for a moment he was unperceived. She turned her head, and her eyes met his. Even the ineffable incident was forgotten, as he marked the strange gush of lovely light, that seemed to say—— what to think of was, after all, madness.

CHAPTER V.

Arundel's Disappointment

THE storm was past. He vowed that a dark thought should not again cross his mind. It was fated that she should not be his; but it was some miserable satisfaction that he was only rejected in favour of an attachment which had grown with her years, and had strengthened with her stature, and in deference to an engagement hallowed by time as well as by affection. It was deadly indeed to remember that Fate seemed to have destined him for that happy position, and that his folly had rejected the proffered draught of bliss. He blasphemed against the Fitz-pompeys. However, he did not leave Dacre at the same time as Arundel, but lingered on. His affairs were far from being arranged. The Irish business gave great trouble, and he determined therefore to remain.

It was ridiculous to talk of feeding a passion which was not susceptible of increase. Her society was Heaven; and he resolved to enjoy it, although he was to be expelled. As for his loss of fortune, it gave him not a moment's care. Without her, he felt he could not live in England, and, even ruined, he would be a match for an Italian prince.

So he continued her companion, each day rising with purer feelings and a more benevolent heart; each day more convinced of the falseness of his past existence, and of the possibility of happiness to a well-regulated mind; each day more conscious that duty is nothing more than self-knowledge, and the performance of it consequently the development of feelings which are the only true source of self-gratification. He mourned over the opportunities which he had forfeited of conducing to the happiness of others and himself. Sometimes he had resolved to remain in England and devote himself to his tenantry; but passion blinded him, and he felt that he had erred too far ever to regain the right road.

The election for which Arundel Dacre was a candidate came on. Each day the state of the poll arrived. It was nearly equal to the last. Their agitation was terrible, but forgotten in the deep mortification which they experienced at the announcement of his defeat. He talked to the public boldly of petitioning, and his certainty of ultimate success; but he let them know privately that he had no intention of the first, and no chance of the second. Even Mr. Dacre could mot conceal his deep disappointment; but May was quite in despair. Even if her father could find means of securing him a seat another time, the present great opportunity was lost.

'Surely we can make some arrangement for next session,' said the Duke, whispering hope to her.

'Oh! no, no, no; so much depended upon this. It is not merely his taking a part in the debate, but—but Arundel is so odd, and everything was staked upon this. I cannot tell you what depended upon it. He will leave England directly.'

She did not attempt to conceal her agitation. The Duke rose, and paced the room in a state scarcely less moved. A thought had suddenly flashed upon him. Their marriage doubtless depended upon this success. He knew something of Arundel Dacre, and had heard more. He was convinced of the truth of his suspicion. Either the nephew would not claim her hand until he had carved out his own fortunes, or perhaps the uncle made his distinction the condition of his consent. Yet this was odd. It was all odd. A thousand things had occurred which equally puzzled him. Yet he had seen enough to weigh against a thousand thoughts.

CHAPTER VI.

A Generous Action

ANOTHER fortnight glided away, and he was still at the Castle, still the constant and almost sole companion of May Dacre. It is breakfast; the servant is delivering the letter-bag to Mr. Dacre. Interesting moment! when you extend your hand for the billet of a mistress, and receive your tailor's bill! How provokingly slow are most domestic chieftains in this anxious operation! They turn the letters over and over, and upside and down; arrange, confuse, mistake, assort; pretend, like Champollion, to decipher illegible franks, and deliver with a slight remark, which is intended as a friendly admonition, the documents of the unlucky wight who encourages unprivileged correspondents.

A letter was delivered to Miss Dacre. She started, exclaimed, blushed, and tore it open.

'Only you, only you,' she said, extending her hand to the young Duke, 'only you were capable of this!'

It was a letter from Arundel Dacre, not only written but franked by him.

It explained everything that the Duke of St. James might have told them before; but he preferred hearing all himself, from the delighted and delightful lips of Miss Dacre, who read to her father her cousin's letter.

The Duke of St. James had returned him for one of his Cornish boroughs. It appeared that Lord St. Maurice was the previous member, who had accepted the Chiltern Hundreds in his favour.

'You were determined to surprise, as well as delight us,' said Mr. Dacre.

'I am no admirer of mysteries,' said the Duke; 'but the fact is, in the present case, it was not in my power to give you any positive information, and I had no desire to provide you, after your late disappointment, with new sources of anxiety. The only person I could take the liberty with, at so short a notice, was St. Maurice. He, you know, is a Liberal; but he cannot forget that he is the son of a Tory, and has no great ambition to take any active part in affairs at present. I anticipated less difficulty with him than with his father. St. Maurice can command me again when it suits him; but, I confess to you, I have been surprised at my uncle's kindness in this affair. I really have not done justice to his character before, and regret it. He has behaved in the most kind-hearted and the most liberal manner, and put me under obligations which I never shall forget. He seems as desirous of serving my friend as myself; and I assure you, sir, it would give you pleasure to know in what terms of respect he speaks of your family, and particularly of Arundel.'

'Arundel says he shall take his seat the morning of the debate. How very near! how admirably managed! Oh! I never shall recover my surprise and delight! How good you are!'

'He takes his seat, then, to-morrow,' said Mr. Dacre, in a musing tone. 'My letters give a rather nervous account of affairs. We are to win it, they hope, but by two only. As for the Lords, the majority against us will, it is said, be somewhat smaller than usual. We shall never triumph, George, till May is M.P. for the county. Cannot you return her for Pen Bronnock too?'

They talked, as you may suppose, of nothing else. At last Mr. Dacre remembered an appointment with his bailiff, and proposed to the Duke to join him, who acceded.

'And I to be left alone this morning, then!' said Miss Dacre. 'I am sure, as they say of children, I can set to nothing.'

'Come and ride with us, then!'

'An excellent idea! Let us canter over to Hauteville! I am just in the humour for a gallop up the avenue, and feel half emancipated already with a Dacre in the House! Oh! to-morrow, how nervous I shall be!'

'I will despatch Barrington, then,' said Mr. Dacre, 'and join you in ten minutes.'

'How good you are!' said Miss Dacre to the Duke. 'How can we thank you enough? What can we do for you?'

'You have thanked me enough. What have I done after all? My opportunity to serve my friends is brief. Is it wonderful that I seize the opportunity?'

'Brief! brief! Why do you always say so? Why do you talk so of leaving us?'

'My visit to you has been already too long. It must soon end, and I remain not in England when it ceases.'

'Come and live at Hauteville, and be near us?'

He faintly smiled as he said, 'No, no; my doom is fixed. Hauteville is the last place that I should choose for my residence, even if I remained in England. But I hear the horses.'

The important night at length arrived, or rather the important messenger, who brought down, express, a report of its proceedings to Castle Dacre.

Nothing is more singular than the various success of men in the House of Commons. Fellows who have been the oracles of coteries from their birth; who have gone through the regular process of gold medals, senior wranglerships, and double firsts, who have nightly sat down amid tumultuous cheering in debating societies, and can harangue with unruffled foreheads and unfaltering voice, from one end of a dinner-table to the other, who, on all occasions, have something to say, and can speak with fluency on what they know nothing about, no sooner rise in the House than their spells desert them. All their effrontery vanishes. Commonplace ideas are rendered even more uninteresting by monotonous delivery; and keenly alive as even boobies are in those sacred walls to the ridiculous, no one appears more thoroughly aware of his unexpected and astounding deficiencies than the orator himself. He regains his seat hot and hard, sultry and stiff, with a burning cheek and an icy hand, repressing his breath lest it should give evidence of an existence of which he is ashamed, and clenching his fist, that the pressure may secretly convince him that he has not as completely annihilated his stupid body as his false reputation.

On the other hand, persons whom the women have long deplored, and the men long pitied, as having 'no manner,' who blush when you speak to them, and blunder when they speak to you, suddenly jump up in the House with a self-confidence, which is only equalled by their consummate ability. And so it was with Arundel Dacre. He rose the first night that he took his seat (a great disadvantage, of which no one was more sensible than himself), and for an hour and a half he addressed the fullest House that had long been assembled, with the self-possession of an habitual debater. His clenching argument, and his luminous detail, might have been expected from one who had the reputation of having been a student. What was more surprising was, the withering sarcasm that blasted like the simoom, the brilliant sallies of wit that flashed like a sabre, the gushing eddies of humour that drowned all opposition and overwhelmed those ponderous and unwieldy arguments which the producers announced as rocks, but which he proved to be porpoises. Never was there such a triumphant début; and a peroration of genuine eloquence, because of genuine feeling, concluded amid the long and renewed cheers of all parties.

The truth is, Eloquence is the child of Knowledge. When a mind is full, like a wholesome river, it is also clear. Confusion and obscurity are much oftener the results of ignorance than of inefficiency. Few are the men who cannot express their meaning, when the occasion demands the energy; as the lowest will defend their lives with acuteness, and sometimes even with eloquence. They are masters of their subject. Knowledge must be gained by ourselves. Mankind may supply us with facts; but the results, even if they agree with previous ones, must be the work of our own mind. To make others feel, we must feel ourselves; and to feel ourselves, we must be natural. This we can never be, when we are vomiting forth the dogmas of the schools. Knowledge is not a mere collection of words; and it is a delusion to suppose that thought can be obtained by the aid of any other intellect than our own. What is repetition, by a curious mystery ceases to be truth, even if it were truth when it was first heard; as the shadow in a mirror, though it move and mimic all the actions of vitality, is not life. When a man is not speaking, or writing, from his own mind, he is as insipid company as a looking-glass.

Before a man can address a popular assembly with command, he must know something of mankind; and he can know nothing of mankind without knowing something of himself. Self-knowledge is the property of that man whose passions have their play, but who ponders over their results. Such a man sympathises by inspiration with his kind. He has a key to every heart. He can divine, in the flash of a single thought, all that they require, all that they wish. Such a man speaks to their very core. All feel that a master-hand tears off the veil of cant, with which, from necessity, they have enveloped their souls; for cant is nothing more than the sophistry which results from attempting to account for what is unintelligible, or to defend what is improper.

Perhaps, although we use the term, we never have had oratory in England. There is an essential difference between oratory and debating. Oratory seems an accomplishment confined to the ancients, unless the French preachers may put in their claim, and some of the Irish lawyers. Mr. Shiel's speech in Kent was a fine oration; and the boobies who taunted him for having got it by rote, were not aware that in doing so he only wisely followed the example of Pericles, Demosthenes, Lysias, Isocrates, Hortensius, Cicero, CÃ¦sar, and every great orator of antiquity. Oratory is essentially the accomplishment of antiquity: it was their most efficient mode of communicating thought; it was their substitute for printing.

I like a good debate; and, when a stripling, used sometimes to be stifled in the Gallery, or enjoy the easier privileges of a member's son. I like, I say, a good debate, and have no objection to a due mixture of bores, which are a relief. I remember none of the giants of former days; but I have heard Canning. He was a consummate rhetorician; but there seemed to me a dash of commonplace in all that he said, and frequent indications of the absence of an original mind. To the last, he never got clear of 'Good God, sir!' and all the other hackneyed ejaculations of his youthful debating clubs. The most commanding speaker that I ever listened to is, I think, Sir Francis Burdett. I never heard him in the House; but at an election. He was full of music, graceÂ» and dignity, even amid all the vulgar tumult; and, unlike all mob orators, raised the taste of the populace to him, instead of lowering his own to theirs. His colleague, Mr. Hobhouse, seemed to me ill qualified for a demagogue, though he spoke with power. He is rather too elaborate, and a little heavy, but fluent, and never weak. His thoughtful and highly-cultivated mind maintains him under all circumstances; and his breeding never deserts him. Sound sense comes recommended from his lips by the language of a scholar and the urbanity of a gentleman.

Mr. Brougham, at present, reigns paramount in the House of Commons. I think the lawyer has spoiled the statesman. He is said to have great powers of sarcasm. From what I have observed there, I should think very little ones would be quite sufficient. Many a sneer withers in those walls, which would scarcely, I think, blight a currant-bush out of them; and I have seen the House convulsed with raillery which, in other society, would infallibly settle the rallier to be a bore beyond all tolerance. Even an idiot can raise a smile. They are so good-natured, or find it so dull. Mr. Canning's badinage was the most successful, though I confess I have listened to few things more calculated to make a man gloomy. But the House always ran riot, taking everything for granted, and cracked their universal sides before he opened his mouth. The fault of Mr. Brougham is, that he holds no intellect at present in great dread, and, consequently, allows himself on all occasions to run wild. Few men hazard more unphilosophical observations; but he is safe, because there is no one to notice them. On all great occasions, Mr. Brougham has come up to the mark; an infallible test of a man of genius.

I hear that Mr. Macaulay is to be returned. If he speaks half as well as he writes, the House will be in fashion again. I fear that he is one of those who, like the individual whom he has most studied, will 'give up to party what was meant for mankind.'

At any rate, he must get rid of his rabidity. He writes now on all subjects, as if he certainly intended to be a renegade, and was determined to make the contrast complete.

Mr. Peel is the model of a minister, and improves as a speaker; though, like most of the rest, he is fluent without the least style. He should not get so often in a passion either, or, if he do, should not get out of one so easily. His sweet apologies are cloying. His candour—he will do well to get rid of that. He can make a present of it to Mr. Huskisson, who is a memorable instance of the value of knowledge, which maintains a man under all circumstances and all disadvantages, and will.

In the Lords, I admire the Duke. The readiness with which he has adopted the air of a debater, shows the man of genius. There is a gruff, husky sort of a downright Montaignish naÃ¯vetÃ© about him, which is quaint, unusual, and tells. You plainly perceive that he is determined to be a civilian; and he is as offended if you drop a hint that he occasionally wears an uniform, as a servant on a holiday if you mention the word *livery*.

Lord Grey speaks with feeling, and is better to hear than to read, though ever strong and impressive. Lord Holland's speeches are like a *refacimento* of all the suppressed passages in Clarendon, and the notes in the new edition of Bishop Burnet's Memoirs: but taste throws a delicate hue over the curious medley, and the candour of a philosophic mind shows that in the library of Holland House he can sometimes cease to be a partisan.

One thing is clear, that a man may speak very well in the House of Commons, and fail very completely in the House of Lords. There are two distinct styles requisite: I intend, in the course of my career, if I have time, to give a specimen of both. In the Lower House Don Juan may perhaps be our model; in the Upper House, Paradise Lost.

BOOK V
[CONTINUED]

CHAPTER VII.

'To See Ourselves as Others See Us.'

NOTHING was talked of in Yorkshire but Mr. Arundel Dacre's speech. All the world flocked to Castle Dacre to compliment and to congratulate; and an universal hope was expressed that he might come in for the county, if indeed the success of his eloquence did not enable his uncle to pre-occupy that honour. Even the calm Mr. Dacre shared the general elation, and told the Duke of St. James regularly every day that it was all owing to him. May Dacre was enthusiastic; but her gratitude to him was synonymous with her love for Arundel, and valued accordingly. The Duke, however, felt that he had acted at once magnanimously, generously, and wisely. The consciousness of a noble action is itself ennobling. His spirit expanded with the exciting effects which his conduct had produced; and he felt consolation under all his misery from the conviction that he had now claims to be remembered, and perhaps regarded, when he was no more among them.

The Bill went swimmingly through the Commons, the majority of two gradually swelling into eleven; and the important night in the Lords was at hand.

'Lord Faulconcourt writes,' said Mr. Dacre, 'that they expect only thirty-eight against us.'

'Ah! that terrible House of Lords!' said Miss Dacre. 'Let us see: when does it come on, the day after to-morrow? Scarcely forty-eight hours and all will be over, and we shall be just where we were. You and your friends manage very badly in your House,' she added, addressing herself to the Duke.

'I do all I can,' said his Grace, smiling. 'Burlington has my proxy.'

'That is exactly what I complain of. On such an occasion, there should be no proxies. Personal attendance would indicate a keener interest in the result. Ah! if I were Duke of St. James for one night!'

'Ah! that you would be Duchess of St. James!' thought the Duke; but a despairing lover has no heart for jokes, and so he did not give utterance to the wish. He felt a little agitated, and caught May Dacre's eye. She smiled, and slightly blushed, as if she felt the awkwardness of her remark, though too late.

The Duke retired early, but not to sleep. His mind was busied on a great deed. It was past midnight before he could compose his agitated feelings to repose, and by five o'clock he was again up. He dressed himself, and then put on a rough travelling coat, which, with a shawl, effectually disguised his person; and putting in one pocket a shirt, and in the other a few articles from his dressing-case, the Duke of St. James stole out of Castle Dacre, leaving a note for his host, accounting for his sudden departure by urgent business at Hauteville, and promising a return in a day or two.

The fresh morn had fully broke. He took his hurried way through the long dewy grass, and, crossing the Park, gained the road, which, however, was not the high one. He had yet another hour's rapid walk, before he could reach his point of destination; and when that was accomplished, he found himself at a small public-house, bearing for a sign his own arms, and situated in the high road opposite his own Park. He was confident that his person was unknown to the host, or to any of the early idlers who were lingering about the mail, then breakfasting.

'Any room, guard, to London?'

'Room inside, sir: just going off.'

The door was opened, and the Duke of St. James took his seat in the Edinburgh and York Mail. He had two companions: the first, because apparently the most important, was a hard-featured, grey-headed gentleman, with a somewhat supercilious look, and a mingled air of acuteness and conceit; the other was a humble-looking widow in her weeds, middle-aged, and sad. These persons had recently roused themselves from their nocturnal slumbers, and now, after their welcome meal and hurried toilet, looked as fresh as birds.

'Well! now we are off,' said the gentleman. 'Very neat, cleanly little house this, ma'am,' continued he to his companion. 'What is the sign?' 'The Hauteville Arms.' 'Oh! Hauteville; that is—that is, let me see! the St. James family. Ah! a pretty fool that young man has made of himself, by all accounts. Eh! sir?'

'I have reason to believe so,' said the Duke.

'I suppose this is his park, eh? Hem! going to London, sir?'

'I am.'

'Ah! hem! Hauteville Park, I suppose, this. Fine ground wasted. What the use of parks is, I can't say.'

'The place seems well kept up,' said the widow.

'So much the worse; I wish it were in ruins.'

'Well, for my part,' continued the widow in a low voice, 'I think a park nearly the most beautiful thing we have. Foreigners, you know, sir——'

'Ah! I know what you are going to say,' observed the gentleman in a curt, gruffish voice. 'It is all nonsense. Foreigners are fools. Don't talk to me of

- 264 -

beauty; a mere word. What is the use of all this? It produces about as much benefit to society as its owner does.'

'And do you think his existence, then, perfectly useless?' asked the Duke.

'To be sure, I do. So the world will, some day or other. We are opening our eyes fast. Men begin to ask themselves what the use of an aristocracy is. That is the test, sir.'

'I think it not very difficult to demonstrate the use of an aristocracy,' mildly observed the Duke.

'Pooh! nonsense, sir! I know what you are going to say; but we have got beyond all that. Have you read this, sir? This article on the aristocracy in "The Screw and Lever Review?"'

'I have not, sir.'

'Then I advise you to make yourself master of it, and you will talk no more of the aristocracy. A few more articles like this, and a few more noblemen like the man who has got this park, and people will open their eyes at last.'

'I should think,' said his Grace, 'that the follies of the man who had got this park have been productive of evil only to himself. In fact, sir, according to your own system, a prodigal noble seems to be a very desirable member of the commonwealth and a complete leveller.'

'We shall get rid of them all soon, sir,' said his companion, with a malignant smile.

'I have heard that he is very young, sir,' remarked the widow.

'What is that to you or me?'

'Ah! youth is a trying time. Let us hope the best! He may turn out well yet, poor soul!'

'I hope not. Don't talk to me of poor souls. There is a poor soul,' said the utilitarian, pointing to an old man breaking stones on the highway. 'That is what I call a poor soul, not a young prodigal, whose life has been one long career of infamous debauchery.'

'You appear to have heard much of this young nobleman,' said the Duke; 'but it does not follow, sir, that you have heard truth.'

'Very true, sir,' said the widow. 'The world is very foul-mouthed. Let us hope he is not so very bad.'

'I tell you what, my friends; you know nothing about what you are talking of. I don't speak without foundation. You have not the least idea, sir, how this fellow has lived. Now, what I am going to tell you is a fact: I know it to be a fact. A very intimate friend of mine, who knows a person, who is a very intimate friend of an intimate friend of a person, who knows the Duke of St. James, told me himself, that one night they had for supper—what do you think ma'am?—Venison cutlets, each served up in a hundred pound note!'

'Mercy!' exclaimed the widow.

'And do you believe it?' asked the Duke.

'Believe it! I know it!'

'He is very young,' said the widow. 'Youth is a very trying time.'

'Nothing to do with his youth. It's the system, the infernal system. If that man had to work for his bread, like everybody else, do you think he would dine off bank notes? No! to be sure he wouldn't! It's the system.'

'Young people are very wild!' said the widow.

'Pooh! ma'am. Nonsense! Don't talk cant. If a man be properly educated, he is as capable at one-and-twenty of managing anything, as at any time in his life; more capable. Look at the men who write "The Screw and Lever;" the first men in the country. Look at them. Not one of age. Look at the man who wrote this article on the aristocracy: young Duncan Macmorrogh. Look at him, I say, the first man in the country by far.'

'I never heard his name before,' calmly observed the Duke.

'Not heard his name? Not heard of young Duncan Macmorrogh, the first man of the day, by far; not heard of him? Go and ask the Marquess of Sheepshead what he thinks of him. Go and ask Lord Two and Two what he thinks of him. Duncan dines with Lord Two and Two every week.'

The Duke smiled, and his companion proceeded.

'Well, again, look at his friends. There is young First Principles. What a head that fellow has got! Here, this article on India is by him. He'll knock up their Charter. He is a clerk in the India House. Up to the detail, you see. Let me read you this passage on monopolies. Then there is young Tribonian Quirk. By G—, what a mind that fellow has got! By G—, nothing but first principles will go down with these fellows! They laugh at anything else. By G—, sir, they look upon the administration of the present day as a parcel of sucking babes! When I was last in town, Quirk told me that he would not give that for all the public men that ever existed! He is keeping his terms at Gray's Inn. This article on a new Code is by him. Shows as plain as light, that, by sticking close to first principles, the laws of the country might be carried in every man's waistcoat pocket.'

The coach stopped, and a colloquy ensued.

'Any room to Selby?'

'Outside or in?'

'Out, to be sure.'

'Room inside only.'

'Well! in then.'

The door opened, and a singularly quaint-looking personage presented himself. He was very stiff and prim in his appearance; dressed in a blue coat and scarlet waistcoat, with a rich bandanna handkerchief tied very neatly round his neck, and a very new hat, to which his head seemed little habituated.

'Sorry to disturb you, ladies and gentlemen: not exactly the proper place for me. Don't be alarmed. I'm always respectful wherever I am. My rule through life is to be respectful.'

'Well, now, in with you,' said the guard.

'Be respectful, my friend, and don't talk so to an old soldier who has served his king and his country.'

Off they went.

'Majesty's service?' asked the stranger of the Duke.

'I have not that honour.'

'Hum! Lawyer, perhaps?'

'Not a lawyer.'

'Hum! A gentleman, I suppose?'

The Duke was silent; and so the stranger addressed himself to the anti-aristocrat, who seemed vastly annoyed by the intrusion of so low a personage.

'Going to London, sir?'

'I tell you what, my friend, at once; I never answer impertinent questions.'

'No offence, I hope, sir! Sorry to offend. I'm always respectful. Madam! I hope I don't inconvenience you; I should be sorry to do that. We sailors, you know, are always ready to accommodate the ladies.'

'Sailor!' exclaimed the acute utilitarian, his curiosity stifling his hauteur. 'Why! just now, I thought you were a soldier.'

'Well! so I am.'

'Well, my friend, you are a conjuror then.'

'No, I ayn't; I'm a marine.'

'A very useless person, then.'

'What do you mean?'

'I mean to say, that if the sailors were properly educated, such an amphibious corps would never have been formed, and some of the most atrocious sinecures ever tolerated would consequently not have existed.'

'Sinecures! I never heard of him. I served under Lord Combermere. Maybe you have heard of him, ma'am? A nice man; a beautiful man. I have seen him stand in a field like that, with the shot falling about him like hail, and caring no more for them than peas.'

'If that were for bravado,' said the utilitarian, 'I think it a very silly thing.'

'Bravado! I never heard of him. It was for his king and country.'

'Was it in India?' asked the widow.

'In a manner, ma'am,' said the marine, very courteously. 'At Bhurtpore, up by Pershy, and thereabouts; the lake of Cashmere, where all the shawls come from. Maybe you have heard of Cashmere, ma'am?'

'"Who has not heard of the vale of Cashmere!"' hummed the Duke to himself.

'Ah! I thought so,' said the marine; 'all people know much the same; for some have seen, and some have read. I can't read, but I have served my king and country for five-and-twenty years, and I have used my eyes.'

'Better than reading,' said the Duke, humouring the character.

'I'll tell you what,' said the marine, with a knowing look. 'I suspect there is a d—d lot of lies in your books. I landed in England last seventh of June, and went to see St. Paul's. "This is the greatest building in the world," says the man. Thinks I, "You lie." I did not tell him so, because I am always respectful. I tell you what, sir; maybe you think St. Paul's the greatest building in the world, but I tell you what, it's a lie. I have seen one greater. Maybe, ma'am, you think I am telling you a lie too; but I am not. Go and ask Captain Jones, of the 58th. I went with him: I give you his name: go and ask Captain Jones, of the 58th, if I be telling you a lie. The building I mean is the palace of the Sultan Acber; for I have served my king and country five-and-twenty years last seventh of June, and have seen strange things; all built of precious stones, ma'am. What do you think of that? All built of precious stones; carnelian, of which you make your seals; as sure as I'm a sinner saved. If I ayn't speaking the truth, I am not going to Selby. Maybe you'd like to know why I am going to Selby? I'll tell you what. Five-and-twenty years have I served my king and country last seventh of June. Now I begin with the beginning. I ran away from home when I was eighteen, you see! and, after the siege of Bhurtpore, I was sitting on a bale of silk alone, and I said to myself, I'll go and see my mother. Sure as I am going to Selby, that's the whole. I landed in England last seventh of June, absent five-and-twenty years, serving my king and country. I sent them a letter last night. I put it in the post myself. Maybe I shall be there before my letter now.'

'To be sure you will,' said the utilitarian; 'what made you do such a silly thing? Why, your letter is in this coach.'

'Well! I shouldn't wonder. I shall be there before my letter now. All nonsense, letters: my wife wrote it at Falmouth.'

'You are married, then?' said the widow.

'Ayn't I, though? The sweetest cretur, madam, though I say it before you, that ever lived.'

'Why did you not bring your wife with you?' asked the widow.

'And wouldn't I be very glad to? but she wouldn't come among strangers at once; and so I have got a letter, which she wrote for me, to put in the post, in case they are glad to see me, and then she will come on.'

'And you, I suppose, are not sorry to have a holiday?' said the Duke.

'Ayn't I, though? Ayn't I as low about leaving her as ever I was in my life; and so is the poor cretur. She won't eat a bit of victuals till I come back, I'll be sworn; not a bit, I'll be bound to say that; and myself, although I am an old soldier and served my king and country for five-and-twenty years, and so got knocked about, and used to anything, as it were, I don't know how it is, but I always feel queer whenever I am away from her. I shan't make a hearty meal till I see her. Somehow or other, when I am away from her, everything feels dry in the throat.'

'You are very fond of her, I see,' said the Duke.

'And ought I not to be? Didn't I ask her three times before she said *yes*? Those are the wives for wear, sir. None of the fruit that falls at a shaking for me! Hasn't she stuck by me in every climate, and in every land I was in? Not a fellow in the company had such a wife. Wouldn't I throw myself off this coach this moment, to give her a moment's peace? That I would, though; d——me if I wouldn't.'

'Hush! hush!' said the widow; 'never swear. I am afraid you talk too much of your love,' she added, with a faint smile.

'Ah! you don't know my wife, ma'am. Are you married, sir?'

'I have not that happiness,' said the Duke.

'Well, there is nothing like it! but don't take the fruit that falls at a shake. But this, I suppose, is Selby?'

The marine took his departure, having stayed long enough to raise in the young Duke's mind curious feelings.

As he was plunged into reverie, and as the widow was silent, conversation was not resumed until the coach stopped for dinner.

'We stop here half-an-hour, gentlemen,' said the guard. 'Mrs. Burnet,' he continued, to the widow, 'let me hand you out.'

They entered the parlour of the inn. The Duke, who was ignorant of the etiquette of the road, did not proceed to the discharge of his duties, as the youngest guest, with all the promptness desired by his fellow-travellers.

'Now, sir,' said an outside, 'I will thank you for a slice of that mutton, and will join you, if you have no objection in a bottle of sherry.'

'What you please, sir. May I have the pleasure of helping you, ma'am?'

After dinner the Duke took advantage of a vacant outside place.

Tom Rawlins was the model of a guard. Young, robust, and gay, he had a letter, a word, or a wink for all he met. All seasons were the same to him; night or day he was ever awake, and ever alive to all the interest of the road; now joining in conversation with a passenger, shrewd, sensible, and respectful; now exchanging a little elegant badinage with the coachman; now bowing to a pretty girl; now quizzing a passer-by; he was off and on his seat in an instant, and, in the whiff of his cigar, would lock a wheel, or unlock a passenger.

From him the young Duke learned that his fellow-inside was Mr. Duncan Macmorrogh, senior, a writer at Edinburgh, and, of course, the father of the first man of the day. Tom Rawlins could not tell his Grace as much about the principal writer in 'The Screw and Lever Review' as we can; for Tom was no patron of our periodical literature, farther than a police report in the Publican's Journal. Young Duncan Macmorrogh was a limb of the law, who had just brought himself into notice by a series of articles in 'The Screw and Lever,' in which he had subjected the universe piecemeal to his critical analysis. Duncan Macmorrogh cut up the creation, and got a name. His attack upon mountains was most violent, and proved, by its personality, that he had come from the Lowlands. He demonstrated the inutility of all elevation, and declared that the Andes were the aristocracy of the globe. Rivers he rather patronised; but flowers he quite pulled to pieces, and proved them to be the most useless of existences. Duncan Macmorrogh informed us that we were quite wrong in supposing ourselves to be the miracle of creation. On the contrary, he avowed that already there were various pieces of machinery of far more importance than man; and he had no doubt, in time, that a superior race would arise, got by a steam-engine on a spinning-jenny.

The other 'inside' was the widow of a former curate of a Northumbrian village. Some friend had obtained for her only child a clerkship in a public office, and for some time this idol of her heart had gone on prospering; but unfortunately, of late, Charles Burnet had got into a bad set, was now involved in a terrible scrape, and, as Tom Rawlins feared, must lose his situation and go to ruin.

'She was half distracted when she heard it first, poor creature! I have known her all my life, sir. Many the kind word and glass of ale I have had at her house, and that's what makes me feel for her, you see. I do what I can to make the journey easy to her, for it is a pull at her years. God bless her! there is not a better body in this world; that I will, say for her. When I was a boy, I used to be the playfellow in a manner with Charley Burnet: a gay lad, sir, as ever you'd wish to see in a summer's day, and the devil among the girls always, and that's been the ruin of him; and as open-a-hearted fellow as ever lived. D———me! I'd walk to the land's end to save him, if it were only for his mother's sake, to say nothing of himself.'

'And can nothing be done?' asked the Duke.

'Why, you see, he is back in Â£ s. d.; and, to make it up, the poor body must sell her all, and he won't let her do it, and wrote a letter like a prince (No room, sir), as fine a letter as ever you read (Hilloa, there! What! are you asleep?)—as ever you read on a summer's day. I didn't see it, but my mother told me it was as good as e'er a one of the old gentleman's sermons. "Mother," said he, "my sins be upon my own head. I can bear disgrace (How do, Mr. Wilkins?), but I cannot bear to see you a beggar!"'

'Poor fellow!'

'Ay! sir, as good-a-hearted fellow as ever you'd wish to meet!'

'Is he involved to a great extent, think you?'

'Oh! a long figure, sir (I say, Betty, I've got a letter for you from your sweetheart), a very long figure, sir (Here, take it!); I should be sorry (Don't blush; no message?)—I should be sorry to take two hundred pounds to pay it. No, I wouldn't take two hundred pounds, that I wouldn't (I say, Jacob, stop at old Bag Smith's).'

Night came on, and the Duke resumed his inside place. Mr. Macmorrogh went to sleep over his son's article; and the Duke feigned slumber, though he was only indulging in reverie. He opened his eyes, and a light, which they passed, revealed the countenance of the widow. Tears were stealing down her face.

'I have no mother; I have no one to weep for me,' thought the Duke; 'and yet, if I had been in this youth's station, my career probably would have been as fatal. Let me assist her. Alas! how I have misused my power, when, even to do this slight deed, I am obliged to hesitate, and consider whether it be practicable.'

The coach again stopped for a quarter of an hour. The Duke had, in consideration of the indefinite period of his visit, supplied himself amply with money on repairing to Dacre. Besides his purse, which was well stored for the road, he had somewhat more than three hundred pounds in his notebook. He took advantage of their tarrying, to inclose it and its contents in a sheet of paper with these lines:

'An unknown friend requests Mrs. Burnet to accept this token of his sympathy with suffering virtue.'

Determined to find some means to put this in her possession before their parting, he resumed his place. The Scotchman now prepared for his night's repose. He produced a pillow for his back, a bag for his feet, and a cap for his head. These, and a glass of brandy-and-water, in time produced a due effect, and he was soon fast asleep. Even to the widow, night brought some solace. The Duke alone found no repose. Unused to travelling in public conveyances at night, and unprovided with any of the ingenious expedients of a mail coach adventurer, he felt all the inconveniences of an inexperienced traveller. The seat was unendurably hard, his back ached, his head whirled, the confounded sherry, slight as was his portion, had made him feverish, and he felt at once excited and exhausted. He was sad, too; very depressed. Alone, and no longer surrounded with that splendour which had hitherto made solitude precious, life seemed stripped of all its ennobling spirit. His energy vanished. He repented his rashness; and the impulse of the previous night, which had gathered fresh power from the dewy moon, vanished. He felt alone, and without a friend, and night passed without a moment's slumber, watching the driving clouds.

The last fifteen miles seemed longer than the whole journey. At St. Alban's he got out, took a cup of coffee with Tom Rawlins, and, although the morning was raw, again seated himself by his side. In the first gloomy little suburb Mrs. Burnet got out. The Duke sent Rawlins after her with the parcel, with peremptory instructions to leave it. He watched the widow protesting it was not hers, his faithful emissary appealing to the direction, and with delight he observed it left in her hands. They rattled into London, stopped in

Lombard Street, reached Holborn, entered an archway; the coachman threw the whip and reins from his now careless hands. The Duke bade farewell to Tom Rawlins, and was shown to a bed.

CHAPTER VIII.

The Duke Makes a Speech

THE return of morning had in some degree dissipated the gloom that had settled on the young Duke during the night. Sound and light made him feel less forlorn, and for a moment his soul again responded to his high purpose. But now he was to seek necessary repose. In vain. His heated frame and anxious mind were alike restless. He turned, he tossed in his bed, but he could not banish from his ear the whirling sound of his late conveyance, the snore of Mr. Macmorrogh, and the voice of Tom Rawlins. He kept dwelling on every petty incident of his journey, and repeating in his mind every petty saying. His determination to slumber made him even less sleepy. Conscious that repose was absolutely necessary to the performance of his task, and dreading that the boon was now unattainable, he became each moment more feverish and more nervous; a crowd of half-formed ideas and images flitted over his heated brain. Failure, misery, May Dacre, Tom Rawlins, boiled beef, Mrs. Burnet, the aristocracy, mountains and the marine, and the tower of St. Alban's cathedral, hurried along in infinite confusion. But there is nothing like experience. In a state of distraction, he remembered the hopeless but refreshing sleep he had gained after his fatal adventure at Brighton. He jumped out of bed, and threw himself on the floor, and in a few minutes, from the same cause, his excited senses subsided into slumber.

He awoke; the sun was shining through his rough shutter. It was noon. He jumped up, rang the bell, and asked for a bath. The chambermaid did not seem exactly to comprehend his meaning, but said she would speak to the waiter. He was the first gentleman who ever had asked for a bath at the Dragon with Two Tails. The waiter informed him that he might get a bath, he believed, at the Hum-mums. The Duke dressed, and to the Hummums he then took his way. As he was leaving the yard, he was followed by an ostler, who, in a voice musically hoarse, thus addressed him:

'Have you seen missis, sir?'

'Do you mean me? No, I have not seen your missis;' and the Duke proceeded.

'Sir, sir,' said the ostler, running after him, 'I think you said you had not seen missis?'

'You think right,' said the Duke, astonished; and again he walked on.

'Sir, sir,' said the pursuing ostler, 'I don't think you have got any luggage?'

'Oh! I beg your pardon,' said the Duke; 'I see it. I am in your debt; but I meant to return.'

'No doubt on't, sir; but when gemmen don't have no luggage, they sees missis before they go, sir.'

'Well, what am I in your debt? I can pay you here.'

'Five shillings, sir.'

'Here!' said the Duke; 'and tell me when a coach leaves this place to-morrow for Yorkshire.'

'Half-past six o'clock in the morning precisely,' said the ostler.

'Well, my good fellow, I depend upon your securing me a place; and that is for yourself,' added his Grace, throwing him a sovereign. 'Now, mind; I depend upon you.'

The man stared as if he had been suddenly taken into partnership with missis; at length he found his tongue.

'Your honour may depend upon me. Where would you like to sit? In or out? Back to your horses, or the front? Get you the box if you like. Where's your great coat, sir? I'll brush it for you.'

The bath and the breakfast brought our hero round a good deal, and at half-past two he stole to a solitary part of St. James's Park, to stretch his legs and collect his senses. We must now let our readers into a secret, which perhaps they have already unravelled. The Duke had hurried to London with the determination, not only of attending the debate, but of participating in it. His Grace was no politician; but the question at issue was one simple in its nature and so domestic in its spirit, that few men could have arrived at his period of life without having heard its merits, both too often and too amply discussed. He was master of all the points of interest, and he had sufficient confidence in himself to believe that he could do them justice. He walked up and down, conning over in his mind not only the remarks which he intended to make, but the very language in which he meant to offer them. As he formed sentences, almost for the first time, his courage and his fancy alike warmed: his sanguine spirit sympathised with the nobility of the imaginary scene, and inspirited the intonations of his modulated voice.

About four o'clock he repaired to the House. Walking up one of the passages his progress was stopped by the back of an individual bowing with great civility to a patronising peer, and my-lording him with painful repetition. The nobleman was Lord Fitz-pompey; the bowing gentleman, Mr. Duncan Macmorrogh, the anti-aristocrat, and father of the first man of the day.

'George! is it possible!' exclaimed Lord Fitz-pompey. 'I will speak to you in the House,' said the Duke, passing on, and bowing to Mr. Duncan Macmorrogh.

He recalled his proxy from the Duke of Burlington, and accounted for his presence to many astonished friends by being on his way to the Continent; and, passing through London, thought he might as well be present, particularly as he was about to reside for some time in Catholic countries. It was the last compliment that he could pay his future host. 'Give me a pinch of snuff.'

The debate began. Don't be alarmed. I shall not describe it. Five or six peers had spoken, and one of the ministers had just sat down when the Duke of St. James rose. He was extremely nervous, but he repeated to himself the name of May Dacre for the hundredth time, and proceeded. He was nearly commencing 'May Dacre' instead of 'My Lords,' but he escaped this blunder. For the first five or ten minutes he spoke in almost as cold and lifeless a style as when he echoed the King's speech; but he was young and seldom troubled them, and was listened to therefore with indulgence. The Duke warmed, and a courteous 'hear, hear,' frequently sounded; the Duke became totally free from embarrassment, and spoke with eloquence and energy. A cheer, a stranger in the House of Lords, rewarded and encouraged him. As an Irish landlord, his sincerity could not be disbelieved when he expressed his conviction of the safety of emancipation; but it was as an English proprietor and British noble that it was evident that his Grace felt most keenly upon this important measure. He described with power the peculiar injustice of the situation of the English Catholics. He professed to feel keenly upon this subject, because his native county had made him well acquainted with the temper of this class; he painted in glowing terms the loyalty, the wealth, the influence, the noble virtues of his Catholic neighbours; and he closed a speech of an hour's duration, in which he had shown that a worn subject was susceptible of novel treatment, and novel interest, amid loud and general cheers. The Lords gathered round him, and many personally congratulated him upon his distinguished success. The debate took its course. At three o'clock the pro-Catholics found themselves in a minority, but a minority in which the prescient might have well discovered the herald of future justice. The speech of the Duke of St. James was the speech of the night.

The Duke walked into White's. It was crowded. The first man who welcomed him was Annesley. He congratulated the Duke with a warmth for which the world did not give him credit.

'I assure you, my dear St. James, that I am one of the few people whom this display has not surprised. I have long observed that you were formed for something better than mere frivolity. And between ourselves I am sick of it. Don't be surprised if you hear that I go to Algiers. Depend upon it that I am on the point of doing something dreadful.' 'Sup with me, St. James,' said Lord Squib; 'I will ask O'Connell to meet you.'

Lord Fitz-pompey and Lord Darrell were profuse in congratulations; but he broke away from them to welcome the man who now advanced. He was one of whom he never thought without a shudder, but whom, for all that, he greatly liked.

'My dear Duke of St. James,' said Arundel Dacre, 'how ashamed I am that this is the first time I have personally thanked you for all your goodness!'

'My dear Dacre, I have to thank you for proving for the first time to the world that I was not without discrimination.'

'No, no,' said Dacre, gaily and easily; 'all the congratulations and all the compliments to-night shall be for you. Believe me, my dear friend, I share your triumph.'

They shook hands with earnestness.

'May will read your speech with exultation,' said Arundel. 'I think we must thank her for making you an orator.'

The Duke faintly smiled and shook his head.

'And how are all our Yorkshire friends?' continued Arundel. 'I am disappointed again in getting down to them; but I hope in the course of the month to pay them a visit.'

'I shall see them in a day or two,' said the Duke. 'I pay Mr. Dacre one more visit before my departure form England.'

'Are you then indeed going?' asked Arundel, in a kind voice.

'For ever.'

'Nay, nay, *ever* is a strong word.'

'It becomes, then, my feelings. However, we will not talk of this. Can I bear any letter for you?'

'I have just written,' replied Arundel, in a gloomy voice, and with a changing countenance, 'and therefore will not trouble you. And yet——'

'What!'

'And yet the letter is an important letter: to me. The post, to be sure, never does miss; but if it were not troubling your Grace too much, I almost would ask you to be its bearer.'

'It will be there as soon,' said the Duke, 'for I shall be off in an hour.'

'I will take it out of the box then,' said Arundel; and he fetched it. 'Here is the letter,' said he on his return: 'pardon me if I impress upon you its

- 277 -

importance. Excuse this emotion, but, indeed, this letter decides my fate. My happiness for life is dependent on its reception!'

He spoke with an air and voice of agitation.

The Duke received the letter in a manner scarcely less disturbed; and with a hope that they might meet before his departure, faintly murmured by one party, and scarcely responded to by the other, they parted.

'Well, now,' said the Duke, 'the farce is complete; and I have come to London to be the bearer of his offered heart! I like this, now. Is there a more contemptible, a more ludicrous, absolutely ludicrous ass than myself? Fear not for its delivery, most religiously shall it be consigned to the hand of its owner. The fellow has paid a compliment to my honour or my simplicity: I fear the last, and really I feel rather proud. But away with these feelings! Have I not seen her in his arms? Pah! Thank God! I spoke. At least, I die in a blaze. Even Annesley does not think me quite a fool. O, May Dacre, May Dacre! if you were but mine, I should be the happiest fellow that ever breathed!'

He breakfasted, and then took his way to the Dragon with Two Tails. The morning was bright, and fresh, and beautiful, even in London. Joy came upon his heart, in spite of all his loneliness, and he was glad and sanguine. He arrived just in time. The coach was about to start. The faithful ostler was there with his great-coat, and the Duke found that he had three fellow-passengers. They were lawyers, and talked for the first two hours of nothing but the case respecting which they were going down into the country. At Woburn, a despatch arrived with the newspapers. All purchased one, and the Duke among the rest. He was well reported, and could now sympathise with, instead of smile at, the anxiety of Lord Darrell.

'The young Duke of St. James seems to have distinguished himself very much,' said the first lawyer.

'So I observe,' said the second one. 'The leading article calls our attention to his speech as the most brilliant delivered.'

'I am surprised,' said the third. 'I thought he was quite a different sort of person.'

'By no means,' said the first: 'I have always had a high opinion of him. I am not one of those who think the worse of a young man because he is a little wild.'

'Nor I,' said the second. 'Young blood, you know, is young blood.'

'A very intimate friend of mine, who knows the Duke of St. James well, once told me,' rejoined the first, 'that I was quite mistaken about him; that he was a person of no common talents; well read, quite a man of the world, and a good deal of wit, too; and let me tell you that in these days wit is no common thing.'

'Certainly not,' said the third. 'We have no wit now.'

'And a kind-hearted, generous fellow,' continued the first, 'and *very* unaffected.'

'I can't bear an affected man,' said the second, without looking off his paper. 'He seems to have made a very fine speech indeed.'

'I should not wonder at his turning out something great,' said the third.

'I have no doubt of it,' said the second.

'Many of these wild fellows do.'

'He is not so wild as we think,' said the first.

'But he is done up,' said the second.

'Is he indeed?' said the third. 'Perhaps by making a speech he wants a place?'

'People don't make speeches for nothing,' said the third.

'I shouldn't wonder if he is after a place in the Household,' said the second.

'Depend upon it, he looks to something more active,' said the first.

'Perhaps he would like to be head of the Admiralty?' said the second.

'Or the Treasury?' said the third.

'That is impossible!' said the first. 'He is too young.'

'He is as old as Pitt,' said the third.

'I hope he will resemble him in nothing but his age, then,' said the first.

'I look upon Pitt as the first man that ever lived,' said the third.

'What!' said the first. 'The man who worked up the national debt to nearly eight hundred millions!'

'What of that?' said the third. 'I look upon the national debt as the source of all our prosperity.'

'The source of all our taxes, you mean.'

'What is the harm of taxes?'

'The harm is, that you will soon have no trade; and when you have no trade, you will have no duties; and when you have no duties, you will have no dividends; and when you have no dividends, you will have no law; and then, where is your source of prosperity?' said the first.

But here the coach stopped, and the Duke got out for an hour.

By midnight they had reached a town not more than thirty miles from Dacre. The Duke was quite exhausted, and determined to stop. In half an hour he enjoyed that deep, dreamless slumber, with which no luxury can compete. One must have passed restless nights for years, to be able to appreciate the value of sound sleep.

CHAPTER IX.

A Last Appeal

HE ROSE early, and managed to reach Dacre at the breakfast hour of the family. He discharged his chaise at the Park gate, and entered the house unseen. He took his way along a corridor lined with plants, which led to the small and favourite room in which the morning meetings of May and himself always took place when they were alone. As he lightly stepped along, he heard a voice that he could not mistake, as it were in animated converse. Agitated by sounds which ever created in him emotion, for a moment he paused. He starts, his eye sparkles with strange delight, a flush comes over his panting features, half of modesty, half of triumph. He listens to his own speech from the lips of the woman he loves. She is reading to her father with melodious energy the passage in which he describes the high qualities of his Catholic neighbours. The intonations of the voice indicate the deep sympathy of the reader. She ceases. He hears the admiring exclamation of his host. He rallies his strength, he advances, he stands before them. She utters almost a shriek of delightful surprise as she welcomes him.

How much there was to say! how much to ask! how much to answer! Even Mr. Dacre poured forth questions like a boy. But May: she could not speak, but leant forward in her chair with an eager ear, and a look of congratulation, that rewarded him for all his exertion. Everything was to be told. How he went; whether he slept in the mail; where he went; what he did; whom he saw; what they said; what they thought; all must be answered. Then fresh exclamations of wonder, delight, and triumph. The Duke forgot everything but his love, and for three hours felt the happiest of men.

At length Mr. Dacre rose and looked at his watch with a shaking head. 'I have a most important appointment,' said he, 'and I must gallop to keep it. God bless you, my dear St. James! I could stay talking with you for ever; but you must be utterly wearied. Now, my dear boy, go to bed.'

'To bed!' exclaimed the Duke. 'Why, Tom Rawlins would laugh at you!'

'And who is Tom Rawlins?'

'Ah! I cannot tell you everything; but assuredly I am not going to bed.'

'Well, May, I leave him to your care; but do not let him talk any more.'

'Oh! sir,' said the Duke, 'I really had forgotten. I am the bearer to you, sir, of a letter from Mr. Arundel Dacre.' He gave it him.

As Mr. Dacre read the communication, his countenance changed, and the smile which before was on his face, vanished. But whether he were displeased, or only serious, it was impossible to ascertain, although the Duke watched him narrowly. At length he said, 'May! here is a letter from Arundel, in which you are much interested.'

'Give it me, then, papa!'

'No, my love; we must speak of this together. But I am pressed for time. When I come home. Remember.' He quitted the room.

They were alone: the Duke began again talking, and Miss Dacre put her finger to her mouth, with a smile.

'I assure you,' said he, 'I am not wearied. I slept at——y, and the only thing I now want is a good walk. Let me be your companion this morning!'

'I was thinking of paying nurse a visit. What say you?'

'Oh! I am ready; anywhere.'

She ran for her bonnet, and he kissed her handkerchief, which she left behind, and, I believe, everything else in the room which bore the slightest relation to her. And then the recollection of Arundel's letter came over him, and his joy fled. When she returned, he was standing before the fire, gloomy and dull.

'I fear you are tired,' she said.

'Not in the least.'

'I shall never forgive myself if all this exertion make you ill.'

'Why not?'

'Because, although I will not tell papa, I am sure my nonsense is the cause of your having gone to London.'

'It is probable; for you are the cause of all that does not disgrace me.' He advanced, and was about to seize her hand; but the accursed miniature occurred to him, and he repressed his feelings, almost with a groan. She, too, had turned away her head, and was busily engaged in tending a flower.

'Because she has explicitly declared her feelings to me, and, sincere in that declaration, honours me by a friendship of which alone I am unworthy, am I to persecute her with my dishonoured overtures—the twice rejected? No, no!'

They took their way through the park, and he soon succeeded in re-assuming the tone that befitted their situation. Traits of the debate, and the debaters, which newspapers cannot convey, and which he had not yet recounted; anecdotes of Annesley and their friends, and other gossip, were offered for her amusement. But if she were amused, she was not lively, but singularly, unusually silent. There was only one point on which she seemed interested, and that was his speech. When he was cheered, and who particularly cheered; who gathered round him, and what they said after the debate: on all these points she was most inquisitive.

They rambled on: nurse was quite forgotten; and at length they found themselves in the beautiful valley, rendered more lovely by the ruins of the abbey. It was a place that the Duke could never forget, and which he ever avoided. He had never renewed his visit since he first gave vent, among its reverend ruins, to his overcharged and most tumultuous heart.

They stood in silence before the holy pile with its vaulting arches and crumbling walls, mellowed by the mild lustre of the declining sun. Not two years had fled since here he first staggered after the breaking glimpses of self-knowledge, and struggled to call order from out the chaos of his mind. Not two years, and yet what a change had come over his existence! How diametrically opposite now were all his thoughts, and views, and feelings, to those which then controlled his fatal soul! How capable, as he firmly believed, was he now of discharging his duty to his Creator and his fellow-men! and yet the boon that ought to have been the reward for all this self-contest, the sweet seal that ought to have ratified this new contract of existence, was wanting.

'Ah!' he exclaimed aloud, and in a voice of anguish, 'ah! if I ne'er had left the walls of Dacre, how different might have been my lot!'

A gentle but involuntary pressure reminded him of the companion whom, for once in his life, he had for a moment forgotten.

'I feel it is madness; I feel it is worse than madness; but must I yield without a struggle, and see my dark fate cover me without an effort? Oh! yes, here, even here, where I have wept over your contempt, even here, although I subject myself to renewed rejection, let—let me tell you, before we part, how I adore you!'

She was silent; a strange courage came over his spirit; and, with a reckless boldness, and rapid voice, a misty sight, and total unconsciousness of all other existence, he resumed the words which had broken out, as if by inspiration.

'I am not worthy of you. Who is? I was worthless. I did not know it. Have not I struggled to be pure? have not I sighed on my nightly pillow for your blessing? Oh! could you read my heart (and sometimes, I think, you can read it, for indeed, with all its faults, it is without guile) I dare to hope that you would pity me. Since we first met, your image has not quitted my conscience for a second. When you thought me least worthy; when you thought me vile, or mad, oh! by all that is sacred, I was the most miserable wretch that ever breathed, and flew to dissipation only for distraction!

- 283 -

'Not—not for a moment have I ceased to think you the best, the most beautiful, the most enchanting and endearing creature that ever graced our earth. Even when I first dared to whisper my insolent affection, believe me, even then, your presence controlled my spirit as no other woman had. I bent to you then in pride and power. The station that I could then offer you was not utterly unworthy of your perfection. I am now a beggar, or, worse, an insolvent noble, and dare I—dare I to ask you to share the fortunes that are broken, and the existence that is obscure?'

She turned; her arm fell over his shoulder; she buried her head in his breast.

CHAPTER X.

'Love is Like a Dizziness.'

MR. DACRE returned home with an excellent appetite, and almost as keen a desire to renew his conversation with his guest; but dinner and the Duke were neither to be commanded. Miss Dacre also could not be found. No information could be obtained of them from any quarter. It was nearly seven o'clock, the hour of dinner. That meal, somewhat to Mr. Dacre's regret, was postponed for half an hour, servants were sent out, and the bell was rung, but no tidings. Mr. Dacre was a little annoyed and more alarmed; he was also hungry, and at half-past seven he sat down to a solitary meal.

About a quarter-past eight a figure rapped at the dining-room window: it was the young Duke. The fat butler seemed astonished, not to say shocked, at this violation of etiquette; nevertheless, he slowly opened the window.

'Anything the matter, George? Where is May?'

'Nothing. We lost our way. That is all. May—Miss Dacre desired me to say, that she would not join us at dinner.'

'I am sure, something has happened.'

'I assure you, my dear sir, nothing, nothing at all the least unpleasant, but we took the wrong turning. All my fault.'

'Shall I send for the soup?'

'No. I am not hungry, I will take some wine.' So saying, his Grace poured out a tumbler of claret.

'Shall I take your Grace's hat?' asked the fat butler.

'Dear me! have I my hat on?'

This was not the only evidence afforded by our hero's conduct that his presence of mind had slightly deserted him. He was soon buried in a deep reverie, and sat with a full plate, but idle knife and fork before him, a perfect puzzle to the fat butler, who had hitherto considered his Grace the very pink of propriety.

'George, you have eaten no dinner,' said Mr. Dacre.

'Thank you, a very good one indeed, a remarkably good dinner. Give me some red wine, if you please.'

At length they were left alone.

'I have some good news for you, George.'

- 285 -

'Indeed.'

'I think I have let Rosemount.'

'So!'

'And exactly to the kind of person that you wanted, a man who will take a pride, although merely a tenant, in not permitting his poor neighbours to feel the *want* of a landlord. You will never guess: Lord Mildmay!'

'What did you say of Lord Mildmay, sir?'

'My dear fellow, your wits are wool-gathering; I say I think I have let Rosemount.'

'Oh! I have changed my mind about letting Rosemount.'

'My dear Duke, there is no trouble which I will grudge, to further your interests; but really I must beg, in future, that you will, at least, apprise me when you change your mind. There is nothing, as we have both agreed, more desirable than to find an eligible tenant for Rosemount. You never can expect to have a more beneficial one than Lord Mildmay; and really, unless you have positively promised the place to another person (which, excuse me for saying, you were not authorised to do) I must insist, after what has passed, upon his having the preference.'

'My dear sir, I only changed my mind this afternoon: I couldn't tell you before. I have promised it to no one; but I think of living there myself.'

'Yourself! Oh! if that be the case, I shall be quite reconciled to the disappointment of Lord Mildmay. But what in the name of goodness, my dear fellow, has produced this wonderful revolution in all your plans in the course of a few hours? I thought you were going to mope away life on the Lake of Geneva, or dawdle it away in Florence or Rome.'

'It is very odd, sir. I can hardly believe it myself: and yet it must be true. I hear her voice even at this moment. Oh! my dear Mr. Dacre, I am the happiest fellow that ever breathed!'

'What is all this?'

'Is it possible, my dear sir, that you have not long before detected the feelings I ventured to entertain for your daughter? In a word, she requires only your sanction to my being the most fortunate of men.'

'My dear friend, my dear, dear boy!' cried Mr. Dacre, rising from his chair and embracing him, 'it is out of the power of man to impart to me any event which could afford me such exquisite pleasure! Indeed, indeed, it is to me most surprising! for I had been induced to suspect, George, that some explanation had passed between you and May, which, while it accounted for your mutual esteem, gave little hope of a stronger sentiment.'

'I believe, sir,' said the young Duke, with a smile, 'I was obstinate.'

'Well, this changes all our plans. I have intended, for this fortnight past, to speak to you finally on your affairs. No better time than the present; and, in the first place——'

But, really, this interview is confidential.

CHAPTER XI.

'Perfection in a Petticoat.'

THEY come not: it is late. He is already telling all! She relapses into her sweet reverie. Her thought fixes on no subject; her mind is intent on no idea; her soul is melted into dreamy delight; her only consciousness is perfect bliss! Sweet sounds still echo in her ear, and still her pure pulse beats, from the first embrace of passion.

The door opens, and her father enters, leaning upon the arm of her beloved. Yes, he has told all! Mr. Dacre approached, and, bending down, pressed the lips of his child. It was the seal to their plighted faith, and told, without speech, that the blessing of a parent mingled with the vows of a lover! No other intimation was at present necessary;' but she, the daughter, thought now only of her father, that friend of her long life, whose love had ne'er been wanting: was she about to leave him? She arose, she threw her arms around his neck and wept.

The young Duke walked away, that his presence might not control the full expression of her hallowed soul. 'This jewel is mine,' was his thought; 'what, what have I done to be so blessed?'

In a few minutes he again joined them, and was seated by her side; and Mr. Dacre considerately remembered that he wished to see his steward, and they were left alone. Their eyes meet, and their soft looks tell that they were thinking of each other. His arm steals round the back of her chair, and with his other hand he gently captures hers.

First love, first love! how many a glowing bard has sung thy beauties! How many a poor devil of a prosing novelist, like myself, has echoed all our superiors, the poets, teach us! No doubt, thou rosy god of young Desire, thou art a most bewitching little demon; and yet, for my part, give me last love.

Ask a man which turned out best, the first horse he bought, or the one he now canters on? Ask—but in short there is nothing in which knowledge is more important and experience more valuable than in love. When we first love, we are enamoured of our own imaginations. Our thoughts are high, our feelings rise from out the deepest caves of the tumultuous tide of our full life. We look around for one to share our exquisite existence, and sanctify the beauties of our being.

But those beauties are only in our thoughts. We feel like heroes, when we are but boys. Yet our mistress must bear a relation, not to ourselves, but to our imagination. She must be a real heroine, while our perfection is but ideal. And the quick and dangerous fancy of our race will, at first, rise to the pitch. She is all we can conceive. Mild and pure as youthful priests, we bow down before our altar. But the idol to which we breathe our warm and gushing vows, and bend our eager knees, all its power, does it not exist only in our idea; all its beauty, is it not the creation of our excited fancy? And then the sweetest of superstitions ends. The long delusion bursts, and we are left like men upon a heath when fairies vanish; cold and dreary, gloomy, bitter, harsh, existence seems a blunder.

But just when we are most miserable, and curse the poet's cunning and our own conceits, there lights upon our path, just like a ray fresh from the sun, some sparkling child of light, that makes us think we are premature, at least, in our resolves. Yet we are determined not to be taken in, and try her well in all the points in which the others failed. One by one, her charms steal on our warming soul, as, one by one, those of the other beauty sadly stole away, and then we bless our stars, and feel quite sure that we have found perfection in a petticoat.

But our Duke—where are we? He had read woman thoroughly, and consequently knew how to value the virgin pages on which his thoughts now fixed. He and May Dacre wandered in the woods, and nature seemed to them more beautiful from their beautiful loves. They gazed upon the sky; a brighter light fell o'er the luminous earth. Sweeter to them the fragrance of the sweetest flowers, and a more balmy breath brought on the universal promise of the opening year.

They wandered in the woods, and there they breathed their mutual adoration. She to him was all in all, and he to her was like a new divinity. She poured forth all that she long had felt, and scarcely could suppress. From the moment he tore her from the insulter's arms, his image fixed in her heart, and the struggle which she experienced to repel his renewed vows was great indeed. When she heard of his misfortunes, she had wept; but it was the strange delight she experienced when his letter arrived to her father that first convinced her how irrevocably her mind was his.

And now she does not cease to blame herself for all her past obduracy; now she will not for a moment yield that he could have been ever anything but all that was pure, and beautiful, and good.

CHAPTER XII.

Another Betrothal

BUT although we are in love, business must not be utterly neglected, and Mr. Dacre insisted that the young Duke should for one morning cease to wander in his park, and listen to the result of his exertions during the last three months. His Grace listened. Rents had not risen, but it was hoped that they had seen their worst; the railroad had been successfully opposed; and coals had improved. The London mansion and the Alhambra had both been disposed of, and well: the first to the new French Ambassador, and the second to a grey-headed stock-jobber, very rich, who, having no society, determined to make solitude amusing. The proceeds of these sales, together with sundry sums obtained by converting into cash the stud, the furniture, and the *bijouterie*, produced a most respectable fund, which nearly paid off the annoying miscellaneous debts. For the rest, Mr. Dacre, while he agreed that it was on the whole advisable that the buildings should be completed, determined that none of the estates should be sold, or even mortgaged. His plan was to procrastinate the termination of these undertakings, and to allow each year itself to afford the necessary supplies. By annually setting aside one hundred thousand pounds, in seven or eight years he hoped to find everything completed and all debts cleared. He did not think that the extravagance of the Duke could justify any diminution in the sum which had hitherto been apportioned for the maintenance of the Irish establishments; but he was of opinion that the decreased portion which they, as well as the western estates, now afforded to the total income, was a sufficient reason. Fourteen thousand a-year were consequently allotted to Ireland, and seven to Pen Bronnock. There remained to the Duke about thirty thousand per annum; but then Hauteville was to be kept up with this. Mr. Dacre proposed that the young people should reside at Rosemount, and that consequently they might form their establishment from the Castle, without reducing their Yorkshire appointments, and avail themselves, without any obligation, or even the opportunity, of great expenses, of all the advantages afforded by the necessary expenditure. Finally, Mr. Dacre presented his son with his town mansion and furniture; and as the young Duke insisted that the settlements upon her Grace should be prepared in full reference to his inherited and future income, this generous father at once made over to him the great bulk of his personal property amounting to upwards of a hundred thousand pounds, a little ready money, of which he knew the value.

The Duke of St. James had duly informed his uncle, the Earl of Fitz-pompey, of the intended change in his condition, and in answer received the following letter:—

'Fitz-pompey Hall, May, 18—.

'My dear George,—Your letter did not give us so much surprise as you expected; but I assure you it gave us as much pleasure. You have shown your wisdom and your taste in your choice; and I am free to confess that I am acquainted with no one more worthy of the station which the Duchess of St. James must always fill in society, and more calculated to maintain the dignity of your family, than the lady whom you are about to introduce to us as our niece. Believe me, my dear George, that the notification of this agreeable event has occasioned even additional gratification both to your aunt and to myself, from the reflection that you are about to ally yourself with a family in whose welfare we must ever take an especial interest, and whom we may in a manner look upon as our own relatives. For, my dear George, in answer to your flattering and most pleasing communication, it is my truly agreeable duty to inform you (and, believe me, you are the first person out of our immediate family to whom this intelligence is made known) that our Caroline, in whose happiness we are well assured you take a lively interest, is about to be united to one who may now be described as your near relative, namely, Mr. Arundel Dacre.

'It has been a long attachment, though for a considerable time, I confess, unknown to us; and indeed at first sight, with Caroline's rank and other advantages, it may not appear, in a mere worldly point of view, so desirable a connection as some perhaps might expect. And to be quite confidential, both your aunt and myself were at first a little disinclined (great as our esteem and regard have ever been for him), a little disinclined, I say, to the union. But Dacre is certainly the most rising man of the day. In point of family, he is second to none; and his uncle has indeed behaved in the most truly liberal manner. I assure you, he considers him as a son; and even if there were no other inducement, the mere fact of your connection with the family would alone not only reconcile, but, so to say, make us perfectly satisfied with the arrangement. It is unnecessary to speak to you of the antiquity of the Dacres. Arundel will ultimately be one of the richest Commoners, and I think it is not too bold to anticipate, taking into consideration the family into which he marries, and above all, his connection with you, that we may finally succeed in having him called up to us. You are of course aware that there was once a barony in the family.

'Everybody talks of your speech. I assure you, although I ever gave you credit for uncommon talents, I was astonished. So you are to have the vacant ribbon! Why did you not tell me? I learnt it to-day, from Lord Bobbleshim. But we must not quarrel with men in love for not communicating.

'You ask me for news of all your old friends. You of course saw the death of old Annesley. The new Lord took his seat yesterday; he was introduced by

Lord Bloomerly. I was not surprised to hear in the evening that he was about to be married to Lady Charlotte, though the world affect to be astonished.

I should not forget to say that Lord Annesley asked most particularly after you. For him, quite warm, I assure you.

'The oddest thing has happened to your friend, Lord Squib. Old Colonel Carlisle is dead, and has left his whole fortune, some say half a million, to the oddest person, merely because she had the reputation of being his daughter. Quite an odd person, you understand me: Mrs. Montfort. St. Maurice says you know her; but we must not talk of these things now. Well, Squib is going to be married to her. He says that he knows all his old friends will cut him when they are married, and so he is determined to give them an excuse. I understand she is a fine woman. He talks of living at Rome and Florence for a year or two.

'Lord Darrell is about to marry Harriet Wrekin; and between ourselves (but don't let this go any further at present) I have very little doubt that young Pococurante will shortly be united to Isabel. Connected as we are with the Shropshires, these excellent alliances are gratifying.

'I see very little of Lucius Grafton. He seems ill.

'I understand, for certain, that her Ladyship opposes the divorce. *On dit*, she has got hold of some letters, through the treachery of her soubrette, whom he supposed quite his creature, and that your friend is rather taken in. But I should not think this true. People talk very loosely. There was a gay party at Mrs. Dallington's the other night, who asked very kindly after you.

'I think I have now written you a very long letter. I once more congratulate you on your admirable selection, and with the united remembrance of our circle, particularly Caroline, who will write perhaps by this post to Miss Dacre, believe me, dear George, your truly affectionate uncle,

'FITZ-POMPEY.

'P.S.—Lord Marylebone is very unpopular, quite a brute. We all miss you.'

It is not to be supposed that this letter conveyed the first intimation to the Duke of St. James of the most interesting event of which it spoke. On the contrary, he had long been aware of the whole affair; but we have been too much engaged with his own conduct to find time to let the reader into the secret, which, like all secrets, it is to be hoped was no secret. Next to gaining the affections of May Dacre, it was impossible for any event to occur more delightful to our hero than the present. His heart had often misgiven him when he had thought of Caroline. Now she was happy, and not only happy, but connected with him for life, just as he wished. Arundel Dacre, too, of all men he most wished to like, and indeed most liked. One feeling alone had prevented them from being bosom friends, and that feeling had long triumphantly vanished.

May had been almost from the beginning the *confidante* of her cousin. In vain, however, had she beseeched him to entrust all to her father. Although he now repented his past feelings he could not be induced to change; and not till he had entered Parliament and succeeded and gained a name, which would reflect honour on the family with which he wished to identify himself, would he impart to his uncle the secret of his heart, and gain that support without which his great object could never have been achieved. The Duke of St. James, by returning him to Parliament, had been the unconscious cause of all his happiness, and ardently did he pray that his generous friend might succeed in what he was well aware was his secret aspiration, and that his beloved cousin might yield her hand to the only man whom Arundel Dacre considered worthy of her.

CHAPTER XIII.

Joy's Beginning

ANOTHER week brought another letter from the Earl of Fitz-pompey.

The Earl of Fitz-pompey to the Duke of St. James. [Read this alone.]

'My dear George,

'I beg you will not be alarmed by the above memorandum, which I thought it but prudent to prefix. A very disagreeable affair has just taken place, and to a degree exceedingly alarming; but it might have turned out much more distressing, and, on the whole, we may all congratulate ourselves at the result. Not to keep you in fearful suspense, I beg to recall your recollection to the rumour which I noticed in my last, of the intention of Lady Aphrodite Grafton to oppose the divorce. A few days back, her brother Lord Wariston, with whom I was previously unacquainted, called upon me by appointment, having previously requested a private interview. The object of his seeing me was no less than to submit to my inspection the letters by aid of which it was anticipated that the divorce might be successfully opposed. You will be astounded to hear that these consist of a long series of correspondence of Mrs. Dallington Vere's, developing, I am shocked to say, machinations of a very alarming nature, the effect of which, my dear George, was no less than very materially to control your fortunes in life, and those of that charming and truly admirable lady whom you have delighted us all so much by declaring to be our future relative.

'From the very delicate nature of the disclosures, Lord Wariston felt the great importance of obtaining all necessary results without making them public; and, actuated by these feelings, he applied to me, both as your nearest relative, and an acquaintance of Sir Lucius, and, as he expressed it, and I may be permitted to repeat, as one whose experience in the management of difficult and delicate negotiations was not altogether unknown, in order that I might be put in possession of the facts of the case, advise and perhaps interfere for the common good.

'Under these circumstances, and taking into consideration the extreme difficulty attendant upon a satisfactory arrangement of the affair, I thought fit, in confidence, to apply to Arundel, whose talents I consider of the first order, and only equalled by his prudence and calm temper. As a relation, too, of more than one of the parties concerned, it was perhaps only proper that the correspondence should be submitted to him.

'I am sorry to say, my dear George, that Arundel behaved in a very odd manner, and not at all with that discretion which might have been expected both from one of his remarkably sober and staid disposition, and one not a little experienced in diplomatic life. He exhibited the most unequivocal signs of his displeasure at the conduct of the parties principally concerned, and expressed himself in so vindictive a manner against one of them, that I very much regretted my application, and requested him to be cool.

'He seemed to yield to my solicitations, but I regret to say his composure was only feigned, and the next morning he and Sir Lucius Grafton met. Sir Lucius fired first, without effect, but Arundel's aim was more fatal, and his ball was lodged in the thigh of his adversary. Sir Lucius has only been saved by amputation; and I need not remark to you that to such a man life on such conditions is scarcely desirable. All idea of a divorce is quite given over. The letters in question were stolen from his cabinet by his valet, and given to a soubrette of his wife, whom Sir Lucius considered in his interest, but who, as you see, betrayed him.

'For me remained the not very agreeable office of seeing Mrs. Dallington Vere. I made known to her, in a manner as little offensive as possible, the object of my visit. The scene, my dear George, was trying; and I think it hard that the follies of a parcel of young people should really place me in such a distressing position. She fainted, &c, and wished the letters to be given up, but Lord Wariston would not consent to this, though he promised to keep their contents secret provided she quitted the country. She goes directly; and I am well assured, which is not the least surprising part of this strange history, that her affairs are in a state of great distraction. The relatives of her late husband are about again to try the will, and with prospect of success. She has been negotiating with them for some time through the agency of Sir Lucius Grafton, and the late exposÂ© will not favour her interests.

'If anything further happens, my dear George, depend upon my writing; but Arundel desires me to say that on Saturday he will run down to Dacre for a few days, as he very much wishes to see you and all. With our united remembrance to Mr. and Miss Dacre,

'Ever, my dear George,

'Your very affectionate uncle,

'Fitz-pompey.'

The young Duke turned with trembling and disgust from these dark terminations of unprincipled careers; and these fatal evidences of the indulgence of unbridled passions. How nearly, too, had he been shipwrecked in this moral whirlpool! With what gratitude did he not invoke the beneficent Providence that had not permitted the innate seeds of human virtue to be blighted in his wild and neglected soul! With what admiration did he not gaze upon the pure and beautiful being whose virtue and whose loveliness were the causes of his regeneration, the sources of his present happiness, and the guarantees of his future joy!

Four years have now elapsed since the young Duke of St. James was united to May Dacre; and it would not be too bold to declare, that during that period he has never for an instant ceased to consider himself the happiest and the most fortunate of men. His life is passed in the agreeable discharge of all the important duties of his exalted station, and his present career is by far a better answer to the lucubrations of young Duncan Macmorrogh than all the abstract arguments that ever yet were offered in favour of the existence of an aristocracy.

Hauteville House and Hauteville Castle proceed in regular course. These magnificent dwellings will never erase simple and delightful Rosemount from the grateful memory of the Duchess of St. James. Parliament, and in a degree society, invite the Duke and Duchess each year to the metropolis, and Mr. Dacre is generally their guest. Their most intimate and beloved friends are Arundel and his wife, and as Lady Caroline now heads the establishment of Castle Dacre, they are seldom separated. But among their most agreeable company is a young gentleman styled by courtesy Dacre, Marquess of Hauteville, and his young sister, who has not yet escaped from her beautiful mother's arms, and who beareth the blooming title of the Lady May.

www.ingramcontent.com/pod-product-compliance
Ingram Content Group UK Ltd.
Pitfield, Milton Keynes, MK11 3LW, UK
UKHW041050100125
453365UK00005B/350